ROSLYN REED

A HEMORRHAGE OF US

A HORROR ROMANCE NOVEL

CONTENTS

CONTENT WARNINGS

A Hemorrhage of Us is an adult novel that is not intended for audiences under the age of 18.

A Hemorrhage of Us is a **dark horror-romance** that includes sexual and explicit content. This story features *morally ambiguous* characters. **There are no heroes here.** This book is intended for adults only and contains subject matter that could be disturbing to some readers. Sensitive material includes, but is not limited to: body gore, violence, blood, frequent profanity, torture, murder, frequent mentions of a chronic disorder, emotional and verbal abuse, exploration of implied mental illness (depression, anxiety, CPTSD), memory loss, scenes of mass death, suicidal ideation, explorations of grief and loss as well as heavy mentions of religion.

This book also contains explorations of BDSM themes.

For those who reached out in the dark and wished someone would reach back.

PROLOGUE

There was nothing miraculous about the little girl.

Were it not for the ocean of scars splattered against her skin like spilled paint, she would have seemed like any other. But her misfortune was on display for all to see.

The warm autumn air kissed the unlucky girl's face as she sat on the porch of her grandmother's house, crushing stray crabapples beneath her heel. She longed to run back into the forest, but above her, the sky bled vermillion, and the night was fast encroaching.

Her grandmother never let her set foot outside once the sun went down.

"Rayne." Her grandmother called from the belly of the house. "Where are you at, girl?"

"Porch!"

Behind her, the house shifted and sighed as her grandmother moved slowly. The old woman and her home were inextricably tied, bones creaking from a life well lived. The door eased open, and with no small amount of difficulty, her grandmother hobbled out, a boar bristle brush, a jar of shea butter, and a small bottle of juniper oil in her arms. The old woman sat down in her rocking chair with a groan that sang of unspoken ails, but she smiled when she caught Rayne's brow furrowing. She wiggled her crooked fingers at her. "Bring me your curls."

Rayne's curls hung loose, bits of leaves tangled in them from the trees that she adored. Rayne crawled over to her grandmother and sat between her legs, absently resting her cheek against the old woman's knee.

The steady pulse of the pinewood rocking chair against the porch beat like an old heart as her grandmother set to her work. Though the little girl felt no exhaustion, her body began to sag, relaxed by her grandmother's touch and the tuneless medicine songs she sang.

"I thought I'd told you about wearin' your hair down when you went out runnin' in the wood." Her grandmother tsked, plucking out dead oak leaves from Rayne's hair. "You want to bring those *manëtuwàk* home, all tangled up in you like a thread caught on the pine?"

"No, Mam'maw," she sighed, picking up a fresh, unfortunate crabapple from the ground, yellowed by autumn's kiss, and rolling it between her thumb and index finger. She'd heard the warning too many times to count.

"Hair is the connection to spirit, puts us right in touch with the Creator. It's a gift he gives us as His Chosen people. Can't just be runnin' through the forest all barefoot and wild, letting any ole' haint follow you home," her grandmother continued. "You hear me? You keep your hair protected and braided at all costs when you're in that wood."

"Uh huh."

Her grandmother caught her shoulder. "Don't you 'uh-huh' me, girl," Mam'maw hissed, and then, a moment later, she sighed and smoothed some hair from Rayne's face. She cupped her cheek and stroked it delicately with a weathered thumb. "I'm sorry. Turn back around for me, and I'll tell you a secret."

Rayne loved secrets, but the ones that her Mam'maw shared with her were always the best. Turning her back, she peeled the skin of her crabapple in anticipation.

A few weighted moments later, her grandmother's fingers returned to her hair, and she spoke again. "You know that wood ain't ours, right? Nature doesn't rightfully belong to any human, but that doesn't mean it isn't owned."

"Who owns the wood then?"

"The Devil," Mam'maw whispered in her ear.

Her eyes went wider than the moon, fear and delight knotting her insides up like taffy.

"The Devil?"

Her grandmother looked around as if she were expecting the Devil to be there, waiting to snatch them both up. It would have been theatrical, too over-the-top for anyone else. But her grandmother was a practical woman. She had worked as a school teacher at a time when women like her were not permitted to do so.

Her grandmother held herself like a secret, and sometimes Rayne liked to imagine that it was because she wasn't human. That Mam'maw was a changeling with a mystery running deep in her blood.

"Call him Old Scratch, The Old Man, whatever you like, but use his name sparingly," her grandmother warned. "You ever seen strange footprints in the dirt while walkin'? Like a goat, cept much bigger?"

Rural life had given Rayne the gift of many strange and wonderful sights; she had seen many such footprints in the dirt. At least, she thought.

Her grandmother's face took on that distant look that she only got when she told her tales. The color seemed to leave her copper skin, as if she was melting into the air she spoke so easily on. "That's him. Old Trickster takes many forms, he does. Owls, goats, cats, and even wolves. Sometimes he'll come as a great shadow to drag you down to Hell by your ankles if you're caught walking alone at night."

At this, the girl stiffened with the desire to correct her grandmother, but she knew better than to interrupt.

Rayne knew of the shadows; she had come to learn them very well.

"Little girls like you, wearing your innocence like a crown of roses, are just his cup of tea. He'll find you sure as sunlight if you aren't careful, my girl. The Devil is cruelest to the innocent ones."

The girl's gaze drifted out to the forest that sat at the edge of her grandmother's property, the forest that she had run and screamed and danced in since she could remember. She thought of the trees that hid her, the ground that held her, and the birds that sang to her. And finally, she thought of the Devil, half shadow and moonlight, with a smile like cracking ice.

But mostly she thought of how she had never once been frightened of him.

"I know it seems unfair. But I only want to see you safe, so you take heed and mind me, Rayne Dorne. You hear?"

The girl crushed the crabapple between her fingers, the bitter guts sticking under her fingernails. "Yes, Mam'maw," she murmured.

Her grandmother was a wise woman; she knew so much of the world and everything that lay between it. And yet, for the first time, Rayne had found something that her grandmother was wrong about.

The Devil was not some cruel monster that sought to hurt her.

No. The Devil was kind.

PART ONE
winter

CHAPTER ONE
rayne

The unknown number flashed across her phone screen for the third time in a row, cutting through the darkness of her room. Russet brown eyes fell on it once more, watching as the area code that she had never wanted to see again danced in front of her eyes.

Bury, Pennsylvania.

"Rayne!" Trisha demanded, and Rayne jumped, nearly toppling out of her chair. She scrambled to regain her balance and whirled to glare at her roommate. Trisha stood in the doorway, toothbrush in hand, her long, dark hair secured in a towel. "Are you going to answer that or what? I start my shift in twenty minutes."

Her roommate worked online as a camgirl and was rarely in their apartment outside of night shifts. Rayne was a shut-in, a luxury her work in remote accounting afforded her.

Not that she had much desire to leave their apartment.

"Sorry," Rayne murmured, snatching her phone off her computer desk where it had been aggressively vibrating.

She and Trisha weren't friends. Outside of when rent was due, they didn't interact and that suited Rayne just fine.

"Just keep your door closed. I've got a big client tonight," Trisha barked, slamming Rayne's door before she could do so herself.

Attention drawn back to her phone, Rayne took a deep breath and swiped right, bringing it to her ear.

It's probably just a spam call or something, she thought. "Hello?"

The other end of the line simmered with static, but a slight breath hitched beneath it. "*Rayne.*"

She shivered, ice sliding down her spine. "Who is this?"

The voice on the other end remained silent before it cleared, some of the static melting away. "It's me, Rainy. Callum."

Callum.

The memory of him, taller than her, jet black, pin-straight hair so different than her own auburn nest of curls. They'd never looked like siblings; everything between them was a contrast, but nothing so much more than the perfect, unmarred skin he had.

"Cal," Rayne exhaled. "It can't be you."

"Strange then, that it is."

Outside, in the street below, an ambulance rushed by, followed by the harsh car horns of city drivers. "How did you get this number? Where are you?"

Callum chuckled low and dark on the other end of the phone. "I could always find you."

Rayne blinked. *I don't remember him sounding like this.* "You could?"

"Yes."

Then why didn't you?

The question danced on the edge of her tongue, where it had hung for nearly twenty years. *Why did you lie?*

"Cal—"

"I am at the house. You should be as well."

The house? Oh.

Rayne scoffed, kicking at the ground with her boot. "I'd rather drop dead than set foot in that hick hell ever again."

"Our parents are dead."

"Oh."

Her relationship with her parents was not good. Callum had run away when he was sixteen, and she had just turned seven. She hadn't heard from him since. That had been nearly twenty years ago. *He sounds so… calm.*

"Are you alright, Rayne?"

"What happened?"

"Oh. Well, haven't gotten the autopsies back yet or anything," he replied too quickly. "But I think they suspect a heart attack."

Rayne's brow furrowed. "*Both* of them?"

"Apparently."

"That's… weird."

"You should come home," Callum said again.

"For the funeral… I guess I could. When is it?"

"You missed it. It took place a few days ago."

"And you didn't call me, Cal? What the hell?"

"I am calling you now, am I not?"

"Wait, you said they didn't give you the autopsy yet. How did you get their bodies?"

"Christ, Ray," Callum sighed into the line, static hissing between. "I don't know, I guess I was kind of distracted by the fact that our parents died to worry about logistical questions like that."

Rayne remained silent, listening to her brother's slow, strange breathing on the other end of the line. She had no reason to be upset that he hadn't called her for the funeral; she wouldn't have wanted to attend anyway. But now, this opened her up to the scrutiny of her wretched relatives. She could practically hear them all shucking their teeth as they shook their heads at her. *See that? Couldn't even be bothered to show up to her poor parents' funeral.*

"I'm sorry," Rayne relented.

"It's fine. How have you been since—?"

Rayne understood that she hardly knew her brother anymore; the only thing existing between them now was time and blood, and she could not shake the wrongness of it all. "Yeah. I mean, it's been a long time, Cal."

"Come home. We can talk. And... there are things that you should see. Things that they left for you."

Rayne scoffed, "Yeah, like what, some trash that they didn't want to throw away?"

"Just come back, and you'll see. When can you leave?"

I have a life! She wanted to shout. *A life that you chose to walk out of.* Instead, she chewed her lower lip. "I can be on the road in an hour."

Static buzzed between them like bees and something like laughter. "Good. I will see you soon."

Rayne hung up and hastily rummaged through her desk to grab a notepad and pen so she could leave a note for Trisha.

> *Hey. Family emergency. I'm going to be gone for a little bit. I don't know how long. Here's the rent for the next month. I should be back before the holidays.*
>
> *Don't use my shower. — Rayne*

Trisha had been jealous of Rayne's shower since the day they'd moved in here, but since Rayne paid more in rent, Trisha had begrudgingly agreed it was fair.

Getting up, she moved across the room toward her bed to snatch a pillow off it and kneel on the hardwood floor. The pillow offered a little protection for her skin, but without her thick, knitted thigh highs, she could still feel the strain. She snatched her shoe box from under the bed quickly and tossed it onto the sheets.

Self-loathing, as familiar as a limb, accompanied her as she rose to find a blister already forming on her left knee. *Fuck!* she thought, plopping down on her bed to examine the damage.

Such mundane tasks often left her just that—damaged.

Rayne had been born with a rare disease that left her skin as delicate as butterfly wings. So many simple, gentle experiences that others took for granted left her bleeding and bruised. She tried to accommodate it as much as possible: thick, knitted thigh-highs, gloves, long sleeves over bandages to protect her.

Still, she found herself a glass girl in a world of stone.

I don't have time for this, she thought as she reached for her medical supplies concealed within a black, floral-printed bag that she kept at her side at all times.

Her body forced her to make time, and she began the tiresome process of caring for the shell that she was loath to inhabit. Pulling down her black tights, she assessed the damage. Dusky, almond skin pooled into palm-pink-like waves against a shore; every inch of Rayne Dorne was scarred. Some were nearly invisible, melting back into her dark skin and remaining only visible in bright lightning, but most were shades of pink and lighter brown, as evident as paint on her flesh.

In her youth, she had grown accustomed to questions about house fires, exploding radiators, or car crashes. No one ever believed her when she said that she had been born this way, and when they finally did, they gave her a wide berth for fear that she was contagious.

There had been moments where she was sure she might have been, her frustration coalescing into something airborne and venomous.

Rayne did not look at her body longer than she had to, focusing her attention instead on her steady fingers, the sterile smell of disinfectant, and the perfect white of the medical gauze against her skin. Her parents used to joke that she should get a job as a nurse with all the medical experience she had in dressing her wounds.

It had never been funny.

Finally freed from her task, Rayne finished the bandage by breaking off a piece of medical tape and securing it over the gauze, careful not to allow it to touch her skin. She rolled off her bed and took in the sight of her room, assessing what she might need for the next few days while she and her brother handled the mess their parents had left behind.

One suitcase and an overnight bag.

That was all she had managed to fill her life with in the seven years since she'd left home. Some clothes, a few pairs of shoes, a small collection of herbs her grandmother would have killed her for leaving behind, her favorite books, and a journal she didn't write in but felt the need to drag along with her just in case.

Rayne watched in her rearview mirror as her apartment and the city skyline faded away, swallowed by the smoke of countless buildings and fuel emissions. It was strange how such a dangerous place had made her feel so safe.

She'd been away from her family, nosy neighbors, and town gossip. It had tasted like freedom.

Now I'm about to throw it away, and for what? Rayne blanched, shaking her head and tousling her curls in the process. *That wasn't what I meant. Callum is my brother. I haven't heard from him in so long; it would be cruel just to ignore him.*

She wanted to be kind to her brother despite the flurry of emotion that came whenever she thought about him for too long. Her grandmother had always urged them to forgive others, and as she would say, *'There's no one on God's green Earth that doesn't have a little shit on their shoes.'*

Rayne wished she could be half the person her grandmother had been, and part of her wished that her Mam'maw had called instead of her brother. But ghosts didn't make phone and her Mam'maw was long dead.

Sighing, she allowed her head to fall back against the headrest of her car seat, watching as civilization slipped further away.

CHAPTER TWO
rayne

R ayne gripped the steering wheel so hard that she was sure her skin would tear.

The late morning winter sun bleached the overcast sky, painting everything in an abysmal shade of gray. She hit the gas as her Jeep crept up the hill that led into town, forcing her gaze ahead to avoid looking at the billboard she knew to be waiting for her.

The billboard depicted a cartoon, a smiling tombstone, and a matching paper-and-steel mill waving. Above them, the words: *'Welcome to Bury! You'll never leave alive!'*

It was supposed to be cute.

Bury wasn't the type of town that anyone ever really left; it was the sort of town one was born into and died in. Every resident had their roots dug for them by some ancestor who came to the town for work.

Her grandmother had been one such person, having left the reservation once her husband was offered a job at the local paper mill. He'd built her a home in the middle of the holler, less than ten miles from the steel mill. Rayne's mother had moved out of her childhood home and settled on the edge of town, close enough to walk but far enough that most people wouldn't want to.

Most of her family had died here.

What a sick joke, Rayne thought bitterly.

Ignorant of her anguish, the town buzzed with the haze of locals going about their day.

More than a few heads turned as her black Jeep Cherokee roared through town. She hadn't left in this car, so she was all but a stranger to them at first glance.

Bury did not take too kindly to strangers.

"I should stop in downtown and get some flowers," she said to no one. "That way, I can stop at the graves and be done with it."

Something her grandmother had instilled in her, though she couldn't quite recall why, was always to leave flowers for the dead while the grave dirt was still fresh to avoid bad luck. If the funeral happened only a few days ago, she should be fine.

It would be good for her to be seen mourning them. Less for people to talk about.

Eyes stared into her car as she sat in the parking lot of the florist. People stopped and looked right at her; some ventured a little closer to get a more precise look at her face—a few she recognized, and she sank deeper into her seat, grateful for her tinted windows.

"They're just flowers, Rayne. It's not going to kill you," she murmured.

Pausing to take a breath and gather what fragments of courage were available, she wrenched open the door to her car. Snatching her bag from the passenger seat, she closed the door behind her and crossed the semi-empty parking lot of the flower shop. She stopped just before entering the building, where a missing person's poster hung in the window. A young woman with walnut brown hair and a pleasant face was plastered across it. Rayne recognized her from high school.

She had been one of the dozens of peers who had made Rayne's daily life hell.

A group of girls that giggled whenever she walked past, cornering her in between class periods when teachers were distracted, pulling her hair. Hours in the school nurse's office while they attempted to tend her wounds, always she would say she fell or knocked into some sharp locker edge. Spending lunch and recess hiding in the girls' bathroom, curled up against the windowsill so that no one could get her, even if they did find her.

Rayne smirked at the thought that something terrible might have happened to her. *Couldn't have happened to a nicer person,* she thought, and then, remembering that it was unkind to believe such a thing, she sent up a silent apology to the ghost of her bitch ex-schoolmate as she stepped into the shop.

"Rayne Dorne!"

Great.

Kirstin Laney had never liked her; Rayne had known that since she'd first walked into the store when she was seventeen and asked for a job.

But Rayne had been quiet, punctual, and minded her business, so Kirstin never had any reason to turn that dislike toward her. None of that had stopped the older woman from making snide remarks about Rayne's choice of dark clothing and her scars. Rayne was sure that Kirstin would wait until she was out on deliveries to gossip about her with the other florists, evidenced by the laughter that always ended abruptly when she returned.

So when Kirstin grinned and padded out from behind the cash register with arms stretched wide, it took everything within Rayne to keep from laughing. Instead, she offered a polite smile and let herself get pulled into an embrace, wincing slightly.

"Bless my stars, I never thought I'd see the likes of you here again," Kirstin said, and then, as if remembering what exactly it was that had brought Rayne back, she fixed her face into a theatrical mask of empathy. "I'm so sorry to hear about your parents, sweetheart."

Rayne reached for her well-rehearsed script from the drive-up. She hadn't spoken to anyone outside her clients or her roommate in years.

"Thank you. That's, uhm... real nice of you to say."

"How are you holding up?"

"Well enough, I guess."

"Of course. It gets easier with time; that's what I've heard."

"I wouldn't know."

Kirsten shot her a strange look, and Rayne bit her lip. *Shit. Was that not a normal thing to say?*

Trisha didn't pretend with her. Trisha didn't engage in small talk or give Rayne the impression that she cared much about her life. There was something in that Rayne was grateful for.

Rayne stood there, staring at Kirsten and unsure of what she was supposed to say now.

"So," Kirsten said, clearing her throat. "What can I help you with today, dear?"

Bristling at the pet name, Rayne forced another smile. "Two bouquets of white roses. I'm heading to the graveyard—"

"Oh! Of course, gimme just a few minutes, and I'll get them all wrapped up for you. You don't mind waiting?"

Of course I do. "Not at all."

The moment Kirstin was out of her orbit, Rayne frowned, wishing she'd never come.

"Do you think you're gonna be sticking around?" Kirstin called from the back of the store. "I saw your cousin, June. She came for the funeral, but you probably already knew that."

Rayne hadn't. Juniper Stern was the last person she wanted to speak to.

"It was good to catch up with her. I think it's been even longer since I've seen her around these parts. She was telling me that you weren't invited to the funeral."

Shame heated Rayne's skin, and she forced her attention down to the run-down tile of the floor.

"It's just awful. Your brother not inviting you like that. They were your folks, too, weren't they?"

Rayne stayed still, counting the cracks in the floor.

One, two, three...

It was all too familiar, the feeling of entrapment.

"Family is family. I don't think it should matter that you up and left without a word to anyone. I mean, 'course if it were my daughter that did that to me, I'd be asking God what I did to deserve a kid like that."

Shut up, shut up, shut up, shut up. Rayne fought the urge to pinch her eyes closed, to fold in on herself. Instead, she focused on the number of cracks in front of her and how they splintered.

Four, five, six, seven, eight...

"So, do you *want* to stick around this time?"

"No," Rayne bit out, relieved, when she finally heard Kirsten moving back toward the front of the store. "After my brother and I deal with everything, I'm going home."

Kirsten tilted her head to the side. "Bury's your home, silly. I mean, where else would you ever want to go?" Kirstin asked, her arms full of the much more extravagant bouquets than Rayne had wanted. "Bury is where your blood is."

"Okay, so, how much do I owe you?" Rayne asked quickly, rummaging through her purse.

Kirstin shook her head and shoved the flowers into Rayne's arms, nearly causing her to drop her wallet. "On the house."

"Kirstin... I can't accept these." Charity was something Rayne had long learned to mistrust, especially from *this* town.

"Rayne, dear," Kirstin began, but Rayne could not hide the knitting of her shoulders. She hated pet names and the false sense of security they were meant to instill in others. "You just lost your parents. I think you can accept some free flowers from your old boss."

A dozen words threatened to fall from Rayne's lips in response, none of them kind. Her grandmother would have been seething to know she had raised such an ungracious child. So before Rayne could say any of them, she pulled out sixty dollars, smacked it on the counter, and rushed out of the shop.

The icy wind was a welcome greeting as she shot across the parking lot and practically dove into her car.

What the fuck am I even doing here? She questioned, sinking into the seat of her car. *This was all a mistake. I should just call Callum and tell him I can't do this and that he can have whatever Mom and Dad left.*

Ensuring that her car door was locked, Rayne grabbed her phone. Taking a deep breath, she redialed the number Callum had called from her phone and brought it to her ear.

"The number that you have dialed is out of service. Goodbye."

Rayne stared down at her phone as if it might crawl out of her hand at any moment. "Disconnected."

She dropped her phone onto the passenger's seat and wrapped her arms around herself. An ache fluttered to life in her sternum.

"Why would he do that?" she whispered. *What if it was all just a cruel joke?*

Maybe her parents weren't even dead but were sitting at home, having a laugh at her expense, at how stupid their daughter was.

They would do something like this.

Rayne could see her mother's smug, amused smirk and hear her father's thunderous laughter—she was their favorite joke.

But Callum... he had no reason to hate her, no reason to do something like this. *That doesn't mean he doesn't hate you just as much as they did.*

No. Callum had called her and asked her to come back home so they could work through all of this *together*.

Rayne jammed her keys into the ignition and started her car. She ignored the dozens of eyes on her as she backed out of the parking lot and onto the main road.

It was easier, she realized, than trying to ignore the fear that her brother had abandoned her yet again.

Standing at the cemetery entrance, a bouquet of roses and a bottle of water in her arms, Rayne had never felt more foolish.

"I can't believe I'm really about to do this. It's not like she's even alive to be angry with me."

'Never enter a cemetery without something for the guardian of that place; you'll regret it if you do.'

Her grandmother never explained why someone would regret this, but Rayne knew she had never been one for idle threats.

I miss her. There was a frigid irony in the fact that her grandmother was the only person Rayne would have come back to visit, and Adele was the only one who was not buried there.

Her grandmother wasn't buried anywhere.

Rayne sighed and closed her eyes. *We don't have time for this today.*

She knelt in front of the juniper tree beside the entrance. "Hello, spirits," she whispered. "I ask for safe passage through the cemetery to visit my family and to leave once I am done." With that, she placed her bouquets down, unscrewed her water bottle, and poured the contents at the foot of the tree. The water absorbed quickly into the soil, gurgling and bubbling.

'If the water gets sucked into the soil, the guardians will pull you down. Bubbles mean they're talkin' to you. Be sure to speak back.' Her grandmother used to say.

Rayne nodded, gathering her flowers back into her arms. "Thank you."

The walk through the cemetery was oddly comforting, damp, rotting leaves sliding beneath her boots. Finding her parents' grave was as easy as following the scent of freshly upturned dirt.

"Thelma Rose Dorne and Cassian August Dorne. Devoted wife and mother, loving husband and father," she read aloud, stopping just in front of the sleek marble headstones.

What a crock of shit.

People who knew her parents didn't care to maintain relationships with them. Her father was too big a personality, and her mother... there was no easy way to describe Thelma Dorne.

Lack ran deep in her family's blood, and so the constant drive to have, to achieve, nearly consumed them all, leaving nothing but their hard-won souvenirs. Her mother had been different—worse—because unlike the other women of their bloodline who never made it off the reservation, she *had,* and it still wasn't enough.

Rayne's grandmother had gathered her meager life savings and paid the remaining balance of her daughter's college tuition, most of which Thelma had earned through scholarships. Then, Rayne's mother had packed up, unbraided her hair, and never looked back.

When people asked 'what she was,' upon seeing the light amber of her skin and her lengthy black hair, Thelma would smile and say something about being Irish or Mexican, anything other than who she was.

Her mother lived her half-life and pretended to forget about everything that she'd come from. She entered this new world of asphalt and neon and did her best to blend in.

Until she met Cassian.

Cassian Dorne was more lightning than man; at least, that was what Rayne heard from the friends who had endured him since youth. He had grown up in Pennsylvania's poor, suburban hills with seven siblings. His father was a steel mill worker, and his mother was a seamstress, something others may have tried to hide, but not her father.

He would grin widely and tell anyone who would listen that he was not defined by his dark skin or thick, coiled hair. That the soot and dust from his father's steel mill had simply stuck to his skin and that if he scrubbed hard enough, you'd wash it all away to find him as white as the Pearly Gates.

Laughter was a weapon he wielded well, and it was ultimately what he used to run right through Thelma's icy heart.

It should have been a love story. It should have sounded romantic—*why did it never sound romantic?*

The treacherous truth was one that Rayne knew well; there were no two people worse for each other than Cassian and Thelma Dorne. She and her brother had been the only result of their union. And Rayne had emerged... as she was.

Rayne had grown up knowing that her mother was embarrassed by her; love had never been part of the equation.

Rayne tossed the bouquets unceremoniously before her parents' tombstones, not even bothering to remove the plastic from around them. Her grandmother would have been sick to her stomach.

I don't care. I won't compromise. Not for them. I won't mourn what they weren't by ignoring who they were.

"I won't kneel in the dirt for you," Rayne said, her gloved hand balling into a fist as she glared down at the ground. *I wonder if the worms have come for either of you yet.* "I won't cry for you."

She imagined her parents in the damp, blackened soil, roots from the plants above ground digging so deep into their rotten flesh that they touched the bone, contorting their corpses into something warbled, crumpled, and small.

Worms squirming through a hole they'd hollowed in her father's cheeks. Her mother's jaw broken, dandelion roots sprouting from her splintered teeth, mud filling her gaping mouth in one final agonized scream.

Rayne bit back a smile. *What a pretty ending for a pretty woman.*

A little way behind her, tangled in the underbrush of pine trees, something moved, rustling the bushes. Bury was filled with all kinds of small animals, creatures accustomed to living alongside its residents. *Probably just a squirrel. Nothing to get worked up over.*

A branch snapped, the sound echoing through the graveyard as it gave out under the weight of something much bigger than a squirrel.

Cold wind whipped against her, running along her spine and the back of her legs, mimicking the touch of a hand. Her spine straightened, the hairs on the back of her neck bristled to life. Rayne moved to turn around, but her foot froze, refusing to take the step.

Manëtuwàk.

Spirits.

Rayne pinched her lips together in a tight line to keep her voice locked away, lest the spirit be one of the cunning ones and know how to compel her to speak.

She glanced up at the milky sky, the sun hiding behind a cluster of grey clouds but still very much visible. Haints shouldn't be feeling this emboldened this early in the day and this close to town. *No, I've got to stop thinking about them, or I'll call more to me.*

Keeping her back turned to the noise, Rayne forced her eyes down to the ground and carefully made her way out of the graveyard, walking backward. Her hands reached out behind her every few moments to ensure she didn't knock into any graves and call the dead.

Once she breached the entrance of the cemetery, she released the breath that she hadn't realized she had been holding.

The drive back to her house was quiet despite the music she blared to drown her thoughts. The turn off of the main road and up the old dirt one that cut through the forest and up the mountain was one that she knew well, and the last time she had taken it, she thought that she never would again.

She felt like a ghost here.

Up ahead, a sign hung from one of the trees, and Rayne slowed to read it. Painted in purple across a large, white canvas: *Persephone's Garden* with an arrow pointing down a dirt road through another part of the forest.

"That's new," Rayne said, her nose scrunching. "When the hell did Bury start getting new things?"

She made a mental note to nose her way back down and see what was what. "I'm no better than anyone else in this town." She laughed, bitter as the rotting crabapples scattered throughout the road.

It was not long before Rayne parked her car and stood before the home that had claimed so much of her life, her gloved hand gripping tightly at her bag. The early winter clouds hung heavy with the promise of biting rain.

Her childhood home sat on a large plot of land, a massive backyard that had been home to a dying garden her mother rarely tended to. A large, Victorian-style home painted a deep rust, almost pink; her parents' house had always stuck out in town. Her parents were not happy unless they were attracting as much attention as possible.

Rayne tried not to think about how her car was the only one in the driveway. She wasn't ready to go inside yet.

"Excuse me," a voice called behind her. "Ma'am, I don't know whereabouts you're from, but it sure ain't here. I'm gonna need you to leave."

Rayne turned to meet the gaze of an elderly woman whom she recognized immediately from her youth. *Mrs. Hamper.* One of the few neighbors she'd had and her least favorite. She remembered how, despite being invited over for tea with her parents, Mrs. Hamper had insisted on setting out plastic wrap for her alone to sit on.

As if the disease that flowed through her veins had been contagious. *Would that it were,* Rayne thought. *I would have thrown a generous dose your way.*

"Hello, Mrs. Hamper," Rayne said as politely as she could manage. "It's... nice to see you again."

Confusion raked over the woman's face, and her eyes drifted down Rayne's form, covered from head to toe in black leg warmers over a pair of tights and a dress. Fully covered and completely protected—as always. This quirk seemed to ignite the old woman's memory.

"Oh—Rayne, dear!" She smiled. "Forgive me, I didn't recognize you! You've grown so much, and you look so different."

Different.

She knew what that meant when it came to her appearance. *Almost normal. Like everyone else,* the woman had probably wanted to say *skin unmarred.*

Rayne smiled until it hurt. "Yes, I guess I do. Happens."

"How the time flies. By the way, I'm sorry about your parents, dearie," she said, gesturing to the house. "Are you moving back in?"

"Just to sort out some affairs. I'll be gone soon," Rayne replied.

"Well, welcome home. Please let me know if you need help with anything. I am here for you, truly."

"That is very kind of you," Rayne lied. "Thank you." Politeness roiled in her stomach, and she was nauseous with it. There was nothing kind in the old woman's offer. She had learned long ago that the difference between kindness and nice was an ocean one could drown in.

She watched as Mrs. Hamper glanced at the door behind her and lingered. The polite thing to do would be to invite her in.

"Well," she began, taking a step toward the door. "I've only just arrived. Got a lot to do."

Disappointment and annoyance flickered across the old woman's face until it settled in that mask of kindness once more. "Of course, dear. I imagine this has been quite a journey for you. Well, you know where I am if you need me."

Rayne smiled, though it felt much more like a baring of teeth. "Sure."

She watched as the old woman turned and hobbled back toward her home. Once she was sure the pest was gone, she carefully made her way up the cement stairs leading to the front door and knocked.

Rayne expected no fanfare, no warm welcome to await her when she'd gotten here, but she at least expected her brother to answer the damn door.

"Callum," she called again, her knock much louder than the previous three had been. "I'm here. Can you let me in, please?"

Cupping her hands to peer through the paneled glass of the door, she looked for signs of movement only to find stillness behind it. *What the hell, Cal?* Rayne turned the handle, and the door eased open. *Unlocked. He left it unlocked?*

Pale light from outside filtered through the windows, brightening the house's dark interior. She closed and locked the door behind her before she ventured further inside.

Seven years since she had set foot here, and somehow, nothing had changed. The foyer walls were lined with pictures of her parents and their various framed awards. There were a few pictures of Callum: his football team from middle school, basketball, and finally from his freshman year of high school—the last full year he'd spent in this house.

There had only ever been one picture of Rayne in the foyer, tucked away, separated from the rest of the family. A simple picture of her at her high school graduation: she remembered the fit her mother had thrown because Rayne hadn't smiled. But now that picture was gone.

"Callum drops out of high school, runs away at sixteen, hardly calls or lets anyone know he's alive, and all of his pictures stay up. I leave at nineteen after doing everything right, and I'm dead to them. Figures." Rayne murmured, a humorless laugh tangling in her throat.

She knew that they hadn't loved her, couldn't, maybe, but she wished that it would stop hurting. Underneath the rage toward them, all she could feel was the pain of that betrayal.

What did I do that was so wrong?

Discarding her luggage on the first stair, Rayne ventured deeper into the house that had always felt more like a mausoleum. She took a right to follow the pathway to the living room, finding it empty save for the couches, fireplace, and her mother's hideous paintings of random animals; cats, lions, cardinals. Rayne had always hated all of them.

"Cal?" She called, her voice echoing down the hall. "Are you here?"

Rayne headed back into the foyer, making a hard left into the kitchen. "I tried calling you," she continued. "But your phone said it was—"

On the gleaming silver refrigerator, a neon-pink Post-It note caught her eye, and she froze.

Rayne's breath hitched, her throat constricted with an emotion she recognized all too well. She knew what the note would say. She knew that he was gone and that she was alone again.

It had been like this since she could remember, coming home to an empty house after she walked back from school, spending quiet weekends in her room while her parents went out on their dates. They never left anything but notes in their wake:

'You're on your own for dinner.'

'Lock all the doors, we won't be back until late.'

Rayne expected this from them, had grown more accustomed to it than she wanted to admit. But her brother? She had hoped that maybe he could like her, at least a little. Love was not something Rayne expected from her family, but she wanted at least one of them to *like* her.

She had driven all this way for him, just for the chance that they could be in one another's orbit for a little bit.

Rayne hadn't even been in the double digits when Callum had gone, but now, her brother was pushing forty, and she wondered who he was. Was he married? Did he live around here? Had she become an aunt? Did he miss the rolling hills of their little mountain town?

Had he missed her?

The last thought terrified her because, regardless of the answer, she did not know what to do with the information. Rayne had missed her brother so much that it nearly clouded all her memory of him—who was Callum Anderson Dorne outside of her desire to be near him?

Memory had a way of robbing life from things. And as much as she missed her sibling, she could remember little about him.

But as she looked around their desolate, pristine childhood home, she knew only one thing: her brother was not here, and the answer to why was in the ominous note, taunting her. She stared at it for a moment before she sighed and grabbed it.

> *I had to go. Sorry. Don't listen to*
> *the house.*
>
> *-Callum.*

"'*Don't listen to the house?*' What the hell does that mean?"

Rayne read the note twice, then once more for good measure, and flipped it over, hoping to find some other message, some inquiry about her health, what she'd been doing with her life, or *anything*. But instead, the message remained the same.

"He's gone. He didn't even say goodbye." The sting of it burned her eyes and dried her throat.

Rayne knew that she had no right to be upset. She and Callum were all but strangers. She shouldn't even care that he was gone; it wasn't as if he were an active part of her life.

But her treacherous heart longed for a connection with someone. Even more than that, she wished someone desired the same of *her*.

It was greedy. It was too much for someone like her to request, but she could not hide from it.

Rayne sighed and tore up the letter, tossing it in the trash under the sink.

The house that had been silent in her childhood remained so now in her adulthood. It was strange to her that even though her parents had been living in this house until only a few weeks ago, it was still so cold and empty. Rayne had seen houses in magazines with more warmth.

It accounted for the things she knew to be true about herself: the odd demeanor, lips that struggled to fix themselves into a genuine smile, and the way she regarded herself like something to be contained.

Tears leaked onto her cheeks, and hastily, she wiped at them. "Well," she said with a sniffle. "No use in pouting about it."

No sooner had the words left her mouth than the stairs creaked, shifting as if someone was coming down them. Raising a delicate brow, she padded back out of the kitchen and into the empty foyer.

No one was there.

"Get a grip. It's just you here," she reminded herself, scrubbing a hand over her face. Now, the weight of the hours-long drive on only a few hours of sleep began to hit her.

Again, she heard movement in the house, a slight rumble beneath her feet like the shifting of pipes.

Rayne shook her head. "You need to get some sleep. Your brain is fried."

With a heavy sigh, Rayne grabbed her bag and headed up the stairs to the room she'd claimed as a teenager. She avoided looking at the other one, directing her attention elsewhere.

I'm not ready to think about that place yet.

CHAPTER THREE
the shadow

The Shadow lurked at the edge of the forest in Bury, floating like mist and waiting, *always* waiting.

They had known the second she crossed the border into Bury, the aroma of her skin was unlike anything they had ever smelled before. A delicate mix of almond and rose, no other human's scent came close to enticing them as completely as hers did.

The Shadow had followed her, latching onto the exhaust pipe of her car until she had arrived at her home. They wanted to get closer, to follow her in, but the House would not allow it. Blood magic was often the strongest, but The Shadow did not mind.

Time did not matter, so they rarely bothered to consider the ticking of moments, the passing of days.

The Shadow had slunk into the thickest part of the forest across from her home, nesting in the shade of pine trees while they watched her. They looked on in vague curiosity as the old woman from the only other house on the road spoke to her.

They wanted her to step off her land, to take just a few steps too far into the forest, but, instead, after knocking at the door a few times, she slipped inside.

Annoyance tangled within them; they had been hoping to get at least a chance to frighten her, to feed on her terror just a little before they hunted her. But then again, where would the fun be in such an early victory? *Winter is not yet here, and it has been too long since a game was had.*

So, The Shadow resumed their waiting game, watching for any more signs of her.

Night bled into day, and The Shadow had shifted from their position in the pines to a thicket of blackberry bushes.

The door to the house finally opened, and she stepped outside. The Shadow opened their eyes and watched as the woman, whom they recognized but did not know, stepped carefully through the forest.

The Shadow may not have remembered how long they had haunted the forest of Bury or how many creatures had been caught between their teeth, but they remembered *her*.

Without much thought, The Shadow slipped from their hiding spot and moved closer to her, burying themself in a bush.

She was tall, much taller now than The Shadow remembered. *Or had I somehow become smaller?* They frowned at the thought as small things were meant for eating.

he woman was covered from head to toe in black—a black hoodie, black tights, black thigh-highs over her tights, and beat-down black boots. The exposed bits of skin were marbled, flecked pink, and light brown with scars, and her curly hair was tied back in a mess of a braid. They drank in her appearance, and the differences in how they remembered her from when she last stumbled into their forest.

She stretched, catlike, and then closed the door behind her before heading toward her car again.

Come toward the forest. The Shadow thought, running their tongue along their teeth.

The woman stopped, her back still to The Shadow, but then she turned slowly and stared into the forest. Into The Shadow. *Like she had heard me.*

How long has it been since I have been heard like this, when I am nothing more than a breeze?

The woman looked around hesitantly before she walked down her driveway and across the street to the forest's edge.

An ocean of scents followed her as she drew closer: amaretto, roses, coffee, sweat. The Shadow's tongue roiled across its lips, pressed against the trees. Their body melted into being.

Hunger had a way of changing The Shadow.

She paused just at the forest entrance, glancing up at the crucifix that had been nailed to a pine tree and the small collection of charms that hung from it.

The locals had a habit of setting up homemade crucifixes and affixing personal items to them, creating crude altars meant to protect them as they entered the forest.

It amused The Shadow more than anything else; the humans and their superstitions would not protect any of them. It hadn't thus far.

They watched her as she searched for her charm, one that they knew well: a brass ornament of a wolf chasing after the moon. The Shadow did not miss the small, soft smile on her lips when she finally laid eyes on it.

"*Kwilumël,* Ma'maw," She whispered. *I miss you.* "So much."

The Shadow cocked its head to the side. I *have not heard that language in quite some time. It is...nice to hear again.* Language was a skill that The Shadow had acquired in their time and travels; there were very few languages that they did not speak or at least understand.

he stepped further into the grass, still too far for The Shadow to reach out and touch her in the light. She was just out of their reach, and The Shadow swallowed a growl of frustration.

"What the fuck was that?" She whispered. Her fear spiked the air, a sharp, bitter scent that made their mouths water. The Shadow's magic spilled out of them, pooling down into the dirt like molasses. They would drag her into the earth with them so that they could eat her in private. No one would hear her scream, and unlike the other poor creatures that The Shadow captured between their claws, they would leave nothing of her for even the vultures to find.

I will have to devour her slowly.

Her arms encircled her small frame to stave off the morning chill. They could hear her teeth clattering together, and The Shadow wondered if her bones were as fragile as the rest of her. All she needed to do was take one more step, and The Shadow would have her, bones and all.

She squinted, peering at them through the underbrush. Her gloved hand moved to push the thick, overgrown branches from her path. The Shadow's teeth were only a few centimeters from it—

"Rayne?"

Behind her, from the house nearly adjacent to hers, an old woman poked her head out of the door. "What are you doing outside so early?"

Rayne stepped away from The Shadow and out of their proximity to turn and face the woman.

"Oh. Just thought I'd go for a walk or... something." Rayne called back.

The old woman beckoned Rayne over. "You've been gone too long. You don't want to go wandering in that wood before midday."

The Shadow snarled in frustration, the branches in front of them trembling with the sound.

Rayne glanced over her shoulder, almost as if she could see The Shadow, and then back to the old woman. "Yeah... you've got a point there."

The Shadow watched as Rayne slunk back into the light, back to the safety of her own land and that damned House. The Shadow would not risk the light when it had so little energy to sustain itself, and it did not want to rush.

They had been prepared to wait, but then the scent of her fear, the taste of it—now they would need something else to sustain themself until they could find a way to get her.

After a brief exchange with the old woman who did not care to listen, Rayne got into her car, backed out of the driveway, and drove down the road that led to town.

I will feed. They decided. *Seeing her has upset my stomach and gored me like a stag's horn.*

The Shadow melted into the shade of the trees until they were no longer formless but the shadow of a wolf. They breathed deeply of the forest's scent and crouched low to the ground, pressing their noses to the cool dirt.

In winter, nothing was safe from The Shadow, for the warmth of life was something that they could always find in the cold. Beating hearts and pumping blood were a magnet to which they would always be drawn.

Scenting the sweet maple scent of deer fur on the wind, The Shadow licked their lips. It was not as enticing as Rayne, but it would do for the time being.

Disappearing back into the darkness, The Shadow sped through the misty morning, following the scent deeper into the forest until the creature's fear soured the sweet smell. Jagged and very real, their teeth latched around the stag's neck and bit down, copper immediately coating their tongue, and The Shadow sighed in delight.

Life was such a sweet thing to snuff out.

Content with its kill, The Shadow dragged the carcass back down toward the entrance of the forest so that they might eat and catch sight of Rayne when she returned, pretending that it was not fur between their teeth but soft skin and sinew.

They were content to gnaw on their kill, filling the forest with a symphony of snapping bones and tearing tendons that began to mimic the sound of her name.

CHAPTER FOUR
rayne

E ven with the forest in her rearview mirror, Rayne could not shake the chill that slipped down her spine as she had stood at the edge of the forest—the sound of... whatever that had been from within the belly of the woods.

This isn't the forest that I remember.

As a child, she had always been taught to be mindful of the spirits and animals that would gobble her up if she let them, but fear had never been an active part of that.

Most of the town feared the forest, regarding it as a necessary evil interwoven into their lives. Rayne had never viewed it that way. From what she remembered, the forest had always been kind to her.

The forest always—Rayne paused at the thought. *Huh. What had the forest always done for me? I could have sworn that I—shit!*

The sign for Persephone's Garden flashed in her rearview, and she hit the brakes and put the car in reverse before rolling down the dirt road. About a quarter of a mile down, a large fruit stand sat in front of a house Rayne couldn't recall seeing before.

The house was small, but even so, elaborately decorated. It looked nothing like the typical Bury house; suncatchers hung above the door in place of crucifixes, stone gargoyles by the front step instead of angels, and not a single bottle tree in sight.

The fruit stand was filled with pears, kale, and jars of honey. Rayne parked on the opposite end of the road and approached, eying it all as if it were the strangest thing she'd ever seen in her life.

Bury was a coal-mining town; at least, it had been before the mines became too dangerous for anyone to work in, and the residents had been forced to scramble to find work elsewhere. The paper and steel mill had saved most of them, but when those closed down too, Bury had essentially been cut off from the world.

People didn't come here, and they didn't leave; everyone scraped by with precisely what they had, venturing no further than the next town over.

Bury didn't *have* any farmers.

"You're the new girl, aren't you?"

Rayne jumped. From behind the fruit stand, a woman poked her head out, beaming at her, and Rayne knew instantly from the other woman's voice that she was not from here. Her words held none of the heavy Bury drawl that Rayne had tried endlessly to purge.

The woman was tall, easily over six feet, and every inch of her was muscular and strong. Her face was soft, delicate, even with the septum and eyebrow piercings. Her clementine-colored hair was swept up, protected by a pale yellow bandana that somehow matched her bright blue overalls.

She's beautiful.

The woman smiled, shoving her hands into her pockets, and Rayne realized that she was staring. "Ain't new," Rayne corrected, clearing her throat.

"Oh, no? Heard quite a bit of talk about you in town. You got here yesterday, and already word spread up the mountain. Gotta love small towns, huh?"

Rayne's nose scrunched. "No, I sure don't," she grumbled. "Are you Persephone?"

The woman stepped out from behind the stand, bringing with her the scent of lemons. "Nah. Just a little joke no one ever laughs at except me." She offered

Rayne her hand. "I'm Persimmon Jaxon. You can just call me Pers, though. Or Persi. Either suits me just fine."

Pretty name.

Staring down at Persimmon's hand for a beat, Rayne carefully slipped her gloved one into the other woman's. "Rayne Dorne."

"That's a pretty name."

Rayne pulled her hand back and looked away. "Oh. Okay, uhm. Thanks."

If her abruptness bothered Persimmon, she didn't let it show. Instead, she rocked back on her heels. "So, what can I help you with, Rayne Dorne?"

Oh. Shit.

Rayne hadn't intended to buy anything, but she also hadn't expected to meet anyone out here either. She had just come down here to be nosy, but now she felt silly. "Uhm. Two pounds of pears, please."

"Five dollars, flat," Persimmon said, moving to grab a fabric bag from the small cluster of them that hung behind the counter.

"That's a weird-looking bag," Rayne remarked, rummaging through her wallet to grab a five. Her eyes went wide at the realization that saying that aloud might have been rude.

"You like it?" Persimmon grinned, looking up as she placed the pears inside. "I make 'em myself. I got a lot of extra fabric from the clothes I make, and I figured it was better than plastic, right?"

"You make clothes?"

"Made everything I'm wearing."

Rayne looked Persimmon over again, as if she could find any evidence that these clothes were homemade. They seemed nearly perfect. "Wow."

Persimmon waved a dismissive hand. "Not much, just something I like doing for fun." Bright green eyes fell to the money in Rayne's hand. "You gonna pay me or am I gonna have to fight you for it?"

Immediately, Rayne shoved the money into Persimmon's hands. "Sorry! I didn't mean to—I wouldn't—"

Soft laughter twinkled between them. "Rayne, I'm kidding. You're fine."

Unsure, Rayne turned her attention back to the ground. "Okay, good." She held out her hand. "I have to go."

"Sure thing." Persimmon placed the bag in her hand. "It was nice to meet you, Rayne. And don't be a stranger, okay? We're neighbors now, after all."

"Yeah. Okay," Rayne said without looking at her.

As she drove away, she caught Persimmon waving at her through her rearview mirror.

Rayne forced herself to focus on the road.

Rayne took a deep breath, trying to steady herself for what she knew was going to be absolute hell. State offices were a nightmare in the city, but in Bury? They were even worse.

With every employee old enough to remember a time before electricity and the tendency to gossip when they should be filling paperwork, Rayne did not look forward to the long, arduous process of probate.

She had no idea what she was doing, but armed with the power of the internet, she'd spent most of the morning researching what would be required of her to own her childhood home legally.

Now there was nothing left for her to do but walk into the county clerk's office.

The first scent to hit her when she entered was that of dust, stale coffee, and beneath that, the faint smell of off-brand Coca-Cola. The building was frigid, too old to have central heating properly installed. Rayne followed the faded signs until she was in a small room, the floor sticky with spilled drinks that had long since dried. Fluorescent lights hummed overhead like houseflies.

Streaky glass separated Rayne from the clerk at her desk, a woman she recognized from her Mam'maw's quilting club, Harriet something. *Too damn old to be working a job like this.*

Rayne approached the desk. "Excuse me—"

Harriet's attention remained fixed on the quilting magazine she clutched in her gnarled hands. "Take a number, please, and step away from the glass."

"There's no one else here," Rayne said, gesturing to the empty room.

"Ma'am, take a number and step away from the glass," Harriet repeated.

Swallowing the slew of swears that danced on the edge of her tongue, Rayne snatched a faded blue ticket from beside the desk and took three steps back.

Harriet sighed loudly, dog-eared her place in the magazine, and closed it. Easing her binocular-esque glasses onto her nose, she pushed the small black button to her left, and over the crunchy, loud speaker came a pleasant voice:

'*Now serving customer number three.*'

"Please, approach, ma'am."

Rayne forced the kindest smile that she could manage. "Hi, Harriet. I don't know if you remember me, but—"

"What can I help you with today?"

"I'd like to see if my parents' will is on file."

"Sure, I can do that for you. Names?"

Rayne blinked. This woman had known her since birth and damn well knew her parents' names. "Thelma and Cassian Dorne."

Harriet somehow managed to type on her dinosaur of a computer, squinting as she plugged in the information. "And your relation to the deceased?"

Curling her hand into a fist, Rayne smiled harder. "I'm their daughter. Rayne Dorne."

"Alright. Just a moment while I get that information for you."

The moment spooled into fifteen minutes, Harriet humming along with the choral gospel music playing softly from the radio on the desk behind her, while Rayne counted every crack in the floor.

"Alright, Ms. Dorne. Says here that there was, in fact, a will. It listed your brother, Callum, as the executor. However... " Harriet squinted and scrolled down slowly with her computer's mouse. "It looks like he filed a quitclaim last week."

"What the hell's a quitclaim?"

Harriet scowled at Rayne's swearing and smacked her thin lips. "Means he wasn't interested in anything your parents left behind, and since you were both listed, it means everything belongs to you now."

"But. How—?"

"Deed should be comin' in the mail soon. Once you've got that, you're officially a homeowner in the beautiful town of Bury."

Rayne's mouth opened and closed as the weight of it all settled over her.

Harriet sighed, already picking up her magazine again. "You have a blessed day, Ms. Dorne. And I'd thank God tonight, if I were you. Ain't nothing He hates more than when people take His gifts for granted."

The drive back up to her home was entirely silent; even music couldn't drown out the thoughts circling her mind.

Why would Callum give up the house to me?

Why did he say they left me everything when, really, it was all for him?

And if he was going to do all that, then why just disappear right after?

Losing Callum at such a young age when she had adored him had been hard, but it was not what hurt the most. What pained her was the fact that she had caught him that night as he was sneaking out of their home.

His entire life was packed up in his school backpack, his long, silken hair braided and tucked under a baseball cap. Rayne had come downstairs in the middle of the night for a glass of water only to see her brother half out the door.

He'd told her that he was leaving, but before she could shed a single tear, he had sworn that he would come back for her, that he would save her from their parents, but she had to keep a secret. Rayne had believed him with every bone in her small body.

But he didn't come back. Years later, her parents mentioned receiving letters from him, and spoke so fondly of him, even though he'd run away.

Callum had never written her.

I just want to know why, she thought, hastily rubbing away a tear. *Why can't he just talk to me?*

Parking the car in her driveway, Rayne leaned back in her seat, covering her face with her hands, hiding her shame though there was no one else there to see it.

"Fuck," she hissed after a few minutes, wiping the remainder of her tears.

Exiting her car, she paused and considered the mailbox at the end of the driveway. Tightening her arms around herself to stave off the chill, she approached it and opened the mailbox. Shuffling through the mail, there were a few pieces of junk, magazines her mother had ordered too many things out of, but beneath all of that, there was a letter addressed to her from the County Record's Office.

She wasted no time opening it, and her hands shook, clutching the deed to the home she had worked so hard to escape.

This town is trying to eat me alive.

CHAPTER FIVE

rayne

S taring into the inky darkness surrounding her, Rayne was beginning to realize that this was not the forest she knew. She reached ahead, grabbing for something to steady herself. The twigs snapping underfoot were the only sound as she maneuvered her way through an indiscernible night.

Rayne tripped, tumbling into nothingness, the scent of dirt and the copper twinge of blood hitting her nose.

"I fell but... nothing hurts," she marveled aloud.

The darkness melted away, revealing a clearing, a single tree in its center. The moon rose from the darkness, fixing itself above her and illuminating the world around her. Silver light splashed over everything, outlining the tree's silhouette.

"A hawthorn tree. Have I—have I seen that before?" Rayne whispered. The shadow of the tree shuddered, moving as if coaxed by the wind, and then it detached from the tree entirely.

Rayne backed away, her spine colliding with an invisible wall, trapping her.

The shadow curled into itself momentarily. A milky eye blinked into existence, followed by another. Pale pupils bulged next and rolled until they came to rest on Rayne.

Rayne held her breath, frozen in place as she watched teeth appear one by one, a dark mouth splitting into a grin. "I did not think it would be so easy to find you."

The creature's voice shook the entire forest, and Rayne felt it in the very marrow of her bones.

"Who are you?" she whispered.

The creature chuckled as its head swiveled toward her, its bones snapping and crunching like gravel. "Come to my tree and ask me that again."

Rayne cast a glance at the tree and then back at the abomination before her. "Why the ever living fuck would I do that?"

It only grinned wider. "Because you always have. You always will."

"I don't know you."

"But I know you," it said, black tongue running along its lips. "Come to my tree, and then you will know me."

The monster did not approach her; it remained across the clearing, watching her.

"Where... where are we?"

"Nowhere."

"Is that a riddle?"

The creature chuckled at her expense again, and Rayne's cheeks flushed.

"Is that what constitutes a riddle to you, Rayne?"

Rayne scowled. "No—I—I want you to go away."

"Hmm," it replied, staying exactly where it was.

"I'm not scared of you, whatever you are," she lied.

"No?" the creature asked, and its grin grew impossibly wider, slicing across its entire face. "Such brave words. I wonder, however—"

It grew in size until the darkness of it lapped at her feet, and it bled into the sky. The creature's massive jaws opened, its tongue curling around the moon. "If you will remain as such after I've snuffed out the light."

The monster swallowed the moon, throwing her and the entire world into smothering blackness.

Rayne shot up, sheets damp with sweat plastered to her skin. Her breathing remained ragged even as she took in her surroundings, even as the realization that she was no longer trapped in the dark with... whatever that had been. Grey morning light filtered in through her bedroom window, streaking across her floor.

I must have been dreaming, she thought as she ran a hand through her curls. *But it felt so real.*

Rayne shuddered, the memory of the shadow's voice slipping down her spine. She could have sworn that it was right in her ear, surrounding her and drowning her all at once.

She swung her legs over the side of the bed with a groan, her toes tapping against the cardboard of the pizza box she'd had from last night.

"No more pizza before bed, apparently," she said as she scooped the trash up and walked stiffly out of her room. Rayne was typically very clean, never allowing her space to ever get above a dull roar in terms of mess.

This house just makes me want to rot, she thought miserably as she carefully descended the stairs.

She heard people her age beginning to complain of aching joints and stiff limbs where there had once been fluidity—it was always so funny to her. People experiencing discomfort in their bodies for the first time, when *all* she felt was discomfort in hers.

The skin disease that ate away at her was a nasty one, attacking all of the soft tissue in her body, making her delicate in more ways than one. It was genetic and not contagious, though the rough appearance of her skin, covered in countless scars, indicated otherwise to people.

That was the real reason Rayne kept herself covered from head to toe, not just to protect her skin but to protect herself from the way that people looked at her, the questions that always followed.

Her legs and hands were where the worst of the damage had been done. Scars that ran deep, sometimes her hands didn't even look human to her.

The mirror had never been a companion.

Sighing as she cracked her neck and rolled her shoulders, Rayne tossed the pizza box into the recycling and plopped down at the kitchen table.

"So... what do I do now?"

None of this was part of the plan.

Rayne had intended to come back, spend a week, maybe two with her brother, and then run as fast away from this town as soon as she could, back to her life.

"If you could even call it a life," she murmured.

It wasn't much, but it was hers and none of her family could touch it.

"You don't own me," Rayne declared, imagining that her parents' ghosts were sitting across from her.

The house's landline rang and she yelped, nearly falling out of her chair.

Why the fuck do they still have a landline in this day and age?

Rayne stood and slowly approached the muted-pink phone hanging on the hallway wall, as if it were a wild animal.

"Hello?" she ventured when she finally picked it up.

"Who is this?"

"Uh, you tell me. You called."

"Where's Callum?"

Rayne bit her lip. "He's... he left. He isn't here."

"Oh. So, this must be Rayne," the voice chirped. "Hey, Rainy. It's June."

I should have recognized that shrill voice. "Hi," Rayne clipped back.

Juniper Stern was Rayne's second cousin and personal nightmare. She had never outright bullied Rayne, but she had a way of making her feel small. Juniper's favorite thing to do was point out every flaw Rayne had. It was her cousin who had given her the nickname 'Rainy' when they were children because of her constant frown and messy hair.

The rest of the family had been all too happy to adopt it.

"Wasn't expecting to hear from you. How are things going?"

Rayne pulled the phone away from her ear for a moment to stare at it, incredulous that her moron of a cousin was really trying to have a conversation with her. "They're... fine."

Before Rayne could get another word out edgewise, Juniper pressed on. "So, do you know when Cal will be back? I tried calling his cellphone, and he didn't answer, but then I remembered how bad the service was out in Hicksville, so I figured I'd try the house phone."

"It's not even nine AM."

"More than half the day is gone! We can't all have cozy work-from-home jobs," Juniper chirped. "In any case, I really need to talk to him about the estate and all that noise."

"Cal isn't coming back," Rayne began, chewing on her lower lip. "And... he left the house to me. Filed a quit claim and skipped town."

Silence stretched between them, so long that Rayne was nearly sure Juniper had hung up on her. "That can't be right."

"It is. Got the deed and everything."

"None of that sounds like Callum," Juniper pressed.

Of course, he kept contact with her and the rest of the family, Rayne thought, splintering at the realization. *But not me.*

"Yeah? Well, I wouldn't know," Rayne bit back.

Juniper remained silent long enough for Rayne to realize that she'd been out of line. "Look, June—"

"I need to talk to Callum. I think there's been some kind of mix-up. I'm going to keep trying his cellphone." And then she hung up.

Rayne slammed the receiver back into the phone, her fingers crying out in protest. She ignored them and rested against the wall, sliding down and curling her knees into her chest.

What did I do? Why can't anyone just fucking tell me what I did?

Beneath her feet, the floor shifted, settling with the movement of the harsh wind.

"No need for any of that now."

Rayne's head whipped up from between her knees, ice settling in her veins. Wordlessly, she moved to her feet and into the kitchen. Grabbing a knife, she peered around the corner of the kitchen entrance way into the foyer.

Seeing nothing, she peeked into the living room and back down the hallway where she'd just been.

I heard someone, she thought, clutching the knife to her chest.

Slowly, she crept down the hallway to the guestroom at the end of it and kicked open the door. When she found nothing, she did the same to the guest bathroom, sunroom, and laundry room.

No one could have snuck upstairs, as there was only one way up, and Rayne had been too close to miss the sound of someone entering the house.

"I'm not crazy," she declared to the house. "I heard what I heard."

I am keeping this knife with me.

After Rayne finished rummaging through the kitchen to find something equivalent to breakfast, she settled on one of Persimmon's pears and a mug of the disgusting coffee her parents had loved so much. She settled onto the couch, pen and legal notepad of paper on the coffee table, along with her sad breakfast and her phone in hand.

Okay, so. I guess I'm Googling how to sell a house.

Rayne had no interest in this place. At nineteen, she had sworn to herself that she would never live in Bury again, and she intended to follow through with that by any means necessary.

She would sell this place for whatever anyone would pay. After a few hours' worth of research, Rayne deemed her best bet to sell through a realtor in another town.

Bury didn't have a single realtor as far as she knew, and it was better that way; none of the locals would want this place knowing that two people had died in it.

Despite the religion that coursed through the veins of the town, there was an undeniable stain of folklore and the old world.

Rayne would have a better chance of offloading the place to a stranger who knew nothing about her or her family.

"Okay," she said, sitting up from the curled position she'd taken. "Step one, clean the house and get rid of all their junk."

One hour later, Rayne found herself in front of her parents' room, her hair piled on top of her head, some ratty old clothes she'd seen in her closet, in case she got dirty. Her parents' room used to be off limits, reserved only for emergencies or when she needed to get their attention.

She was twenty-six years old, and yet standing at the foot of their door, Rayne was seven years old again.

When her Mam'maw had died, it rippled through everything Rayne had been. She had been too young at that time to understand that her parents were not the people she should have sought comfort from.

She had tried to vent to her mother, crying about how much she missed her Mam'maw and how she didn't understand where her Mam'maw had gone or why Rayne couldn't go to her house anymore.

"She's gone to Heaven, Rainy," her mother had said, in the middle of painting her nails when Rayne had wandered in. Her grandmother had been gone only a week, and Rayne couldn't remember if she'd seen her mother shed a single tear. "Ain't no use in crying when God's got her in His hands. We should all be so lucky."

Rayne swallowed the sudden dryness in her throat, clearing it. "I'm not a child anymore. They're dead, and I'm not."

Still, she hesitated, her fist clenching and unclenching as the moments ticked by. When she crossed the threshold, she half expected her mother's sharp voice to cut her down, endlessly correcting the wrongness of her daughter.

When nothing happened, Rayne sighed. "Time to grow up and get to work."

Rummaging through their things was like playing in a graveyard, kicking up the dust of everything her parents had been.

Rayne started with the paperwork to ensure nothing significant had been left behind. Then she would just tear through the room and get rid of every hideous thing she could find.

She made an event of the occasion, taking a break to get more coffee and discovering hot chocolate in the cupboard.

Sitting on the edge of her parents' bed, she scattered the contents of their dressers and file cabinets around her.

The crisp apple scent of her mother's perfume clung to every paper, and her father's nameless knick-knacks were tossed in with them. Even though her parents had been married for nearly twenty-five years before they'd passed, nothing about them had ever seemed compatible.

Rayne had never dreamt of marriage, could not imagine what life would look like with another person at her side after seeing what her parents had been like.

I'd rather be alone than a thorn in the side of another.

Her fingers brushed over the crinkled, stained papers, her eyes scanning for anything that could have been important. The scent of roses flooded her nose, and Rayne dropped everything.

Mam'maw.

Her grandmother had loved roses. She'd filled her garden and her house with them, drying the petals out to make potpourri. Every time Rayne caught a whiff of the scent, it comforted her, reminding her of summer evenings on her grandmother's porch, the cicadas singing along with the old woman.

The scent alone was enough to fold her in memories of the only time she could ever remember feeling loved.

Rayne wore perfume oils to match the scent as best she could, but nothing ever smelled the same.

An old, browning envelope was the source of the smell, and Rayne held it to her nose, breathing in the scent. She pinched her eyes shut to keep the tears at bay. After a few moments, she opened it, delicately pulling out the letter within—her grandmother's distinct scribble.

Adele hadn't learned to read or write until after she'd married Rayne's grandfather, Henry. She'd taught herself out of spite; her handwriting had never quite become legible enough for most people outside of the family to discern it.

"*Ntan'të,*" The letter began, addressed to Rayne's mother. "*I know that you are upset with me, but it's what I want for her. You already have a home, one that you and your husband share. You said that you wanted Callum to have it, and that is your right. But this is my home, and I have every right to give it to her."*

Rayne's nose scrunched in bewilderment as she read on. *"I know that... you struggle with her, that she is not the daughter you imagined. But she is yours as you are mine. I love her, and I want this for her. Forgive me if you feel I have disrespected you. That was never my intention. Could you come over next weekend and help me draft the paperwork? All of these legal papers with their fancy words, they never speak truly, and I want to make sure that little snapdragon gets everything."*

After her Mam'maw had died, her house, along with everything within it, had been put up for sale by the bank. That's what Rayne's mother had always told her. It ended up being sold to a real estate company looking to buy up land, so after they acquired it, they demolished the house and leveled the ground.

Only to end up not even building on it, abandoning the land for a more profitable region.

Everything Adele had worked for, all of her memories, her stories, her history, was destroyed with nothing to show for it.

But why would my grandmother have tried to give me the house if she was drowning in so much debt? Rayne wondered.

Thinking back, her grandmother had never struggled for money as far as she remembered. Rayne remembered overhearing her mother explaining Adele's situation to him one afternoon. After her husband had been accidentally killed on the job and the state had been ruled at fault, Adele was set to receive a payment every month for the rest of her life, so long as she never remarried.

Adele hadn't, not for the money but because her husband had been the love of her life.

So then why would the bank take her house? *Unless... unless my mother had been lying.*

The letter slipped from Rayne's fingers, and she dove into the paperwork, digging through every single file. The sun's position had shifted in the sky by the time she found them, tucked away in a manila folder with a blue star sticker, and written next to it was her grandmother's old address.

8 Huckleberry Rd
Bury, Pennsylvania

Inside, she found her grandmother's will listing Rayne as the sole executor. Trembling fingers slid through the rest of the paperwork: another listing Thelma as the guardian of Rayne's property due to her being a minor, and a copy of a petition Thelma had filed with the probate court asking to sell the house "for the minor's benefit."

Rayne scrambled to her feet, pacing the room. Her ears rang, every fiber of her being radiating with fury.

I could have had everything. My grandmother's journals, her paintings, her garden, and my mother, she—

Her parents' wedding picture stared at her, proudly displayed beside the TV. Rayne snatched it and stormed into the hallway, tossing it over the railing.

Glass shattered over the marble floor, and Rayne was sure she'd never heard a more beautiful sound in her life.

"I will not die your daughter," she shouted. "I will not carry anything of yours!"

Rayne blew through her parents' room like a hurricane, sparing nothing. She gathered every picture of the two of them and shattered it on the floor. She broke every item her mother might have loved: her Tiffany glass lamps, her laptop, ripped the pages from her books, and tore her expensive clothes.

"I'm glad you believed in Hell because I know you're there now. I hope your skin is bubbling off the bone and your eyes are boiling in your skull!"

Tremors ripped through her even as she surveyed the damage she'd done. *It's not enough.*

It was not enough to destroy what her mother had cared about; Rayne wanted—*needed*—to erase every trace of the shell of a childhood she'd had. Everything save for the sole picture she had of her and her grandmother.

What few pictures of Rayne existed in the house were tucked away in random corners, a drawer in her mother's side of the closet, on her father's bookshelf. Rayne grabbed them all. She tore them out of frames.

"If everyone wants to act like I don't exist, then I won't. I'll cut out every ounce of me, I'll change my fucking name. I will never be Dorne again."

Pausing only to put on her boots, Rayne gathered every picture of her and headed downstairs. She disregarded the crunching of glass under her and went outside through the sliding door in the living room, out onto the balcony, and out in the backyard.

Outside, there was a pear tree with rotten and half-eaten fruit on the vine from where squirrels and birds had made meals of them. A shovel would have been smarter, but Rayne's patience was threadbare.

Rayne knelt into the dirt and dug, gloves and all, ripping up the cold ground and focusing on her rage instead of the pain in her screaming knees. When the hole was deep enough, she shoved the pictures into it and began piling dirt on.

Her face, soft and round, eyes sad even in pictures where she was smiling, looked back up at her. Bile rose in her throat, and she hastened her pace in response, desperate to be done with all of it.

Even when she was buried, dead in the ground like the two who had created her, Rayne felt tethered.

Tied to them, locked into some role she had never asked for.

I could burn this whole place down, she thought, her vision long since blurred with tears. *Leave the stove on and just walk away.*

She didn't.

Instead, she grabbed her keys and sped into town like a bat out of hell.

CHAPTER SIX
rayne

R ayne drove with no real destination in mind.

Somehow she ended up downtown, parked in the public lot just a few blocks down from the grocery store. Since she hadn't planned on being here so long, she hadn't accounted for needing to buy food. She couldn't just survive on pears and shitty coffee. It occurred to her, vaguely, how terrible she looked at the moment; her hair a mess, her face flushed, cheeks tear-stained, wearing a ratty old band t-shirt and leggings littered with holes. She hadn't even remembered to grab her thigh highs for protection.

"What the fuck does it even matter? What can anyone say about me that they haven't already?" She mumbled.

Unaware of her suffering, the day was crisp, a brief blimp of autumn weather before the real winter came in to devour everything. The sun bled into the forest's mountains, pinks and oranges kissing the dark trees. Her grandmother used to say that all of God's glory could be found in the mountains. She'd always said she wanted to be buried in those hills.

Instead, her grandmother had been cremated, her ashes scattered to the wind.

Rayne didn't even have a place to visit her.

As she crossed the street, a couple passed her by, tangled in one another, laughing and whispering between themselves as they walked.

Rayne's chest tightened with the all too familiar tension knotting within her: envy.

It was not the romance that she craved but the proximity; someone who wanted to be near her and who didn't spike her anxiety when they *were* in her orbit. Rayne could not imagine what that would look like, let alone feel like, but her stubborn, weak heart could not let go of the desire.

When she finally made it to the store, Rayne froze. *I forgot. His family owns this place—how the fuck could I have forgotten?*

As quickly as she'd come, Rayne turned on her heel and walked back the way she'd come. Her day was bad enough already; no need to add *him* to the mix.

"Rayne! Hey!"

Persimmon waved at her from the parking lot, a fabric bag of leeks in her arms as she approached. Rayne stared blankly at her.

Why is she calling me?

"I wasn't expecting to see you out and about," Persimmon said conversationally. Her eyes traced over Rayne as she really looked at her. "Are you... okay?"

Rayne blinked up at Persimmon, her mouth opening and closing as she fought with what to say.

I should just lie. It was what she typically did when, on the rare occasion, someone asked how she was doing.

It was easier for her that way; she didn't have to worry about accidentally needing someone for something.

But Persimmon, there was something genuine in her expression. *Besides,* Rayne thought, *we're strangers. What do I care if she knows about how shitty things are for me right now?*

"I'm having a bad day. Things are... not good."

"I'm sorry to hear that," Persimmon said, her expression softening. Like she meant it.

Rayne balled her hand into a fist at her side to keep from fidgeting. "It's... I should be used to it. That's on me, I guess."

Persimmon pursed her lips like she might say something, her lips pressed into a tight line.

"I'll see you around," Rayne murmured.

"Did you want to come over?" Persimmon asked as just as Rayne was about to slide past her.

She turned to face the other woman, confusion furrowing her brow. "To your house?"

"Yeah."

"What for?"

Persimmon shrugged, "I made too much soup. You could have some if you wanted. Better than letting it go to waste."

Rayne opened her mouth to decline, to find some excuse for why she had to go home, but then she thought about the house she would be returning to.

The ghosts of her anger still haunting the halls.

"Instead, Rayne nodded. "Okay."

Persimmon drove a mustard-yellow pickup truck, a cluster of colorful daisy stickers plastered on its rear. Rayne knew she had only just met Persimmon, but it somehow matched her perfectly.

People reacted differently to her than they did to Rayne. On the brief walk to her car, several people came up to her, smiling and asking how she was doing. She knew them all by name, knew about their lives.

How does she make it look so easy? Rayne wondered. *I would combust if this many people tried to talk to me.*

Even as Persimmon bade Rayne to follow her car, Rayne thought about her. Bury did not take kindly to strangers, and anyone who was not born and raised here was considered a stranger.

And yet here Persimmon was, clearly being accepted into the fold.

How had she done that?

When they finally arrived at Persimmon's house, Rayne parked where she had the first time they'd met. "Is that alright?" She asked, gesturing to her Jeep.

The orange of the sky had melted into a deep purple, the last fragments of sunlight leaving the sky. Persimmon chuckled, waving dismissively as she locked her car. "No one typically comes up here this time of night anyway, so you're good."

Persimmon did not hurry inside as most other Bury residents did; she took her time and flashed Rayne a smile as she unlocked the door.

Rayne bit her lip, unsure if she should smile back or not.

"Welcome to my little corner of the world," Persimmon announced, and Rayne took a tentative step inside. The first thing that hit her was the scent: rosemary, peppermint, and something floral beneath it, like lavender.

Despite the bright exterior, the interior was dark, with low lighting, small chandeliers hanging from the ceiling, and dark fabrics draped and hanging from the walls. Along the walls, murals decorated every surface. The largest mural depicted a sunflower in the middle of a garden.

It's so beautiful in here. Rayne marvelled. "Your house is pretty," She said.

Persimmon shrugged her shoulders, shoving her hands into her pockets. "It's not much, but it's mine, and that means more than anything else, you know?"

Rayne understood the sentiment all too well but couldn't find the words to articulate it.

"Well, let me show you to the kitchen," Persimmon said after a few moments, nodding to Rayne's left. Rayne followed her quietly.

The kitchen was just as beautiful. All along the windowsill sat various raw crystals of all sorts. Rayne recognized a few: rose quartz, aquamarine, and amethyst. Suncatchers hung in the window in the shapes of stars, moons, and the sun. A mug was tucked away with them, with 'Ohio Strong' written on it, and inside sat a mini pink, white, and baby blue flag.

Where have I seen that flag before? Rayne thought, cocking her head to the side. *I know it means something... Oh!*

As if she could read Rayne's mind, Persimmon was at her side, brow raised as she stared down at Rayne. "Problem?"

Rayne jumped. "Oh! No. Not at all. I would never judge you for—"

"For being from Ohio?"

Rayne's cheeks flushed. "No, I meant—"

Persimmon's smile was all warmth, reminding Rayne of summer. "I know, Rayne. I was just messing with you."

"Oh. Yeah. Okay." Rayne replied, chewing on her bottom lip.

"Sorry," Persimmon sighed. "Here you are, hungry after a shitty day, and I'm teasing you. I'm a terrible host."

I couldn't host to save my life, so I know exactly how you feel. "It's okay."

Persimmon gestured to the small table in the center of the kitchen. "Have a seat, and I'll heat it for you."

"Thanks."

Rayne took the chair closest to the window and stole glances at the outline of Persimmon's massive garden in the backyard.

"Did you want to talk about it?" Persimmon asked over her shoulder, her head in the refrigerator.

"Sorry?"

"Your day."

Rayne stared at the back of Persimmon's head as if she'd just sprouted a second one. Her palms grew clammy, even through her gloves, and she clenched her fists, shoving them into her lap.

Suddenly, she's ten years old again, her parents are asking her about her day, but it's not real. It's always a trap. No matter what she tells them she did, there was always something she could have done better. Study harder. Keep her room cleaner, do more yard work, and get better grades.

Does she really want to know? Is she just trying to be nice, or... should I have come here?

"You don't have to, you know. It's just, well, if you wanted to, you could."

Rayne took the out. "Thank you. So. Bury, have you been here long?"

"Five years next month," Persimmon said over the metal clanging of pans. "Heard you grew up here."

Rayne pressed her fists tighter into her lap. "Yeah."

"What made you come back?"

"My parents died."

Persimmon turned to face her. "Oh, Rayne. I'm so sorry."

"Don't be," Rayne snapped, frowning at how harsh she sounded, even to her own ears.

Persimmon simply nodded, turning back to her soup. "Okay."

"Why did you... I mean, what made you want to live in Bury?"

Persimmon shrugged, pouring soup into one of the pans and turning on the stove. "I just wanted somewhere quiet where I could start over. Build something that was just for me, you know?"

Yes. I did that too. I ran and built myself up from nothing. I don't have much, but it's all mine; no one can touch it. Diminish it. "Yeah."

"I like it here. People are nice enough. Nosy, but what town isn't full of nosy neighbors?"

People are friendly to you. You're beautiful, you smile so easily and you're easy to talk to. How could anyone be unkind to you? "It's good that... you have that."

"So, you gonna stick around here?" Persimmon inquired, cocking a hand on her hip. The scent of pumpkin and sage warmed the air, and Rayne wanted to melt into it.

"Not for long. I have to sell the house—"

"Shit!" Persimmon swore, her hand coming to her forehead. "I forgot to ask if you have any allergies. I don't want to poison you."

"Oh, uhm, no."

"Okay, good. Now, what were you saying?"

Rayne shook her head. "Nothing, it's okay."

Persimmon cast her a side-long glance but returned to stirring the soup. "Okay."

Rayne wasn't sure if she was making a mess of this, but she liked that Persimmon didn't force conversation on her.

They sat in relative silence, the wooden spoon scraping against the metal pan an oddly comforting sound.

It was not long before Persimmon was pouring its steaming contents into an olive-green bowl and placing it in front of Rayne with a spoon. "It shouldn't be scalding, but just be careful when you take a sip, yeah?"

"Aren't you going to eat?"

"I did earlier. I have too many leftovers, and I have to use this pumpkin up before it goes bad. If you like it, you can take some home with you."

Rayne bit her lip. "You don't have to do that."

"I know. Look at it this way, you're technically doing me a favor. If you don't take it, then I'll have wasted food, and how am I supposed to live with myself then?" Persimmon asked, flashing Rayne a grin.

Rayne looked away, pretending to find something terribly interesting about the spoon that had been placed in front of her. "Okay."

Carefully, she dipped her spoon and brought it to her lips. Sweet, buttery pumpkin hit her tongue followed by the robust taste of sage and another herb she couldn't place. "This is amazing," She said, looking between the bowl and Persimmon. "Are you a chef?"

The other woman threw her head back, laughing so long and hard that Rayne was almost certain she'd misspoken.

"No, Rayne. Not at all. But thank you for the ego boost. It will go straight to my head, I assure you."

"It's just true," Rayne said under her breath, her cheeks hot.

Later, after the sun had long since disappeared from the sky and the crescent moon took its place, Rayne was standing at the door of Persimmon's home, her arms full of tupperware with frozen soup cubes inside them.

"Thank you again, Persimmon," Rayne said, attempting to smile. A real one. "This was nice. I will bring your containers back soon."

"Don't worry about it, Rayne. It's not like I don't know where you live and can't just knock down your door for my tupperware when I need it."

This time, Rayne picked up that Persimmon was joking. She didn't laugh, but she tried another smile. "Okay, yeah. Uh. Goodnight."

"Night!" Persimmon called as Rayne backed away and went down the stairs. "Oh, and Rayne?"

"Yes?" She asked, turning back.

"You can call me Persi. If you want to,"

"Okay."

It didn't hit her until she was in her car, driving up the long dirt road that led to her place, that Persimmon was the first person she'd had a genuine conversation with in years.

By the time Rayne had pulled into her driveway, the warm, soft feeling she'd had while she was at Persimmon's house had crystalized into the icy realization that she was going to have to spend another night in this place. Alone.

The sigh that she let out was bone deep. *I don't want to go back in there. I just want... I don't know. Someplace warm.*

After taking a few moments to gather herself and her soup, Rayne exited her car and walked up the narrow pathway toward the front door, climbing the few steps with heavy feet. The porchlight beside the door kicked on, and Rayne leaned down to place the containers on the ground when she saw it.

A photo. Bent slightly and covered in dirt, she flipped it over. The picture was of her; she couldn't have been more than eight years old. Rayne was sitting in her bedroom at her bubblegum-pink plastic table, a faux tea kettle in her hand as she poured imaginary tea. "What the fuck?" Rayne whispered. "I don't remember this. And where did it—"

The backyard. The photos she'd buried.

Someone had dug them up. Or at least this one. And then they'd left it on her front porch, like they'd wanted her to find it.

Slowly, Rayne looked around, searching for movement or any sign that someone else might be near. Mrs. Hamper's home was dark, except for the electric candles in each window. Hers was the only other house on this road, and save for the single streetlight at the far end, there was no light.

As far as she could see, no one else was here.

Rayne's attention returned to the picture between her fingers. *Why would someone want me to see this? It's just a normal pic—wait.*

Squinting, Rayne realized that her younger self was not just having a tea party, but she wasn't looking at the camera; all of her attention was fixed on the empty seat directly across from her, her mouth open as if she was mid-conversation.

With someone.

This doesn't make sense. Rayne could remember almost everything about her childhood; she remembered the plastic tea set her grandmother had gifted her, the plastic table her father had built for her. She even remembered this exact outfit and how it was her mother's favorite thing to see her in: pink, frilly, and ridiculous. All of the memories wove together except for this moment, which was peering back at her.

A rare flash of joy caught on film, and yet it did not belong to her.

Her beloved stuffed penguin, her constant companion, was discarded on the floor, lying at her feet as if he wasn't there. That penguin had acted as the only friend she ever had.

But if I'm not playing with him, then who the fuck am I talking to?

A branch snapped like bone in the forest behind her. Rayne whirled, staring into the thick, blackness of the forest.

I won't be scared away so easily, she thought, managing to slip her key into the lock with trembling fingers while she kept her eyes on the woods. *I am not afraid.*

CHAPTER SEVEN
rayne

R ayne sat up, gasping as she did. She hadn't meant to fall asleep, even curled in her bed, blankets tucked up to her chin.

I have to stay awake until morning, she told herself, rubbing her eyes and rolling her shoulders. The alarm clock beside her bed offered the only light in her room.

3:23 AM.

Damn it! Not even close to sunrise. I can't sleep, not until the sun is up and I can see again.

The mountains were not well lit; only six streetlights stretched from her home along the three miles into town. The dark took all else. So if there were someone in the forest watching her house, waiting for an opportunity to get in, Rayne would not see them coming before the sun rose.

She'd played the scenario in her mind, over and over again, since she'd gotten home. Rayne had buried her past, literally shoving what physical proof there was of most of her childhood into the ground. But someone had seen her and had decided to dig them back up.

Instead of all of the pictures, they'd focused on only one. A moment she couldn't remember spent speaking to someone she couldn't see.

Why?

"It doesn't make any sense," Rayne murmured, turning to lie on her back and stare up at the ceiling.

Could Callum be messing with me?

He may have never really left town, but was instead hiding out at the motel on Main Street. Perhaps this was all just some ploy to... to what, freak me out? To what end?

Rayne's brow furrowed, and she groaned, her arm moving to cover her face. Sunrise could not come quickly enough.

When Rayne opened her eyes again, she found herself in that black clearing once more, the moon hanging fat and lazy in the sky.

"I must have fallen asleep." She gasped, her voice rippling through the dark like a stone through water.

The hawthorn tree stood just as it had before, alone in the moonlight and a clearing that she could not discern. "You did not come to my tree."

Rayne spun on her heels, scanning the dark for the same abomination that she feared had followed her into another dream. "Where are you?" She hissed.

It laughed, her knees trembling, with the timbre of its voice. "It does not matter. Now that I've caught wind of your scent, it is only a matter of time."

Rayne's heart screamed in her chest, her blood thrumming in her ears. "Until what?"

The monster sighed wistfully, air brushing against the back of her neck. Rayne jumped away and the beast chuckled again. "Until the dirt clots your throat and the cold closes your eyes."

"Try it," She spat, searching for the source of the creature's voice. Perhaps it was the fact that she knew she was dreaming and that this thing, whatever it was, was not real and could not touch her.

"I won't go down so easily."

"Won't you?" Its laughter skeleton leaves in the wind. "I have brought down creatures with strength you could not imagine."

Air tickled against her bare palm this time, and Rayne swung her fist.

"You are nothing more than a rabbit to be caught between my teeth, Rayne."

In her fear and the confusion of the night before, she had not realized that the monster called her by name. That it had been calling her that this entire time.

"How do you know my name?" She whispered. "You said you knew me, how?"

The monster remained silent, and something shifted around her. Rayne felt the cold, a shiver trickling down her spine.

"I told you to come to my tree, and then you would know me in turn."

"Why would I come to your 'tree' when you're threatening me, when you keep intruding on my dreams? If I don't know you, I surely couldn't have invited you."

Finally, Rayne caught a flash of white, a milky eye blinked open on the ground beneath her, and moved with the shadows, closer. "I have told you where the answers lie."

"And I told you that I'm not going to some cursed—wait," Rayne took a step toward the shadow, and it paused, cocking what she assumed to be its head at her. "I have to come to you, don't I?"

The world stilled, holding its breath. The monster did not reply.

Emboldened, Rayne took another step forward. "You can't get me where I am, can you? That's why you're trying to get me to go to the tree You can't touch me—"

Another eye shot open, and the monster snarled. Rayne's hands flew to her ears, and she crouched down.

The shadow rose above her, towering until the moon was blotted out. "Hear me, Rayne, and know that I will be the one to put you in the ground. There is no place where I cannot reach you."

The darkness seeped into her mouth, her nose, her eyes, drowning the sound of her screams.

The floor awoke Rayne, her shoulder colliding with the hardwood. She swore, rubbing her smarting shoulder. Blinking the sleep from her eyes, she was greeted with the pale light of morning.

I'm not dead. At least no one snuck in here in the middle of the night to stab me.

Rayne sat up slowly, a hiss slipping between her teeth. Discomfort sparked from her hands, shooting all the way down her legs.

She sighed, her fingers tracing a delicate path down to her knees. Raised and swollen, she knew all too well what blisters felt like beneath her clothes. Her head fell back against the edge of the mattress.

Might as well get my day started.

Her black, floral medical bag in hand, Rayne limped down the hallway and to the stairs, her body aching from the day before and the hard fall out of bed. *I'm going to be covered in blisters if I'm not careful.*

It was not until Rayne reached the final step of the stairs that she noticed the difference in temperature between upstairs and downstairs—upstairs had been comfortable, cozy from the heat that had kicked on at some point in the night. But downstairs, it was sweltering.

"What—"

The fireplace danced, the flames fat and strong. The couch cushions lay scattered in the center of the floor, and the sliding glass door to the back porch was wide open.

Someone had been in the house. I had been asleep, and someone was in the house! But how could they have gotten in? This door locked from the inside, and I had locked every single entrance.

It was a mystery that would have to be left to the police, as far as she was concerned.

Muscle memory had Rayne in front of the phone before she could even think to do anything else. Her finger hadn't even begun to dial 911 when she watched with her own eyes, the door creep closed, the lock turning itself. The flame of the fireplace died down before extinguishing like a sigh, leaving only toothy embers in its wake.

Rayne dropped the phone and backed against the wall. A breathless laugh escaped her lungs, and she shook her head, cursing whatever God there might have been.

Of course, this house is fucking haunted.

CHAPTER EIGHT
the shadow

The Shadow was discontent.

Rayne had been here for nearly a week now, and their patience was threadbare.

I did not think that this would be the way the wheel has turned. I should have expected it, especially from her.

Annoyance hummed behind their eyes like a cicada song, and the sudden influx of emotion did nothing but disrupt their stomach. Feelings were not something that their kind used; emotions were strange accessories, and they much preferred to observe them rather than ever allow the strange sensations near them.

Rayne filled their chest with the flutterings of irritation, and they longed to be rid of it all.

Once I have eaten her, they thought, *I will leave this place for a while. I will return when the air is not soured by the stench of almond and rose.*

The Shadow kept close to her property, edging as near as they dared in the daylight. To cross the threshold of her yard at night was one thing, but during the day, that wretched house was impenetrable.

The sun was nearly at its midpoint in the sky when the front door opened, and Rayne stepped out in the chill, bringing with her a wave of fresh smells. There was the unmistakable scent of her and, beneath that,t the sterile sting of ointment and gauze.

Their center softened as they watched her toss a small floral bag into the passenger's seat of her car and close the door behind her.

There it was again. That—

The Shadow scowled, baring their teeth at her.

I could simply eat her on her way back inside and be done with it all, The Shadow thought. *If there is enough shadow for even a moment, I will need only a second before I drag her into the woods with me.*

But then the sport of the hunt would be gone. There would be no adrenaline to sweeten the taste of her blood, no fear clotting her heart.

I would rather starve.

The rumble of her car's engine hooked their attention back to her and, remaining in the curve of the forest, followed after her into town.

A flurry of surprise tangled in their throat as they followed her to the last place they would have expected to see her; her dark car pulling into the gravel lot of the only church in town.

Religion was a strange beast to The Shadow. Through every place that they had traveled, the names were different but the sentiment was always the same: purity, perfection, chasing out the dark.

The church sat just on the outskirts of town, more of the wood than of the people that resided there. It was painted that same shade of blue most of the town was fond of, a ward of sorts. At least, as far as they believed. No color could protect anyone from The Shadow.

The Shadow slunk along the shade of the oak tree in the back of the church, peering around the building just in time to catch Rayne as she entered.

They pressed closer, listening to the sound of her worn boots against the dust ridden wood floors. They did not have to see her to imagine her expression; heavy frown souring her face, nose scrunched, gloved hands shoved into her pockets to keep from accidentally nicking against anything sharp.

The Shadow, as most spirits were, was more animal than anything else. They heard and saw more than human eyes could perceive. But even with their recent kill, The Shadow needed more to sustain themself. Winter was not yet here.

"Can I help you?" An elderly man asked after Rayne. "Don't I know you?"

"Might," Rayne said and The Shadow focused their attention into the building, able to discern her figure through the dry rotted wood and pews. She looked away, dark eyes fixing only the floor. "Name's Dorne."

"Ah, Rayne. I'm so sorry about your parents," the man offered and The Shadow snarled, teeth catching on the corner of the church. "The service was beautiful."

The Shadow drifted up the nearest window for a better look at Rayne only to be met with her russet gaze, her attention fixed solely on them. The Shadow stumbled back a step.

She cannot see me in the light. It is not possible.

Rayne's eyes remained locked on theirs for another moment and then back to the priest's. "I'll take your word for it."

The priest's expression changed into an emotion that The Shadow could not decipher. "It's a shame you weren't able to make it."

"I need holy water," Rayne interrupted.

The Shadow's ears perked at that. *Do you truly think that some 'blessed' water will save you?*

The priest gestured for Rayne to follow him to the back of the church, toward a small, baby-blue basin, sunbleached by the high, bright windows. Rayne stayed a few paces back, watching as the priest opened a small compartment at the base of the basin and produced a small, plastic bottle with a golden crucifix on it. "Do you need any additional blessings? I imagine that this has been a difficult time for you."

The Shadow watched her eyes follow the bottle into the water. "No. I'm fine," After a moment, she added, "Thank you."

Once the bottle was full, the priest offered it to her but then pulled it back at the last moment. "You didn't come to service much, did you?"

Rayne chewed her lower lip, her hand clenching into a fist as she shoved it back into her pocket. "Not since my Mam'maw."

"Your folks came. Every Sunday."

"I'll bet."

"And Adele, well, your Mam'maw, she was a wonderful woman. God fearin' to the bone," the priest said. The Shadow watched Rayne's jaw work, her mouth a tight, pinched line. "She'd want to see you in the congregation, Rayne."

Her spine straightened "You don't know shit about my family!" The priest's scowl matched the one on her own lips. "Excuse my mouth, but if it's all the same to you, I'd like that holy water now, *Father.*"

The Shadow pressed closer to the glass to catch the intricacies of their talk; the slight tremble to Rayne's knees, the sharp breathing of the priest, his finger tapping against the plastic.

Humans communicate in such strange ways.

After a few more tense moments, the priest handed over the holy water.

"Thank you," Rayne said and then, softer, "I'm sorry for cussin'."

Discontent rumbled in The Shadow's stomach, their lips pulling back from the razors of their teeth. *Backing down. Where are your teeth, Rayne?*

The Shadow shuddered the moment the thought rippled through them;

It matters not. She will not need them when I am done with her.

CHAPTER NINE
rayne

Rayne was not an exorcist.

She knew no more of spectres and spirits and than she did of God and His angels.

But what she did know was that this was her house now, and she would be damned if the ghosts of her parents were going to terrorize her in death as they had in life.

Her Mam'maw had always spoken of ghosts as if they were fruit flies, simple enough to get rid of but a nuisance nonetheless.

"Worse things walkin' this world, snapdragon," she'd say while her crooked fingers slid into Rayne's curls.

Her grandmother had removed a ghost from the house once while Rayne had been over for the weekend. They'd sat in the garden, bumblebees dipping near enough to Rayne that they'd tickled her ears. Her attention had been fixated almost entirely on that while her grandmother had warred with the supernatural.

Rayne could not remember all of what had happened, her grandmother had mentioned a wayward ghost that had followed her from a dream, drunk the sorrow of her loss, as it had been a dream of Rayne's late grandfather.

When Rayne closed her eyes, she saw flashes of her grandmother walking
backwards though the house with the abalone shell that Adele's mother had
passed down to her, felt her hair freshly washed, braided and anointed with
oil, heard the bees and her Mam'maw's soft singing, smelled the burning cedar
chips, dried juniper and sage. But the memory ended there, splintered into a
dozen other precious moments between them.

There were fragments of sentiments her grandmother had shared with her
that tangled in the quagmire of her memory; keeping the windows open so
the spirits could leave, always starting from the furthest and highest corner of
the house and working down when banishing, walking backwards so the spirit
couldn't sneak up on her, only cleansing on an empty stomach, asking the spirits
of the plants from the herbs she burned for help, praying to The Most High for
strength and blessings.

It would have to be enough.

Rayne sat on the floor of her parent's bathroom, sprinkling a pinch of juniper, cedar, and rosemary onto the lit charcoal disk she had placed in a small
pan and lined the bottom with salt to keep it from getting too hot.

She kept a little bit of the herbs with her everywhere she went, another
beautiful stain left behind from the only person who'd ever really cared for her.
Her Mam'maw had said that the herbs would keep evil at bay, and while Rayne
wasn't entirely sure about that, she kept them with her regardless.

Sweet grey smoke danced in front of her, and she stuck her hands into it,
'washing' them in it as best she could. Her hands would have to be clean to keep
the spirits from sticking to them.

Rayne stood, the pan handle clutched tightly in her ungloved hand, and
slowly she began to walk backwards through the room, smoke trailing behind
her. She was supposed to pray now, to ask for help from the depths of her soul.

I don't know any prayers and I've never known any healing songs.

Sucking in a breath, Rayne swallowed years of discomfort, of resentment,
and then vomited them back up.

"Kètanëtuwit," *Greatest Spirit,* she began, nearly choking on the name that
she had not spoken in over two decades. "I should not be asking you for help

but... I need it. Please just... get rid of them. My parents. It's not fair that I can't get away from them. It's bad enough that they have my name, my blood, my hometown, there are so few things of me that they did not seep into."

When her voice caught, the back of her throat tingling, she wrote it off as the smoke.

"I don't want them. They never wanted me so why... Why are they still here? Please, just get them out. Cast them into the lake of fire or take them to Heaven, anywhere that is not this house. Not while I'm here."

After moving out of her parents room, Rayne paused to glance down at the white door further down the hallway, painted off-white with pink ballerina slippers lining the border.

I should go in there, she thought, swallowing, approaching it cautiously. *I'm supposed to cleanse every room.*

Her finger brushed the brass door handle, bile rising almost immediately.

No. I can't do it. This has to be enough.

Rayne buried the thoughts of that room as deep as she could and returned to the task of finally ridding herself of her parents.

The process was slow, awkward but eventually, her back hit the sliding door to the back porch and reaching behind her, she undid the lock and slipped outside.

The smoke whispered its dying breaths and Rayne put it down on the ground, flipped her head and allowed the last of the smoke to soak into her hair to cleanse any wisps that might knot in it. When the smoldering charcoal was finally done, Rayne took it into the garden, poured dirt over the embers and smooshed it into the ground with the heel of her boot.

"Earth, I offer you this knowing that you will make new what was once impure," Rayne whispered, pressing her index and middle finger to her lips and then into the soil.

With an exhale, she plopped back into the bed of daffodils, still green and stubborn despite the whispers of winter and the flowers having long since passed.

When I die, she thought, *I want to come back a daffodil. Screw haunting houses, I'll bloom in frozen ground alone in the snow. No parents to claim me.*

The sun was only just beginning to set when Rayne finally set foot back in the house with a relieved exhale. The air was sweet and all felt calm.

Rayne kicked her filthy shoes off onto the carpet, *I've got to scrub the floors and vacuum anyway.*

"I might just have the last of Persimmon's soup tonight," she declared, sliding on the linoleum floor, her knitted thigh highs the perfect vehicle for it, allowing her the motion with as little friction as possible.

Her head was entirely in the refrigerator, rummaging for something to go with it when a voice, soft as television static whispered:

"Let me keep you warm, cherub."

Rayne jolted, knocking her head on the inside of the refrigerator in her scrambling.

When she looked up and around, the fireplace in the living room had flickered to life, burning as if it had been this entire time.

"No. There's no way. You—you can't still be here," Rayne whispered. "I don't understand. I did everything right! I—"

That room.

No, no, no. I can't go in there. I won't.

The walls shifted, the stairs shifting with them, a symphony of moving wood. **"I will never leave."**

Rayne's brow furrowed, her eyes searching in the fading light for movement, for even an outline of a spirit. "Where are you?"

This time, it was the floor directly under her feet that moved, warmed like skin. **"Where I have always been. Cradling you."**

Rayne rested her hip against the counter, her fingers brushing the pale granite and something—the air, *sighed.* The linoleum peeled off of the wood panel by her right foot and curled toward her, tickling the top of her foot before it righted itself again.

The fear that she had initially felt those first few haunted nights here had shifted. The space didn't feel the same. It felt warm. Alive.

The house.

It wasn't haunted, it was—

"Are you... alive?"

It would make sense, more sense than the idea that her parents had come back to taunt her from the grave. Things had been too harmless for Thelma and Cassian Dorne, she realized. The floors that had caught her, rising to meet her as she walked, pipes that shuttered.

"Of course. You are in the whole of me, nestled in my stomach just as you always have been."

Rayne looked over at the fireplace and the flames rose in response. "Holy shit! So you're really the house."

Or I've finally gone and properly lost it. "How do I know you're real?"

Haints and vengeful ghosts were one thing, but living houses seemed too far out of the scope of possibility. When her Mam'maw spoke of the supernatural, it had always made sense.

"Is my fire not warm enough for you?"

Rayne glanced at the fireplace and for a few minutes she allowed the sound of the simmering wood to be enough.

She couldn't remember her house feeling unique in her childhood. It had always been cold. "Okay," she began. "Maybe you are alive. Then why did you never speak to me before now?"

The House exhaled, the wood within the fireplace crackling like clittering laughter and Rayne scowled.

"Could you imagine how that would have gone, dearest? Your mother cleaning the kitchen and your father working in his little office and then I say 'Won't someone come and clean the leaves from the back porch? They are so dreadfully itchy.'"

Okay, it's got a point there. "Why didn't you at least talk to me?" she murmured. "You could have come to me one of the days that I was home alone."

"I did not yet know what to say. I was not used to the act of speaking. Language must be taught, you know."

"Then how did you learn?"

"By listening. I leaned in close and memorized every word that ever passed behind my walls. Rather clever, aren't I?"

"Yeah. I suppose you are."

"I gave you as much love as I could, tried to cushion you where I was able. It was not easy to protect you with your flower petal skin. Yet here you are, whole and unharmed."

Rayne thought back to all of the wounds she had sustained as a child; knocking her knee against a tree, scraping her hand on cement, other children that played too rough with her and left her tender skin raw and bleeding. All of that blood, and though she had been hurt outside of the house, she had never been hurt *inside* her home.

This is madness, she thought. *I have finally gone and properly lost my mind. Too much time on my own and now I'm imagining a company where it could never exist.*

It was the only thing that made sense, wasn't it?

In her youth, Rayne's imagination had run rampant. Her lack of tangible connections outside of her grandmother had given her a large gap to fill. She'd done so with imaginary kingdoms and creatures, friends that lived in moss, companions trapped in stars. The finer details of her games escaped her, but she knew down to her core that they were there.

Her loneliness had never disappeared and so, then why would her imagination?

Rayne bit her lip as she paced the kitchen. *Does it really matter if it's all in my head? The house is much easier to talk to than my cousin or anyone else in my family.*

Delicately, she ran her hand along the wall, the pads of her fingers brushing against the wallpaper. "Okay. Maybe you *did* protect me. But why?"

"Because you are mine, cherub. Those that made you may not have cared to claim you, but I will never deny you. You have been mine since the first moment that you bled me to life."

"Bled?"

"As much as you are mine, I am yours. Your blood soaked into the floorboards, the grout in the bathrooms, the carpet. You fed me with the whole of you. So now I will shelter you in the whole of me so long as I stand."

Rayne remained silent, crossing her arms and carefully leaning her cheek against the wall. It was as close as she dared to an embrace and the house sighed in delight. "Okay. Do you have something you'd like me to call you?"

"I care not for names. Call me what you wish."

"House?"

"Yes, cherub. That will do."

"Why do you call me cherub?" she asked, looking up at the ceiling, half expecting to find a face staring back at her.

"That is what you will always be to me."

Rayne swallowed, her mouth pinching into a tight line. If she were braver, she would admit to House that this was the kindest thing anyone had said to her in years and she did not know how to hold it.

House pressed on, shifting ever so gently behind her feet. *"I have missed your warmth behind my ribs, dear one. You were gone from me for much too long."*

Later that night as she lay awake in bed, it hit her that she was going to be leaving House again, and this time for good. For the first time, she felt guilty for wanting to run away.

CHAPTER TEN
the shadow

L icking the blood and viscera from their lips, The Shadow stared up into the window of Rayne's home. The lights had gone out a few hours ago, and soon, it would be three am. The Witching Hours, they'd heard humans call it. They were close enough in their superstitions; it was the point in the day when the Veil that separated worlds was thinnest.

The easiest time for dreamwalking.

They had been strategic in their planning and had fed before they tried to slip into her dreams.

She will not get the best of me again.

The Shadow had not intended for her to learn of the limitations that existed between them both, but it could not be helped now; they would have to pivot.

The thinning of the Veil felt like a break in humidity, granting spirits such as The Shadow a breath of fresh air when it came walking amongst humans. The Shadow crept as close as they could to the property line before they felt the house prickle.

"Calm yourself, wretch. I will not set foot over your precious border," The Shadow snarled.

"Leave her be, wraith. You know how this will end."

The Shadow ignored House and instead focused on the steady pulse of Rayne's heart through the wall.

Their power was a nebulous thing, expanding with age and hemorrhaging into the world around them. The Shadow could compel and slip into a mind as ink into water. They could have slipped into Rayne's mind at any time she was within their proximity. They could have forced her to walk into the forest and sit right between their jaws.

They refused.

To enter a sleeping mind was a less delicate process. The Shadow always ended up as a bull within a china shop, destroying more than they intended.

When they tumbled into Rayne's dream, it was easy enough to craft the image of their clearing from the shadows of her mind.

She did not make them wait long.

Rayne entered the clearing, and they watched as she took in her surroundings.

As they did twice before, The Shadow spilled into the darkness under her, melting into the night. They shifted, adjusting their appearance to what they knew would scare her, and opened their white, glowing eyes and stared at her.

No sooner had they opened their eyes when Rayne charged forward and stomped her heels into their pupils.

The Shadow recoiled, not in pain but surprise. In dreams, there was no pain or pleasure to be felt, a vacuum solely for sight and sound. *She just tried to blind me.*

"*What* is your problem with me?" Rayne demanded, and then, before The Shadow could answer. "You keep showing up in my dreams, doing weird shit, and trying to drag me into the forest. What do you *actually* want from me?"

The Shadow blinked, swirling near her as they regained themself. *This is unexpected.* They had thought of countless ways in which they would hunt her down, and not in a single one of them had she fought back.

This is much better.

A grin cut through the darkness of The Shadow. "I have told you. Come to the forest."

"What exactly is in it for me?"

"I do not understand," The Shadow said, curling their misty head toward her.

"What do I get out of going to see *you* in the forest?" Rayne snapped. "You're just some monster in my dream."

"We will see about that."

"*No,* we won't. I don't even know your name."

The Shadow blinked down at her, moving back to put some distance between her and them. "I will not give it."

"So you do have one then?" The Shadow did not miss the smug smirk on her face when asked, and another strange feeling bit into their stomach like a thorn.

"I may," The Shadow replied, shifting away from her. To speak of names made them uncomfortable. To know something's name was to have power over it, to have an intimate level of control that The Shadow could not bear to fathom.

Rayne Dorne would never know it. *She's taken too much already.*

"You know mine," Rayne pressed.

"Yes."

"How?"

The Shadow cocked its head to an unnatural angle and only smiled at her.

"That's not fair."

The Shadow's smile soured into a frown. "Fairness is a fable. A pretty lie for soft, weak things."

Rayne scowled up at The Shadow, and for a moment, all they both did was stare at one another in complete and utter discontent. She broke first, sighed, and rested her back against the invisible barrier The Shadow made to keep her from wandering too far into the dream forest. "First House, and now you. I have a much easier time talking to monsters and houses than I do with real people."

The Shadow shrank, hovering only a few inches taller than her, staring down its nose. *I do not like it when she speaks as such. It upsets my stomach and sours my tongue.* They considered telling her as much for a moment, but they held their tongue.

"You are strange," they remarked.

She flashed them another frown, her entire face scrunching into displeasure. "*You're* calling me strange? *You're invading my dream.*"

Fire licked up their spine. "The same way that you have invaded this town with your presence?"

Rayne crowded them. "*I* don't want to be here."

At this, The Shadow flickered, fading for a moment before darkening into a more corporeal state. "Why?"

Curiosity was a dangerous thing to their kind, The Shadow knew. A weakness that every creature from their world shared.

Longevity was both a gift and a curse for spirits; The Shadow knew that they would long outlive the human race as it was now, but with that came boredom. They had seen so much in their long life, had experienced a great many sensations and surprises. But the novelty wore off long ago, and humans were terribly repetitive.

They rarely did anything new. But when they did? The Shadow and all of their kind were drawn to it like moths to a flame.

That smug smirk returned to Rayne's full lips. "Tell me why you want me to come into the forest, and then I will tell you."

I should just eat her now, The Shadow thought. *She is a thorn in my side and will remain so until I am free of her.*

"You struggle with listening, it seems."

"Leave me alone then, and you won't have to deal with my listening problem," Rayne bit back.

You started this. You are the one who needs to leave me alone.

"Are you... really not going to tell me your name?" Rayne asked again, softer. There was something in her tone that they did not like, although they could not place it.

"Call me whatever you like. It will make no difference."

From the corner of their eye, The Shadow caught her looking at them and then their tree.

"Hawthorne," Rayne said suddenly. "I'll call you Hawthorne."

Hawthorne. Like my tree.

It suits me. The Shadow shivered, and the entire clearing rippled in response. *How had she been able to choose a name for me, something that suits me so well, when she does not know me? Is it the same reason that she could see me when I followed her?*

The Shadow, Hawthorne, existed solely on their own. They could not bear a tether of any sort, and their solitude was their freedom. They loved it, craved it more than bloodshed, than flesh sliding down their throat. But this, being known, being seen, was a pleasure that they had not experienced in a very long time.

It rippled through them with its power, and they needed to understand how she could have known this without knowing them.

"I like that," Hawthorne said. "I like it very much."

This time, when Rayne smiled at them, it was different, and there was nothing they could do with the knowledge.

"Hawthorne," she began, chewing her lower lip. "If I go to your tree, are you going to hurt me?"

Hawthorne turned to face Rayne fully. They noted the tension in her jaw, her hand bunched into a fist at her side.

A lie was born and died just as quickly on their tongue as they looked down at her. It would be better to lure her into a false sense of security before they killed her; it would give a headier flavor to her fear. Still, their curiosity prickled against their skin, settling in their chest.

Perhaps I will wait a little longer to eat her. I will extract the knowledge from her, and once that is done, so is she.

"Let us meet somewhere different then," Hawthorne said. "The graveyard, perhaps."

"Are you going to try to hurt me there?"

"The spirits of that place would not allow it."

Rayne's dark eyes widened, her pulse quickening, and it took everything within Hawthorne to keep from licking their lips.

"You didn't say that you wouldn't try," she whispered.

"No." Hawthorne's grin spread like cracking ice. "I did not."

CHAPTER ELEVEN
rayne

Thoughts of Hawthorne trailed Rayne all day.

Why did they speak about my arrival as if I've committed some crime against them? Rayne wondered, watching the coffee drip steadily into the holder, steam rising.

She had decided somewhere between her first coffee and vacuuming the hallway that she *would* go to the graveyard. If her House could speak then maybe her dreams could spill into the real world.

"What's stolen all of your attention, cherub?" House asked, the refrigerator rumbling to her left.

"What? Oh. I was just thinking about a dream I had," Rayne replied, tasting blood. Her tongue drew over the seam of her lip, bloody and raw from where she'd been chewing it. "It's nothing, House."

"Rather greedy of you to keep all of those dreams to yourself when I cannot follow you."

Rayne's battered lip shifted into a small smile, and she brushed her fingers along the edge of the kitchen counter. "I'm sorry, House. Can I do something for you instead?"

The temperature dropped and then spiked, sweat beginning to bead at Rayne's nape from the sudden influx of warmth.

"A gift, for me? After so long without you? Yes, yes, yes. I think that's rather fair. What will you give me?"

"Are you making it hotter in here?"

"Well, what can you expect? Gifts are so rare, of course my blood will sing for you. Tell me, what will I have?"

She laughed a little, patting the counter. "Well, what would you like?"

House sighed, as light as spring rain. *"Oh, what I would give for one of your ribs, cherub. Or a little bite of your heart. I could stand for a hundred years then! Oh, what about an eye? Yours were always so pretty. Think about how lovely I will be once I have one of those!"*

Rayne stepped back, shaking her head. "What?"

House huffed. *"Perhaps a finger then, if you must be so stingy."*

"I don't—why do you want parts of my *body?*"

"I told you, cherub. I am as much yours as you are mine. I will crave the taste of you until I am returned to the dirt."

Rayne blinked at the ceiling, her teeth working her lower lip again. *Okay, so my house is alive and wants to eat me. But then... have I ever been wanted like this before?* she wondered, licking her lips, her blood coating her teeth.

The pad of her finger ran along the rough skin of her lower lip, blood beading. "Would blood work?"

The air hummed with electricity and the hair on the back of her neck rose.

"Oh, yes. Blood will do just fine."

As there was not enough to drip off of the ends of her fingers, she grabbed a fresh paper towel and padded it against her lip, blotting most of it away. "How do I give it to you?"

"My fire, cherub. Think of it as the back of my throat."

Rayne approached the fireplace slowly, her hand hesitating above the flames before she released it. She watched it ignite, her blood the last thing to burn.

House quaked and the floor felt warmer even through her socked feet.

"You taste like a dream. If I could sleep, it would be only to think of you."

Heat kissed her cheeks, flushing her skin. Rayne patted the wall stiffly. "You're welcome, House. I have to leave now but I'll be back later."

"Where are you going?"

Rayne paused and pretended to busy herself with putting on her shoes once she was in the foyer. "To the graveyard."

"Oh, I see."

As she was leaving, House called to her. *"Cherub?"*

Rayne paused in the doorway. "Yes?"

"Don't go into the forest."

Brow furrowing, she frowned at the ceiling. "I said I was going to the cemetery."

"*Yes,*" House continued. *"I know."*

"Why shouldn't I go into the forest?"

The House remained silent, the crackling of the fireplace dying down until the flames were nothing but embers, bleeding into black.

"House?"

"There are—rabbits in the wood and all other sort of creatures. You should be careful."

Rayne scoffed, rolling her eyes. "I don't think rabbits are my biggest concern at the moment. But thanks, House. I will."

House sighed as she closed the door behind her.

Rayne hadn't expected there to be anyone else in the graveyard when she arrived, it was a public place of course, but in all her time in the town, she had never seen anyone else there.

An old man stood toward the back of the graveyard, near the iron fence. He watched her, scowling, and Rayne ducked her head.

In town, she had grown accustomed to eyes following her, trailing her and yet she was distinctly aware of the moment that Hawthorne laid eyes on her.

It was the same feeling she'd gotten in the church.

She looked around, the low autumn sunlight painting the damp grass in shades of yellow and auburn. On the other side of the graveyard, where crumbling, unmarked headstones lay there was a willow tree, casting heavy shadow.

In the shadows, she caught movement, distortion like heating rising off of the pavement.

There.

Rayne approached carefully, her hands tight at her side, fingers playing against the edge of her satchel. *I don't know if holy water will work on whatever the fuck Hawthorne is, but it's better than nothing.*

She stopped a few feet away from the willow. "You didn't tell me what time to meet you."

The distortion rippled closer but, she noted, not directly in the sunlight. "Did I need to? You are here."

"I guess."

Well, at least I know I'm not crazy. I mean, I think I'm not? I wonder if anyone else can see what I am?

She cast a quick glance over her shoulder, relieved that the old man's attention returned to the grave he'd been kneeling in front of.

"What are you looking at?"

"Nothing," Rayne replied hastily, turning back to Hawthorne and clearing her throat. "Okay, so. I'm here, finally. Aren't I supposed to know you now or whatever?"

"How did you choose the name Hawthorne?"

Rayne blinked. "What?"

"The name you gave me. How did you acquire it?"

"The weird tree you kept showing me. It's a hawthorn, isn't it?"

"Yes, it is."

"And you climbed out of it that first night, so I assumed that it had something to do with you."

Hawthorne made a noise that sounded somewhat thoughtful but then again, Rayne did not know what sort of noises monsters were supposed to make.

"And that is the whole of it?" Hawthorne asked.

Rayne raised a brow. "Should there be more?" When Hawthorne did not answer, she pressed on. "I should be the one asking questions here. Why do you keep showing up in my dreams, Hawthorne? I don't dream of shadow men—"

"I am not a man," Hawthorne replied, shifting closer. "I am not a woman either."

Rayne's brow furrowed in confusion. "What are you, then?"

The willow branches moved with the wind but Rayne swore there was another sound under it, like laughter.

"I've had many names."

"That doesn't answer my question."

"No, it doesn't."

Rayne frowned, annoyance settling in her stomach, and her arms crossed over her chest.

"Are you seeking the knowledge so that you might splash me with that holy water in your bag?"

Rayne stepped back, clutching her bag to her side. "How did you know I had holy water?"

"I can smell it. Just as I can smell the blood singing in your veins."

"Are you a haint?"

"Do I seem it?"

I don't know what the fuck that even means. Answering a question would be nice. "I don't know. I don't even know how I'm supposed to refer to you."

"By my name, I imagine."

Whatever you are, I wish I could punch you. "It? They?" Rayne ventured.

Hawthorne made another noise, thoughtful, this time she was nearly sure. "They would suit me. I do not enjoy the idea of him or her."

"Is it because you're a monster?"

Am I really discussing the nuances of gender with a fucking shadow creature?

"It is because those terms do not fit me, no more than that."

"Okay."

Rayne's eyes flickered down to the edge of the shadows that Hawthorne danced behind before returning back to where she imagined their face was. "So, I was right."

"Right about what?"

She pointed down to the ground. "You can't approach me, not really at least."

The distortion curled with the distinct sound of chuckling. "You are certain of this?"

Rayne took a step back into the light, her hand dipping into the satchel for her holy water. "Yes," she said around the lump in the back of her throat.

The nebulous outline of Hawthorne darkened until they were visible in front of her, shifting like a cluster of gnats. There was nothing she could recognize even remotely as human, their jaw canine and their eyes reflecting scarlet, catching in the light.

Their face so near to hers that she could smell them; like damp earth and heavy rain.

"You reek of uncertainty." Rayne's pulse hammered away as she stared up at them but Hawthorne's attention caught over her shoulder and they melted back into nothingness. "*Nothing* is staring right at you."

Rayne glanced over her shoulder to find the old man watching her, his eyes wide in horror.

Shit. So much for keeping a low profile.

Ducking her head, she hastily made her way out of the graveyard but not before she caught what the old man said, spat under his breath like a curse.

"*Witch.*"

CHAPTER TWELVE
rayne

"I really need to go shopping."

Dinners of noodles with only olive oil and lemon juice and slices of pears or canned peaches for every other meal were beginning to lose their charm. But the idea of visiting the town grocery store was less charming.

Bury had only one grocery store and two small corner stores on opposite ends of town. The corner stores were fine, except that most of the time they served as hangouts for locals. Most teenagers opted to spend their free time at Devroe Mine, drinking in the long tunnels on weekends.

Rayne had never been herself, but in high school, it had been the only thing anyone in her class could ever talk about.

The Kapplers owned the grocery store, and she had no interest in seeing them ever again, especially not their son.

Rayne shook the thoughts of him away and hopped up onto the kitchen counter, crossing her legs.

My mother would blow a gasket if she ever saw me doing this.

She settled in, resting her back against the wall and pulling her steaming bowl of noodles into her lap. While the house wasn't clean yet, Rayne wanted to make the most of her time. She didn't want to spend a moment longer in this town than she had to.

"Okay," Rayne said, her finger hovering over the number she'd found online for the closest realtor. "Here goes nothing."

The phone rang, and she put it on speaker, placing it down in front of her so she could blow on her food.

"Eden Reality. This is Judith speaking," chimed a bright voice, and Rayne dropped her fork into the bowl altogether.

"Hi. Uh—My name is Rayne Dorne, and I'm looking to sell my home."

The steady pulse of computer keys sounded faintly in the background.

"Well then, I guess you called the right place, huh?" Judith asked with a pleasant laugh.

Rayne tried to mirror the action, but it sounded more like she was choking. If Judith noticed, she didn't say anything.

"Okay, so. How soon are you looking to put your house on the market?"

"As soon as possible."

The typing continued. "Hmm. Alright, well. I've got to be honest with you, Miss. Dorne, with the holidays coming up, most people are looking to stay right where they are. So, just know you might not get any offers till the middle of January."

No! I need to get out of here.

"I was... looking to sell sooner than that."

"Any particular reason why?"

Rayne chewed her bottom lip. "It's my childhood home, and I'm just... trying to cut ties."

"Hm, yeah, I can understand that. What's the address?"

"3 Erial Rd, Bury, PA."

The typing stopped. "Bury?"

"Yes." Rayne swallowed.

On Judith's end, a chair rolled, pushing back, and the stretch of leather. "You really expect me to sell a house all the way up in Bury?"

It's not so bad here! She wanted to say, but the lie was too bitter for even her. "I'm just tryna get outta here."

Judith smacked her lip. "Well, I'm sorry, Miss Dorne. But a place like Bury is... out of my radius. Best of luck to you. I'm sure you'll need it."

The line went dead before Rayne could even think to respond. Rayne stared down at her food, all semblance of an appetite scrubbed clean. She was not sure how long she sat like that, silent.

Is this town cursed, or is it just me? Why can't I get away from this place? What limb do I need to sever to free myself?

"You want to leave me again?"

"It's not you, House. It's... the memories here. The people," she whispered.

"Ignore them, cherub. They know nothing of you. Why should any of it matter?"

"Ignore them?" Rayne hissed, her head shooting up to glare at the ceiling. Her bowl clanked into the sink, broken ceramics and pasta coating it. "Ignore them? How can I ignore them when every move I make comes with dozens of eyes? Every inch of this town is a reminder of how miserable I was here, how I was never good enough for anyone. Tell me, House, how exactly do I ignore the fact that this place is and was Hell?"

"Cherub—"

"No! Fuck you and fuck this town!"

Rayne stormed out of the kitchen and out of the house, barely pausing to snatch her keys from the holder by the door.

She did not get into her car; she stomped past it and up the dirt road that led to the river.

Near the foot of the mountains, there was a river that Rayne loved. It might have been the only thing within Bury that she did like, but she realized that was because it felt as though it were hers.

Downstream, the people of the town would fish, even kayak, but upstream was considered the badlands, The Devil's playground. That part of the mountain was considered too wild, and nearly everyone in town, or their parents or grandparents, had a story about something wicked they'd seen amongst the trees.

Sarah Butcher had sworn she'd seen Old Scratch himself one Sunday morning, hissing at the sound of the church bells as service ended. Jeremiah Suthers said he'd heard his wife calling his name, telling him to meet her beneath the pines, and he said he would have gone, had she not been six feet under the ground for nearly two years.

Everyone had seen something wrong, swearing the ghosts of the old miners walked between the trees, looking for someone to drag back down into the sweltering soil with them.

Rayne, in all her years, had never once seen or heard anything strange here. If anything, this part of the river was deathly quiet save for bird song and the summer scream of cicadas.

The river did not have a name, or if it did, it was not one that she had ever heard. Her grandmother had sworn that the river was the mouth of the mountains, and so Rayne spoke to it as if it could speak back. Sometimes, she remembered that it did.

She longed to peel her boots off and race into the frigid water and splash around. She wanted to tell the river about everything she'd done and seen since she'd been here last and listen to what it had to say to her in return.

It was dangerous work for her, navigating the small pebbles and rough dirt of the riverbed with her bare feet, but her body seemed to remember how. Rayne sat at the edge of the river, allowing the cold water to rush over her toes and splash against her ankles.

I don't know what to do anymore. I could just walk away from the house, leave it here for someone to squat in.

Her chest tightened with the memory of House's words, how it had spent years waiting for her to return. It deserved someone to keep it company, even if it wasn't her. *House hadn't asked to be created. It shouldn't be punished for it.*

House was her responsibility, if she really was what had given it life. She wanted to ensure that she could give a decent one.

I could give it to Juniper. Immediately, she frowned and shook her head at the idea. *Juniper will strip House bare, gut it, or worse, wreck it, just like my grandmother's house.*

Her lower lip trembled with the effort of swallowing the sob that wanted to escape. Ryane buried her head between her knees, hiding from the world as she finally lost the battle with her tears.

She did not know how long she remained there until she felt it; a chill that slipped down her spine, tickling her very bones. Rayne looked up and turned her head away, wiping at her tears with her sleeve.

"I know you're there, Hawthorne."

Their voice came from behind her. "How?" They sounded almost confused.

"I just do," she murmured. "What do you want?"

"Why are you crying?"

Rayne felt them hover closer. "Don't come near me," she snapped.

Hawthorne paused but did not step back. "Will you answer my question or not?"

"Why do you even want to know?" She sniffed.

"Is curiosity no longer a valid response?"

All they ever do is ask me questions. And threaten me, mainly that, but questions too. "I'm trapped in this town, and I just want to leave," she said, finally.

"Perhaps the town is not ready to let go of you yet."

"I don't have anything left for this town to take from me." Rayne admitted. *My grandmother. My parents. My brother, wherever he is. He could have been swallowed up by the mines for all I know.*

Hawthorne laughed, the sound rumbling like an avalanche, and she shivered at the icy air that followed their presence. From the corner of her eye, the distortion she had come to know as Hawthorne collected near her. "There's always more to lose, Rayne."

Rayne turned to face them fully. Within the movement, the shifting darkness, she could see the curve of their lips, the shape of their strange chatoyant eyes. She should have been running. "Why are you following me, Hawthorne?"

The river's song swallowed the sudden silence between them, and if she could not see Hawthorne, she might have assumed that they had left.

"Perhaps," they said, barely audible above the water. "The town and I have more in common than it seems."

Her brow furrowed. "What does that mean?"

Hawthorne stood and moved away from her, further down the shore. "You ask too many questions."

"*Me?*" Rayne scoffed. "All *you* do is ask *me* questions!"

Hawthorne laughed again, and it was, admittedly, beginning to frighten her less the more that she heard it. "I am entitled to my curiosity."

"And I'm not?"

Hawthorne remained silent again, and Rayne felt as though she'd made some misstep.

"We could... play a game," she offered. *What are you thinking? This is the same creature that has mentioned wanting to eat you time and time again. The only thing that you should be doing is running away.*

Hawthorne burst into form, more solid than she had ever seen them, and their eyes caught the sunlight, reflecting it. She looked away when it began to hurt her eyes. "What kind of game?"

"A question game."

Hawthorne's head cocked to the side. "And how do we decide who wins?"

I hadn't thought of that. "I guess, whoever refuses to answer a question first loses?"

Hawthorne made a thoughtful noise, curling like a cat. "And what are the stakes?"

Rayne balked. "Stakes?"

"What shall one of us get if we win?"

"Oh." Rayne chewed on her bottom lip. "If I win, then... you'll help me sell my house."

Hawthorne's voice was the rip of skin against gravel. "And what makes you think that I have that ability?"

I hadn't thought of that either. "I mean... well, you were in my dreams, so I thought that... are you saying that you can't?"

Another tense pause fell between them. "No," Hawthorne said finally. "I am not."

"Okay. Yeah. Then those are my terms. What do you want if you win?"

"When I win, you will come to my tree."

Rayne swallowed, lifting her chin. "Fine."

"Then it is set. You shall go first."

"What are you?" Rayne asked the question, stumbling out before she could think of a better one.

"I am... old. Humans have given me many names, though I like Hawthorne best. I am from a world under this one. There was a time when humans gave me the title of 'god'."

That doesn't really answer my question, but I guess it doesn't not answer it either. Rayne considered Hawthorne carefully; their shadowy body, their teeth, the way that they had looked in her dreams like some hellhound had dragged itself up from the depths itself.

"My turn then." Hawthorne shifted from the shoreline to one of the trees behind her. "What do you remember of your time here?"

"What?"

Hawthorne leaned in closer, dark lips pulling back into a grin. "Shall I ask it again, or have you chosen not to answer?"

"No, I just... " Rayne shook her head, turning her attention back to the river as if it held the answer for her. "I remember my grandmother and her home—the crabapple trees. I remember when she died. I remember walking alone from the bus stop back to my house. I remember spending so much time in my room that I thought I'd melt into the carpet. I remember hearing my parents fight, yell at one another, and then me. I remember hating school, always trying to act sick so I wouldn't have to go. And I remember the day that I graduated high school, I packed up all my things and never looked back."

Hawthorne remained close for another moment before drifting away again. "I see."

Again, that feeling of having misstepped reared its ugly head. "Was there something that I'm supposed to be remembering?"

"Is that your question for me, then?"

"No," she murmured, working her lip again. "Why have you been following me?"

"I like the way you smell."

"Wha—"

"Asking another question, are we? That seems like cheating."

"I wasn't." Rayne frowned. "Ask yours."

"When you left, where did you go?"

"A city. It's nothing like things are here, and I like that."

"A city?" Hawthorne echoed, something bitter in the way that they said the word.

"I—" Rayne paused. She wanted to say that she liked cities, that she enjoyed the constant brigade of noise and scents, the steady flow of people through the street outside her apartment. That she didn't miss the stars or the smell of damp leaves and the taste of mountain air. "I like where I live."

If Hawthorne did not believe her, they said nothing of it, only sat back, waiting.

Rayne thought for a moment. "Am I the only one who can see you?"

"No. Anyone can see me if I choose."

If I choose. They want me to see them, to know that they're there.

Rayne looked Hawthorne over again; even with what they'd told her of themself, she could not grasp what they actually were. *A god? Maybe. I don't know what kind of god would be nothing more than a shadow and spend their days in the wood.*

She wiggled her toes, numb from the cold water and chilly air. She grabbed her socks, breathed into them to warm them up, and slipped them onto her feet.

"Run out of questions to ask?" Hawthorne pressed.

"I'm thinking," she snapped, sliding her shoes back on.

I wonder if my Mam'maw ever told me a story about them? Most of her grandmother's stories had been about haints, haunts, and the occasional good folk. There was not much else that she spoke about. Except for...

"Are you the Devil, Hawthorne?"

The movement around her ceased, stilling as if they'd deflated.

"Ask me another question."

Rayne stood, her limbs heavy and aching from the cold. "That's my question."

Hawthorne was in front of her again, their breath tickling against her forehead. "Ask. Another. Question."

She rose to the tip of her toes, glaring back up at them. "No. Answer it or lose."

Hawthorne dissolved into the air, and Rayne saw nothing of them. What she did see was the splitting of the tree nearest to her, splitting and splintering as if lightning had struck it.

Rayne winced, covering her face with her hands to protect it.

"I will help you sell your beloved house," Hawthorne snarled a moment later.

"A sore loser, are we?"

Hawthorne hovered too close, and Rayne stumbled back a step, falling onto her side. Even through her clothes, she could feel the skin on her thigh split and the warmth of blood blooming.

Rayne swore, glaring up at Hawthorne. "What's your—"

The shape of Hawthorne was an inky blot in the winter sun, their wide eyes settled directly on her hip, as if they could see through her clothes. "You're bleeding."

They sound... hungry. She scrambled back, rocks crunching under the thick heel of her boot. "It's nothing. I'm fine."

Hawthorne did not say anything, only continued to stare at her. Dread sank deep into her gut, her pulse fluttering. "Stay—stay away from me, Hawthorne," she warned, willing as much iron into her voice as she dared.

They shifted, moving from the breeze and cold into shadow, into warmth, and into something terribly real. Rayne's eyes went wide as she watched them solidify. *"No."*

CHAPTER THIRTEEN
hawthorne

.

O
f all things for her blood to smell like, it had to be citrus.

There was the unmistakable metallic kiss that all human blood carried to them, but beneath that, there was a biting sweetness, a bitter, somehow saccharine smell that left them salivating.

Rayne was up in an instant, dashing up shore and into the forest in a blink.

They had eaten already, finally feasting on something more satisfying than screaming foxes and frightened little rabbits. They should not have been hungry. But everything about Rayne Dorne was begging to be torn into.

Nothing could ever taste better than her.

Hawthorne turned their head to get a better look at her as she bolted for the forest. *I am faster. It is only fair that I give her a head start. Let her think that she will make it home.*

They waited to see her curls disappear down the trail that led to her home before they followed. Hawthorne cut through the grass and bramble, a tangled web of shadow, teeth, and appetite. It was not just the scent of her fear that compelled them and numbed them to all outside of their desire; it was the hummingbird of her heart, the fluttering pulse rushing through her veins.

They aimed to slip under her feet, snag one of her ankles, and trip her, but as if sensing their thoughts, she changed the pattern of her running, zigzagging through the grass and slipping through their dark fingers.

Amusement rumbled in their chest. *No matter. I can always keep up with you, little wolf.*

Hawthorne skidded to a halt, the term a guillotine to all that they'd sought only a moment before. Their stomach roiled with that sensation that they couldn't name, could not find an origin to other than *her*. Her face. Her smell. Her voice.

They thought of her face, contorted in agony as her entrails gushed between their teeth. The soft rose and sweet almond scent of her that would go cold and fade as her blood seeped into the black soil. The deep rasp of her voice that would disappear into the night after her dying screams like the pulse of a bird's wings.

Hawthorne scowled, displeasure settling in.

There would be no joy in her suffering... but why?

Her skin was so easy to tear, a fact that had delighted them in every thought they'd ever had of her. Pain was nearly as sweet as fear, but the more they tried to envision it, the less they desired it.

The realization pooled in their gut like spilled honey as they let Rayne escape.

I do not want to see her suffer.

The thought rippled through them, shifting every cell. Hawthorne sought a distraction, something to focus their body on while their mind could not stray from Rayne.

Hawthorne hated the taste of black bears. Their fur was too thick, their meat oily and tough, their blood sharp as rotten berries. Hating their taste did not stop them from hunting the creatures for sport.

But halfway through their pursuit of the creature, Hawthorne lost interest in the chase. The ghost of Rayne's scent still coated their senses.

Friction clicked between their rib bones, a sensation that they were beginning to recognize as annoyance. Irritation. *It is irritating to think of her as much as I do. It is irritating that, as much as I want to eat her... now that I have spoken to her, I do not want to hurt her.*

They should, they did, and yet something within them stumbled over the idea and kept stumbling over everything about her.

Hawthorne had not intended to walk all the way back to her home, and yet, they found themself at the edge of her property, waiting for the sun to dip beneath the cover of the trees. While they could not cross this threshold during the day, at night, they could make it all the way to the front door, and there would be nothing that her wretched House could do about it.

If I do not want to hurt her, then I will kill her without doing so, Hawthorne thought, brushing the dying grass. The lawn both overgrown and dying at the same time. It reminded them of her and the thing she'd made of them. *I will compel her to me and lull her into a dream that she will never wake from. Then we shall both have what we want; I will be free of her, and she will be free of this town.*

The lights were on within the house, and Hawthorne could see her shadow moving through the living room, ducking into the kitchen.

The moment that the sun disappeared and the sky melted into shades of orange and purple, Hawthorne slunk to her front door. The porchlight burst on, sensing their heat and presence.

"Go away, wraith," The House snarled, barely hushed. It was such a ravenous thing when it came to Rayne. Unlike the rest of the spirits of this world and the next, House only had a taste for its maker. **"She came back to me fair and square. You'll not dig your teeth into her!"**

"It will be easier if you let me in."

"I would rather rot than bring you a moment of ease."

Inside, her footsteps stopped abruptly, her attention fixed on the ceiling. "House? Who are you talking to?"

"No one, cherub. Come sit by the fire."

"Liar, liar," Hawthorne sang, brushing a clawed finger along the doorframe.

Through the paneled glass, Hawthorne could see her, outlined by the warm, orange light. She turned, and even half-covered in shadow, they could see her frown.

"Is someone outside?" Rayne whispered to the House.

"No one you need concern yourself with, my pretty. Aren't you hungry? You've barely eaten—"

"Who's out there?" she demanded, stepping closer to the door.

Hawthorne could not help the smile that tugged at their lips. That courage would be the end of her. "Hello, Rayne."

She paused. "What are you doing here, Hawthorne? I told you to stay away from me."

"You also told me that you wanted my assistance in selling your house. Or has your mind changed already?"

"You chased me earlier," Rayne said, venturing closer to the door. "You looked like you wanted to eat me."

I do, but you tangle my stomach up with thoughts of what your blood will taste like and the sound of your voice caught in the pines. "That was a misunderstanding."

"A misunderstanding? You chased me!"

"You were bleeding. Blood has a way of... robbing me of my control."

Though Hawthorne could see her, the paneling in the glass obstructed her face, keeping her eyes shielded. Their spell could not work its way into her unless they met her eyes.

"Are you a vampire?" Rayne asked softly, pressing close to the wall beside the door, as if to hide from them. The movement stirred something soft in the back of their throat, coating it like tar. The inside of their chest fluttered. *What does that mean?*

"Why would you think that?" They did not bother to hide their amusement. It was a ridiculous accusation, although not unfounded.

"You said blood makes you weird. And you can't come into my house."

"And how do you know that I cannot come in?" Hawthorne challenged.

"Because you would have already."

"Perhaps I am merely polite?"

Rayne shook her head. "You're not the type for manners."

There. That tiny invisible thread that she kept plucking but refused to pull on completely. It would drive them to madness before want of her ever could. "What do you know of me, Rayne?" Hawthorne did not recognize their own voice when they spoke. Soft. *Weak.*

"All I know is that you haven't said you weren't a vampire."

"I am not a vampire. None of my ilk can enter a home uninvited. A rule as old as the passing of time."

"Oh," Rayne paused and then said quickly, "Well, I'm not letting you in here."

"Then come out."

Her brow furrowed. "What for?"

"How can I help you if we can't see one another?"

"We're talking now. Besides, strange things happen when I stand out on the porch at night."

Curiosity tickled their nose. "Such as?"

"Someone—something dug up one of my pictures and left it out there."

Hawthorne opened their mouth before closing it again. *I must tread carefully.* "Would it comfort you to know that I am the one who left it here for you?"

Her hummingbird pulse kicked to life behind the wood. "Why?"

"I saw it in your yard. You did not do a very good job of burying it," Hawthorne said, juggling the truth and the almost lie on the edge of their tongue. "It is you as a child, is it not?"

"You should have left it!" Rayne hissed. "I buried it for a reason. It's none of your business what I bury in my yard!"

Hawthorne did not know what to say. They had thought that she might have been relieved to learn that it was they who had done it and not some other spirit. They frowned, that unnamed sensation settling in their chest, bitter as ever.

"Are you—" Hawthorne searched for the proper word. They knew of human emotions, but it was difficult to remember the names for each of them. "Angry with me?"

"You snooped in my yard, and now you've tried to eat me."

"Yes. But, that is not an answer."

When Rayne did not immediately answer, their attention honed in on her, a falcon circling a rabbit.

She is so close to opening the door. I need only—

"It doesn't matter how I feel about it."

Her voice sounded so small when she spoke, and in that moment, Hawthorne remembered what it felt like the first time they understood hatred. It was not the sweet tang of fear, but the fire of some unspoken animal that they did not know how to leash.

But it was not for Rayne. Despite the tempest of their discontent, they had never felt that strange, feral emotion toward her.

It has been too long since I have uttered the words, Hawthorne thought, tangling like a string in the wind. *I have carved out every soft thing in me.*

"I do not ask questions unless the answer holds... some value to me," Hawthorne ventured, toeing that invisible line once more.

Rayne's cheek rested against the glass, and she chewed her lower lip, tearing it to shreds again. Her smell soaked through the glass and into them. Her heart was as soft as they'd ever heard it, as distant as summer thunder. Their fingers ghosted along the outline of her face. "Will you answer me?"

Rayne shook her head.

Hawthorne smiled. "So, I suppose that I will have to wait outside your door all night until I receive it."

Her sigh fogged the glass, the scent of peaches and cheap coffee creamer coming with it. They had never craved the taste of either more in their life.

"I'm not... mad at you. I should be, but I'm not. You're the first person who hasn't made me feel out of place. And then you tried to eat me."

"I am not a person, Rayne." It was the truth, as much as they could give her. "I will not deny my nature. All spirits, haints, wisps, or otherwise are the same: we are hungry." She inhaled sharply as the words settled over her. "As to what we are hungry for, that may vary."

Even your precious House would chew you up and hoard your bones if you let it.

"I am not going to let you inside."

"As you said. I will wait for you outside."

"Do you promise not to kill me if I do?"

Hawthorne scoffed, their voice nails across cement. "I do not make promises."

"What if we make a deal?" Rayne asked, lifting her head from the glass to peer at them through it, her eyes still obscured.

Instantly, Hawthorne livened, their eyes alight. Deals and games were cut from the same cloth, and they adored both in equal measure. "What are your terms?"

"I will come outside," Rayne offered. "But only during the day."

"Mm. What are mine?"

"If you catch me outside at night, then... you can eat me."

It was too simple a deal, but it flicked Hawthorne's interest nonetheless. Rayne truly knew nothing of them or their world, as her deal left loopholes large enough for Hawthorne to swim through.

I will play her game fairly. When I win, she will be all the more filling.

"Yes. We have a deal, Rayne Dorne."

"Okay. Good. Hey, Hawthorne?"

"Yes?"

"Get off of my porch," she punctuated the sentence by slamming the inner door and locking it loudly.

Laughter burst out of their chest so suddenly that they took a step back, startled by the sound.

She made me laugh. I have not laughed since—

"Look what you've done. Are you happy now?" the House whispered in the flickering of the porchlight beside their head. ***"There's still time. Go back to your forest, no, another forest far from here. Let her remain within my walls."***

"You've grown greedy."

"And you've grown cruel. Let me keep her."

Hawthorne said nothing as they stepped out of the amber light of the porch and into the black of the night.

Speaking with Rayne had distracted them from all else, and now that they were alone again, they felt a distant ache in their chest, familiar as it was foreign.

I think I want to keep her too.

CHAPTER FOURTEEN
rayne

Rayne swore at the empty refrigerator shelves and did the same when the barren pantry greeted her. She'd gone through her last of the canned food the night before, and she'd meant to go to the corner store, but Hawthorne's sudden appearance had thrown her off the track.

I wonder where they are and what they do during their days.

But then she remembered the feral glimmer in their eyes yesterday, the feeling of running from them when she was sure that their breath was ghosting the back of her neck.

I shouldn't be thinking about them at all. They'd kill me if I gave them the proper chance.

She dressed like a criminal, in a black zip-up hoodie, thick matching sweatpants, and knitted gloves. Black was her favorite color to wear most of the time, and it was the only one that she never had to worry about bleeding through if she accidentally hurt herself.

"Where are you going now, cherub?" House yawned. **"Not back to that wood, I hope."**

"I'm just running to the store, House. I'll be back in twenty minutes."

House groaned miserably, and Rayne paused in the doorway. She hesitated a moment before brushing the knitted pads of her finger along the wood panel.

"It's okay." The words stumbled off her tongue, and she wasn't sure that she was doing this correctly. *I've never comforted anyone before.* "I—uhm, I'll be back soon, and I'll put some extra wood in your fire."

House purred like a cat, and she took that as answer enough.

After settling in her Jeep, Rayne shifted the car in reverse, looking to her rearview mirror.

Hawthorne sat curled in the back seat, a collection of smoke. "Hello."

Rayne screamed, slamming down on her brakes. Her body surged forward, and if it were not for the cushioned cover she had on her seatbelt, it would have cut her from throat to her navel.

"What the hell are you doing in here?" she shouted over her shoulder, craning her neck to glare at them.

Hawthorne cocked their head to the side. "Waiting for you to drive us wherever we are going."

"Were you waiting for me all night?"

"No. Only since you got in the car," Hawthorne answered. "You are rather oblivious when you enter and exit this machine. Something might snatch you and drag you off into the forest."

"*Something* is seriously wrong with you and—" Across the way, movement in the window of The Hampers' house caught her eye. Mrs. Hamper stood, watching her, the old lady's thin lips pinched into a sneer. It occurred to Rayne how this must look, her in the middle of her driveway, screaming at what looks like an empty seat.

Hastily, she backed down the rest of her driveway, into the road, switched gears, and raced down the path.

Hawthorne shifted to the passenger's seat, collecting on the cushion like honey. "She is a nosy vulture."

Rayne did not immediately answer them, her anxiety rising. *I hate when people look at me like that. Especially when I'm not prepared for it.*

Memories of her childhood here rushed into her vision: the eyes that followed her wherever she went or how small she made herself, the barely concealed whispers about her scars, the constant bandages she wore. Eventually, she'd started covering up with long sleeves even in the summer, double-layering everything. But it never mattered. People had seen, and they never forgot. They never let her forget either.

"Where are we going?" Hawthorne asked, their voice plucking her from the sea of her past.

"*I* am going to the corner store to grab food as quickly as possible. You are going to stay here."

"You do not govern me. I will go into your 'corner store' if I wish."

"Someone will see you!"

"You forget that I am of shadow. I can return to that, and no one will catch sight of me."

Rayne paused. "Why were you watching to see when I'd get into my car? Were you waiting for me?"

Hawthorne shifted. "You said that you wanted to get out of here. I am trying to help you hurry that process along."

It's so hard to read them, she thought, glancing sideways at them. Their voice lacked any of the intonation she had taught herself to dissect in others.

Rayne turned on her music to distract herself from the creature that she could not unravel.

B-Quick Mart sat beneath a rotting apartment building in a nearly abandoned shopping center. The parking lot was an empty square of cracked, graffiti-covered asphalt, weeds sprouting between the painted words and symbols. It was a stomping ground for teenagers and the town's lowlifes.

Outside the store, two teenage boys and two young men had rooted themselves. One of the teenagers circled in front of them on his bike, showing off his tricks. The oldest-looking one of them, Rayne, recognized from high school as one of Len Kappler's friends. *Ian something.* He was wearing a *Bury High School* letterman jacket that had seen better days. He fished a pack of cigarettes out of his oil-stained, acid-wash jeans and lit it up just as Rayne pulled into the parking lot.

All of them turned to stare at her, eying her and her car. Rayne stalled. Even from across the lot, her and Ian's eyes met, the cherry of the cigarette simmering like a warning.

There's no way that they don't try to hotwire my car while I'm in there or go for my converter. Even if they didn't do either of those things, Rayne only had cash on her. *It's like I'm just begging to get mugged.*

"Goddamn it," she murmured.

She put the car in reverse, flipped a U-turn, and pulled out of the lot.

"Why did you do that?" Hawthorne asked

"I'm not in the mood to get robbed," Rayne bit back.

"They would not have done anything to you."

With a scoff, Rayne replied, "You don't know that."

"But I do," Hawthorne stated as if it were something she should have expected. "I would have made a meal of them all before they could think to cause you any discomfort."

Rayne did not know what to say to that. She tightened her grip on the steering wheel and forced her attention forward.

"There is no one waiting outside of this store, and yet you are still hesitating." Hawthorne cocked their head to the side, watching her.

Frustration flared once more that she could not read the meaning behind their words.

The parking lot of Kappie's was nearly empty this late in the morning, but Rayne couldn't bring herself to exit the safety of her car yet. Kappie's Market was the only real grocery store in town, and it just so happened to be owned by the family that had made her school life a nightmare.

Maybe they just own it now and don't work the floor anymore? She hoped, even though she knew damn well that no one in this town could afford not to work.

I just need to get it over with and stop being such a baby. I'll be in and out before anyone can spot me.

"Are you... going to stay in here?" Rayne asked, glancing over at Hawthorne.

"No," Hawthorne answered after a moment. "I will follow in your shadow. Walk, and I will walk with you."

It was madness, she knew, to find comfort in someone who had only the day before attempted to kill her, and yet, knowing that Hawthorne would be with her calmed the frightened animal in her chest.

Kappie's was nothing like the big, beautiful, and spacious grocery stores she'd grown to love in the city. Instead, it was a cramped space in a rundown building that looked much worse on the outside than it was on the inside.

Wow, she thought as shining, automatic doors slid open for her. Silver, shining and clearly brand new, they were entirely out of place in the out-of-date building. *Guess they're moving up in the world.*

Upon entering, the new doors proved to be the only part of the store that had changed. Rayne was hit with the familiar scent of slightly rotten lettuce and lemon cleaner. *Okay, let's do this.* She snatched a bright yellow plastic basket. Muscle memory directed her down the aisles as she barely glanced at the things she was tossing in: pasta, oats, as few perishables as possible, though she would need to get at least a few fresh items.

"This place is strange," Hawthorne said from somewhere behind her. Rayne jumped, almost having completely forgotten that they were with her. "It is odd to see so much food."

"Have you never been in a grocery store before?" she whispered over her shoulder, darting down the produce aisle toward the deli.

"Of course not. What need would I have for someone to catch and kill my food for me?"

"Fair enough."

Something tugged at her foot, and she glanced back, assuming that her shoelace had snagged on the corner of something sharp, only to find Hawthorne's fingers against her ankle.

"There are oranges here," they said, their voice the most emotive that she had heard thus far. It almost sounded like they were *excited*.

Rayne looked to the display in front of her and slightly to her left; lemons, grapefruits, and of course, oranges.

"Yeah. Grocery stores usually have those."

"All of them?"

"I guess?"

"I would like some."

Rayne's brow furrowed. "Then take some. You said yourself that you're ungovernable."

"I cannot take one without becoming fully physical here. I will be seen," Hawthorne answered.

Rayne frowned. "Okay, well, what do you want me to do about it?"

"I would like you to buy me an orange."

"What? No."

"Can you not afford an orange?"

"Of course I can, but—" Rayne sighed. "Okay, fine. Just let go of me."

With six oranges tucked carefully into her basket, she whispered over her shoulder. "Anything else in this store that you're dying for me to get you?" she snapped.

"No, the oranges are more than enough."

Hawthorne allowed her to shop in relative peace, slipping back into her shadow. When she was finally ready to leave, she stepped up to the checkout counter and rang the bell on the table.

Please don't be someone I know, please be a stranger.

"Yeah, I'm comin'. Gimme a minute," someone called from the dairy aisle. All it took was one glance for Rayne to recognize him: Todd Kappler—Len's older brother.

He had the same mousy-blond hair as his brother, buzzed short, like his time in the military had ingrained the style in him. His presence brought not only the scent of sweat and tobacco but the memory of the last time she'd seen him.

Rayne shrank, her shoulders knitting together and her gaze staying fixed on the ground in front of her as he settled behind the register.

"Sorry 'bout that," Todd said. "Just me today, and we got a whole new shipment in, so I'm runnin' around like a chicken with my head cut off," he said, the Bury hilt so deep in his voice that she was certain an outsider might not have caught everything he'd said.

"It's fine," Rayne murmured, nearly sighing in relief when she heard the beeping of the scanner.

"Shit load'a oranges you got there for the middle of winter," he remarked, and Rayne willed herself to nod instead of mentioning that it was still November and winter didn't officially start for nearly an entire month.

Todd stared at her, his attention creeping over her like ivy. Rayne's fingers dug deep into her wallet as she forced herself to breathe normally.

"Hey. I recognize you." Rayne felt sick. "Yeah. You had those scars. Rayne, right?"

How many other scarred black girls who look like me do you know that live in this nearly all-white town, you idiot? She wanted to snap at him, but she swallowed the words. "Yeah."

"Heard about your folks. Must be terrible, couldn't imagine losin' mine."

Please stop fucking talking to me.

Unsure of what else to do or what to say in a moment like this, Rayne kept her attention pinned to the floor while he rang up her purchases and placed them in large, brown paper bags, slower than drying paint.

"You sure look... different from the last time I saw you," he continued, and Rayne's breath hitched as his attention on her sharpened. "You always were wearin' black but... you ain't like a Devil worshipper or nothin', are you?"

"Nope," Rayne said too quickly, her accent catching like wildfire. *I am going to have to beat this back outta me. I refuse to sound like this. I refuse.* "How much do I owe you?" she asked, careful to enunciate every syllable.

Todd raised a brow, scoffing at her. "Ain't you just a regular city girl now?"

"I guess. How much?" she pressed.

"Fifty-five flat."

"Keep the change." Rayne whipped out three twenties and popped them on the counter in front of Todd. She scrambled to gather the two bags in her arms so she could get out as soon as possible.

"Don't need your charity, Dorne. You ain't no better than the rest of us. Talk all posh if you want, but you're Bury through and through."

Rayne swallowed, speed walking toward the door. *Don't react, don't react. You know it's always worse when you give them the reaction they're looking for. Just keep walking.*

"I'll let Lenny boy know you're back!" he called after her.

Rayne kept walking, and it wasn't until she made it to the lot that she was able to breathe.

"You did not like talking to him," Hawthorne stated, their voice brushing against her ear. She turned, but they had melted away, a vague outline barely visible if she squinted.

"No, I didn't," she replied.

"Then why did you not leave?"

"I had—" Rayne had turned around to fix them with a glare when her attention caught on the window of the grocery store. A fresh missing person's flyer right in front of the shopping carts, and pictured on it was a man she recognized, but only barely. Stepping closer, she squinted at the picture of him. He was grinning in the photo, surrounded by what she could only assume to be grandchildren in front of a glowing Christmas tree.

Missing: Jeffery Harris

Age: 76

Last Seen: November 13th. Leaving

his home on Mulberry Street,

heading for the cemetery.

Please contact the family for any

information on Jeffery.

That man. I saw him in the graveyard that day. Was I the last person to see him?

"Are you concerned for this man's whereabouts, and that is why you are staring at his picture so intently?" Hawthorne inquired, this time from directly beneath her.

"No. Well, yes. I think that I saw him at the graveyard that day and that maybe I was the last person to see him alive."

"You were."

"How could you know that?"

"Because I ate him," Hawthorne answered, and it sounded so... simple. Rayne wasn't sure if it was simply the way that their voice sounded or if they genuinely felt no guilt in admitting what they'd done.

"You... ate him?"

"Yes, and I did not enjoy the taste of him. Too bitter, but meat is meat. I should have known by the way he spat at you."

He spat at me?

Rayne remembered the way he'd slung the word 'witch' at her, but she had been so busy trying to leave that he could have spit at her on her way out. *It wouldn't surprise me at this point, really.*

She clutched her bags closer to her chest. "Did you eat him because of that?" Rayne whispered as if speaking it aloud would alter the truth of it.

Hawthorne remained silent for a few seconds. "It seems that you still do not know me, Rayne." Before she could press them for more information, they interrupted. "Let us leave. I would like my oranges now."

CHAPTER FIFTEEN
hawthorne

Hawthorne was bewildered.

Their days had become a strange tangle of events that Hawthorne could not understand. A schedule had been born between them and Rayne.

Every day she rose in the late morning, and Hawthorne would meet her in the garden out back, hovering close by while she drank her coffee. The season was beginning to grow its teeth. Hawthorne watched the blood rush to her dark skin, her nose and cheeks reddening in the cold.

Sometimes they would both sit in silence, but more often than no,t Rayne would speak, her words rising with the grey smoke of her breath. She spoke in rivers and waterfalls of words, barely pausing to breathe, and Hawthorne found that they liked to listen. They liked knowing about what her life looked like outside of this town, and they liked that she seemed to enjoy it when they formed opinions on her world.

"Your employment is very boring," Hawthorne replied one day after she had finished explaining to them what exactly an accountant was and why they were necessary.

Rayne took a sip of her coffee before she responded, huddled on the stone bench under the pear tree. "Yeah," she agreed, licking the milk foam from her upper lip. Hawthorne's attention hooked on the movement. *Why?* "But it's consistent work, and I'm good at it. And it pays my bills."

Hawthorne made a soft noise of discontent. Of all the things she shared with them, they disliked the knowledge of bills and rent most of all. "It is moronic to have to pay to exist."

"I agree with you, but that's just the way things are for us," Rayne said, placing down her mug beside her. "I imagine in your world there have never been any landlords or kings, right?"

Discomfort trickled down their spine at that thought, and they chose their following words carefully. "Hierarchies exist in all things. Even my world."

"Really? So, there are what, kings, queens? Rulers of the forest?" Rayne asked, and Hawthorne had come to learn her voice well enough to read the curiosity in it.

They did not want to talk about this.

"Perhaps." They floated upward until they were tangled in the amber leaves of the tree. Hawthorne shook the branches hard until a few pears toppled down on her.

Rayne's sharp laughter cut into them every time they heard it. They wanted to chase the sound but could not understand where it would lead them if they did. They distracted themself with dodging the fallen pears she tossed back up at them.

Sometimes Rayne would drag cardboard boxes of junk her parents had left behind out onto the back porch and rummage through them while Hawthorne remained close by. Other times, she would head into town, and they would filter into her car to tag along and hide in her shadow while she went about her day.

But every day, just as the sun was beginning to set, she would go inside for the night, but not before saying "goodnight" to them. It was an entirely human custom, they understood, and while they did not know the intention behind it, Hawthorne liked that it was something Rayne gave them every day, like a trinket.

Occasionally, they would go to the river, and it was those days that Hawthorne thought might be their favorite.

On those days, Rayne removed her thick, large socks and rolled up her leggings to her knees, exposing more of her skin to the elements. Marbled, soft brown and pink in some places, her scars painted her skin like seafoam.

It was not just the sight of her legs that drew them nearer, but the sweep of her thick curls, their constant tangling. The way that she scrunched her nose when she was annoyed or thinking too hard. Every gesture, every movement made Hawthorne draw closer to her. There were moments, flashes, where she looked at them and they could not understand the expression on her face.

She does not smile often but when she does... she is beautiful.

It wasn't until after she did this that Hawthorne remembered they were supposed to be trying to keep her outside past sunset so that they might win their game and finally eat her.

Why do I only ever seem to forget around her?

Memory was a gift and a curse for spirits. They could remember everything in perfect clarity, but with it came the knowledge that they could only experience something once. These remained ingrained in their kind long after things were rotting in the ground.

For the first time that Hawthorne could remember, they began to second guess themself, doubt creeping in like frost.

Rayne *made* them doubt.

Is killing her what will bring me peace?

Hawthorne did not exactly know what peace was, but they imagined that it was what life had been like before her. Who they had been before their paths crossed.

"Hawthorne?" Rayne called.

She stared up at them, half in her car and half in the driveway, the engine rumbling low and steady. Their attention fell back to her, leaving their confusion behind, and they swept closer to her. "Yes?"

"I asked if you were going to come with me to the DMV?"

Hawthorne frowned and tangled in her hair like smoke. "If that is the place you spoke of yesterday, then no. I will not suffer such torment."

Rayne scoffed. "You're so dramatic. But suit yourself. I'll be back in a little bit."

"With oranges?" Hawthorne asked, undoing a knot in one of her curls.

There were few foods that Hawthorne could say they sought, but oranges were always at the top of their list. Every bite of them was a burst of summer and sunlight, and even though they were a winter beast, the flavor brought them endless pleasure. Not every place that Hawthorne traveled had them so readily available, especially not in winter. *Had I known, I would have wandered into those smelly grocery stores much sooner.*

"You've still got three left."

Rayne was a cruel thing and rationed their oranges, keeping them inside the house so that they could not snatch more. If they could not hear its rhythm in her chest, Hawthorne would have thought her heartless. "I would like more."

"You're rather demanding," Rayne replied, lifting a gloved finger, and Hawthorne swirled around it before manifesting above her.

"Yes."

"And what exactly do *I* get in exchange for spending all of *my* money on oranges for you?"

"What do you want?" Hawthorne asked, peering down at her. Her heart answered before she did, kicking to life as if they'd just threatened to eat her.

Rayne opened and closed her mouth a dozen times, and Hawthorne tilted their head, curious.

"I'll be back," Rayne declared, and just before she closed her car door, she added. "With oranges."

Hawthorne watched her back out of the driveway. *I could leave.* They thought as she drove away. *I could return to the forest, and she would never see me again. I do not have to eat her. But then it would—*

"You can still leave," the House said, echoing their thoughts back at them. It did not matter that they had just thought the same thing; hearing it from the House set a flurry of irritation behind their eyes. **"*There is time. Now, while she is still—*"**

"You should know better than to try and dictate what I need to do," Hawthorne replied, cutting it off without bothering to look over their shoulder. "When have you ever had sway over my choices, House?"

Perhaps it was solely to spite the House or because no matter what other choices Hawthorne might have had, none of them compared to following Rayne Dorne. *That is what I will do.*

The House sighed miserably, **"Yes, I suppose it always has to be this way, doesn't it?"**

Hawthorne pretended not to hear.

When Hawthorne decided that they could wait for her no longer, and their curiosity got the better of them, they went off into town in search of Rayne.

Her scent was warm against their nose, gentle as a caress but strong enough that they could taste it, could taste her. The thread of her led them back to the accursed grocery store, but even under the scent of rotting greenery and leaking air conditioning, Hawthorne could still smell her.

Scouring the parking lot, they came upon her Jeep and slid under it, nestling in its shadow while they waited for her. Luckily, she did not make them wait for long. She rushed out of the grocery store as she always did.

The grocery store and the man who worked there were two topics she refused to discuss; every time Hawthorne mentioned either, she'd frown and mumble that she didn't want to talk about it.

They wanted to know, but they did not want to make her upset. It unsettled their stomach.

Hawthorne slunk into the car when she opened the door, barely visible as they dripped into the back seat. Rayne tossed the bag of oranges in the back with them, and Hawthorne sighed in pleasure at the mere scent of them.

"Okay, that could have been worse," Rayne murmured, clicking her seatbelt into place.

Hawthorne had witnessed the behavior of many humans, but Rayne was the only one they had seen who spoke to herself as much as she did. They could not deny how odd it was, nor could they deny that they found it pleasant in a way they could not name. Endearing.

Yes. That it is.

They liked it when she was outside the House, it meant that they could get as close as they wanted and not make her nervous. When she felt them looking at her too long, she would begin to shift and shrink in on herself. Hawthorne did not like it when she did that.

They much preferred her when she was laughing or so lost in a story that she seemed to even forget they were there.

Ignorant to their presence, Rayne had turned on her music. Typically, Hawthorne found themself indifferent to most music, but this did not sound like any music they'd ever heard before.

Hawthorne swept into the passenger seat, closer to the speakers. "What is this music?" they asked.

Rayne screamed, and the car swerved hard to the right, nearly off the road. She swiveled the steering wheel hard to get the vehicle back to the middle of the right lane.

"Hawthorne!" she hissed at them, fixing them with a glare. "You can't just do that. You can't just appear out of nowhere without announcing yourself. I nearly drove off the road!"

"And yet you didn't." Hawthorne shrugged before they gestured to the car's speakers. "The music? What is it?"

Rayne rolled her eyes and turned the volume down. "If you wanted me to turn it down, that's all you had to say."

Hawthorne huffed. "I do *not* want you to turn it down."

Rayne turned to look at them, and they recognized the bewilderment on her face. "Do you like music?"

"No. I like *this* music, whatever it is," Hawthorne replied. On the screen of her dashboard, the album cover flashed; a red-haired woman's back was turned, her hands covered in paint, and a denim jacket that had been spray-painted on. "Is there more?"

Rayne laughed a little. "Oh yeah, big time. I've got every album of theirs. Do you want to hear more?"

"I want to hear all of it."

When they arrived back at the House, Rayne kept her car running for them while she carried the oranges and a few other things she'd bought inside, and they could keep listening to her music. They were disappointed when she returned a few minutes later to turn the car off.

"Sorry," she said, smiling a little as the engine kicked off. "But, I think I've got my old CD player inside somewhere. I know I've got at least one album in my room. Might be in the garage, and there's at least an hour or so before the sunsets."

Hawthorne tilted their head. "What does this mean?"

"It means that I can plug my CD player into the outlet out on the porch and you can keep listening."

"Oh. This is good news, then." Hawthorne swirled through her hair for a moment. "Yes, I would like that."

Rayne laughed a little, and Hawthorne watched her disappear into the House. They dipped along the side of the House and stopped at the edge of the back porch. From inside, they could hear Rayne as she moved through the House, her feet against the linoleum in the kitchen, the hardwood of the hallway that led to the garage.

"***Do not try to enter, wraith,***" the House mumbled, low so that Rayne could not hear.

"I am not. *She* is coming to me," they said, grinning and flashing their teeth at House.

"***So smug in your cruelty,***" House continued, jealousy radiating off of it like heat. "***You are the greediest thing.***"

The sliding door opened, and Rayne peeked her head out. "Hawthorne?"

They moved closer to the door, careful not to touch the wooden ground of the deck, and instead hovered nearby. "I am here."

"Okay. So, I don't think you can actually come all the way up here without an invitation, right?"

"I can go no further than the top step of any residence."

"That seems rather specific," she remarked, closing the door behind her, a pink and white "*CD player*" as she referred to it tucked under her arm along with a couch cushion.

"Most things for spirits are," Hawthorne said with a shrug, floating behind her. Rayne tossed the cushion down on the top step and plugged the dangling white cord into the grey box along the outside wall of the house.

"I don't think that I'll ever understand your world," Rayne said with a sigh, making herself comfortable on the cushion.

I hope that you never have to. Resilient as you are, you would not make it out alive.

They did not say as much, knowing that it would only ignite her curiosity. Hawthorne had begun to learn Rayne, to know her as they might have known an extension of themself. There was a part of her that sought a fight, something about her that screamed silently.

"I could say the same of yours," Hawthorne said instead, settling at the step just below her, her knee dangerously close to their lips.

"Fair enough."

Rayne turned the music on, and the pair of them fell into a comfortable silence. Even with the music, Hawthorne was painfully aware of Rayne. The smell of her, the sound of her heart, and her breath as she mouthed the words.

"You're staring at me," she murmured, looking away from them.

"Yes. I like to," they admitted.

Rayne paused, her heart skipping a beat. "Why?"

I should give her the truth. "You are—"

Inside, the landline rang, the sound wedging between them. Rayne looked at them a moment longer before glancing over her shoulder toward the door. "I should... get that. I'll be right back."

Hawthorne nodded, watching after her.

"Hello?" Rayne said from inside. "Oh, June. Hi."

Hawthorne snarled. *I hate that woman.*

"Rainy. Have you... heard from Callum yet?" Juniper's shrill voice snapped over the phone. Even over the music, they could hear her.

I should not eavesdrop, Hawthorne thought. *But then again, she did not ask me not to.*

"No," Rayne replied, much gentler than that woman deserved. "I haven't. I promised I'd let you know if I did."

"Something just isn't adding up," Juniper pressed on as if Rayne hadn't said anything at all. "I've been calling him non-stop, and he hasn't answered me. Not even a text. Now, apparently, his phone is disconnected."

Hawthorne could hear Rayne beginning to chew her bottom lip. "Maybe he just wants to be left alone, June. Our parents just died, so maybe—"

"Cal doesn't run away from his family," Juniper hissed into the line. "I know him better than anyone, and last time I talked to him, he said he was going down there to see your parents."

"What?" Rayne asked. "I thought that he only came down here to handle the funeral arrangements. I didn't know that he had left before that."

Silence stepped between the pair, and Hawthorne could hear Rayne's weight shifting as she rocked uneasily.

"You telling lies, Rayne Dorne?"

"No. Why would I lie about that, June?"

After a long moment, Juniper said, "I think I should come up there. Help you look for him because something—something just isn't right about all this."

"I—I would really prefer if you didn't," Rayne said, quiet as a mouse.

I hate it when she sounds like that.

"There's a lot of stuff I'm trying to manage right now with the house, and everything is a mess, and I just need some space to get everything settled."

"I *will* get to the bottom of this, Rainy. And I *will* find Callum." The line clicked, and Rayne's breath hitched as she hung the phone back on the receiver.

Hawthorne returned to where they had been sitting previously and waited for Rayne to return. When she did, there was a certain heaviness to her that

Hawthorne did not care for; her arms circling herself, like she was trying to keep from spilling over.

There is an appropriate response to this situation, I am sure, but I do not know what it is. "Hello, Rayne," they said in place of anything else to think of.

She tucked a strand of hair behind her ear from her ruined braid, not looking at them. That sensation returned, as uncomfortable as ever, as they watched her. "Hi, Hawthorne." She sat back down on the cushion and turned the music down, though Hawthorne did not need it. They could hear her over everything.

"I really need to sell the house. The sooner I leave Bury, the better. I just want to be free of all of this. Do you think we could put a rush on getting me out of here?"

Hawthorne frowned as they felt something inside of them shrink. "Yes. If that's what you want."

Rayne nodded and turned up the volume on the CD player as they both sat in silence.

Hawthorne couldn't hear anything over their desire to keep Rayne in Bury.

I do not know that I can let her go again.

CHAPTER SIXTEEN
rayne

D esire had kicked up a storm within her, and now, she was left with only the dust.

I want to leave. I've always wanted to leave this town. I've dreamt of nothing else since I was ten years old. I built something outside of these mountains, and I want to go back to that. So then, why am I even hesitating?

Rayne knew the answer: Hawthorne.

They wanted to kill her, and yet they hadn't hurt her. Not once despite every opportunity that they'd had to do so. Instead, they sat with her, spent most of their days talking to her, and she didn't know what it meant.

I really want us to be friends, and we might be.

At least, she hoped. Rayne had never had a friend before, and so she wasn't entirely sure what the criteria was. She'd read dozens of books, seen hundreds of movies, but none of them really explained friendship to her or what it meant to be inside of one.

She'd thought to search online for an answer, but even typing the question felt pathetic and so she buried the thought.

Nearly thirty years old, and I don't know what a friend looks like.

All Rayne knew was that she liked Hawthorne, no matter how foolish it might be. They listened to her; they never said anything unkind to her. Blunt, maybe, but never unkind, and she was not sure what to do with that knowledge.

"The sun is setting," Hawthorne said, cutting through the buzz of her thoughts. They smirked at her. "Perhaps I should drag you off into the woods and keep you to myself."

Heat crept up her spine but she ignored it, jutting her chin out in defiance. "Try it. I'm not scared of you anymore, Hawthorne."

Their head tilted at that strange angle, so undeniably other that it made her stomach clench. "No?"

She shook her head, standing on the tip of her toes to get closer to looking them in the eye; they had nearly a foot on her. "Not at all," she bit back a smile. "You're nothing but a harmless little puppy."

Shadows tangled around her limbs and locked around her waist, knocking her back against the outside of the house. Not hard enough to hurt her, she noted. Hawthorne's shadows were warm, much warmer than she ever would have anticipated.

"A puppy am I?" Hawthorne asked, flashing her the dark daggers of their teeth. "Are you certain about that?"

Rayne swallowed. "Yup."

A wispy shadow slithered up her body and around her neck like a snake and wrapped around the hollow of her throat. It tightened for a moment, taking Rayne's breath with it, but only a fraction of a second. Hawthorne watched her with one of their unreadable expressions on their face.

Tension spiked behind her eyes, fading the moment that Hawthorne released their grip on her airway. It hadn't been nearly as unpleasant as it should have been. *I want them to do it again.*

"Careful, little wolf," Hawthorne murmured, leaning down to brush their lips close to her ear. "One day, something might just come along to grant that death wish."

Little wolf.

That's the second time they've called me that.

"I can handle myself," she said, not even sounding convincing to herself.

Hawthorne laughed, their voice the sound of gravel underfoot. She liked how frequently they changed, how sometimes their voice was as soft as leaves in the breeze and other times it was an avalanche, heavy and shattering.

"You talk quite a bit. How will you back it up if someone were to test you?"

Hawthorne pressed closer, bringing with them the scent of petrichor and damp leaves. They were warm, so warm, and they were touching her and nothing hurt.

When was the last time someone was ever this close to me without my skin splitting like paper?

Never.

The realization knocked the breath out of her lungs, stole whatever answer she might have had for Hawthorne. Their eyes traced along her face, her messy hair, and a shadow carefully tucked a strand behind her ear.

Hawthorne leaned closer, and Rayne's pulse hammered in response, though she wasn't certain that it was from fear.

"Cherub," House whispered.

Rayne yelped, shoving Hawthorne away, and they slunk back to the bottom step. "House! What's wrong with you? You scared me half to death!"

"Apologies, beloved, but there is someone at my door. A policeman. He knocks so ungraciously."

A cop?

Rayne cast a glance back at Hawthorne, and she frowned at the sudden distance between them. "I've got to go. But I'll see you tomorrow?"

Hawthorne nodded. "You will."

"Okay, then. Goodnight, Hawthorne."

"Goodnight, Rayne."

A shiver slipped down her spine, shaking her shoulders at the sound of her name on their tongue.

It's just the wind, she assured herself as she closed the sliding glass door behind her and locked it. *It's cold out tonight, that's all.*

Rayne hesitated at the door, watching the outline of the officer through the glass. "How long has he been standing here?" she whispered.

"At least ten minutes, cherub. I do not think he will go away until he speaks to you."

Shit.

A sharp inhale to ground herself, and Rayne pushed open the door. The officer stood eye level with her, tanned, sun-wrecked skin and dark hair to match his eyes. Time certainly hadn't been kind to him, though Rayne recognized him.

"Evenin', Rayne," he said, smiling tightly at her, and she did not miss the way his eyes scanned her. "Heard you were back in town, almost didn't believe it. You remember me?"

How could I forget the asshole who used to hide my math textbooks before class and laugh when I'd get in trouble for not having them? Or how you used laugh at every shitty thing Len ever did to me? Rayne did not return his smile. "Brian Creed. Yeah, I do."

Brian nodded, slipping his hands into his back pockets. "Good to have you back. Bury misses its own. We're a dying breed, you know? Not many towns are left like this in the world."

Thank God for that. "I suppose not," Rayne murmured. "Is there... something I can do for you?"

"Yeah, if you don't mind. I just had a few questions for you if you got the time. Can I come in?"

Rayne tensed. "Prefer if you didn't. The house is a mess."

"Suit yourself," he shrugged, but something in the gesture felt performative, as if he was trying to seem more at ease than he was. Rayne bristled, scrutinizing every movement as he pulled a notepad from his pocket. "Have you been out to the old cemetery recently?"

"Yeah. Stopped by a few times to visit my parents' grave."

Brian nodded again, though his pen wasn't moving. "Figured as much. Sorry about your folks, by the way. Awful to lose your family at any age."

"Thanks."

"When you went out there, did you remember seeing anyone else?"

It must be about that old man. The one that Hawthorne—oh, shit. "I think so," Rayne said, swallowing the rising nerves. "I saw an old man on my way out to my car."

"Did you?" Brian asked, his pen moving slowly over the paper now, and it took everything in her for Rayne to resist peeking down at the words. "Remember when that might have been?"

"A couple of weeks ago, I think."

"Around what time, do you think?"

"The sun was still out."

"And did you two talk at all?" Brian asked, finally looking up from his notepad.

Witch, the old man had spat at her as she left. Rayne shook her head, "No, can't say we did. I keep to myself when I can help it."

Brian's attention remained glued to her for a long moment before he flashed her another tight smile. "I remember that about you. Well." He pushed the notepad and pen back into his pocket. "Thank you for your time."

"Sure. Is everything alright?"

"Suppose you ain't seen all the missing person posters up around town?"

Rayne lied, shaking her head. "Can't say I have."

"Well. An old man went missing a while ago. Names Jeffery. Ever met him?" Rayne shook her head, and he continued. "Nicest man I ever met. Family is worried sick about him."

"That's awful," Rayne replied, unsure of how she should sound, what she should say to convey her innocence. "I'm sorry to hear that."

"Yeah, real terrible. Everyone in town is keepin' an eye out."

"I will too," Rayne promised around the dryness in her throat.

"Appreciate it," Brain said. He glanced her up and down one more time before he took a step back off the porch. "Thanks again for your time, Rayne. I'll see you around. Oh, and welcome back."

Rayne tried to smile and waved as he walked back to his patrol car parked by her mailbox. She waited until he was in his car for her to exhale, closing the door behind her as quickly as she could.

"You handled that so well, cherub," the House crooned. *"Let us hope that he does not return. I do not like the smell of him."*

"I didn't have anything to do with that man's death," Rayne murmured, hardly hearing House. "Hawthorne was the one who killed him. Not me."

But then that hadn't stopped me from spending time with Hawthorne, or from letting them closer than I should. They killed a man. They kill people.

Rayne paced the kitchen, chewing her lower lip. *It wasn't as if I had been exactly horrified when they'd told me. More surprised, I guess. But then what does that say about me? Some poor old man is dead and being mourned by his family, and I—*

"I don't care," she whispered, pausing. "I don't... care that he's dead."

When the confession came with no lightning to strike her down, no thunder clap of God's fury condemning her to Hell, a small breathless laugh slipped from behind her lips.

All those years of hearing how kindness was the only way, her parents hissing at her to 'be kind' despite their own cruelty to her, even her Mam'maw's harsh warnings to always keep a pure heart, otherwise the Lord would ruin her life and drag her down to hell.

Mam'maw.

Whatever joy she'd felt in that moment melted at the memory of her grandmother and how she felt about spirits that did evil, how she would feel about Hawthorne.

Her grandmother would have fasted for weeks, sharpened herself into some holy weapon and waged war against Hawthorne the moment she caught sight of them.

But what would she think of me? Allowing myself to get so close to a spirit so dangerous, a monster?

Would she start to hate me, too?

A knock at the front door jolted her from her thoughts, and she froze. "House, is it him? Is the cop back?"

"No, not him. I like the smell of this one. Like lemons and fresh sage."

Rayne crept closer to the door, and through the panels, she caught clementine hair glowing under the porchlight. *Persimmon.*

"Hey, neighbor!" Persimmon beamed as Rayne cracked the door. "How's everything going with you? I just saw Officer Creed's squad car heading back to town from up this way. You okay?"

Did she really come up here just to check on me? "Oh, uhm. Yeah. He just wanted to drop by after hearing I was in town."

Persimmon rolled her eyes. "Ugh, what a pain. But I'm glad you're alright."

Rayne nodded. "Yeah, thanks for checking."

"Actually, that's not why I came up here." Rayne's hand stilled, and she pushed the door open a little wider. "I wanted to invite you over tomorrow for the holiday."

"Holiday?"

"Thanksgiving," Persimmon began. "Although it feels kind of icky to celebrate that sort of thing, especially since most of this town sits on Native American land."

"Yeah, I know. My family is from around here. I'm Indigenous," Rayne said, the words harsher than she meant them. "Sorry. It's just—it's fine. I'm not, like, offended or something."

Persimmon exhaled as if Rayne were the intimidating one. "Okay, good. I'm making a mess of this but what I'm trying to say is that I'd like for you to come over for dinner. Holiday or not."

Why does she want me to come to her place?

Rayne eyed Persimmon, watching her face for any signs of dishonesty. "Okay," she said after a few moments. *She seems like she means this. I just don't know what that means.* "What time?"

"Great. Awesome. Yeah, okay." Persimmon looked so excited that Rayne wondered for a moment if she'd even heard her correctly. "How about five-thir-ty?"

"Sure."

"Okay, cool! So, I guess I'll see you tomorrow then?"

Rayne nodded, bewildered at the other woman's excitement. "Yeah. Tomor-row."

It wasn't until Persimmon was walking back down the road and the door had closed behind her that it occurred to Rayne she would be expected to bring something.

Fuck.

Rayne Dorne was many things, but a good cook was not one of them.

Back home, she rarely cooked for herself and instead relied on ready-made meals from her subscription service. Everything was fresh, and all she had to do was throw something in the oven or on the stove, and it was ready in under thirty minutes.

Trisha's boyfriend was a chef, and usually when he came over, the two of them hogged the kitchen. Not that Rayne minded, she hated everything that went into food preparation and serving. It was convenient, but now, standing in the middle of her kitchen, staring down her refrigerator, she was beginning to think that she'd bitten herself in the ass.

All of the stores in town would be closed for the day, and if she was lucky, the diner on the other side of town would be open, and she could grab something from there. But, lucky was not something Rayne would ever consider herself, and she did not want to waste what little time she had before dinner at Persim-mon's looking for ways to get out of cooking.

A few panicked online searches led her to a recipe for stuffed peppers she could manage. Really, the *only* thing that she could manage on such limited time and skill.

Rayne paced the kitchen, wringing her hands as if to wring the nerves from herself. *What if I screw this up? What if I mess up so badly that she starts hating me? Oh god, what if I get her sick?*

Rayne rushed over to the sink for the third time to wash her hands, turning the water as hot as she could bear and scrubbing her hands and under her nails.

"What are you doing?" Hawthorne asked from outside the window above the kitchen sink.

Rayne shrieked, sloshing water and soap onto the floor and all across the countertop. "Jesus, Hawthorne!" she hissed. "I hate when you do that!"

Even with the late morning sunlight filtering in behind them, she could make the outline of their grin. "That is a shame because I quite like doing it. You are easy to frighten."

She bit back the smile threatening to spread and snatched the nearby roll of paper towels and dried off her hands. "*You* are an asshole."

They tilted their head, something she was becoming fond of watching them do. "Perhaps that is true."

"What are you doing outside of my window?"

"You did not come out into the garden this morning, and it is nearly afternoon," Hawthorne said, their brow furrowing. "I was curious as to what you were doing that was more interesting."

"I am *trying* to cook dinner."

"That is not interesting at all."

This time, Rayne could not hide her smile, even as she tried to sound frustrated with them. "Okay, well, I'm not your entertainment, Hawthorne. If you're so uninterested, then go find something more interesting to do."

As soon as the words left her lips, she regretted them. She did not want Hawthorne to leave, nor did she want them to find something more interesting. She hoped, selfishly, foolishly, that she might be the most interesting part of their day.

But Rayne knew better.

That's a one-way ticket to getting your feelings hurt, and you know it. You don't matter to anyone and no one matters to you, and that's fine.

"I am content where I am," Hawthorne answered after a moment. "What are you making and why so early in the day?"

"Persimmon invited me over for dinner," Rayne replied, pretending to be too distracted by cleaning the peppers to meet Hawthorne's eyes. "I've got to make something too. I just really hate cooking."

"Why?"

"Because I'm bad at it and it's time-consuming and a pain in the ass and a dozen other reasons."

Hawthorne rested their elbows on the windowsill. "In that case, I will watch your attempts at making something."

Rayne frowned and splashed water at the glass. "Easy for you to say. You eat all your food raw."

"What makes you say that?" Hawthorne asked. "I can cook quite well."

"What? How? You never told me that you could cook."

Hawthorne smirked. "You never asked."

Rayne glared at them before returning to her task, drying and cutting the peppers in steamed silence.

"Should you not be pre-heating the oven?"

Rayne glanced up at them, down at the recipe she'd looked up on her phone to confirm before she stomped over to the oven and turned it on. Hawthorne chuckled, and her scowl only deepened. *I think I hate them.* "Why is it that you know anything about ovens?"

"I am old, not a neanderthal, Rayne. I have ventured enough into the human world to know of technology and all the other conveniences that you distract yourself with."

"You don't seem like you'd be interested in any of that."

"I am not. It doesn't mean that I am ignorant of it."

Rayne's mouth crooked in thought. *I assumed that they just hunted people down and hid in the forest. Maybe I should stop doing that. I don't know them any better than they know me.*

"You should be tending to the meat now," Hawthorne said, nodding toward the package of ground beef on the counter.

"You're bossy," she murmured. *I was going to do that anyway, not just because they told me to,* she assured herself.

"I believe 'helpful' is the term you meant. Do you know how to season it?" *No.* "Yes."

"Mhm. Tell me what herbs you have, and I will tell you which to use."

Rayne scowled. "So you're ungovernable but are fine with telling other people what to do?"

"Not other people, Rayne, *you*," Hawthorne replied. Rayne could hear the amusement in their voice as they spoke. *Of course, they're emotive when they're fucking with me.* "Continue your pouting if you'd like, but none of that will get your flavorless meat seasoned."

She opened the spice cabinet and made a show of rummaging around, much louder than she needed to be. "Onion powder, salt, pepper, fennel seed, garlic powder—"

"Those will do. Grab them all."

Rayne tossed them all onto the counter, folding her arms over her chest.

"A bowl next, you'll need to mix them."

"Good girl," they purred when she grabbed one and placed it beside the stove. Rayne nearly dropped it, her knees trembling. She cleared her throat, praying that they didn't notice.

Heat licked at her spine, her nerves alight by their voice as they issued gentle instruction to her. Every fragment of praise settled into her core, and the sensation it brought was as foreign as it was pleasant.

When the peppers were fully prepared and in the oven, Hawthorne's smile pressed against the glass. "You did well."

Rayne pursed her lips, fumbling with what response to give them. Praise was not something she knew how to hold. "You did most of it."

Hawthorne eyed her strangely for a moment, but then their usual smirk appeared. "I will accept an orange as payment."

Of course. "You've only two left now, you know." She snatched one from the fruit bowl on the island and headed to the back porch.

Hawthorne met her at the door, careful not to touch the ground. "We can go to the store and get more, yes?"

"Fine, yes." She sighed, sliding open the door, offering the orange flat in her palm as if to a wild animal.

Hawthorne opened their mouth, and their tongue rolled down, locking around her wrist. It slid up between her fingers, cool and surprisingly damp. Shivering, her hand opened, and Hawthorne's tongue released her, wrapping around the orange and drawing it back up to their mouth. "Thank you." Their teeth split the fruit skin, sliding through the orange folds like butter until it was shucked and peeled, discarded.

Their tongue slowly parted the center of the orange, and Rayne blinked, suddenly lightheaded.

"I have to shower."

She did not give Hawthorne a chance to respond before she closed the door and sprinted upstairs as if she could outrun the desire nipping at her heels.

Okay, so they're only a little burnt. Rayne thought, inspecting the peppers through the plastic lid of the Pyrex container she'd rushed to shove them into.

After Hawthorne and their orange, Rayne had taken a long, cold shower. But even curled on the tile, her spine aligned with the grout; she could not get the image of Hawthorne's teeth ripping into the fruit with such ease out of her head.

The image brought with it a thought, quiet and treacherous that she could not dare allow herself to give weight to: *What would it be like if they were to bite me like that?*

A quick shake of her head, and she brushed the thought aside. *Nope. I'm not unpacking that right now.*

Resting the container against her hip, Rayne rang the doorbell. Persimmon answered almost immediately. "Hey! I'm so glad you could make it."

Rayne tried to smile, hoping it was enough. "Thanks for inviting me."

"Oh! You brought something. You didn't have to do that, that's so sweet of you."

Her cheeks flushed with the compliment, and Rayne shrugged as Persimmon eased the container out of her hands.

"Come on in, don't want you to freeze. It's cold out there."

As Rayne closed the door behind her and followed Persimmon into the house, she noticed that Persimmon wasn't wearing her usual overalls.

She was wearing a powder blue sundress, her muscular arms and toned legs clearly visible. Her orange hair was much longer than Rayne had realized, brushing along her waist as she moved.

She's even prettier than before.

Envy coiled within Rayne, and she shoved her hands into her hoodie pocket, making a fist. Jealousy was a lifelong companion of hers , and yet it still knocked the wind out of her when it arrived at her side. It swept in during quiet moments, when her attention fell to someone walking confidently in their skin. A woman with beautiful hands or carelessly allowing the sun to kiss her bare legs.

I don't even know what it feels like to wear a dress like that. Does she feel pretty in it?

The interior of Persimmon's home was even warmer and more beautiful than Rayne remembered. Every inch decorated with bits of the season, dark red and brown leaves strung on fishing line, cinnamon sticks and dried oranges in small glass bowls. House may have been alive but Persimmon had breathed life into her space.

She's like one of those princesses in fairytales. I didn't even know that people like this could exist.

"Rayne?"

Jolting, Rayne's attention snapped to Persimmon. "Sorry. Yes?"

"I asked if you wanted something to drink. I've got non-alcoholic and otherwise. Coffee, flavored seltzer, dandelion wine. Pick your poison, whatever you want, I've probably got it in here somewhere."

Rayne perked at the mention of wine. She was not particularly a drinker but she enjoyed trying new things when the opportunity arose. "Dandelion wine sounds good. Thank you."

Persimmon winked. "I knew you'd go for that." *What does that mean?* "Give me a minute and I'll grab you a glass. Have a seat."

She dipped down out of the kitchen and down into the basement by the back door. Rayne took a careful seat at the kitchen table, running her gloved fingers over the smooth, streakless glass tabletop. *Everything here is so perfect. Even her,* Rayne thought, averting her gaze from the outline of her reflection. *She must have made a deal with the Devil.*

When Persimmon returned with the wine, Rayne worked to keep from staring and marveling at how one person could show up as themselves so completely.

Dinner was pleasant, and if Rayne were braver, she might have ventured to say that she was having a good time. Persimmon had made more food than the two of them could have ever possibly hoped to finish, with Rayne having to tap out long before dessert could even be pulled out of the refrigerator.

Persimmon pouted, "I made pear tart. If you're not going to eat it now then you're taking some home with you. I will not accept arguments."

Two glasses of wine had loosened the laughter out of her. "Okay, okay. I'll take some back home."

Persimmon grinned and set to work, flitting through the kitchen. Rayne glanced out of the window into the blackness of the night, searching for two familiar orbs floating somewhere nearby. She was enjoying herself, more than she ever could recall while in another's presence but she was also keenly aware of Hawthorne's absence. *If they were here tonight might be perfect.*

"Oh, I meant to ask," Persimmon began, tugging Rayne's attention back to her as she focused her attention on slicing the tart. "How has everything with the house been going? Are you all settled in?"

Rayne sighed, resting her elbows on the table. "I'm settled but that's just the problem. I'm trying to get unsettled. I want to sell it and get the hell out of here."

Persimmon's shoulders knitted together. "Oh, are you? That's kind of a shame. It's a beautiful old house. Prettiest in town, I'd say."

"Are you joking? Your house is gorgeous. Nothing in Bury could compare." Rayne scoffed, though she could practically hear the House's indignant huffing from here.

"Don't get me wrong," Persimmon began, glancing over her shoulder. "I love my house, I've poured all of myself into it. But there's just something about a house like yours. It's different. Good bones, so much character. You know what I mean?"

"Not really."

"I don't know, it's kind of hard to describe. There's just an energy to places like that, just begging to be tended to."

Rayne opened her mouth to disagree when the thought flashed into her mind like lightning: *I should sell the house to Persimmon.*

Persimmon. Rayne couldn't believe that she hadn't thought of her before. House was a hungry, needy thing and it required near constant attention. Persimmon would be the perfect match with all the care and affection that she poured into her own home. House would be content for the rest of its days.

House deserves that. It is a good house no matter how demanding.

"You could tend to it, if you wanted. I'd sell it to you," Rayne offered.

Persimmon whirled on her. "Me? Rayne, look, I'm honored, but I don't have the kind of money that house is worth—"

"Make me an offer," Rayne blurted. "Whatever you can pay, I'll take. You'd be doing me a favor."

Placing the knife down, Persimmon turned to give Rayne her full attention. "You're not drunk, right?"

"Tipsy, maybe? But even if I wasn't, I would still make this offer. I—need to get out of here, Persimmon. I can't stay in this town."

Persimmon tapped her nails against the counter, staring out at the window behind Rayne. "Okay," she said after a long moment. "If you're serious then I'd like to at least come check the place out."

"Yeah, 'course," Rayne said. *Goddamn this accent!* "I don't mind that. Could you do tomorrow?"

"Yeah. Thank you for this, Rayne."

Rayne shook her head, relief rising like the tide. "No, Persimmon. Thank *you*."

"I'm fine," Rayne assured Persimmon for the fourth time as she reached for her keys. The wine had brought with it a surge of warmth, flushing her skin and dizzying up her vision. "It's only a mile or two. I can drive."

"Yeah, I don't know about that," Persimmon chuckled, dropping Rayne's keys into one of the small bowls filled with dried oranges and cinnamon. "Why don't I just drive you up to your place and then I can drive your car up to you tomorrow when I stop by?"

"That seems a little excessive."

Persimmon shrugged. "Maybe, but I don't want you wrecking your car. Then how would you ever leave this dreadful place behind?" There was nothing malicious in Persimmon's tone but Rayne felt the stab of shame none the less.

I must seem so ridiculous to her, trying to run away like a little kid.

"Yeah, okay," Rayne murmured.

"Thank you."

Rayne had no idea why Persimmon was thanking her, but she simply nodded and grabbed the large plastic container of leftovers Persimmon had forced on her, including the pear tart.

Persimmon's mustard-yellow truck would have been an eyesore if it belonged to anyone else, but somehow it seemed to work for her, even the little purple flowers painted on the back side of it. The interior was drenched in the rich lemon scent of her perfume and every bit of her; pressed, crocheted flowers hanging from the mirror.

The drive up the hill was quiet, and Rayne was glad for it; it didn't feel like the ones where she had to force herself into silence while she waited for someone else to speak, afraid of taking up any space. It almost felt like the ones that she and Hawthorne fell into.

They were in her driveway before she knew it and she was unclasping the seatbelt and spilling out into the night as soon as the car parked.

"Thank you for tonight," Rayne said, pausing, half way out of the car door. "It was really nice."

"Of course. Thank you for coming. I've never really gotten the chance to host anything before."

Confusion flickered across Rayne's face. *She was such a natural. Who wouldn't want to spend time with her in her home?* Unsure of what else to say, Rayne nodded. "Okay. Well, goodnight."

"Yeah, night. I'll see you tomorrow afternoon, alright?"

"That works fine," Rayne replied, closing the door.

Persimmon's headlights turned the other way before fading back down the hill, leaving Rayne bathed in the darkness of the night.

Rayne stood there in the middle of her driveway for a long moment, the porchlight's faint glow the only illumination.

She'd made a deal with Hawthorne, a dangerous game of cat and mouse. If they found her outside of the safety of her home after the sun had set, they told her that they would drag her back to the forest. Eat her alive.

I should be running. They could be out here right now.

It was a mixture of exhaustion and alcohol, she told herself that slowed her movements and kept her from hurrying into the house like she should have. It was that same cocktail that kept her standing at the door even when she had fished her house key out of her hoodie pocket, hesitating.

When she finally made it inside, instantly greeted by House's delighted chatter, she did not know what to tell herself.

Rayne had no explanation for the disappointment that trailed her when no monster had come for her.

CHAPTER SEVENTEEN
rayne

"**W**ake up, cherub!"

Rayne rolled out of bed and toppled onto the carpet with a shriek that immediately melted into a groan of discomfort. She was grateful for the pillows she'd tossed onto the floor last night when she'd thrown herself onto her bed.

She hadn't been drunk but her head was still throbbing with the pulse of too much wine. *I should have known better. I don't ever drink, so two glasses was way too much.*

"What the hell, House?" Rayne grumbled, her cheek buried in the carpet.

"**I'm sorry, beloved but your lemon girl is at the door. Waiting for you it seems.**"

"Lemon girl? Who—" *Persimmon. But I thought she'd said she wasn't going to come by until this afternoon?* "House, what time is it?" Rayne asked, feeling around for her phone.

"**Noon has long since passed. It's closer to evening now.**"

"Shit!"

Rayne scrambled to her feet, slipped her thigh highs over the tights she hadn't bothered to remove last night before getting into bed and hurried down the stairs to the front door.

"Hey, Persimmon!" she nearly shouted, swinging the door open. "Sorry I didn't hear you knocking."

Persimmon smiled down at her, looking as perfect as ever, not so much as a brightly colored strand of hair out of place. She was back in her overalls, her hair braided back in two neat pigtails. "No worries, Rayne. Brought your car back, safe and sound." She gestured to Rayne's Jeep in the driveway and plopped Rayne's keys into her hand. "Did you get any sleep?"

Immediately, Rayne realized how terrible she must look; her wild curls framing her face, ruddy skin heavy with yesterday's grime, and her rumpled clothes. She shrank further into the house. "Oh, yeah. I kind of passed out and just woke up."

Persimmon laughed, though it didn't seem as though there was any malice in it, but Rayne could never be entirely sure. "You don't drink much, do you?"

Rayne shook her head.

"Sorry that I forced all that wine down your throat. I'll be more mindful of it in the future."

Rayne's brow furrowed. *You didn't force me to do anything. I drank because I wanted to, I was... having fun.* She swallowed the words, keeping them buried where they couldn't be used against her later.

"So... mind if I come in?"

"Oh!" Rayne stepped aside to allow Persimmon to step inside. "Yeah, sorry. Welcome in."

Persimmon stepped into the foyer carefully, her attention circling the room with a whistle. "Wow. Some entrance."

Rayne had never found her parents' home to be beautiful, but for a moment, she allowed her eyes to follow the same path of Persimmon's and pretend that this was her first time here. *Maybe it could be beautiful.*

"So, this might be an odd request but do you actually mind if I look around the place by myself? I find that I get a better read on energy if I'm alone,"

Persimmon asked, fishing out a small notepad and pen from the pocket of her overalls. "But if that's too invasive, I understand."

Rayne hadn't even considered the idea that Persimmon might have wanted a guided tour from her. "No, that's fine by me."

"Perfect. Anywhere you'd rather I didn't go?"

"Upstairs. There's a white door at the end of the hall with pink slippers painted on the door," Rayne said immediately. *Oh. If I do sell this place, I'm going to have to go in there and clean it out myself at some point.* The thought made her sick. *Maybe I can just sell as is. Someone else can deal with that mess.*

"Heard." Persimmon nodded. "Okay, well, don't mind me. I'll be back once I've checked everything out."

Rayne nodded and watched as Persimmon padded delicately into the living room. She placed her keys down and hung back in the foyer, unsure of what to do with herself while Persimmon explored the house.

"Why is she rummaging through my innards like some beast?" The House demanded, low and angry. *"What kind of guest sneaks around?"*

Rayne bit her lip to keep from answering House, terrified that Persimmon would hear her and think that she was mad.

"She is writing, is it about me?" House demanded. *"All of this investigating and she has brought me nothing sweet to eat! No hair, no blood or bone. Cherub, you cannot be condoning this savagery. Why do you not throw her out into the cold where she belongs?"*

"Do you mind if I go outside and check out the backyard and porch?" Persimmon asked, reappearing from the guestroom at the end of the hallway.

"Not all at. You've got free rein," Rayne said and then, once Persimmon was outside, she placed her hand against the wall. "House, calm down. Persimmon is just looking at you. She's thinking of buying you, won't that be nice?"

The floor shuttered and shifted. *"Buying me! I will not be sold off, cherub."*

"House." She began as gently as she could. "I already told you that I can't stay here. I can't live here. But Persimmon, she would love you properly. You should see how beautiful her home is. She'd breathe so much warmth and life into you." *More than I could ever give you.*

"Don't you understand, beloved?" House sighed with the wind. *"You are the marrow of me. It does not matter who walks my halls, the foundation of me was built upon your name. We are tied to one another; we have always been and must remain so. She may live here but she will have none of me."*

Rayne opened her mouth to speak, to find something that might comfort it, but the back door opened, and Persimmon returned, so she clamped her mouth shut, offering a tentative smile.

When Persimmon finally disappeared upstairs, Rayne tried again to speak. "I understand that you... are accustomed to me. Attached to the memories of me that you may have but I'm not that girl anymore. You don't know me, House. Learn someone new, you'll be happier."

"There is no one living or dead who knows you better than I, sweetling. There might have been once but no longer. If I cannot have you, I would rather the fire take me."

Rayne's chest tightened with the House's words. She did not know what it meant to be desired or sought. She did not know how to hold it. "House—"

"I have nothing else to say." The House huffed before going silent. Despite her attempts to get it to respond, House remained as quiet as winter.

"This really is a beautiful home you have here," Persimmon said, announcing herself as she reentered the kitchen where Rayne had slunk off to speak to House. "I took some notes on a few things that probably will need some fixing up. But, based off of everything I've seen, I'm interested."

Persimmon slid her notebook into Rayne's hands. "That's my offer."

Rayne's eyes widened at the number. It was much more than she was expecting. *So much for being a humble farmer.* "Deal."

"Wait, are you sure? Don't you want time to think about it?"

"No. I was ready to let this place rot. This is a perfect offer."

Persimmon grinned, her smile enough to light up the entire sky. "Really? Oh my god, okay. Okay, cool. Thank you."

"Yeah, of course. So, when do you want to draw up the paper work?"

"Well, the holidays are coming up and while I don't particularly care for them, you know how people around here get. It will be impossible for us to get anything official done until at least after New Years."

Rayne's heart dropped into her stomach. *New Year's? That's more than an entire month here.* Another month of rent paid for a place she wasn't staying in. But really, what other choice did she have? "Okay," Rayne replied, nodding and swallowing the dryness in her throat. "After New Year's is fine. I can keep cleaning everything up here in the meantime."

"That's perfect," Persimmon said, taking back her notebook. "Although, I'm not going to lie, I am kind of sad to see you go. I wish you could stay, it's nice having you around."

It's nice having you around.

Rayne stared blankly at Persimmon, her mouth opening and closing as she fought for the proper response. *No one has ever said that to me before. What do I do with that? What's the right thing to say?*

Persimmon did not seem to mind her foolishness, simply offered Rayne another one of her kind, dazzling smiles. "Well. Thank you for this. I hate to run but I've got some kale to clean before I drop it off in town and I want to finish up before dark. But I'll see you around?"

Rayne could only nod, waving lamely as Persimmon headed out the door.

The silence in the house was deafening but its weight had shifted, tilting into something like freedom. *I can really leave town for good this time. I don't ever have to set foot here again.*

It should have felt like it had the first time when she'd been eighteen and gotten her first taste of life outside of these hills. Where no one cared about how she looked or knew her mother's grocery order by heart or how her father ordered his burgers at the diner. Being Rayne Dorne meant nothing out there, and it had been the most addicting feeling she'd ever encountered in her life.

But now something felt different and she wasn't sure why. There was a weight, something tethering her heart and weighing on her emotions.

Is it because of what Persimmon said? Or could it be Hawthorne?

Hawthorne was the companion Rayne had never expected. Leaving them felt like a betrayal, an incision deeper than what she would be inflicting on her House or Persimmon, and she could not understand why.

They could visit me in the city, she thought. *They mentioned that they could go anywhere they wanted. They might not like it but they still could. Maybe I should ask them?*

No. Who are you to ask anything of them? You've got another month with them. Enjoy it and then move on.

It was not until the sun had begun to kiss the hills that House spoke to her again, startling her as she forked some of the pear tart Persimmon had given her into her mouth, hunched over the kitchen island.

"The Devil is coming for you, sweetling. Do not let it in."

There was something like recognition, something like a memory in its words.

"What do you mean, House?" she asked around a mouth of tart. "What Devil?"

It shifted closer to her in an embrace that she could not return. **"It's too late, my dove but it doesn't have to be. It does not have to end this way this time."**

"This time? What are you talking about?" Her pulse jumped, kicking to life. House had never sounded so emotive, so frightened.

"Listen to me, Rayne. Do not answer the door. Stay within me and I will protect you from the cruel hands of fate."

A memory that had slipped her mind until now slid back in as if had never left: the note that Callum had left her. The only thing he'd written: *"Don't listen to the house."*

Could he have... known that the House was alive and been trying to warn her? Had the House been leading her astray this whole time?

The knock at the door should have startled her, should have given her cause to jump.

Instead, Rayne's heart leapt into her throat, pounding a million miles a minute. Slowly she approached the door like a needle set on its path, pulled to whatever sat on the other side.

She knew, somehow, that it was Hawthorne before she opened the door and met their strange eyes, looming over her. The House was speaking, she was sure of it but the words were smothered by a wave of relief that came with seeing Hawthorne again. Behind them, the winter sun bled easily into the ink of night as dusk settled. With every passing moment of the fading light, Hawthorne came more and more into her view. "Hawthorne."

"Rayne," they breathed, every hair along the back of her neck raising. "You are leaving."

"How did you know that?"

"I heard you speaking with her. You are leaving."

She swallowed. "Yes."

"After the winter festivities have ended?"

"Yeah. I guess I didn't need your help after all," Rayne offered humorlessly. Hawthorne did not laugh.

"You will stay until that time?"

Rayne nodded. "I have no choice."

Hawthorne brushed closer. "Will you invite me inside?"

"Don't let them in!" The House hissed, the heater crackling in warning. *"There will be no saving you if you do."*

Rayne took a step closer to the threshold though every nerve sang with life, adrenaline spiking. "Will you hurt me if I do?"

Hawthorne leaned down, their face only a few inches from hers. "Would it matter so long as it is what you want?"

She remained silent as she watched her reflection in their eyes, how small and fragile she looked. Rayne was delicate; the scars that covered every inch of her skin were proof alone. Pain was something that she had grown accustomed to, her body had been built for it against her will. She hadn't chosen this body, this pain.

What if I can choose this one?

"That isn't an answer," she stammered.

"Then ask me the right questions."

A dozen thoughts danced through her mind: *Why are you the only person I've ever felt so comfortable with? Why haven't you killed me yet?*

None of them seemed right or what Hawthorme might have been looking for. Nothing about them made sense, especially not when it came to her.

"Why do you want to come in if not to hurt me?" she whispered.

"*Cherub, close the door,*" the House begged, groaning with the wind.

"It's cold," Hawthorne said barely above the wind. And that was her end, the great undoing of every wall she had constructed around herself.

It didn't matter that Hawthorne would surely tear her apart, that they barely concealed their hunger for her; in that moment, Rayne understood them. And they were right, it was all so terribly cold.

"Come in," Rayne whispered to the night and the monster at her door.

CHAPTER EIGHTEEN
hawthorne

T he invitation once extended melted the invisible barrier that barred Hawthorne from entering. They stood at their full height, their chest only just reaching the top of the door's frame.

Hawthorne knelt and materialized into the house as a great cloud of black smoke and their eyes ignited open, two glowing garnets. Immediately they were swallowed by the scent of Rayne, she drenched every bit of the house and beneath that they could smell the remnants of the orange woman which hardly concerned them. But under that a symphony of familiar scents found them, remnants of a life from the past.

Rayne had backed away from them although they smelled no fear from her. Hawthorne halved themself, concentrating all of their attention into a physical form, solidifying. *Perhaps a more human form would be appropriate in this place.*

Their jaw cracked, splintering into something more humanoid. Their legs elongated until they were standing like a man before Rayne. The House hissed in displeasure, the floor warming with its fury. Hawthorne paid it no mind, instead fixing all of their attention on Rayne.

It is strange. I never noticed how small she is out there. In here she is but a mayfly in the great web of the world.

"You look different in here," Rayne said, her dark eyes wide with an emotion that Hawthorne could not recognize. The lack of this knowledge irritated them.

"I am more solid now, I'm a human shape."

"No," Rayne began, shaking her head. "That's not what I mean. Outside you're like the wind.

"And now?" they tilted their head.

"I don't know what to call you," she admitted, raising a gloved palm. "Do you feel the same?"

Hawthorne stared at her hand, searching for the meaning in the gesture. *Does she want me to touch her?* In this form, Hawthorne was capable of touch, of experiencing the vaguest sensations outside of eating their fill.

I think I would very much like to touch her in a way that is not eating her.

"No," Hawthorne began, carefully raising their hand to press against hers. "It is... warmer in here. I am not accustomed to it." The moment that their skin brushed against her hand, they recoiled in displeasure. The silky fabric between her skin and their hand felt nauseating, wrong. "Remove your gloves."

"What?" Rayne clutched her hand to her chest.

"You heard me well and clear, Rayne."

"Why?"

Irritation flickered to life. *Must we continue on with these barriers?* "You see me as I am now and feel what there is of me. I ask you to extend me the same courtesy."

She scrunched her nose at them, frowning in that way that they had only seen her capable of. "I am less myself because I wear gloves?"

It pulled a smile from them regardless of how annoying they found the idea. "Nothing could lessen you," Hawthorne replied and she gaped up at them, wide eyed. "But I cannot experience you as you truly are if layers of fabric and material sit between us."

Rayne did not move immediately and Hawthorne did not press her, they simply allowed the patience that they could only ever find with her to bloom in the silence. *I wonder what it is you are thinking of when you're like that. When you look at me like that. Do you regret this?*

She took a deep, steadying breath and slowly pulled the silk glove from her hand, starting with her index finger until she had peeled it all away, revealing her hand. The skin of her hands and arms was flecked with pink scars, floating against the warmth of her dark skin. *Like stones within a river, catching light from the sun. Beautiful.*

Hawthorne traced the scars with their eyes. Their smoky hand wrapped around hers with a gossamer touch, mindful of how delicate she was, and they brought her hand to their lips. The kiss was no more than a flutter of wings against the back of her hand. *Has anyone ever kissed your skin like this, Rayne? Would you tell me if they had?*

"Why did you do that?" Rayne asked, her eyes wider than the moon. They half expected her to tear her hand away, and yet she let them continue to hold it.

Why did I do that?

"You are beautiful. I like beautiful things," Hawthorne answered, though they were not sure what was truth and what wasn't between them anymore.

"I'm not. You can't just—"

Hawthorne did not mean to move, had no intention of it, but their body decided for them; they pressed Rayne against the nearest wall. *"Do not do that."*

"I told you not to let them in, cherub. Look what you've done now. Why must the field mouse always chase after the fox?"

They reached behind Rayne, flexing their claws against the wallpaper in warning. *I may not be able to speak to you directly, but just know that I will find your heart and tear it out if you do not shut up,* they thought at the House, and though it could not hear them, its immediate silence told them that it understood.

Hawthorne's teeth brushed against her forehead as they leaned down, the scent of her skin on the edge of their tongue. "Do not think that you can dictate my vision of you. I can and do see you, Rayne. I will not allow you to diminish yourself right in front of me. Shrinking is for lesser beings."

Rayne's heart hammered against her ribcage, every pulse plucking at some invisible thread around Hawthorne's throat. Despite their proximity, they did not detect her fear. *Such a strange little wolf.* "Do you understand what I am saying, Rayne?"

"Yes," she breathed.

"Good." They hesitated a moment before sweeping away from her. An ache followed, the desire to be near her again. "I would like for you to show me around."

"For what?" Rayne snapped. Hawthorne liked her sharp edges; they liked that she did not give in to them.

"It is considered polite to show a guest around your home, is it not?" Hawthorne asked without turning to face her.

"Oh, *now* you're concerned with politeness?"

Hawthorne chuckled. "Such a cruel little thing."

"Why are you so... physical now?" Rayne inquired. "Why didn't you appear like this before?"

At this, Hawthorne did turn to meet her gaze, chewing on their answer for her. "It takes a great deal of energy. If I have not fed adequately, it is irritating."

Rayne's brows rose. "Will you... like fade if you don't eat?"

"Do you die if you miss a meal? It is much the same with me. I have less energy, but I am still here. Now, will you show me around, or must I stalk through your home like a bear?"

Rayne narrowed her eyes, and Hawthorne only smiled at her. Without a word, turned and led them out of the foyer and into the kitchen. "Kitchen. This is where I keep your ocean of oranges."

Hawthorne sniffed the air as they followed behind her. "Do you have anymore?"

"I have one. You can get a tour or an orange, you can't have both."

They sighed miserably. "You are made of ice and venom, I am sure of it."

Hawthorne did not miss the slight smile on her lips when she brushed past them into the living room. They kept only a few paces behind her, trying to balance their attention between her and her home. There was nothing in this house more interesting than her. However, there was one thing that they longed to see almost as much as they wanted to watch her.

"Where is your room?" Hawthorne asked as casually as they could manage, running a clawed finger along the end table in the hallway.

"It's upstairs. If you must see it."

"I must."

"Fine. Come on."

Their hands brushed as Rayne ascended the stairs, magnetized to one another. Touching her sent electricity down the column of their spine, igniting every nerve beneath their shadowed skin. *The world is so full of sensation when she is near. Is there magic in her? Some craft she has mastered that I have yet to know of.*

They should have known that the House would not stand for the secret magic buzzing between the two of them. It was such a jealous creature.

The walls shifted as it whispered to her, hushed and urgent. ***"You don't know what this means. Your grandmother did, didn't she tell you not to let anything from the wood set foot here?"***

Rayne's shoulders knitted together in front of them, and Hawthorne scowled. ***"What will you do when their teeth are in your heart, and the worms have come for your eyes?"***

They swallowed the growl that bubbled in their throat at the House's words. It knew nothing of what it was saying; it spoke of some ominous future, foretelling some imaginary end.

"You will rot here," it continued. ***"Lichen will fester along your spine and—"***

The moment that Rayne's foot reached the top step, she stomped her foot hard on the ground. "Shut up!" Rayne screamed, her voice echoing throughout the halls and carrying through the house. She glared up at the ceiling.

Finally, they thought with a smirk. *Someone needed to set this brick-and-mortar straight, and I am glad it is her.*

Rayne looked down at them, sheepishly tucking a bit of her hair behind her ear. "Sorry."

Oh, yes. She does not know that I can hear it. It is best that I keep it that way. "I said nothing."

"I wasn't snapping at you. It was the House. Can you—can you really not hear it?"

"I hear only you," they responded, and it was more honest than they cared to admit.

Rayne had looked at them strangely after they said it, and they wanted to prod at her, to ask her why, what that expression meant. But then she turned, and they continued down the hallway in silence. Upstairs was divided into wings; the largest room was to the immediate left of the stairs, and at the end of the hallway, there was another room, a white door with pink ballerina slippers painted along the edge.

Hawthorne froze, all of them zeroing in on it. "That door," they began, their voice barely above a whisper. "What is it to?"

Rayne followed their gaze, and they heard the sharp intake of her breath. "It doesn't matter. No one goes in there."

"But—"

"No, Hawthorne." Something in her voice wavered, heavy with an emotion that they could not name. "Just drop it. *Please.*"

Hawthorne dipped their head lower to get a better look at her face, her trembling lip, her eyes suddenly wet, fixed on the floor. Their insides felt like shattered glass, and they swallowed more of it when they said simply, "Very well. Let us continue."

"Thank you." Rayne's hand slipped into theirs as she led them to the other end of the hall. Hawthorne marveled at the sight of their skin pressed against hers, how small her hand was in theirs, and how warm her flesh was against the winter of them.

They stopped at a chestnut-brown door, with plants mimicking the shape of ivy hanging from it. Even through the closed door, Hawthorne could smell the ocean of her scents. Her hair conditioner, the sweet alcoholic kiss of her rose perfume, dried sweat, old blood, the sharp twinge of ointment and medical gauze.

Her space smells just as good as she does. How can one woman make everything smell so sweet?

"This is my room," Rayne announced, and then, seeming to realize that she was still holding their hand, she dropped it with a soft grunt of surprise, her cheeks flushing.

Hawthorne pretended not to notice, fixating on the strange fake ivy hanging. It reminded them of a story they'd heard once: Rapunzel. *A girl locked away in her ivory tower.* They swallowed. "It suits you."

"Do you even know what it is?" she asked with a frown.

"No, but I do not need to. It reminds me of you. May I go inside?"

Rayne huffed and shrugged her shoulders. "If you want."

Hawthorne ducked into her room, folding in on themselves, evaporating and appearing again in a burst of dark mist. Smaller now but still towering over her, they glanced around the room. Everything from the checkered rug across the light blue carpet to the thin glowing lights in the shape of roses that hung from her skylight sang of her.

A clawed finger traced along the delicate lights, and something fluttered in their stomach, moving up toward their chest.

"Look how well I've kept you," the House purred, creaking under Rayne as she shifted her weight. ***"See how I will cushion the curve of you forever? They will never be able to do the same."***

Rayne shushed it, and the floor of the attic above them snapped loudly in rebellion. Hawthorne pretended to remain unaffected, moving around her room. They brushed the dust off the polaroids taped to the walls, pictures of trees, butterflies, and the river.

Hawthorne ran their fingers along the cracked spines of her old books on her mahogany bookshelf. Titles that they recognized: *Rebecca, Wuthering Heights, A Midsummer Night's Dream.* They paused to sniff the half-burnt white and pink candles smelling distantly of roses, jasmine, wax, and dust. It was such a small thing, yet it was charming.

They could feel Rayne watching them. *I cannot say what I would like to.* "This room suits you well. It is drenched in you."

The strange, pretty color returned to her cheeks. "It was my brother's before he left. I spent a lot of time... making it mine."

"Yes, I imagine that you did," Hawthorne replied, smirking a bit at the little plastic figure of a howling wolf on the corner of her bookshelf. "Did you spend much time in here?"

"Yes. Too much time."

"Is that why you made it look like this?"

"Yeah. I guess I thought that it would make things better. Sometimes it did."

"And the other times?" Hawthorne asked, fixing her with those bright garnets.

"The other times it was just lonely."

Lonely. That was a word Hawthorne had come to learn well, along with its meaning.

That hollow thing within their chest cracked, and that sensation, warmth, and discomfort, alive and burning, rose in them. It was similar to how they felt when hunger kicked at them, but the shape was different. When they looked at Rayne, they wanted.

What do I want from her if not to kill her? Do I want to kill her?

Death was an end, one that Hawthorne had never hesitated to issue to living creatures. It did not matter to them what or who died; it was simply the way of the world.

But Rayne. Her death would be the end of her; even if they ate her eventually, the taste of her sweet blood and pretty skin would fade. They would no longer be able to watch her strange expressions or hear the deep rasp of her voice.

I do not want to lose those things about her. But then, what do I want?

When Hawthorne turned to her, she was already watching them, and their eyes met. Hawthorne half expected Rayne to turn away from them, to look anywhere else, but she didn't. They stepped closer, and what they wanted suddenly became crystal clear.

"Can I kiss you, Rayne?" Hawthorne asked, far enough away that she could move, push them even if she wanted to.

"Kiss me? You want to kiss me?"

"I would not have asked if I did not."

"Why?" she rasped.

A dozen answers raced through their mind: *Because you're beautiful. Because I need to know what you taste like. Because this is the closest I can get to eating you.* "Because if I don't, I think I'll eat you whole."

"Is that a threat?" she whispered, even though she took a step closer to them.

"Always."

Hawthorne longed to touch her, *needed* to touch her, but more than that, they needed her to want it just as much as they did. Their fingers ghosted along the halo of her hair. She stayed exactly where she was, frozen, and they gave her another moment to move, to heed the advice of her fretting house.

"The door is right there, Rayne," they said over her hammering heart. "I will not block your path if you choose to leave."

"I don't want to leave."

Hawthorne felt a flicker of gratitude in the space within their chest where their heart might have been. *I do not want you to leave ever again.* "Then answer me."

"Yes. You can... kiss me."

Rayne rose to the tip of her toes, and Hawthorne lifted her to keep her from hurting her delicate feet. *She is but a feather in the palm of my hand. Porcelain waiting to be shattered.*

They tilted their head down, watching her every move, seeking any signs of distress. She chewed on her lower lip so hard that Hawthorne was sure she'd bleed. "Rayne."

"I don't know what to do."

"Stop this to start." They drew her bottom lip from her assaulting teeth.

"And then?"

"And then, *this.*" Their lips did not collide with hers, nor did they crash like some violent tide. No, Hawthorne kissed her as if she could answer every question dancing behind their eyes. *What is this? Do you feel it too? What is its name?*

Rayne answered not only with her lips but with her fingers against the curve of their shoulder, her chest pressed against theirs like a flower seeking the first light of spring.

Hawthorne was a tangle of sensation, and their core liquified, threatening to melt them back into nothingness. They held onto their body and rooted themself in the heat of her lips, the whisper of her curls against their skin.

She pulled back on a fraction of movement away from them, and Hawthorne was off of her in an instant, placing her back down carefully. *Did I hurt her?* "Are you alright?"

Rayne nodded, wide-eyed and trembling. They wanted to shift closer, steady her in some way, but they needed to know that they had not harmed her. They waited, allowing her the room to find the rest of her words.

"I just couldn't breathe. I kind of panicked."

Ah, yes. Humans do need their breath, don't they? I will remember this.

"I'm sorry."

Hawthorne cleared the distance between them, drawn back into her orbit. "Sorry. I have heard this said by humans before. What is its meaning?"

Rayne brushed closer, and Hawthorne allowed their fingers to play with the hem of her shirt. "It means that you are regretful about something that you did. Or that is happening to another person."

They frowned. "You regret my kissing you?"

"No!" She jolted closer. *Did she mean to be so close?* "I'm just sorry that I had to pull away and ruin it."

"Hear me now, Rayne," they began, using her shirt to yank her forward. "Do not attempt to put words in my mouth or thoughts in my head. You ruined nothing. You have nothing to be sorry for. If I am displeased with something you've done, I will voice it. Until then, do not offer me your sorrow." *There are much sweeter things I would rather you give me.*

"It's just the polite thing—"

Again with her accursed politeness. Their hand snaked under her chin, catching her cheeks between their palms. "Do we understand one another? I deeply dislike repetition."

She swallowed. "Yeah, I understand."

As they released her, they indulged in the briefest touch of their finger against the hollow of her cheek.

"I should head to bed. I've got to handle the garage tomorrow, and that's gonna be a lot so—"

Humans and their sleep. "Alright."

"Would you—I mean, you could stay tonight, if you wanted. The guestroom I showed you downstairs is open to you if you want it."

Memory dug its claws into Hawthorne's core, the words that they longed to say jagged in their throat. "I would like to stay the night," they said finally.

"Okay. Good." Rayne bounced on her heel, her hands behind her back, and her heart singing yet another drumming song for them.

Hawthorne remained rooted in place, allowing her space to tell them the rest of what was on her mind.

"Thank y—"

"Do not thank me, Rayne," Hawthorne warned, somberness clouding their expression. "Do not ever thank one of my kind. It is a debt, and it *will* be collected. You will not like what is taken."

Her pretty eyes went wide, and Hawthorne licked their lips. "What does that mean?" she asked.

"It is as I said. Spirits will always collect, and they will take all." It was true, but Hawthorne knew that she would not understand, that her humanity limited her in the ways of their world. "Even your *beloved* House."

Rayne glanced at the walls around them both, and Hawthorne could practically see the realization that her sweet, charming little House was not just a spirit but something that could and *would* eat her settle over her.

Nails from beneath the carpet pushed up and stabbed into the soles of Hawthorne's feet, one against their heel, dangerously close to piercing their dark skin. The House did not have to speak for them to understand the warning.

'Spill my secrets, and I will start spilling yours.'

Fair enough, you wooden wretch.

"I will see you in the morning, Rayne," Hawthorne said, drawing her attention back to them, and the nails slipped back into the carpet.

"Okay." She took a step closer to them, but something stopped her, and she moved back. "Goodnight, Hawthorne."

Hawthorne frowned, unsure of what this meant. "Goodnight, Rayne." They slipped out of the room, spilling like smoke into the hallway.

Their eyes were again drawn to the room at the opposite end of the hallway. Something within their chest constricted, squeezed as if by a great python.

"Leave it be, wraith," the House whispered, the wall beside them shifting. ***"You are here now, and that is damage enough. Let the past stay where it belongs."***

I can't. I won't.

CHAPTER NINETEEN
hawthorne

Houses weren't particularly interesting, Hawthorne had come to find. It had been years since they had last been in a home, and without Rayne to entertain them, their skull buzzed with monotony.

They had crept through every corner, slipped into every space, but nothing was able to hold their attention long. Above them, through the floorboards, they could hear the gentle hush of Rayne's breath as she slept.

She is fast asleep. She will never know if I look around.

Hawthorne slipped under the crack of her bedroom door, spilling in like sand. Rayne was curled within her bed like a field mouse in the dirt. Her thick curls had fallen out of her silk cap and wrapped around her. It was some unknown force, some magnetic pull that brought them closer to her, hovering over her as she slept.

Her face softened in sleep, no frown tugging at her full lips, no tension knotting her brows. She was just... still.

It would be all too easy for me just to kill you where you lie. Hawthorne brushed a stray strand of hair from her face, twirling it around their finger. *You'd fight back. You'd want to take a piece of me with you, wouldn't you? You'd try to blind me and go for my eyes.*

As if she could hear their thoughts, she sighed and turned her face closer to them. *Why is it so strange? Why do I feel like this? Why does seeing her like this make me feel...*

I cannot spend this entire morning staring at her. They thought, wrenching their hand back when it threatened to brush against her hair. Some part of them ached when they did finally turn away, but they ignored it. *It cannot bother me if I do not name it.*

Without her watching them, Hawthorne took the time to properly examine her room the way that they had longed to before. In the corner of her room, across from her bed, there was a line of small polaroid pictures, clipped to a line of plastic lights. Tombstones, trees, mountain rocks, and abandoned buildings, Rayne had filled her camera with how she saw the world: sharp angles, overcast days, close-ups of gritty textures.

Even the way that you see the world is beautiful, little wolf.

"Hawthorne?" Rayne murmured, her voice still rough with sleep. She blinked awake, her gaze settling on them in the powdery morning light. "What are you doing sneaking around my room?"

"Sneaking." Hawthorne smirked, shifting into something more solid but not yet taking their humanoid shape. They crouched on the ground, all of their limbs cracking as they settled.

Rayne watched them, wide-eyed and fully awakened by their shifting. "Does that hurt?"

"Does what hurt?"

"Changing shapes like that, becoming all solid."

Hawthorne tilted their head as their spine snapped into place, rolling their shoulders to align all of the vertebrae. "No, not in the way that you mean. There is always pain in becoming."

"I guess I get that." Rayne sat up and winced, rubbing her hips gently with the heel of her palm.

Displeasure licked at their spine, watching discomfort tarnish her expression. They had too many thoughts about the disease that made a meal of her, but if they allowed themself to wander down that road, they would never get off of it. Hawthorne wanted to ask her if she was alright, but they already knew the answer. *How could she ever be alright when her body is the way that it is?*

"I want to tell you something," she said, glancing over her shoulder at them.

"I am listening."

"If you wanted to stay here sometimes, in the house, you could," Rayne began, and the working of her lower lip followed soon after. "With me."

Something deep in the forest of them bristled to life at the offer. They could hear the unspoken weight of expectation there. She expected them to come when she beckoned them, to crawl at her feet like some pet. She would expect them to be there, at her side, leashed and tethered.

Hawthorne felt the rumble of disdain growing in their chest, an avalanche of disgust. *No. If there is one thing that I will not tolerate, it is a collar. A cage. Even from you, little wolf.*

"I could leave the door unlocked for you. You could come and go whenever you'd like. I—I don't mind. But, only if you wanted."

The steam that had been building up in their belly, simmering in their gut like a fight, escaped just as quickly as it had come. Hawthorne sighed, and the desire to fold into her, to smooth their palm in the curve of her soft hand, nearly locked around their throat like the collar that they'd feared.

Of course, she would never see you that way, would she? Who else but her could come as close to domesticating the wilderness of you?

Hawthorne moved closer to her; they hesitated only a moment before they sat on the bed beside her, their thighs brushing against one another's. They remained still, giving her space until they felt the rigid tension in her limbs loosen. She did not pull away, but after a moment, she leaned into them. "If I ever were to be kept," they admitted. "It would be by your hand."

"It doesn't hurt when you touch me," Rayne continued, and Hawthorne swallowed, knowing exactly where this was going. Carefully, they moved away from her.

"Should it?" Hawthorne inquired, unsure of what emotion they should attempt to portray to distract her from this line of questioning. *Now would be a perfect time for you to interject, you wooden wretch,* they thought at the House.

"Well, it always does. When other people touch me, at least. But you, you're not even human. How can you do that?"

A lie bubbled and died, but the truth pebbled their tongue. "I have crushed many things underfoot," Hawthorne began carefully. "Some time ago, I learned how not to." *It is all that I can give her at this moment.*

"You and the House sound so much alike." Rayne said, throwing her legs over the side of the bed.

Hawthorne huffed indignantly at the exact moment that the House's pipes shifted. "That is not true."

Rayne giggled a little. "Not like that, but the way that you speak. Do all spirits speak the same?"

"Yes and no. There is a language in our world, a way to speak in-between," Hawthorne replied. It was proving difficult to explain their world to her from the outside; it was like painting a picture but never showing it. "We... rarely speak in absolutes in most cases."

"Why?"

"Why does the sun rise? Yes, there are your human explanations for it, but there is no why. Not really."

Rayne scrunched her nose as she stood, stretching. She was wearing an over-sized, dark shirt and oversized shorts, and even in what looked like rags to them, her beauty was undeniable. She had worn those thick, black socks of hers to bed, and they scowled at the barrier between them and seeing her skin. "Fine. Keep your spirit talk if you must."

"I will."

"Speaking of your spirit talk, I have another request to make of you. Since I don't need your help selling the house anymore."

The offer she dangled in front of them nearly had their mouth salivating without even hearing the meat of it. It spilled like blood into the water. "Make your offer, and I shall tell you what I desire in exchange."

"Could I... learn magic? Or whatever it is that you can do?"

Oh. What an odd request. The novelty whetted their appetite in a way that they could not name. "Elaborate on your meaning, Rayne."

"Well, the shifting or whatever it is that you do. And you slipped into my dreams. Is that something that I could learn how to do?"

It was a *thought*. One that they did not entirely know how to answer. Hawthorne looked away from her as if the answer lay elsewhere. On the surface, the answer was simple: *yes*. Many humans taught themselves or stole the ways of spirits. Knowledge was a rare gift from Hawthorne's kind.

Even then, the humans' stolen fare never measured up to the power they sought. It would not be difficult for Hawthorne to teach Rayne a parlor trick or two; it would be more than she could ever hope to achieve researching on her own.

But Hawthorne had come to know Rayne better than that, and they could see that beneath the fear, the shrinking, the hesitation, there was something in her that hungered the way that they did.

No paltry magic will quell that want.

There was only one offer Hawthorne could make her, and neither of them was ready for that. *Or might never be.*

"I... think so," Hawthorne managed, their voice hesitating. Open honesty was a discomfort to their kind; it was too vulnerable, a way of placing too many cards on the table.

"You think?" Rayne spat back, thick brow raising in distaste.

Hawthorne did nothing to hide their amusement. "I have already expressed my thoughts on repeating myself."

"You're not sure? Shouldn't you know?"

"It is not every day that a human asks me to teach them the ways of my kind," they retorted.

"Well, what do the humans that you make deals with usually ask for?"

Surprise brushed along their spine. *She expects that I speak to other humans, that I offer them anything?* "I do not make deals with any other humans, Rayne. There is only you."

Silence unspooled, and between them, Rayne stared at them with her wide, dark eyes, and Hawthorne stared back, their confession leaving their throat raw.

"Okay. Uhm, I'm going to make breakfast. Do you want an orange?"

Hawthorne exhaled. "Yes. I would like one very much."

The rest of the day passed by in something that Hawthorne could only deem as peace. They watched Rayne as she worked, clearing out her parents' junk, and sat with her during her breaks. Hawthorne was not one for idleness, but they were coming to enjoy slowness with Rayne. She made everything more enjoyable.

It was not as though they had never observed other humans before; in all of the years of their long life, they had seen humans do many things. But watching Rayne was different; the way that she went about everything was different from the other humans.

After several hours spent rummaging through her parents' hoard, she wandered out into the garden, and Hawthorne trailed quietly behind her. She sat beneath the barren pear tree and peeled off her boots. She wiggled her socked toes into the icy soil. *I wish that she would trust me enough to show me more of her skin.* There was no heat to the desire; it was a simple ache to see more of her unrestrained.

"Will you not remove your socks?" Hawthorne inquired, settling under the brambles of a nearby blackberry bush.

"I will not," Rayne replied. "You got a fear of fabric?"

"I fear nothing," Hawthorne pouted. "I have already told you my thoughts on these layers."

Rayne laughed, her head falling back into a ray of cold sunlight in her amusement. The way it flashed against her skin danced behind their eyelids long after she moved. Hawthorne melted in the light, unable to focus on anything else outside of the small details of her.

They were not sure whether she had forgotten she was not alone or simply didn't care, but soon she began to hum, murmuring to herself what sounded like a list of tasks to complete around the home.

Hawthorne was content to listen to them until her soft murmurs came to a halt as she laid eyes on something moving slowly through the bushes to her left. They scented warm fur and burrow dirt. *A rabbit.*

"Oh, hello there!" Rayne crooned, her voice softer than snowfall. They stared at her and then back at the unremarkable rabbit.

Why is she so happy to see something so small? they wondered, frowning. *It is a rabbit; she must have seen hundreds in her time here. What is so special about this one?*

Something sour tasted on Hawthorne's tongue, and their chest constricted with the realization that Rayne had never spoken to them that way nor looked at them half as affectionately as she did that rabbit.

I do not know why I want this, but I will not deny myself, Hawthorne thought. *Perhaps I should kill the thing, tear it apart, and see what makes it tick? I will find its charm and take it for myself.*

Rayne had leaned closer to the creature, and it did not run from her. Hawthorne could see her reflection in its eyes, though they smelled no bitter twang of fear.

It is not scared of her, Hawthorne marveled.

Above them, their ears caught the sharp slice of wings cutting through the air, and a hawk swooped down, descending upon the rabbit.

Rayne let out a horrid shriek and scrambled to her feet, racing towards it. Hawthorne did not recall moving, but they were suddenly at her side as she stumbled across the garden toward the rabbit. She swatted at the hawk with her bare hands and it released the rabbit but not without nicking her palm in the process.

The air split with the stench of blood, the earthy kick of the rabbit's and the sweet tang of Rayne's. Their tongue darted out against their lips as they solidified, moving to stand at Rayne's side. It didn't matter that her blood whetted their appetite; all of their attention was fixed on the pained, wet breath sounding from her chest.

"Rayne?" Hawthorne asked.

She did not answer them, crouching over the small creature as it clung to life. Its eyes were wide with shock, and its heart beating at a rapid pace, but Hawthorne could hear each beat growing slower than the last.

"It's still alive," Rayne whispered, kneeling into the cold dirt to try to gather the wounded thing into her lap. "It's still breathing."

"Yes," Hawthorne began, finding the way her fingers curled into the matted fur much more interesting than a dying rabbit. "But not for much longer. Death will come for it soon enough."

Rayne whipped her head around and fixed them with a venomous glare. Her brows furrowed, and her eyes, wet with unshed tears, were nearly searing. If Hawthorne had breath, she might have stolen it. *Her anger might be even more beautiful than her.*

"Don't fucking say that!" she hissed before turning back to the rabbit. "It will not die!"

Blinking, Hawthorne crept closer; the sweet scent of death, like rotten fruit, was dancing just at the edge of their nose. "It will. I can smell it. Why does this upset you?"

"It's hurt!" Rayne cried.

"It is dying," Hawthorne corrected. *Why is she so upset by something natural?*

"It couldn't protect itself," she said, her voice cracking with what Hawthorne assumed to be emotion.

Hawthorne could not take their eyes off her hands, bloody and covered in fur. The gash on her palm was thin but ran deep, her skin split. There was a desire, a want that coalesced into a need as they watched blood dry against the chestnut of her skin. *I do not ever want to see her bleeding again,* they thought.

Confusion tumbled after. *When have I ever denied the scent of blood, the ripping of skin?*

"It was weak," they said to distract themself from their turmoil.

"So it deserved to die?"

"Yes. As we all will. When our bodies or minds weaken, then Death will come. It is the way of the world... are you crying?"

Hawthorne had seen many human tears in their time; their expressions often varied when the tears fell. Sometimes they smiled or wailed; it was difficult to discern what emotion was behind the tears.

This is worse than her blood, they thought, their frown nearly cleaving them in half as they melted back into the shadows.

The rabbit's heart had slowed to a stop, and the subtle kiss of rot was already beginning to set into it.

Rayne did not respond; her hands trembled as she held the dead thing, and they could not understand it.

Silently, she tore off her hoodie and folded it on the ground in front of her before she knelt into it, wincing slightly. They opened their mouth to tell her not to do this, that surely her knees would blister and bruise, but the hard look on her face silenced them.

She dug her fingers into the dirt and began digging. Hawthorne pressed close enough to smell the sweet tinge of the thin line of sweat beading at the nape of her neck. Once the hole reached a depth she seemed content with, Rayne snatched dead leaves and bits of grass from around her before she laid the rabbit delicately in its soft grave. Rayne tucked her head in prayer, though her voice was anything but smooth as she spoke.

She whispered. "The hammer cannot always come down on the nail. May the Creator open the way for you, especially."

Hammer? Why are you so angry?

Hawthorne stilled. It had been so long since they had heard someone pray, but Rayne's song, her voice hushed with reverence, set fire to a need for more.

Would you pray for me, little wolf? If I asked it of you?

Rayne hummed low and familiar, a song they had once heard and recognized immediately as a mourning song. *She is mourning this creature. How can she mourn something that she does not know?*

She covered the rabbit's body in dirt and used the heel of her palms to compact it. The harsh expression on her face had not softened despite her tears.

"The hammer can't always come down on the nail," she repeated to herself. Rayne stood and headed back inside, leaving Hawthorne to stare after her.

Eventually, Hawthorne joined her inside. She stood in the kitchen, washing the dirt and dried blood from her hand while the House fussed.

"What have you done now, cherub? Always hurting yourself, always bleeding. What—don't waste such beautiful blood and wash it down the drain! Oh, you selfish, lovely girl."

"House," Rayne grit out without turning her attention away from her work. "Not now."

The House sighed. *"It is always 'Not now, House.' 'No food for you, you useless thing!' One day you will learn to love me truly, dear one."*

Hawthorne gave Rayne her space but never allowed themselves to drift too far from her. The image of her fiery anger, her biting tone, danced recklessly through every thought.

After washing her hands, she returned to the porch to burn cedar chips in the fire pit and run her hair and hands through the smoke. They understood why she did this, a practice passed down to her meant to cleanse her body and spirits from the energy of death. She did so silently, without the song or prayers that Hawthorne would have expected with the gesture. Then she'd come back inside, fed herself, and curled up on the couch until the sun had fled the sky. Hawthorne had not left her side for a moment.

They could not if they tried.

"You are tired," Hawthorne declared, glancing down at Rayne as she curled on the couch, caught between sleep and wakefulness. She'd been drifting in and out for the last fifteen minutes, her book discarded on the coffee table. Why she did not simply go upstairs to her comfortable bed, they did not know, but it irritated them to watch her make herself so small on the seat.

Some of her curls had wiggled loose from her nearly perfect braid and framed her face. They could not look away even as her eyes blinked open and found them in the low light.

"I'm fine. Just resting," she mumbled.

"Why not rest in your bed then, as it was created?"

She frowned at them and rolled over so that her back was to them, pressing herself deeper into the old couch. "I don't want to," she snapped.

Uninterested in the idea of picking a fight with her, but curious to see what would happen if they simply remained, Hawthorne folded in on themself and sat on the floor beside the couch.

Rayne shifted only twice before going completely still, sleep relaxing the tenseness in her limbs that she never seemed to lose other than in the depths of her slumber.

"You should let her be." the House whispered with the crackling of the fireplace.

Would you agree with your needy House were you awake?

As if in response, the wood in the fire crackled loudly, and Rayne groaned in her sleep, rolling over again so that the amber light of the flames illuminated her face. Hawthorne blinked, transfixed, and some invisible thread tugged them forward to brush the curls from her face so that they could get a better look at her. With all the tension of the day relieved from her, she looked so different.

No. She looks like herself.

Looking at her now set an odd symphony of emotions that they could not name. She was beautiful and they—

Hawthorne pulled away, slowly so as not to wake her. *I cannot think here. I should go.*

"Don't just leave her there, you great beast!" the House snapped. **"Her bones will ache, and she'll toss and turn; the rough material will cut her skin."**

"You told me to leave her alone."

"Since when have you ever listened to me?" the House retorted. **"Don't just stand there."**

Unease settled in their marrow as they looked down at Rayne's sleeping form. "What would you have me do?"

"Make yourself useful and carry her to bed."

There was a bit of strength left in this humanoid form for them, so carrying her up the stairs in this form would not prove difficult.

Silently, Hawthorne stood and moved to the fireplace. With a breath of their darkness, they snuffed out the flames, leaving only the two candles on the windowsill over the kitchen sink.

They made quick work of those as well before they returned their attention to their little wolf. *She isn't mine*, they reminded themself, correcting the thought. *I can lay no claim to her.*

Hawthorne knelt to her so that they were at eye level with her. Even in the darkness, they could make out the minor beauty marks that lived on her face, a constellation. Their thumb ghosted along the one on her right cheek. *Had she always been so beautiful?*

Stop. Get her in bed. Put some distance between you both so that you can think.

As carefully as Hawthorne could, they eased her into their arms so as not to hurt her.

Hawthorne's hand slid into her curls, supporting her head as their other hand caught behind her knees and they pulled her close. Immediately, the scent of her washed over them.

The rose scent of her soap that they knew she used, had used since her grandmother's death because it reminded her of the old woman. But there was another smell tangled in her hair, that soft, sweet almond that they were coming to adore.

They brushed their nose against her hair to get another wave of the scent.

Rayne nestled in closer to them and let out a sigh that sounded dangerously close to their name.

"You can't have her!" the House hissed at them through the creaking of the stairs as they carried her up. *"You will not take her from me. Put her to bed and then leave, wraith. I will keep her safe. I will hold her as you never could."*

Hawthorne swallowed the growl that threatened to tear out of their throat, and were it not for Rayne, they would have torn into The House.

Once inside her room, Hawthorne shifted her in their arms so that they could pull back the sheets of her bed and fold her into it. Immediately, she nestled into her bed, clutching her pillow to her and nuzzling into its softness. "Hawthorne," she sighed as if they were a breath of fresh air.

As if they were a relief to her.

Hawthorne leaned in closer to her, beckoned by the scent of her and the desire to hear her repeat their name. They smoothed her hair out of her face, less out of necessity and more, they realized, to have an excuse to touch her. A touch she leaned into.

There was a thought, a thrumming thing that pulsed beneath their skin when they looked at her. It was not hunger. At least, not a hunger that Hawthorne could ever remember feeling before.

But instead of allowing this thought to have a voice, they whispered in hopes to snuff it out: "Goodnight, Rayne."

It took no small amount of effort to tear themselves away from her, but they managed to do so, the door closing behind them acting as the knife that severed the thread between them.

The sound of their name on her lips followed them down the hall and to the stairwell.

Why am I responding this way to her? Hawthorne wondered, settling down at the top of the stairs. *She's not—I have never felt this way about her before.*

Hawthorne wanted her. They wanted to be closer to her; they wanted to learn all of the things about her that changed. But it was the desire of proximity that haunted them now. They wanted to bury their nose in her hair and taste the salt of her skin.

Fucking was not a foreign concept to spirits and definitely not Hawthorne. Men, women, and everything in between, Hawthorne fucked indiscriminately. If they were attracted to someone and they were consenting, Hawthorne was interested. But their interest existed only before and during the interaction; never once had Hawthorne *longed* for someone.

Their body, while not fully human, was not devoid of feeling or response, and their cock twitched to life with the thought of fucking Rayne. The thought of her full, perfect lips wrapped around their cock, the warmth of her wet cunt, and the scent of her enveloped around them.

The House creaked under them in something that felt distinctly like disapproval. Yet their mind was not on the stubborn structure but on the sleeping woman on the other side of the cherrywood walls and what it would be like if they dared to open the door. If they woke her and dared to ask her if she wanted the same way that they did. Their hand seemed to move of its own accord, sought and found their aching cock. Shadows of precum beaded at the head of their cock, and the heat coiling in the pit of their stomach was quickly becoming an inferno.

Hawthorne closed the embers of their eyes and imagined that it was Rayne's hand stroking their cock instead of their own cool fist, the warmth of her skin, and the delicate touch of her nimble fingers. Their head rested against the wall as they lost themselves to the fantasy of her. *Fuck, just like that,* they praised the ghost of her, draped in figment and the heady veil of their need for her. *Touch me just like that. Good girl.*

Their fantasy Rayne batted her thick lashes up at them and fixed them with a playful smirk before she leaned forward and took the head of them into her mouth.

Hawthorne's thumb swirled over the head of their cock, imagining that it was her tongue. Their fingers tangled in her curls to keep them out of her face and to keep her just where they wanted her. They swore again, feeling all too clearly the smooth slide of her throat as they bucked their hips into their fist.

Their other hand moved to their mouth to stifle the moan that spilled off their tongue in the shape of her name. In their mind, she says theirs back to them and manages to beg for more around their cock.

The thought of her desire, unabashed and unhindered for them, sent Hawthorne over the edge, and in the darkness, their orgasm dragged them under. Hawthorne bit down on their fist until they tasted the pine of their own blood to hide the strangled cry that came from them in an attempt to keep Rayne undisturbed. In the throes of their pleasure, they melted back into the shadow, losing control of their corporeal form and becoming nothing.

When they emerged, coming up for air, they were lying back against the carpet, staring up at the ceiling. *Have I ever thought of anyone like that before?* they wondered, catching the breath that they didn't need. "No," they murmured aloud, answering their own question. "No one but her."

"*Let her be,*" the House demanded again, reminding them of its infuriating presence.

Hawthorne groaned, rolling their shoulders. "Don't you ever shut up?"

"*My cherub need not get wrapped up in the likes of you now. She deserves to have a real life, to own a home, and grow fat with joy. You will feed her pears and lead her to that wood, and then that will be the end of her.*"

"House," Hawthorne said finally, and the structure froze, an eerie silence filling the space as it leaned in closer to listen. "Be quiet. You know as much of her as I do. You have known me since she was a child. Have I ever sought to force her to do anything?"

"*I will tell her that she's welcomed a liar into her home. I will tell her the truth of you and her past—*"

At this, Hawthorne sat up, pressing a clawed finger to the wall in a silent threat. "You. Will. Not. You will not disturb her. I will tear you apart before you can utter a word."

"*How can you stomach lying to her? Keeping the pearl of her past tucked under your tongue? As if you have any more claim to it than you do of her!*"

Hawthorne did not want to talk about this now, did not want to think about the past, as it could only make these newfound sensations, kicking to life within them, even more complicated. "Have you ever seen true darkness, House? The gnashing teeth of oblivion? I can ensure that you do if you speak anymore of the past."

The House shivered with mirth. "*You will not harm me. She loves me so, and you, soft thing that you are, will not hurt her in such a way.*" Hawthorne growled at the truth of its words. They would not hurt Rayne, not unless she opened that pretty mouth and asked them for it. "*Worry not, my shadow. I will not share your sins so long as you gift me something of you. Leave it in my hearth so that it may burn when you next light my fire.*"

Hawthorne sighed. "You blackmailing terror. Yes, then if that is what it will take."

An unexpectedly comfortable silence slid between them, and Hawthorne allowed their mind to wander back to the thoughts of their little wolf. There was something within in their chest that ached, like a muscle pulled, though they had not exerted themselves in any way. There was pain in being so close to Rayne and yet so far, hiding beneath the veil of a promise that hurt them.

"She will choose you, you know," the House whispered, shattering the gossamer hold of their thoughts. *"It is inevitable. She will eat pears from your outstretched hands, lick eternity from your fingers, and she will burn. We all will. We will go out as stars enflamed in the silent night only to ignite again."*

She will choose you.

Silently, Hawthorne stood and descended the stairs. Like a record set to play, they set out on a path that they felt they'd walked a thousand times before. "I will be back," they murmured by way of farewell. "Keep her warm for me. The wind has teeth tonight."

If the House responded to their request, they did not heed it, deaf to all but the thought that there might be a chance Rayne felt the same strange ache they did, and that the remedy might be accessible to them both. All that they would have to do was reach for one another, and the need to be close would simply disappear.

Perhaps the House sees something in me that I did not, for it is right and has made a liar of me again, they thought as they slipped out of the front door and into the biting chill of the night. *I cannot let her leave again. Should she choose to go, then I will follow her.* The dark and the cold called to them, coaxing them back into the wind, into the rattling of dead leaves and the frozen moss that lined the forest floor. Only their thoughts kept them from disappearing completely, anchored to the world by a pair of burning brown eyes and shipwrecked skin.

Hawthorne had always been hungry, had always sunk their teeth in the tenderest bits of weaker creatures, but the idea of digging into Rayne... she would make a meal of them. She would have them, bones and all, and Hawthorne would let her.

She may be the one who would eat pears from their hands and lick their sticky fingers clean, but they would drag her down into the dirt with them, belly exposed, waiting for the dagger of her kiss to spill their entrails like a procession of rose petals.

'Inevitable,' the House had said.

If I am to kneel into this aching and see what lies on the other end of this sorrow, it would not be without blood.

CHAPTER TWENTY
rayne

Rayne had never been happy before. The shape of the word was foreign on her tongue, but she thought that the last few weeks with Hawthorne might have been something close to that.

She loved the moments that they spent together, regardless of what they did or didn't do. The moment they shared took place beneath the glow of Kappie's. Rayne was making her biweekly trip into town to grab as many supplies as she could and then hole up in her house until she had to do it all over again. They came with her, buried in her shadow and falling in step behind her, content to linger and watch as she fretted about the store.

Rayne dumped as much pasta as she could fit into her arms into the cart. She worried about her lip, all but assaulting it with her teeth as she weighed her loot, crunching the numbers in her head. Randomly, Hawthorne would brush against her legs, against her fingers, and tug at her hair, pulling laughter from her.

They teased her constantly, but it was never unkind. Hawthorne was nothing but gentle with her.

"I wish that things could stay like this." Rayne sighed.

"Why can't they?" they asked, feathering a whisper against the back of her neck.

Shit. Didn't mean to say that out loud. She pressed her lips into a tight, stubborn line, pretending not to have heard them over the Christmas music blasting through the crunchy speakers overhead.

Hawthorne's teeth nicked her shoulder without drawing blood, and Rayne shuddered at the sensation. "Rayne."

"What?" she murmured, a slight hitch to her voice. They chuckled and leaned in closer, their breath fogging against the shell of her ear.

"You said that you wished things could stay this way. I want to know why it is that you think that they cannot."

Indecision kicked up a storm within her, her lip quirking as she chewed on what answer she wanted to give them. The truth was a dangerous thing, Rayne had found. The more she spoke, the worse people's response to her became.

But Hawthorne isn't most people. They aren't even a person. And they like me. Somehow.

Rayne opened her mouth to tell them, but clamped it shut a moment after. She turned away and forced her cart through the produce aisle. She felt Hawthorne trail behind her, having been trained in the sensation of their presence.

They always followed. She did not know what to do with this knowledge.

"How many bags of oranges did you say that you wanted again?"

Rayne was cheating a bit; she knew that mentioning their beloved oranges would distract them. They loomed over her like a vulture. "I would like two bags," they replied. "And do not think that your talk of oranges will distract me from my question, Rayne."

"I don't belong here, I never have," she began, trying to focus on the oranges instead of Hawthorne. "No matter how... nice things can be here. This place isn't for me."

It didn't matter that her grandmother had rooted her bones into the land, that her family was rotting in the soil and fertilizing the flowers that would arise next spring—Rayne did not belong to Bury.

"What if I don't let you leave?" they asked.

Do they... not want me to leave?

Rayne opened her mouth to speak, but her words were lost around the hiss that she let out as her hip bumped too hard into the sharp edge of the shopping cart. Pain bloomed, and her hand moved to her side. Blood stickied her palm, and she felt Hawthorne brush nearer, solidifying.

"Rayne."

The hum of the fluorescent lights above, the sharp sting of her skin, and the hot kiss of shame overstimulated her senses. "Don't!" she snarled, grabbing the end of her cart and pulling it along out of the aisle and toward the checkout line.

Rayne pretended not to notice the way the teenage cashier eyed her, her gaze lingering on paying and bagging her items. It was not until she was outside in the parking lot, tucking all of her groceries away, that Hawthorne spoke again.

"Are we going back to the house?"

"Did you have somewhere that you wanted to go?" she asked, pressing another hand to her hip. The blood had slowed but was still soaking through her clothes. Going home would be her best bet, but if she had to, she could dress and handle her wound in the car. She would if Hawthorne needed her to.

"That does not answer my question," Hawthorne replied.

"Can you just answer my fucking question?"

"Answer mine then."

Overstimulated by her discomfort and every single sensation outside of her, Rayne snarled and swung open the door to the driver's side of the car, and Hawthorne melted into the shadow of the passenger seat, claiming the space beside her.

Hawthorne granted her a few minutes of quiet before they spoke again. "May I see your wound?"

There was a rational part of her that remembered the look in Hawthorne's eyes when they'd admitted to wanting to eat her, when they'd spoken about their bloodlust. But there was another part of her, lonely, desperate, longing to be seen by someone. If only for a moment. *Hawthorne has the stomach for blood. For the ugly things. They will see me... I think.*

Keeping her eyes on the road to avoid their eyes, Rayne lifted her hips to peel down the waistband of her leggings and allow Hawthorne to look at the cut.

Her skin had sloughed off, the friction of the collision enough to harm her. It was embarrassing being such a soft thing.

"Does it hurt very badly?" Hawthorne asked after a few moments of silence.

Rayne blinked. *No one ever asked me that before.* "Not really, it won't truly until the morning."

"I am sorry." Hawthorne breathed against her shoulder, freezing her. Stiffly, she rolled the leggings back, adjusted herself, and backed her car out of the parking lot.

"For what? You didn't do anything to me."

"That is what is said, yes? When someone is hurt and it... *upsets* you as well."

Rayne's grip on the steering wheel tightened as if she could squeeze out the parts of her that didn't know how to respond or what to do with the knowledge that Hawthorne felt something for her.

"Yes," Rayne managed. "That's what is said."

The rest of the car ride continued in gentle silence, Rayne's mind filled with thoughts of the monster beside her.

Once they returned to the House, Hawthorne slid out of the car before she could get the chance to do so. "Go inside. I will meet you there."

"Okay. Are you leaving?"

"Of course not. I am going to bring in your groceries for you."

Rayne threw them a confused glance. "I can carry them."

"Yes, you're very strong," they teased, and she resisted the urge to toss her keys at them. "But go tend to your hip. I will do this for you."

Part of her wanted to fight, to push back, but her lips fixed into a tight line and she simply nodded, tucking her head and heading inside.

"Bleeding again, my cherub?" the House sighed as she ascended the stairs. *"Always outside of me. I'm beginning to think that you do this on purpose to leave me out."*

"No, House. I am not trying to leave you out of my bleeding," she replied with a roll of her eyes. "Next time I hurt myself, I'll be sure to do so inside of you."

Her hands moved of their own volition, her limbs existing on autopilot when it was time for her to take care of herself. If pressed, Rayne could not speak about the first time that she had to dress her own wounds. Her mother had taught her when she was old enough to hold anything, as she had been taught at the hospital after giving birth to Rayne.

Most of her youth had been spent tied in bandages and soaked in ointments. Caring for the soft, rotting vessel she'd been thrust into came as second nature to her.

"Rayne?" Hawthorne asked. Rayne jumped and glanced down to find her hip already wrapped, her hands washed, and all her medical supplies neatly tucked back into her black floral bag. "Are you alright?"

"Oh, yeah. Uhm, you can come in."

Halving themself, they stepped into her room and sat beside her on the edge of her bed. It was some kind of strange magic that pulled Rayne toward Hawthorne, her head coming to rest against their shoulder. The magic did not grant her the proper words to give Hawthorne, but they did not seem to care. They leaned into her as well.

Carefully, her hand coasted up their dark shoulder, the shadows of their flesh swirling around her fingers as she did so. Hawthorne's long, clawed fingers traced the outline of her waist, avoiding the bandage at her hip as if they knew exactly how to keep her comfortable.

I want more. I want Hawthorne closer.

Rayne had never wanted like this. Everything about Hawthorne should have repelled her, their teeth, their otherness, but instead, she pressed closer. They were the flame and she the foolish little moth.

I don't care if they hurt me. Even if they eat me. I want whatever this is as long as I can have it.

Rayne lifted her face towards theirs to find them already looking down at her. Their hand moved from her waist to tilt her chin toward them. Hawthorne kissed her, and her arms locked around their neck almost instantly. Their mouth was cool as river water, but their skin seared like summer sunlight. The urge to bite them was maddening but she knew that they would bite her back and one touch alone would split her fragile skin open, her blood spilling into the carpet.

The thought sent electricity sparking down her spine. It would be so easy for Hawthorne to tear her apart, to unmake the poorly stitched-together thing that she was.

Their hand ghosted along the hem of her hoodie. "I'd like to touch you more," Hawthorne said, breaking the kiss enough to speak. "May I?"

"Yes. *Please.*"

Wait. If they touch you then they'll feel your scars, they'll see all of your strange skin. As other as they may be, how could they want that?

Tension knitted her shoulders.

"What's wrong?" they asked, brushing their lips against her cheek.

"Nothing," she lied, shaking her head and trying to smile at them.

Hawthorne pulled back, completely to fix her with their full attention. "That is untrue. Where are you?" Hawthorne asked, watching her.

She shook her head, but her expression did not change. "Nowhere."

"You've always been such a terrible liar," Hawthorne sighed, offering her their hand.

"You don't know what sort of lies I've told," she shot back, accepting their outstretched hand.

They pulled her to them so that she was half on their lap.

"If you say so," Hawthorne replied, amusement tickling their throat.

"What does that mean?" she asked, drawing in a breath at their touch. They moved her further onto their lap until she was straddling them, and while they didn't answer her, their fingers continued to draw patterns idly against her stockings.

"You won't remove your clothes, will you?" they asked.

Rayne shook her head. "No, I won't."

They nodded. "Not a problem." Their clawed fingers drew a line down her thigh, tearing into her stockings without so much as even nicking her fragile skin. Rayne's breath tangled in her throat as she watched them, but she couldn't move away, didn't want to. "Can I keep touching you? More than this."

Rayne nodded, and Hawthorne frowned at her. "No. I need you to speak. Your words."

"Yes," she whispered. "You can touch me more than this."

"Are you comfortable?"

"No."

Hawthorne immediately withdrew their hand, and Rayne pulled their hand back. "No, not like that. I mean, I've just... I've never had someone this close before."

"Ah. I see. We will go as fast or as slow as you like."

"Okay."

They split her stockings just enough to grant them access to her panties and everything beneath it. "And if something is a problem, you'll tell me. Won't you, little wolf?" they asked as they ever so gently rubbed a finger against her through her underwear.

Pleasure pooled at her core from their touch, and her fingers dug into their wispy shoulders, her nose burying against the rise of their collarbone as she melted into them. This close to them, they smelled of the earth bloated with rainfall. Like every summer she'd ever spent making mud pies in her grand-mother's backyard.

Rayne let out a surprised moan, catching in her throat around the sound of their name. "Hawthorne—"

"Answer my question, little wolf," they breathed as their claw split her panties.

"Yes!" She gasped. "I will tell you if something is a problem."

"There's my girl," they murmured, and her thighs trembled with that simple phrase. Being claimed by someone.

Their girl.

"I've laid claim to you for much longer than that wisp of teeth and branches!" The House snarled with the angry lurch of the windows as they were pressed with the winds outside. ***"Do I mean less? Should I threaten to eat you, too?"***

"Shut up, House!" she spat.

"Trying to distract you from me, is it?" Hawthorne asked. "When you are with me, Rayne, I will not share your attention with another. Are we clear?" Their finger moved to rub the sensitive bundle of nerves between her legs, and she moaned, latching onto their broad shoulders in surprise.

"Yes!"

"Much better," they purred, pressing another burning kiss to her lips. She wanted them to brand her with the heat of what she was feeling for them, the way that this nameless thing that existed between their bodies was burning her alive. Rayne bucked her hips against their finger.

Hawthorne stopped and withdrew.

Rayne whined and pushed against their shoulder. "What the hell?"

"Not yet, little wolf. Did you think I'd go so easy on you?"

Just as Rayne prepared an array of every swear that she knew to throw at them, they flipped her onto her back, pressing her deep into the mattress. The breath was forced out of her lungs with the quickness of it, and they kissed her again as if they could drink it in.

"Tell me what you want, Rayne," they whispered in her ear, their teeth dangerously close to her flesh and sending a shiver down her spine.

"You're an asshole. Don't just ask me something like that when we're like this."

Hawthorne grinned, exposing their teeth to her once more, and her eyes lingered a moment. "Call me whatever you'd like, but it will not change what I'm asking. Tell me what it is that you want and I'll give it to you."

"Why?" Rayne murmured. "Why should what I want matter to you at all?"

Hawthorne could have lied to her, could have gifted her soft, flowery words. But she would not have believed them. Instead, they said, "I do not know. But it does. I want to give to you. I have never wanted that before."

Rayne swallowed. "You said that spirits don't give gifts. That nothing comes for free."

They smiled a little. "We don't. Even my giving cannot come without an exchange."

Of course. There was something comforting in that knowledge. She nodded as her hand snaked up their chest. "Tell me what it means."

"If you give me your faith, your absolute devotion, then there is nothing that I cannot and will not lay at your feet," Hawthorne murmured. "Anything you want, I will give you."

"Could you make this—" Rayne gestured to her body and the skin that had never felt like hers.

Hawthorne silenced her with a kiss, her stomach fluttering before she could continue. "No. Magic cannot fix everything."

Rayne swallowed. *No. I will learn magic. I will change what can be changed about this body. There must be something.* "So *not* anything that I want then," she grumbled.

Hawthorne smirked. "Let me rephrase: anything within my power to give you, I will."

Rayne ran her fingers over the groves of their flesh, where bones should have been. There were things like bones, she realized. They felt like what bones should have felt like under skin, but wrong.

"Faith," she repeated, careful not to look at them. "What does that really mean?" Rayne had never paused to consider religion outside of the stories she'd been fed as a child. Her grandmother believed in God and the Devil, good and evil, but she also believed that certain stories could only be told in winter or worms would work their way into your throat.

Faith had always been a tangled thing for her, caught between damnation and indifference. She was not sure if she really had anything to give.

"You feed me, and I will feed you," Hawthorne explained.

"Feed?"

"Yes. I will peel back the flesh of the world for you, and in exchange, you will give me some of you. Your blood, your tears, your fear."

Rayne swallowed. "Why my fear?"

Hawthorne brushed a curl from her face with their claw. "It is the purest form of devotion. Lay your prayers at my altar, and I will give you the world."

"At a price."

Hawthorne shrugged. "All things come at a cost. This is one that you may choose. But know that once you've devoted yourself to me, you cannot escape. I will find you anywhere you go, Rayne."

Rayne's heart felt as though it was going to burst out of her chest. "And will I be able to do the same?" she asked. *Shit. I shouldn't have asked them that. They don't seem as though they would ever want to be followed, least of all by me.*

Hawthorne stared at her with that unreadable expression of theirs again. "Yes. I imagine that you could. Tell me what you want then, Rayne Dorne."

The look that they gave her set a fresh wave of panic. *What does it mean when you look at me like that? Can't you just tell me?*

I could find them even when I go back to the city, she thought. *I could even sneak away to wherever they are on the weekends. That could be nice.* "Does this offer have an expiration date?"

"No," Hawthorne replied, their hand coasting along the valley of her hips, sinking lower. "It does not. I could wait forever, but I will not. You do not have that long."

"This might be the worst pillow talk that I've ever heard." *Not that I'm exactly an expert.*

Hawthorne tilted their head, glanced over at her pillow, and then back at her. "Why would I speak to your pillow? It is inanimate."

Rayne brushed her nose against their shoulder, swallowing down her amusement. "No. Pillow talk is intimate talk when you're alone with someone in bed."

"Ah. I see. Another bit of your human slang," they murmured, leaning closer to her while their hand slipped between her legs. "Would you like me to show you just how well I can use your 'pillow talk?'"

The pad of their finger traced her clit from the outside of her underwear, eliciting a sharp intake of breath, her hand latching onto the hollow of their throat. Surprise, as clear as day, flashed across Hawthorne's face, and then a delighted smile.

"Choking me does not count as an answer, you know."

"I want it. I want everything. But your claws—"

Hawthorne removed their hand from between her legs, and she whimpered at the loss, they held it up for her, and she watched as their claws melted into their dark skin. "I will not harm you unless you beg me *very* sweetly for it."

Their words turned her core molten and their lips captured hers before she could even think to respond. The gentleness of their touch continued to catch her by surprise, even how their lips moved against hers. They seemed to remain conscious of the threat friction posed against her skin. *How could they know? I didn't tell them, at least, I think I didn't.*

The material of her underwear slid away, leaving only her wet entrance waiting for them. She accommodated them immediately, the hills of her thighs warm around their hand.

Their middle finger found the wet, welcoming warmth of her cunt and they both sighed as Hawthorne entered her. Her head fell back with a moan, all thoughts giving way to the bonfire of pleasure heating between her legs.

They sank their finger deeper slowly, allowing her to adjust but her body moved of its own accord, her legs hooking around them, the heels of her feet at the base of their spine and she ground back against their finger. Hawthorne pulled out and sank back in, knuckle deep until she had taken the entire digit. Her head fell back against the pillow with a sigh that they drank in when they kissed her a second time.

"Look at you now!" the House fretted with a nervous creaking of the stairs outside of her room. *"Why do you never listen, why does death have such a hold on you, my cherub?"*

Now is really not the time, House. Please shut the fuck up.

"Perfect," Hawthorne whispered, cutting through House's chatter. They broke the kiss to trail a series of them down her throat, chasing the rush of her pulse. "Just perfect, Rayne."

Her core liquified at the combination of their praise and the ever-so slight curling of their finger inside of her with each thrust. Her nails dug deeper into them with each movement, her hips rising to meet every thrust. Rayne could hardly recognize herself or the sounds that Hawthorne tugged from her. It was not until they brushed some tender, untouched part within her that she swore, nearly choking on their name.

"There you are," they purred into her ear, nipping at her earlobe. Sensation plucked at her every nerve. It was good, too good. Pleasure was not a feeling that Rayne was used to; her body was unaccustomed to such.

As if sensing her overwhelm, Hawthorne slowed their motions, pulling back enough so that they could meet each other's eyes.

"Take a deep breath for me," they crooned in her ear, and she pinched her eyes closed and did exactly as they asked, her muscles loosening. "Slower?"

"It feels good, it's just... a lot," she whispered, shame blanketing her. *At this age, you should have more experience; you should know your body better than this. Oh God, how many people have they been with? They must think I'm a mess.*

"Okay. Do you need me to stop?"

They're so... why are they so understanding? Why don't they talk to me like everyone else? She shook her head, swallowing the lump in her throat. "Please, don't. Just... talk me through it?"

She expected some of their warm teasing, their playful nudging but it never came. Their other hand slid into her hair, caught in her curls and held her close so that they could watch her expressions. Hawthorne fucked her again, slower this time but deeper, their longer finger claiming every inch of her. Their thumb moved to draw steadying circles against her clit as they did and she nearly screamed.

"Oh, fuck, Hawthorne!" Rayne's back arched and her thighs trembled around them, her heels digging into their back.

"Just like that, Rayne," they purred in her ear, their breath just as heavy as hers. "Cum for me."

Rayne pulled Hawthorne down closer to her as she came, her nails digging into their odd bones as stars danced before her eyes. She had chased her own pleasure before, had made herself cum more times than she could count but not a single time had felt even a fraction as good as it did with Hawthorne.

"You orgasm the way that stars die," they murmured into the thickness of her curls. Rayne buried her face against their chest, unable to hold that statement and desperate not to be seen.

"In bed with monsters. Why seek such a depressing destruction?" The House wailed with the wind. *"You'd grow with me, little darling. They could never hold you as I would."*

Rayne ignored the House and instead focused on Hawthorne's scent and how comforting she was beginning to find it.

"I've always known you were good, Rayne," The House snapped. *"You never needed to prove it to me. Your parents never saw but I did. I-"*

"Your house is irritating." Hawthorne sighed. "It is set on not allowing us a moment of peace, it would seem."

Rayne's head snapped up. "You—you can hear it?"

"Much too well for my liking."

That means that they've heard everything it's been saying to me. Fuck. Wait. They said that they couldn't hear it before. Rayne shoved against their shoulder. "You have the nerve to call me a liar when you could hear the House all along. I had asked you before, and you said you couldn't!"

Hawthorne smirked, pleased with themself. "I never said that. What I said was that I could only hear you, which is true. You are the only thing worth listening to in this place."

"What a wretched spectre you are! I will lock you out, invitation or not. There is no place within me for the likes of you."

"Ignore it. It's a jealous thing, it is. I have you in a way that it never can and it—" Hawthorne froze, sniffing the air. They pulled out of her; their fingers were pink with blood. *"I hurt you."*

Rayne stared down at their hand blankly until realization stabbed into her, her pulse immediately rising to a fever pitch. *Of course, I bled. That was my first time, and I didn't even say anything to them.* She pushed against them, wiggling out from under them to scramble off the bed. "No, you didn't. It's okay."

"You are *bleeding.*"

"It's normal. You were... the first person I've ever been with."

Hawthorne looked down at their hand and then back at her. "I was your first?"

Please don't make me talk about this. I don't want to. I can't.

"I see. Can I help you clean up?" Their voice was so soft, too delicate for her to hold in her trembling hands.

Rayne shook her head, eyes fixed on the carpet as she sat up, gathering her tattered clothes, backing toward the bathroom. "No, it's okay. I don't need help. I'll—I'll be right out. You can use their old bathroom if you want to... uhm... wash up too," she said before slipping into the bathroom and closing the door behind her.

The moment the door closed, Rayne's back rested against the door, and she exhaled a long, shaky breath.

On the other side of the door, she heard the House's hushed voice, muffled through the wood. "Look at what you've done. Condemned her and you don't even bother to take care of her!" The House spat, shifting angrily under their weight.

"I would if she would only allow it," Hawthorne whispered, rocking Rayne to her core.

CHAPTER TWENTY-ONE
hawthorne

Hawthorne had never been in an awkward situation before. Shame was not an emotion that they understood before this moment. But, watching Rayne as she desperately tried to avoid their gaze while she made herself coffee might have been the closest that they'd ever come to it.

I should have known that she had never been with another, they thought. *At the very least, I should have asked her. If I'd have known I would have done things differently.*

Despite her avoidance of their eyes, she orbited them, opening and closing her mouth into a tight line.

"Did you want to ask me something, Rayne?" Hawthorne asked, settling on the kitchen island.

"No. Well, I mean, kind of."

"Alright."

"Last night. You were... bossy."

"And this is news?" they asked, hoping to pull a smile from her.

She fought it, her eyes flashing down to the coffee mug between her slender hands. "Well, no. But it felt different."

"Good different?"

"Obviously." She blushed.

"Not obviously. Answer the question, I need to hear you say it."

"Yes, I liked it. A lot. I felt... softer, freer, I guess?"

"And would you like for us to do it again?" Hawthorne pressed, leaning closer to her.

"Yes." Came her immediate response, and Hawthorne chuckled, pressing a kiss to her temple.

"Then does it matter why you enjoyed it? Allow yourself if you want something. Because I am more than happy to give."

She pulled back, not away but enough that she could finally look in their eyes. "Just like that?"

"Just like that. For as long as you'd like it. I enjoy the things that happen between us very much, Rayne. If that changes, I will tell you."

"And if I want to stop?"

"Then we stop." Hawthorne shrugged. Rayne was a frightened animal in many ways and though they'd never sought to comfort something smaller than themself, they were beginning to understand that she needed to talk through the fears and voices that picked at her like birds of prey.

"What if I struggle to say it or I don't know how to ask?"

"Well, why don't we find a word that you can use to tell me when you'd like to stop?" Hawthorne offered.

"Okay. How about... Howl?"

Hawthorne smiled and smoothed a bit of her hair from her face, unable to keep from touching her, magnetized to her. "Howl it is then, Rayne," they purred.

"And if I can't say it?"

You are much stronger than you believe, little wolf. Hawthorne took her hand and brought it to their shoulder. "Then you touch my shoulder like this and you tap twice and I'll know that you'd like to stop. How does that sound?"

Rayne practiced, tapping her fingers twice against their shoulder. "Okay."

"You're pouting," Rayne teased as she dragged the final trash bag of her parents' items.

Hawthorne sat at the top of the stairs, curled like a cat at the base of the banister, glowering down at her. "I am not pouting."

She laughed and it was almost enough to bury their displeasure. "You absolutely are. I will only be gone for twenty minutes, max."

Instead of throwing away all of the garbage that her parents filled their home with, Rayne was set on driving into town and donating it. *I do not know why anyone would want anything owned by those bastards but she seems set on the idea.*

"You could come with me if you wanted to," Rayne continued, sitting at the bottom stair and slipping her thick thigh highs over her tights along with her slick gloves. Despite their irritation at her constant covering of her hands, there was something comforting in watching her fold into her fabric armor. "Or if you'd really rather stay here with House you could always rest in the basement. Plenty dark and damp down there for you, you great bat."

"Absolutely not," the House bristled. ***"I'll let them nowhere near the root of me."***

"I will accompany you," Hawthorne said, stretching. "You are much better company than this collection of brick and wood anyday."

Rayne blushed, her almond skin flushed pink. *I love when her skin does that.*

"Come on," she said, clearing her throat. "The sooner we get there, the sooner we can leave."

Rayne allowed Hawthorne to choose the music while she drove them into town, although they only ever wanted to listen to the same band. Hawthorne fixated on her, watching her from the corner of their gaze. They watched the way her hair fell over her shoulders, her curls falling out of her messy braid, framing her face. The fullness of her lips, the light scarring on her brow and along her jaw.

How could I ever want to look at anything else?

Hawthorne was so engrossed in her that they hardly noticed when she pulled into the parking lot of the duplex downtown.

"Okay," she said, parking the car. "There's a Goodwill store in here so all I'm going to do is drag these bags in the drop off in there and then we can go home, alright?"

Home.

The word was an oily, wretched thing that burned harsher than bile. Home was not something Hawthorne had ever considered for themself, it was hardly something that they ever wanted.

But to share a home with her...

"Hawthorne?" Rayne asked. "Are you coming?"

"Yes. Go and I will follow."

Hawthorne allowed themself to slip back into the air, loosening the grip on themself and tangling in her hair like the breeze. Their cheek rested against her shoulder, drinking in the warmth of her body and the scent of her hair.

"Oh."

"Something wrong?" Hawthorne inquired as she came to a stop, peeking through the curtain of her curls.

"I guess the Goodwill store got combined with another store."

"Is that so surprising?"

"Nothing ever changes here. The last new store that opened up here was before I was even born."

"Perhaps change is good. Maybe—"

"Rayne Dorne!"

Rayne stumbled a step, beneath them her muscles tensed and her breath came in quiet, short bursts. The scent of her fear perfumed the air, knotting around their throat. *She's terrified. But of what?*

To her right, a man approached and Hawthorne swallowed the growl that started in their throat. Dirty blond hair and muddy brown eyes, he smirked down at Rayne as if she was a joke only he knew the punchline to. *I want to rip that smile off of his thin lips.*

"Who is that?" they muttered in her ear.

Her only response was another shuttering breath.

"Aw, come on. Don't tell me that you've forgotten after all this time," he continued and Rayne took a step back, a slight tremble to her step. "Len? Len Kappler?"

"I know who you are," she said without any of her usual fire. "I've got to go."

"You can spare a few minutes for a *friend*, can't you?" The way that the word fell from his lips paired with the clenching of Rayne's fist in response did nothing to indicate any truth to the sentiment. "My brother told me he sees you at the store all the time. Can't say I've seen you at church and my Ma is real sad you didn't at least come by so say hello."

Rayne didn't apologize nor did she look at Len. "I've been busy."

"Yeah. Sorry about your folks. Still. Ain't right for you to just lock yourself up in that old house like some recluse."

"I'm not staying here. I'll be gone soon."

Len scoffed. "Too good for this town, huh? Listen to you, tryna sound like some city girl when you grew up in these same weeds like the rest of us."

"I need to go," Rayne said, her voice even smaller than it had been before. Fury had been building beneath Hawthorne's barely there skin but it crested at the sight of Len reaching out for Rayne's hand, grabbing her as if she were some low hanging fruit.

"Jesus, take a joke, will ya? Always so up tight and weird. I'm tryna be friendly and you're making it real damn difficult."

Hawthorne heard her before they saw her, the door to the store in front of them swung open and that orange haired woman that Rayne had been spending time with stepped out. Her bright eyes narrowed at the sight of Len and then fixated on Rayne.

"There you are, Ray!" She beamed, waving at Rayne. The tension in her shoulders dropped, but only slightly.

What was her name again? Tangerine? Or was it Clementine?

Len's pointed attention turned from Rayne to her. "Hey, Persimmon. Didn't expect to see you off the mountain this early."

Persimmon stood close to Rayne, gently knocking her shoulder into her and flashing her a tiny smile. It seemed that she was placing herself between Rayne and Len. "Rayne and I were going to hang out," Persimmon said before raising a brow at Len. "Unless you wanted to spend some girl time with us?"

Len sneered.

I like this woman, Hawthorne thought.

"I've got to get back to the station anyway," he murmured, eyes roving over Rayne once more. "See you around, *Ray.*"

Hawthorne inhaled Len's scent; cheap soap, motor oil, and wintergreen toothpaste. *Now, I've caught wind of you, I will find you again, Len Kappler.*

Once he was gone, Persimmon turned to Rayne. "You okay?"

Rayne swallowed, nodding at Persimmon and they nuzzled against her, reminding her that they were still there.

"Don't mind Len. He's a fucking asshole."

"Don't I know it," Rayne whispered under her breath and then, louder to Persimmon. "Is he a cop now?"

"Nah. Firefighter. He's friends with a bunch of 'em though. I hope I've never got to deal with any kind of fire. He's the last person I'd want saving me." Persimmon laughed. "So, what's with the bag?" she asked, nodding at the black trash bag in Rayne's hand.

"Oh. I was just trying to donate some of my parents' old stuff. I didn't realize that there was a new store here."

"*Timeless Thrift?* Yeah, it's been here for a few years. Want some help carrying things in?"

"You don't have to do that—"

Persimmon was grabbing the bag out of Rayne's grip and swinging it over her shoulder before Rayne could even finish her statement.

Hawthorne could not think of a single human that they enjoyed outside of Rayne but they liked that Persimmon seemed to notice Rayne in the way that they did.

She trailed Persimmon as she used her foot to ease open the door. Inside of the store the scent of dust and musty rose air freshener hung thick in the air, the floor was covered in thin, dark blue carpet decorated with bright shapes. The shop was filled with aisles and aisles of products yellowed with time.

Rayne walked around the store, spinning on her heels as she took in the faded paper Halloween and Christmas decorations that hang from the ceiling. She looked around and Hawthorne could only look at her. She ran her gloved fingers along the pale artificial flowers that decorated one of the aisles in the back of the store.

"I knew the Halloween decorations would get you," Persi said with a smile.

Rayne so rarely let joy grace her face and so even the ghost of it was gorgeous. "It's so... this place is great. Do you come here a lot?"

Persimmon shrugged, placing the bag down on the ground. "Yeah, a bit. But mostly for the old children's books. I like to use them in some of my mixed media pieces."

"I'd like to see some next time I come over," Rayne said. "If that's alright?"

"That's more than okay, Ray. I'll be right back, I'm going to see if there's anything new since last time I was in."

The books that sat on the shelves were coated in a thick layer of dust and the edges of the page were so yellow that they were nearly golden. She laughed a little to herself, casting a glance up at the buzzing fluorescent lights, humming like flies.

"You like this place?" Hawthorne whispered once Persimmon turned down the opposite aisle.

"Of course, I mean, look at it!" she whispered back.

"I am. *Are you?* This place looks like it's been rotting for years. Some of this dust is older than you."

"Isn't it great? I love it. This is just the sort of shop I'd want to have. I wouldn't change a thing—okay, well, I'd clean it really well. Maybe get in some more Halloween decorations, but other than that? Not a thing."

Such a strange thing she is. Still, they liked when she allowed herself to want, to crave.

"You could have this place if you so desired."

Rayne started, turning her head slightly toward them. "What? No."

"Why not?"

"I can't just steal things because I want them."

Hawthorne laughed at her naivety. It was almost endearing how little she expected from the world. "Yes, Rayne," they spoke in her ear like thunder. "You can. You wanted to make a deal, didn't you? Any desire that you have, if it is within my power then it is within your grasp. If you want this place, you can have it."

Rayne looked around at the store once more and all of its fading glory under the hideous fluorescent lights, her brow furrowing with thought. The smell of lemon and sage drifted toward them as Persimmon made her way back to Rayne.

Persimmon returned, her arms full of Halloween decorations, all of the Halloween decorations that Rayne had lovingly brushed her fingers across. Her brow furrowed and Persimmon's grin only grew wider.

"What are those?" Rayne asked.

"They're for you." Persimmon grinned.

Rayne scrunched her nose and Hawthorne was able to make out the confusion on her face. "What for?"

"I missed your birthday."

Rayne scowled. "I didn't even tell you when my birthday was. We didn't know one another in March."

"Well, now I know your birthday is in March," Persimmon said triumphantly. "We know each other now and I can buy you belated birthday presents if I want to."

"But I haven't gotten you anything," Rayne protested.

Displeasure settled. "Must you always give something back in order to receive?" Hawthorne whispered in her ear and her head turned toward them.

"I'm not stopping you from showering me with birthday presents too if you want," Persimmon teased.

"Okay. Well, I think I've officially cleaned out their books for the season," Persimmon said, nodding toward the back of the store. "Checkout counter is back here."

"Persi, you really don't have to do this—"

"I want to, Rayne. End of story."

At the checkout counter, much too far back in the store, an older woman, decked out in a pink dress littered with flamingos, sat reading a dusty romance novel. She was nearly a head shorter than Rayne and familiarity nagged at their gut. *I have seen this woman before.*

"Oh! Hello," the woman said with a smile, adjusting her thick-rimmed glasses. "I thought I heard someone come in. How can I help you, ladies?"

"Just these, please, Mrs. Modie," Persimmon said, throwing her spoils onto the counter. "And a bag if you don't mind. You can just hand it to me and I'll toss everything in myself once you've rung it up. Oh! And my friend here wanted to drop off a couple of donations."

"Oh, yes. Of course," Mrs. Modie said, adjusting her glasses to stare at Rayne.

Rayne set that polite smile onto her face that Hawthorne hated and folded her gloved hands in front of her, shrinking behind the taller woman while her heart rate picked up.

"Rayne? What's wrong?" Hawthorne pressed.

"Forgive me, but you look terribly familiar. What's your name, dearie?"

"I'm Rayne Dorne."

The woman looked at her long and hard, blinked slowly until recognition flashed in her eyes. "Rayne? Cassian's daughter with all the scars?"

You old miserable bitch. I will tear your throat and spit back your bones.

Hawthorne did not like how the other humans treated Rayne when it came to her body. They did not like the way that they looked at her as if she were contagious.

Persimmon looked between both Rayne and the woman, something heavy in her gaze that Hawthorne could not name.

Rayne inhaled. "Yes. That's me."

The woman whistled, looking her up and down. "Well, look at you. The clothing is a little... dark but I suppose that's always been your way, hasn't it? Do you remember me? I'm Mrs. Modie. Terri's mother?"

"Yes. I remember you," Rayne replied and Hawthorne hated how her voice deflated again. "This shop is nice. When did you open it up?"

"Oh, probably about a year or two after you'd left." Mrs. Modie shrugged. "How've you been, dear? How are things with the house? I'm so sorry to hear about your parents. Just terrible that both of them went at the same time. They will truly be missed around here."

"If you could hand me a bag, please?" Persimmon cut in, wedging herself between Rayne and Mrs. Modie.

Rayne shielded herself behind Persimmon, not meeting the other woman's eyes. "Things are progressing. I'm working through clearing out some of their old stuff. I actually brought some things down here to donate to Goodwill, but if you wanted them, you're more than welcome to them."

Mrs. Modie shot Rayne a look over her glasses that set anger to boil in Hawthorne's gut. "Oh. No, dearie. I appreciate the offer but who knows if that... Well, whatever it is you've got," she began gesturing at Rayne, "can transfer from your things."

Rayne's cheeks flushed and her eyes immediately fell to the stained floor. Hawthorne slipped out of her curls, their power seeping into the floor and stretching to the ceiling, the lights overhead flickering.

"Excuse me?" Persimmon hissed, snapping her head up so quickly that Rayne jumped with the motion and Hawthorne froze. "I'm sorry, but there's no way that I heard you correctly. What did you say to her about *'whatever it is she's got?'*"

"Oh," Mrs. Modie said and her gray skin flushed. "I meant no harm by it. You're rather new around here, Miss Jaxson, in comparison. Rayne and I go way back and see she's always had this—"

"I don't give a shit how long you've known her," Persimmon said, taking another step in front of Rayne. "What makes you think that you talk to her like that? And even though it's none of your damn business *'what she's got'*, don't you think if it was contagious, this whole town would have gotten it by now?"

Their attention fell back to Rayne, to the slight tremble of her knees, the way that her fingers dug into the meat of her palm.

"I think you owe her an apology," Persimmon demanded.

"Rayne?" they whispered, moving back to her side.

She shook her head and rushed out of the store, the door barely having time to close behind her. Hawthorne stared after her and then back to the wrinkled bitch fumbling over her words. *I am going to kill you, old woman.* They wanted to do it now and watch her blood seep into the floor, but the sight of Rayne retreating like some frightened mouse unsettled them more than their desire for blood.

Inhaling, they took in the old woman's scent, recognizing the fragrance of the dirt beneath her sneakers, the exact point in town where that smell congealed. *I will come for you later.*

When they came to Rayne, the trembling had overtaken her entire form and she struggled to get her key into the door of her car. They tumbled between her silken fingers and hit the asphalt, she swore as she knelt to grab them. Hawthorne's fingers swept through her hair like a breeze.

"Do not allow her words to follow you, Rayne."

She shook her head, eyes wet as she looked up at them. "It's not just her. It's—"

Hawthorne growled in irritation, melting back into nothingness at the sound of Persimmon.

"Rayne!" Persimmon called, padding after her, brown paper bag in hand. "Wait, are you okay?"

"I'm fine," Rayne managed around a sniffle, wiping at her eyes with one hand and snatching her keys from the ground with another.

"I'm sorry. I didn't mean to make a scene." Persimmon sighed, stopping a few paces away from Rayne. "She just... I can't believe she said that to you? Like it, like it was fine, normal?"

Rayne swallowed and Hawthorne waited for her to play it off, to say that it was fine.

"Can I open the door for you at least and put your stuff in there for you?" Persimmon asked.

Rayne nodded and handed it to Persimmon, looking away from her. Persi plucked the keys from her hands gently and opened the car door. She leaned in to place the brown paper bag in the back and then handed Rayne the keys.

"Is that... is that how people in town talk to you?" Persimmon continued. Rayne nodded and she then asked, "Has it been like this your entire life?"

"Always."

Persimmon sighed, shaking her head. "I get it. You wanting to leave this place, I mean. For me, a town like this is just what I need. But for you? If this is how people see you, how they think they can treat you... you should get out of here as soon as possible."

Rayne nodded and accepted the keys. "I'll, uhm, see you later. And thank you for the gifts... they were nice. This was nice."

Without another word she got in the car, Hawthorne dripping in after her, and backed out of the parking lot.

Hawthorne materialized beside her in the passenger seat. "Rayne."

"Don't!" she hissed, blinking away the searing tears. "I don't want to talk about it."

Hawthorne reached across her to brush the tears off of her cheeks and she leaned into their touch. They did not speak, allowing the silence to hold her as they could not.

"I should be used to it by now." She sniffed, stealing a glance at them.

"No, you should not. The only one who deserves your sweet tears is me." They smoothed a tear away from her cheek with their clawed finger and brought it to their lips. Their eyes locked with hers as they lapped it up. Salt sweeter than they ever could have imagined splashed against their tongue.

Delicious.

Hawthorne pretended not to notice the way that she squeezed her legs together, pretended not to smell the change in her.

"Don't try to hide from me, Rayne," they whispered in her ear. "I'll always hunt you down, sweet girl."

"I'm not sweet," she shot back.

They smirked, ready to prod at her for the rest of the day if it meant getting her to smile again. "No, you aren't, but you cum so sweetly for me."

She swore as she nearly swerved the car into the wrong lane. Hawthorne's biting laughter lit up the car in response.

Once they returned back to the house, Hawthorne turned to her. "I meant what I said. I will tear her apart for talking to you like that. It would be too easy. Then you can take her strange little space. Make it your own."

They watched her jaw and the way that it worked, her pursed lips, and her gaze flickering toward the house and back to them. "That's not how things work, Hawth. She probably has a will and a plan for what happens to the shop after she dies. I can't just take something from someone because they hurt my feelings."

"She did not just hurt your feelings, Rayne," they hissed. "And yes, you can. It would not be difficult to rid the world of her and set the necessary paperwork with your name on it if that is your concern."

Her heart gave her away, as it always did. "I don't know, Hawth."

She is lying to me again.

"Hello, House!" Rayne sang as she slid her key into the front door and stepped inside, Hawthorne a moment after carrying her groceries. If Hawthorne cared much for appearance, they might have considered how strange a sight she had to witness as she watched a seven-foot-something eldritch creature materialize to carry her gift from Persimmon for her.

The House sighed in delight. "***You were gone so long, cherub.***"

"Must we be greeted with your dramatics every time we return from the outside world?" Hawthorne asked as they slipped past her into the kitchen and plopped them down on the kitchen island.

"Why do you always pick a fight with it?" Rayne asked as she peeled off her boots. "You certainly don't make things simpler between the three of us."

Three of us? Oh, no, Rayne. There is only you and I.

"You are just as difficult, little wolf," they murmured, their lips brushing against the sensitive flesh of her ear. "You're lying to me."

"I'm not lying to you about anything," she said over her shoulder, heading into the living room to tend to House's fire. When she turned back around, Hawthorne was there.

"What do you want, Rayne?" they inquired.

"Right now I want to warm the House up."

"No need for its gaudy fire. I will keep you warm," they countered. The House hissed indignantly as the refrigerator groaned in the kitchen.

"I protect her better than you ever could!" It snapped at them. *"Can you do anything but make her colder? Shall you drag her out into the wood to die of exposure next?"*

Hawthorne unsheathed their claws and tapped them against the marble countertop, thrumming a silent threat. "House," they purred. "This is a private conversation. Why don't you go back to fretting about the snow?"

The House shivered at the thinly veiled threat but responded all the same with a creaking in the wood of the top stair. *"Why don't I just have a private conversation in between your rib cages then? Ah, yes. You have none, you spectre."*

Hawthorne disappeared in a cloud of thick mist and appeared at the fireplace beside Rayne. "Show me your heart, wretch, since you speak so bravely?" they snarled. "Is it this fireplace? Shall I rip out the bricks and see if you can bleed?" They dragged their claws down the fixture of the fireplace's mantle and dug a claw into one of the bricks, working to begin ripping it out.

"I'll bleed before you do, wraith! What is there of you but branches and dust?"

"We'll see just how much you have to say after I find your beating heart and peel it apart layer by layer. I'll make you watch."

"I told you that they were a brute, Rayne! How does it feel to live with a bull in a china shop?" The House whined miserably.

"Hawthorne, please," Rayne sighed, rubbing the bridge of her nose.

Hawthorne growled low and ,in that same cloud of smoke returned to her, kneeling in front of her. "Tell me what you want, Rayne," they demanded again.

"I—I just want to warm up," she said again despite her wide eyes.

"Stop lying to me." Frustration crested.

"I'm not lying to you!" she shot back. "Why does this matter to you so much?"

A dozen answers flooded their minds, and they realized too quickly that they could give her none of them.

"Just tell me, Rayne."

"Can you taste the deception, dear one?" The House asked, laughing. *"Just as bitter as crab apples."*

"Shut up, House!" Rayne exclaimed. "Just—just let us speak privately, please!"

The House sighed and slunk away without really going anywhere at all.

"You're so stubborn," she whispered, and Hawthorne could feel her resolve giving way.

"No more stubborn than you," Hawthorne countered, a hand slinking to her waist.

"Wanting is weakness," she answered as they gathered her against them.

"Not with me," Hawthorne chuckled into her hair, washing, bathing themself in her scent. "You can want all you like. But you have to tell me, little wolf. Why is that so hard for you? Am I so frightening?" they asked, nudging her playfully.

She rewarded them with a small huff of laughter. "Yes and no." Moisture streaked her cheeks and she drew her hand to her face to wipe it away. They frowned. *When did that happen?*

"Tell me what you wanted today." Hawthorne pressed, their voice softening.

"I wanted that shop," Rayne admitted finally, with a shaky breath. "I wanted to wring that old bitch's neck. I wanted to rip out both of her eyes so she could never look at me like that again." Hawthorne's hand stroked up and down her back idly as if she was just venting about a bad day as opposed to confessing to the desire for homicide.

There's my girl. I knew you were not as delicate as they made you out to be.

"And I want you to fuck me so I don't have to think about today. I want you to take me apart so I don't have to remember that I look like this. I don't want to be Rayne Dorne for at least a little while. That's what I want, Hawth," she confessed against their misty flesh.

Hawthorne blinked and tilted their head down to search her face. While they were still learning how to read her face, they were beginning to understand what discomfort and pain looked like on her. They saw none of it on her now.

They pressed their lips against her forehead. "Done."

Hawthorne lifted her and carried her over to the couch and pressed her into the cushions. The floor would offer too much friction against her skin and they refused to hurt her.

They nipped lightly at her lip and chuckled again at her responding moan. She wrapped her legs around their waist.

"Ah, ah. Not this way, little wolf."

They pressed a kiss to her shoulder as they set some space between them, their claw disappeared and their finger sought her entrance through her sheer black tights. The material split, parting easily for them. They growled in approval when they found her wet and ready for them. "You're perfect," they whispered

"You keep destroying all of my tights," She pouted. "These aren't cheap, you know."

"Then don't wear them when you're begging me to fuck you. I'll buy you a new pair if you're so upset."

"Buy?" Rayne asked, sitting up. "With money?"

She is dreadfully adorable. They laughed, slicing down her tights and through her panties. "Would you prefer I use livestock?" They laughed as she bucked against them in response, trying to kick their chest but they held her fast. "You've got such a bite to you, little wolf."

They punctuated the statement by slipping a finger inside her warmth. Rayne nearly melted into the cushions as she relaxed back into the couch, her head falling back. "But all it takes is one finger in that hungry little cunt and you go soft."

"Don't tease me," she hissed before she let out a little yelp as they swatted at her bare ass.

"You're mine, and I'm going to take care of you exactly how you need but not until you beg for it. Now, watch that pretty little mouth, hm?"

Rayne moaned as they carefully worked a second finger into her and she swore. Hawthorne was half convinced she was going to liquify and seep into the couch.

"Not yet, beautiful," they said into her ear. "I meant what I said when I told you that you weren't ready for that yet. We're going to work up to it."

She whined and they raked a claw up the back of her thigh, eliciting a shiver from her. *Gods, she's so responsive.* "I know, I know." They pressed a kiss to her ear and then a second to her temple. "You'll like this though, I promise."

Their fingers moved from her cunt to grasp both of her wrists and clamp them together over her head, firmly but as always, not enough to cause her any discomfort.

This was not something that they had ever done with anyone else before. There was no one that they had ever wanted to expose this part of themself with. But Rayne? They longed for her to know every inch of them, for her to see the entirety of them without looking away.

Hawthorne had never concerned themself with what they were or were not. In their time in different places, they had been seen as a god. Humans had gifted them offerings of blood and flesh, the occasional hymn around the shape of the names that they'd been given. They took many forms, spilling into whatever they wanted to be.

It was this gift that allowed their shadows to take the shape of tendrils, pouring out of their shoulders and abdomen. Two of them wrapped around Rayne's ankles and a third braced itself at her entrance. She tensed and instantly Hawthorne's hand was at her hip, caressing the faint scars there. "It's alright," they assured her. "I'll go slow and we'll stop if you want. Do you trust me?"

She nodded and they tsked. "I need to hear you say it."

"Yes, I trust you."

"There's my girl."

There it was again. There was tenderness to it that set their teeth on edge. *Why do I feel so much when I look at her?*

They chose instead to focus on the sweet warmth of Rayne's center and the sweet music of her pleasure. Hawthorne could feel the ghost of sensations from inside of her. She let out another desperate moan as they worked another inch deeper into her.

Rayne pushed back onto it, her hips rolling and Hawthorne chuckled. "I told you that you'd like it. And you do, don't you?"

"I love it," she moaned and Hawthorne let out a pleased growl against the shell of her ear, nipping at her lobe.

"Would you like for me to actually fuck you now?" they asked.

"W-what? Were you not doing that before?"

"Not at all, gorgeous. Just letting you get used to it. You said you wanted me to pull you apart, didn't you? You're much too composed to suit my idea of shattered."

They paused, waiting for her to back out, to signal that this was too much for her to handle.

She didn't.

Hawthorne chuckled, patting her ass a bit. "So stubborn. Open your mouth then, we can't have you disturbing the neighbors and upsetting your *precious* House, can we?"

Hawthorne did not know or understand envy but they did know that they did not like how protective she was of House and how much she seemed to enjoy its attention.

I want her to enjoy me like that. No more.

Like the perfect girl that she was, she opened her mouth for them and a tendril slid between her lips. Her eyes widened in surprise and her core clenched around their tendril, pulling a groan from them both.

Hawthorne's second appendage pulled out and pushed all the way back inside of her.

"Oh, fuck, Hawthorne!" she whimpered around them. They pulled out of her again and then all the way back in with much more force, another of their tendrils locked around her slim waist, keeping her in place.

Rayne arched with each thrust meeting them exactly where they were. The image of her riding them, taking what she wanted from them, their blood coating her full lips and that fire in her eyes flashed in their mind, and a pleased shudder ripped through them.

I would give anything to see her like that.

Hawthorne adjusted her position, moving so that her ankles were up around their shoulders. She whimpered and her thighs quivered. *Fuck.* "Coming already, gorgeous?" They slid the tendril out of her mouth and it moved to her clit. "Are you going to say my name again?"

She gritted her teeth, nearly white-knuckling the cushions behind her. "Ask me nicely."

They laughed and their attack on her reached a fever pitch as their tendrils filled her completely. She was nearly sobbing when her orgasm tore through her and their name flew off of her tongue.

I will never get over the sight of her like this.

She sagged against the couch and Hawthorne tugged her into their lap, folding her into their embrace. *She fits so perfectly,* they thought, feathering gentle kisses against her temple and forehead.

Like she belongs.

CHAPTER TWENTY-TWO
rayne

S unlight woke Rayne, bathing her eyelids in light until she could bear it no longer. She groaned and rolled over, away from the light. The familiar material of her bedsheets greeted her, but not the scent of pine and moist earth as she expected. The realization roused her fully. Rayne blinked as her vision refocused and glanced around her room.

I must have fallen asleep on Hawthorne last night while we were on the couch. I guess they carried me to bed and then left.

Hawthorne was not a man, they had made that very clear, and they had also made their need for freedom just as clear. They would not be kept and she liked it. She liked knowing that they were still themself and that she had not set some change within them like toppled dominos.

Though she wished that she could have awoken to a note telling her when they would return, she was content. They cared for her and that was more than she had ever expected to have.

"Good morning, my light!" The House sang to her, the windchimes on the back porch shuddering happily under the late morning sun. *"Come light my fireplace, boil some tea on my stoves, and cook in my oven. Warm me with your presence or are you simply going back to bed?*

While all of that sounded lovely, the idea of leaving her warm bed, with the faintest scent of Hawthorne soaking the sheets and into the chill of the rest of her home, felt herculean. "Back to bed, House. I'll read with you in front of the fireplace later." She yawned, pulling the sheets over her head.

Pain sudden and sharp bit at her legs, and she swore. Rayne pulled back the sheets, looked down at her legs and sighed. It didn't matter that Hawthorne had been so gentle with her, the skin on her hips was pink and swollen, the beginnings of a blister on the edges of each. The friction of her writhing paired with that of Hawthorne's movements and the rough fabric of the couch had been a recipe for disaster.

Time to piece yourself back together.

At her bedside dresser sat her black bag, flowers printed on the outside. She tucked it under her arm, grabbed a pillow, and made her way to the bathroom.

There was nothing Rayne hated more than having to deal with her body and its limitations in the morning. She imagined that others her age were settling into routines, finding their flow when it came to their days. She had been awarded no such luck. Whatever cosmic power had decided to curse her with the disease that wracked her skin had not seen fit to allow her any sense of normalcy. Somedays, when things were good, she woke up next to normal. Rayne could simply roll out of bed and begin her day.

But most days she woke aching, some wound needing to be tended to before she showered. And then the long and painful process that came after.

By the time her day was ready to actually start, she was exhausted from what her body required of her.

She had always envied people that could just roll out of bed and start their days, jump in the shower without a thought. They didn't have to access any damage that had been done, they didn't have to take painkillers on particularly bad days just to be able to tolerate the water hitting their skin.

Rayne pushed the bathroom door open, flicked the light on, snapped the toilet lid down and placed the pillow on top of it. *Please let this just be quick.*

But as she accessed her skin in the light, she realized that they were worse than she'd thought.

Hot, angry tears slid down her cheeks as she ripped open her bag and began picking apart her medical kit.

Bandages, antibacterial sprays, over the counter painkillers, gauze and a dozen other things that kept her body functioning. Things that she couldn't afford to leave home without.

What good are you? she hissed, her thoughts mimicking the barbed tone of her mother. *What can you do other than bleed?*

Rayne swatted away at the tears that burned her eyes, staining her vision. She sprayed the cleansing solution on the tender, raised skin, dabbing it dry after a few seconds to ensure that the surrounding area was clean before she could get to work. She sprayed her hands next, giving them a few moments to dry before she reached for one of the sterile needles she kept. If she did not pop the blisters, they would take weeks to heal, paining her the entire time.

Rayne tore into the package and with practiced hands, drove the needle into her the edge of the blistered skin. As blood and liquid seeped out, she pressed a clean piece of gauze to catch it, a soft intake of breath at the sting.

Breathe, she reminded herself. *You've felt worse. This is next to nothing.*

Rayne sprayed more of the anti-bacterial solution onto her skin, hissing as the open flesh of the blister bubbled. After a few more moments, she applied antibiotic ointment to a thick white dressing pad, pressed it to her hip and carefully began the process of wrapping the gauze around her waist to keep the pad in place.

Okay. One down. One more to go.

She repeated the same arduous process on the other side of her hip and before she knew it, an hour had passed. Years of practice had quickened her hands and she could dress most wounds in an hour or less. But it was not the time that drained her, it was what she didn't have.

Rayne didn't have a body that could easily be touched, and it stung to think that Hawthorne's gentleness had been wasted on her. They had taken every precaution and it still wasn't enough. *She still wasn't good enough.*

Hawthorne had given her everything, and yet her treacherous body still had the audacity to blister and split, to bleed?

Who am I to think that someone would want to be a part of this? That someone could stomach being with a body no more durable than tissue paper? Why would Hawthorne want any part of this?

Memories that she could not swallow down hit her all at once; every nasty look that she'd ever received while she had been out, every whisper, every icy word from her peers. They'd all been right, hadn't they?

"Rayne?" Hawthorne called softly from the other side of the door, shaking her from the grips of her sorrow and dragging her head first into another.

Her shoulders tensed, knotting together as she tried to fold in on herself.

"I can hear you crying. What is wrong?" they pressed.

"Nothing, just... leave, please," she managed, burying her head in her hands.

"Why would I leave you when you are distressed like this?"

"Because I asked you to. I just—I don't want to talk about this. Can you leave?"

"I am not going to leave you, Rayne," Hawthorne said, and the statement pressed somewhere delicate within her, somewhere between her ribs. "I can open this door by force but I would rather you opened it for me and told me what has distressed you so."

"I—" Her breath splintered, the words tangling in her throat. "I don't know how."

They're going to yell. They're going to tell me how foolish I am for not knowing the language of my own emotions.

"Alright. I will ask you questions and you will answer them. Can we agree to this?"

What? "I guess, yeah. I—we could try that."

"Are you in physical pain?"

"No. Not anymore."

"Did something occur while you were in the bathroom?"

"No, not really."

"So, you are simply feeling bad, yes?"

Shame heated her cheeks. "I—yeah, yeah. I guess that's true."

"I see. Well, there is no need for you to do it alone since I am here now. If you are resolved to feel poorly then you might as well do so at my side. May I come in now? Or would you prefer to come out here?"

There was something so simple, so easy in the way that they spoke to her. Hawthorne did not complicate situations, always they cut to the root of the thing. It was the closest thing to safety that she'd ever felt.

When she opened the door and stepped out into her room, Hawthorne had almost materialized fully, if she squinted she could see the other side of the room through their shadowy body.

They halved themself, leaning down to kiss the top of her head. "There, see? Now, your misery has a companion. That is the human saying, is it not?"

Rayne laughed, wiping at the remnants of her tears, blinking up at them.

"Yeah, that's the saying, Hawthorne."

When the phone rang late that day, Rayne almost didn't answer it. She and Hawthorne had been sitting across from one another on the kitchen island as she taught them how to play Mancala. She'd fished the game out from under her bed and though she should have been focusing on clearing out her old things, Hawthorne was such an entertaining distraction.

And if she was honest with herself, if she allowed herself a moment of self reflection, she knew that it was greed that motivated her. December was nearly over and her time here in Bury was numbered. She would be here for another few weeks and she wanted to soak in every moment with Hawthorne that she could.

So when she hopped off of the counter and picked up the phone, Rayne was surprised to hear Persimmon's voice on the other end.

"Hey, Rayne," the other woman chirped cheerfully. "I was going to stop by but then I figured you would have preferred me calling instead."

Yeah, now that you mention it. "Uh, yeah. What's up?"

"I wanted to talk to you about yesterday," Persimmon sighed. "I haven't been able to stop thinking about how that woman felt comfortable speaking to you. And you said it's been like this for as long as you can remember, right?"

Rayne began chewing on her lower lip. "Yeah, basically."

"Yeah, that's fucked. I want to help you. I don't want to make you wait any longer to get out of this place. So, let's do it. We've got a few days before Christmas and everyone officially starts to slack off. If we hurry up and push through, I can buy the house from you immediately."

From the corner of her eye, Rayne caught the way that Hawthorne stilled on the kitchen counter.

"Immediately?" Rayne asked.

"Yeah. I mean, since we're both pretty much agreed on everything already, we can push the sale through in a week at the bare minimum and three max. Either way, you could be out of here completely by the middle of January."

Rayne's mouth opened and closed, searching for the words that should have been on the edge of her tongue.

"Rayne, you still there?"

"Yes! Yeah, uhm, yeah, okay," Rayne stammered finally, shaking her head. "Let's do that. Uh, did you, like have a date in mind or—"

"How about tomorrow?"

Rayne winced. "Tomorrow."

"Yeah. Does that work for you?"

Her nails found their way into her mouth, a recurring habit from her youth that she could never fully predict. "Tomorrow is... perfect."

Persimmon sighed in relief on the other end of the line. "Okay, great. We can make a night of it. I'll get some more dandelion wine for us."

"Okay," Rayne said, glancing over her shoulder at Hawthorne only to find the kitchen empty. "Okay, yeah. That sounds good."

Hanging up felt like the closing of some great door that she hadn't realized had been hanging open for her.

Rayne was unaccustomed to this feeling although it rode on the back of a familiar sense of shame. She had grown up knowing that something about her was incorrect. She was accustomed to this knowledge, made friends with it and allowed it to rule her life. And yet this current feeling hissing through her veins was something foreign to her.

The House remained perfectly silent, though she could still feel the slight shifting in the walls, like its lungs were expanding and contracting; breathing.

Hawthorne sat in front of the fireplace, their back to her as the fire roared.

"It's done then," they stated, their voice softer than she had ever heard it. "You are leaving sooner than you said?"

Rayne swallowed the dagger in her throat. "Yes. I have to, Hawthorne. You don't understand."

"I understand you, Rayne," Hawthorne said, the flashes visible through their skin. "Shall we say our goodbyes now?"

"No," came her immediate response. "Not yet, please?"

Hawthorne nodded, but still their back remained turned to her, like they were too disgusted with her to even dare to spare her a glance.

But that's more than fair of them, isn't it?

The silence between she and Hawthorne was foreign to her, so unlike the comfortable quiet that often bloomed between them.

"So, what now?" she asked lamely by way of avoiding what she assumed had begun festering within their shadowy body. *They're angry with me. They are going to hate me now.*

"I would ask something of you, Rayne Dorne," Hawthorne began over the crackling of the fire. She shivered at the use of her full name, every time they said it, it felt as if the very marrow in her bones was singing their name.

"Anything."

They shook their head, a dark chuckle rippling through them. "So enthusiastic in offering yourself. You have no idea of which I'm asking of you."

"Ask me then." *Please.*

"Three days from now, the darkest day of the year will take place: The Winter Solstice. I would—spend that day with you, if you would allow it. It is the one day a year when I am flesh and bone and I—"

"What!" Rayne nearly shouted. "Flesh and bone, like, *a body*? You have a body?"

Hawthorne turned to her then, their eyes catching the light of the fire behind them, glowing like embers. "Yes, I have a body, but only for those twenty four hours. After that, I go back to myself as I am now."

Rayne's mind struggled to keep up with the knowledge Hawthorne had just so casually dropped upon her. *They have a body. They can be physically, fully here. With me.* "How?"

Hawthorne shrugged, sitting back onto their palms. "I do not know. Perhaps it is the day that I was created or maybe The Sleeping King simply thought that it would be interesting to do such a thing on that day. All I know is that when I crawl out from under my tree, I am as human as you. At least, in appearance."

"The Sleeping King?" Rayne inquired. "Who is that?"

Hawthorne only smiled in that strange manner of theirs, their wide jaw always looking so unnatural when they did. "Will you spend that day with me, Rayne? Come to my tree and find me?"

You will not distract me, you great beast. I will know who this King is eventually. "Yes. I will come to your tree and spend that day with you," she said. "And, I would ask something of you now."

Hawthorne raised a brow. "Ask it."

Her eyes cast down as a wave of shyness washed over her. "I—last night was great. I really, really enjoyed it and I want to do it again. But," Rayne swallowed, wringing her hands in front of her, "I got hurt. My skin is just... difficult. I was wondering if we could try again but if you could visit me in my dreams again like you did before? In my dreams, I don't hurt and it's easier. And I—I want you."

Rayne did not have the soft feminine language that she imagined other women had. She did not know how to entice or speak delicately. It was abrasive but she knew no other way to communicate the thoughts within her head or the fire in her blood.

"Rayne," Hawthorne called. "Come here."

She did not remember moving to them but suddenly she was at their side, folded against them. She closed her eyes and allowed the scent of rain, damp earth, and pine to envelope her.

"I will always find you," they whispered in her ear. "When you close your eyes, I will be there."

She was pulled into her dream, like a weed uprooted. She was solid, grounded in her reality one moment and the next, stumbling through a world that rippled. Around her the walls of a house that mirrored her own, but wrong. The ceiling was too high, the hallway too narrow and the light too fleeting.

Though she could not see them, Rayne sensed Hawthorne moving in the shadows, spilling down the opposite end of the hallway. Outside of her awareness of them, she could not feel much of anything. No dull ache, no sting of fabric against a fresh scar, nerve endings singing to life.

Finally.

"I want to hear you say it," Hawthorne demanded, their voice taking on that rough lilt that it had when she first met them in her dreams before.

"Say what?"

"You asked for me to create a dream for you. So, mold it."

The usual nausea that accompanied being asked such a direct question did not come or perhaps here, in this small container of her mind Hawthorne had chased it away.

What do I ask them for?

"Can I... see you? What you really look like when you're not trying to fit inside of houses or stand like a human? I know that it's not you."

Every wall leaned closer, echoing with their laughter. Two torches flickered to life at the end of the hallway and in the dull amber light of them, she recognized the door from her home. *That door.*

Moonlight, sudden and silver, filtered in through the windows, illuminating the Hawthorne shaped mass writhing on the carpet until she watched it separate into something she did not recognize. Flesh gave way to fur matted with bramble and roots, limbs snapped and contorted until Hawthorne was on all fours. Their jaw elongated, snapped open and hung low, tongue lulling over needle sharp, canine teeth.

Like a wolf. Or maybe a coyote?

Rayne gasped when they took a step toward her, almost retreating. *No, I asked for this. I will see them as they are.* "Is—" She cleared her throat. "Is this you, the real you, I mean?"

They smiled—a terrible thing that split their entire face, showing her the dark path down their throat. "Are you frightened of me?" they asked. In their time together, she had begun to understand just a few of the many nuances to their voice, their tone. *They love that I'm scared of them.*

Irritated at the thought being their entertainment, she jutted her chin out. "I'm not scared of you," she lied, glaring into their searing eyes. "You couldn't scare me if you tried."

In response their eyes went white, empty as a shark's. Rayne stumbled backwards until her spine cracked against the wall. Hawthorne cornered her, their breath hot against her forehead and sweet with rot and dirt.

Hawthorne laughed and the shadows melted into something that was no longer human. "I thought you were not afraid?" Their tongue slid along her shoulder. "Why can you never remain as brave in the dark?"

Something was tainting her fear, intermingling in the nest of nerves at the base of her spine. She was scared of Hawthorne, yes, but that unnamed thing ran deeper. Rayne's dark eyes met their pale ones, caught on their fur, their ears, the large, flickering tail behind them. *I want to stay here.*

The truth was a hideous thing and Rayne hated how it had snuck up on her. *I want them. Not just like before or even like this but everything, in every ugly way.* It did not matter that they were most likely some demonic abomination from Hell or that they reveled in murder and terror. *They might be the best friend I've ever had. They might be the only person in this world that knows me, that wants to.*

Briefly Persimmon flashed in her mind; gorgeous, grinning and dripping in sunlight. *We aren't friends. She wouldn't want to be friends with someone like me, she's just... kind.*

"Trying to slip away from me again?" Hawthorne breathed. "Then do it properly."

"What?"

"I will even give you a head start. Now, *run*."

Rayne ducked under Hawthorne, making a dash for the stairs. She scrambled down the hall, her hands on either side of her to brace against the walls as she ran. It was not until the moment that her foot hit the top stair that Hawthorne moved, like an avalanche tumbling toward her.

Even though it was a dream, even though her body was not truly hers here, she could remember the sensation of a hammering heart, of lungs that couldn't snag enough oxygen even if they tried. Their breath tickled the back of her neck and shoulders. *Fuck the stairs.*

Rayne climbed over the banister and leapt down into the foyer. The ghost of discomfort sang in her knees with her landing though she felt nothing. She scrambled to her feet and raced into the kitchen. Behind her, Hawthorne's nails scratched against the marble floor and they hit the ground after her.

Can't hide. They're too close.

The downstairs hallway was narrower than the one upstairs and the rug too small and old to be safe. Her boot slipped, catching on a fraying end and pulling her down. She moved quickly to her knees and reached for the knob of the basement door only to be ripped away.

Hawthorne's jaw clamped around her ankle and she shrieked at the phantom pain.

"Aw," Hawthorne purred, shifting before her eyes into some strange mix of the way she was used to seeing them and their true self. A humanoid animal with human eyes and the mouth of a wolf. She attempted to roll on to her side to get back to her feet but Hawthorne held her in place with the contorted mass of their hands; caught somewhere between paws and the daggers of their claws. "You did not stand much of a chance, did you? You could not even make it out of the house."

Rayne kicked at their chest, jamming her heel into their collarbone as hard as she could. Their resulting smile dripped straight into her core. "Let's try it again, then. See how far I get."

"No," Hawthorne crooned, parting her legs and sliding between them. "I quite like where I have you now."

Rayne's world narrowed to the friction of their hands falling to her hips, the back of her knees as they situated her where they wanted. Their tendrils, which in the waking world were cool and misty, were rough, warm, vines that tangled in her hair and around her wrists. She arched into them and they chuckled against her neck, licking the soft skin with that long tongue of theirs.

"I think you like this quite a bit too, don't you?"

It's just a dream. Shouldn't I be allowed to speak openly? To want dreadfully?

"I want more. You can't hurt me here and I—"

Hawthorne leaned back enough to meet her gaze. "You want it to hurt? No, you want *me* to hurt you?"

Rayne nodded but then remembered their preference for her voicing her desires. "Yes. If I were an animal, something you'd caught between your claws." *I will never be strong. I will never be more than a moth burning in an open flame. I want to know what it's like to lose a fair game.*

"I would pick you apart, piece by piece," Hawthorne said, holding her attention as they dug a claw deep into the flesh of her thigh. Blood spilled down her leg, her skin giving way to them. They dipped their finger in her blood, tonguing it off of the edge of their claw. "I would taste you, savoring every drop of your sweet blood. Not even the dirt would get a sip of you. You'd be all mine."

Sick, saccharine pleasure rumbled through her, their words alone weaving a spell of hunger. Rayne bucked her hips against theirs, grinding as she desperately searched for friction.

Hawthorne tsked, smirking. "You asked to be trapped under me and now you're trying to escape."

"Hawthorne," she whined. "Please."

They adjusted so that their thigh was settled against her. "I'm going to take my time with you, but if you must, then chase your pleasure, you greedy thing."

Rayne was past the point of shame here and ground her cunt against the bulk of their leg.

"After I've had every ounce of your blood, I would want to see under that pretty skin."

Hawthorne continued and their hand moved to slice her sternum open, then sticky with blood, they cupped her chin and tilted it down. Her hips kept moving even as she was drenched in her own blood and she could see the pink, squelching flesh of her stomach. Rayne's moans molded into a howl of pleasure as Hawthorne sunk their hand into her chest at the same moment they tore through her clothes and entered her soaked cunt.

Rayne could feel the fingers in her chest tearing and parting muscles and sinew. "Look at you," Hawthorne marveled, tender and hungry. *Eat me. Find the pearl of me and shuck it out.*

As if they'd heard her, Hawthorne's hand brushed against the inside of her ribcage and finally latched onto her heart. "You wretched, *gorgeous* thing," Hawthorne managed, their voice hindering on something that teetered on the edge of reverent and angry. "Begging to be torn apart, so close to cumming while bleeding for me, howling for more like some wolf baying at the moon."

They kissed her, tongue, teeth and all but it wasn't enough. She needed more. Rayne bit their lip, willing her desires into the feel of her teeth in their flesh.

Hawthorne groaned and roots spilled from their arms, locking around her throat and squeezing the breath out of her. Another finger accompanied the one between her legs, soaring to a fever pitch as Hawthorne worked to rip her orgasm out of her. Rayne's eyes rolled back, and through her blurry vision, she was able to make out Hawthorne with a clotted, red mass of tissue in their palm.

Her heart.

They bit into it at the exact moment that her orgasm shattered her into a million pieces.

CHAPTER TWENTY-THREE
hawthorne

Hawthorne wretched themself out of her dream as a blood fat tick. As always, the world was a smudged, blurred thing in those first few moments outside of a mind, and they blinked until they righted itself. Rayne was still tangled in their arms, her cheek pressed hard against their sternum and her arms squeezing around them. Every few moments her breath would hit their skin in a deep, slow exhale. They could hear the calm beating of her heart despite what they had just done in her dream.

I do not understand how one so small can hold so much. Where do you keep it all?

A soft sigh fell from Rayne's lips and her nails dug into their back. Hawthorne could not help but smile down at her, nuzzling the frizzy hair at her temple. *Trying to claw your way through me, are you? I would let you, if you asked.*

"**Are you just going to leave her asleep on the floor?**" The House fussed.

Hawthorne rolled their eyes, already drawing her closer and moving their knees to keep from jostling her. "Quiet, you fretting gnat. I was planning on taking her to bed, now be silent lest you wake her."

The House huffed, snuffing out the flame of the fireplace with an indignant hiss.

Carefully, Hawthorne carried Rayne from the living room to her bedroom, her head falling to their shoulder despite the vice grip she kept on them. It wasn't until they had peeled back the sheets of her bed and attempted to detach from her that her eyes sprung open. Her dark eyes blinked rapidly as if she could blink the sleep away and then her attention settled fully on them. "Hi."

"Hello."

"Are you—were you—"

"No, Rayne. I was not yet going to leave you, but I will have to soon. I am hungry and it will soon be winter." *Why am I explaining myself to her?* they wondered. *I have never explained myself or justified anything of mine before.*

"Okay."

"That is," they teased, "if you could pry your little claws out of me for a moment."

Except Rayne did not laugh, instead she curled tighter against them, tucking her face into the crook of their arm. "Could you maybe lay with me until I fall back asleep?" she whispered.

That fluttering of wings tickled against their insides again. They realized too late that such a joke brushed too close to the raw parts of her. If there was one thing Hawthorne refused, it was to take on the shape of anyone who had ever harmed her or to ever mirror any of those words back to her. Even in jest.

"Yes, Rayne. I will stay here with you until then," they answered, kissing her forehead. Affection was not foreign to Hawthorne, but with Rayne they couldn't help themself, the way she leaned into every touch, the odd tenderness in which she looked at them. Hawthorne did not bother trying to get her to move, instead they shifted their weight to get her in bed as gently as possible and pulled the blanket over them both after.

Warmth was a fleeting thing for Hawthorne, they felt it in pieces, in fleeting moments but they had never craved it more than when it came to Rayne.

"Hawthorne?"

"Yes?"

"What do you look like when you're human?"

They opened their mouth to answer but quickly thought better of it. *If I tell her then it could ruin everything. This might be the last chance that exists between us for her to understand. I will not risk that.* "You will have to wait and see."

Even half asleep, she scrunched her nose in displeasure. "You're really not going to tell me?"

"No, I am really not going to tell you."

She huffed before turning her face more against their chest. "Absolute asshole."

Quickly after her breath evened out and her grip on them loosened enough for them to feel comfortable slipping out of her grasp, they moved. Before they left, they found a notepad in one of the drawers down in the kitchen and scribbled a note for her.

But now, it was time for them to hunt.

Rayne was a lovely distraction, but they had not forgotten what they had intended to do. That decrepit woman from the rotting store, the smell of the fertilizer around her home was distinct, bitter, and easy enough to follow.

Bury was a different place at night whether its residents realized it or not. Hawthorne's kind roamed, seeping down from the wood to stretch their legs and seek what entertainment they could from the humans. Lesser beings avoided stepping directly into Hawthorne's path and they much preferred it that way. *I hunt alone.*

The old woman lived near the center of town, a small cottage, the yard littered with plastic light up snowmen and Santa Clauses. Hawthorne paused in her yard, tilting their head to get a better look at her decorations. The light up candy canes by her front door and cheap multicolor lights outlining the roof.

I do not mind these Christmas decorations. The lights are pleasant but I have seen much better.

Hawthorne bore no creed of their own nor were they interested in whatever the root of this holiday was, but they had a soft spot for the celebrations and the decorations it brought. In the dead of winter where the sun was scarce and warmth even more so, it was nice to see light. *Even if it is artificial.*

They swept through her yard, peering through the window inside of her house. A living room. *Dull kitchen. No, I must find her bedroom.* Hawthorne moved two windows down, toward the back of the house. *Ah. There she is.*

Tucked comfortably in her bed, buried under a knitted blanket, she slept like someone who was perfectly content with her life. It was a look Hawthorne had come to recognize in humans all too well. *Rayne has never had that look. And it is humans like you that keep her from that.*

Their claws scraped down the glass of the window. Inside the old woman started, felt around on the dresser beside her bed and hastily placed her glasses on. She flicked on the lamp and finally found them at the window. *Got you.*

Their magic spread over her like pitch, her eyes widening and reddening around the edges. "You will not scream," Hawthorne said, crooking their finger toward her. "You will get up quietly, walk outside and meet me in the backyard. You will not put on your shoes."

They watched her nod, helpless tears sliding down her cheeks. *Good.*

Hawthorne had no desire to hunt this woman. No. This was a lesson to her and to every other wretched human in this town that had made Rayne a pariah for nothing other than their own ignorance. This kill would offer no sport.

The back door of her home creaked open, the wood shifted with her first step though it never felt her second. As quickly as she had stepped outside, Hawthorne had her frail ankle between their jaw. Her skull cracked against each step as they pulled her down, dragging her into the damp grass.

Her skin split, blood bursting against their tongue and they bit down until bone crunched like ice. They spat the discarded foot out, watching as she tried to drag herself back and away from them on trembling hands. She whimpered, sobbing small and pathetic. *What a pathetic creature you are.* Their magic was still pressed just as tightly against her; she could not scream even though they imagined that she desperately wanted to.

"Know that is not some random act of violence or you being forsaken by some divine force," Hawthorne rumbled through a jaw that was no longer shaped for speech. "You were so concerned with her skin but look where that has landed you."

Hawthorne launched themself at her, catching her throat between their teeth and ripped the tough meat of her trachea, delighting in the snapping of tight muscle as they tore it out of her. *I promised you that I would tear out your throat, old woman. You and anyone else who would speak against her. I will hunt you all down one by one.*

CHAPTER TWENTY-FOUR
rayne

I have gone to hunt. I will be back
in time for the Solstice. Come to my
tree at morning's first light. I will be
waiting for you.

- H

Rayne's gloved fingers slid along the edges of the note she'd found this morning for the dozenth time. *I know they said that they were hungry, but why couldn't I have just cooked something for them?* She immediately crooked her mouth at the thought. She already knew the answer to that; she was a terrible cook and they both knew it. *But what if they never come back and this is just their way of letting me down gently? I mean, they would have looked like the worst kind of asshole if they dumped me after—well, what we did in my dream. And I don't think that they would do that to me, but then what if I'm wrong? They are some ancient monster and they have made it abundantly clear that they don't care about manners or etiquette. What if—*

"Rayne, did you hear anything that I said?" Persimmon asked with a gentle nudge of her shoulder.

Rayne jolted at the sudden touch, nearly slamming her head against the window of Persimmon's truck.

"Oh, jeez. I'm sorry, I didn't mean to scare you like that. I probably should have asked before I just—"

"It's fine. What were you saying?" Rayne interrupted, shoving Hawthorne's note back into the pocket of her hoodie.

Persimmon pursed her lips, her attention returning to the road. "I was asking if you were sure about this sale. I get that you want to get out of here and you should but I almost feel like I'm taking advantage of you here."

"You aren't," Rayne bit back, her voice sounding more aggressive than she realized. She took a deep breath and continued, softer. "I'm doing okay in life. The money is nice but I was fine before and I'll be fine after. Leaving Bury is the most important thing for me right now."

Persimmon nodded. "Okay, heard."

The rest of the drive into town passed in relative silence save for a few bits of gossip Persimmon chirped at her as they passed by certain people's houses. Today they were going to head down to the municipal office to get a list of title companies that would actually work to close on houses in Bury. It was going to be a remarkably small list, she knew. But it was one step closer to freedom.

Why don't I feel how I thought I would?

Maybe it was some kind of psychological block that kept her from getting excited about it until the deed was done? *Yeah. That makes sense, that's what it has to be.*

Outside the wind bit into her skin and Rayne pulled her hood up to protect her ears, sinking further into her hoodie and grateful for the multiple layers she had worn in anticipation for the weather. She and Persimmon rushed up the cement steps, attempting to outrun the wind but when Persimmon reached to open the door, it was locked.

"What?" she asked, pulling harder on the door handle.

Rayne's nose scrunched, pink and wind bitten. "They can't be closed. It's Wednesday."

Persimmon cupped her hands over her eyes and peered through the glass panel of the door. "I don't see any lights on in there." She sighed, flapping her arms in exasperation. "Well, what the fuck? It's not some holiday or something today is it?"

"I don't think so."

"What the hell!"

Below them, the mail truck pulled up to the curb and Jeremiah Johnson stepped out in full mailman gear, a small handful of manilla mailers in his hand. *Great. Another one of Len's asshole friends.* Jeremiah made no move to hide his distaste for her, eyeing her up and down with a sneer as he jogged up the stairs.

"J! What's the deal with this place being closed?" Persimmon asked, gesturing behind her.

"Hey, P," Jeremiah said, smiling at her as he brushed past to slip the envelopes through the door's mail slots. "Quit playin', I know you know."

Persimmon frowned. "I can assure you that I don't. What's going on?"

"Aw, come on, this ain't—oh shit. You really ain't heard?" he marveled, clutching the strap to the mail carrier bag closer. "You know Mrs. Modie up on Tanenbalm? Owns the thrift place in town? Her husband found her in their backyard this morning all torn up. Looked like some wild animal got to her. He said there wasn't much left."

Hawthorne.

Rayne froze, her hand moving to clutch Hawthorne's note in her pocket.

"Jesus," Persimmon breathed. "And they don't know what did it? A bear or something maybe?"

"That's what the sheriff said but no one knows yet. Pastor thinks it's somethin' different." Jeremiah looked over Persimmon's shoulder at Rayne. "Somethin' unnatural. He's holdin' a prayer service around eleven for her. And for all of us who might need to wash away any sins. Keep the Devil out."

"I see." If Persimmon noticed the way he was looking at her, she did nothing to indicate it.

"I'm headed that way soon as I finish my rounds. You should come with."

"Yeah, I'll see. I've got a lot to handle today but I'll see about sending over some flowers or something."

The rest of their conversation was lost on Rayne, her thoughts occupied fully by the news they'd just received. *Mrs. Modie was dead. She had been rude to me in front of them and now she's dead. They tore her apart.*

For me? No. Maybe. Even if it wasn't for me, she's dead.

Rayne bit her lip to keep from giggling. *Finally someone gets to pay for something that they've done.*

The drive back up the mountain was silent, Rayne lost in her own thoughts and Persimmon's grip tight on the steering wheel.

"Why don't you hang out at my place for a little bit?" Persimmon said suddenly. "I had originally planned on celebrating you getting to take the first step outta here. But, well, I don't want to waste the wine."

"It's 10:32 in the morning," Rayne replied, glancing at the car's clock.

Persimmon shrugged. "Gotta be 5'oclock somewhere. Plus, what's the point of being an adult if you don't get to indulge in terrible choices every once in a while?"

The smile flashed before Rayne could stop it. "Okay."

Later, the sun bled into the overcast sky, blinding and stark against winter sky. "Like bleach," Rayne remarked out loud.

"What?" Persimmon inquired, reminding Rayne that she was not in fact alone.

Rayne shook her head "Sorry, nothing." The other woman shot her a conspiratorial glance before she returned to her own glass of wine. The pair of them sat outside in Persimmon's garden, bundled in dozens of blankets as they drank. The contrast was surprisingly pleasant: a nest of warmth as a refuge against the cold.

Rayne dug her toes deeper into frigid dirt, ignoring the bite of it against her skin. She felt like a wound, a bit of flesh that had been torn into and left to bleed out, raw and vulnerable. It was this feeling, paired with the haze of liquor that yanked the confession from her. "I never thought I'd come back here," she said before swallowing another gulp of dandelion wine.

Persimmon nodded and scooted a little bit closer to Rayne without crowding her space. "But you're here."

"I'm here," Rayne sighed. "And now I am leaving again."

"We're celebrating that," Persimmon reminded her.

Rayne downed the rest of her glass unceremoniously and nodded. She should feel more lighthearted, she knew. She should stop dragging the spirit of the day down. And yet Hawthorne was the anchor that had rooted her so securely in the harbor of this town. Was it really right for her to leave them?

Fuck, she wanted more wine. It had simultaneously warmed and numbed her.

"You're getting out of this place. You can go anywhere," Persimmon pressed. "Have you thought about any places in particular?"

"No," Rayne lied. She had thought of nothing else and yet the answer always remained the same: it didn't matter where she went. The rot of her would follow until she seeped into everything. "I used to love this town," she admitted suddenly, surprising even herself.

"Really?" came Persimmon's incredulous laughter. "Rayne Dorne loving the wretched little town of Bury?"

Rayne laughed a bit at the idea. "The forest, at least. The river and the mountains where my grandmother used to live. I would have given anything to just stay there, in her cold, empty house. It still smelled of her even after she went. I used to think that maybe she was there sometimes."

She had never spoken of her grandmother to another person before, only whispered it to Hawthorne when there was no one but the stars and their stillness to hear the confession. She held onto her grandmother's memory, pressed it tightly between her ribcage for safe keeping. All this talk of her threatened to crack Rayne wide open. But what did it matter?

What had anything she endured as a child amounted to more than a pile of rubble? A haunted house and a secret she cut her teeth on?

"I didn't know you had any more family that lived in town," Persimmon replied softly. "I've never seen a house in the mountains, it must be really well hidden."

"It's gone," Rayne said, voice sharper than she had intended. "Sold and destroyed as if I wasn't still here to receive it. She'd left it for me."

"Why didn't you get it?"

"Wasn't fit for it, apparently. My mother sold the house before I was old enough to do anything with it. She didn't even tell me. I only found out when I was going through her belongings." Rayne laughed mirthlessly as if it meant nothing, as if the hate had not made a home of her. "But I can imagine her mindset: If she and my father had to work so hard their entire lives, why should I be given something for so little?"

Persimmon frowned. "But they had to have changed their mind? The House is—"

"For my brother," Rayne smiled, reaching for the bottle of wine, and realizing that it was nearly empty, brought it to her lips and gulped it down. "But he couldn't be bothered to deal with it or to see me, so I suppose it worked out for the best, didn't it?"

Her disease had given her a unique understanding of pity and how it could be used as a weapon. Rayne had learned to spot it a mile away to protect herself from whatever barbed words were going to get caught under her skin. So when Persimmon looked at her like that, Rayne knew what it was before she even spoke.

"Ray, I'm sorry—" Persimmon began.

Rayne rolled her shoulders as if to shake it from her. "It's fine. I won in the end, didn't I?" she asked without waiting for an answer. "They're dead and gone, nothing but a portion for foxes now, and my brother, a specter tangled in the wind. But I'm here and playing in the spoils of the war they'd waged."

It was funny and she laughed but Persimmon did not join her. Instead her face pinched with that sting of pity and Rayne's stomach rolled with nausea.

"I have to go." The announcement erupted so quickly from her that both she and Persimmon started, but she was already on her feet, already stumbling toward the garden gate. "Thanks for the food and the wine. I'll call you in a few days."

"Wait. I mean, we could try to go back into to town tomorrow, right? Get everything started then?"

"Ye–oh, no. Not tomorrow. I can't. I have someone... important visiting me from out of town."

Persimmon blinked. "Oh. Oh! That's great, Rayne. How about the day after then?"

"Okay. I'll see you then. Thanks for today."

"Are you sure that you're going to be okay walking home? I could come with you," Persimmon offered.

There was a part of Rayne that wanted to say yes and have some company on the brief journey back to House. But the liquor was singing in her veins, the wind was kissing the back of her neck, and despite the company Persimmon had offered her, it was not her attention that Rayne was craving.

"Nah. Thanks though. I'll call you on the landline in two days," Rayne said before she headed out.

The dirt road was as much a part of her as the scars that lined her body, a path that every version of her had walked time and time again; she could walk this path with her eyes closed, with the ground slick and muddy.

Rayne remembered the stories that she would tell herself as a child, the tales that she would weave herself into from her storybooks. She had imagined herself as a princess, the world rising to meet her with birdsong and butterflies that kissed her hair. Sometimes she was the witch, powerful and aloof, the forest closing rank behind her like a shield. And then, on days when the words of the world around her melded with the harsh critiques she received from her parents, she imagined herself as the dragon. She would see herself as serpentine, ugly and roiling like bile in the belly of the world. Everything she laid her hands on burned.

But I am none of these things now. Right now I am simply Rayne, following a thread back to the place I've always been.

"Like in Rapunzel," Rayne murmured aloud, her breath puffing out into a warm cloud before her, tickling her nose. "That Prince, his eyes bloodied and blinded from falling into a blackberry bush. He'd wandered—"

Her mind stole the rest of the sentence from her as the tale continued in her mind. The Prince, thrown from Rapunzel's tower when he'd been discovered by the witch, suddenly blinded, had spent years wandering the world. And then like magic, like a needle set to a record, he found his way back to her.

If I wander far enough, she thought, ducking between the overgrown blackberry bushes, swollen and sweet with rot. *Will I still find myself here? Back in this darkness, walking right back to this fucking house?*

I could burn it to the ground. Burn this entire forest.

Nothing can call me back if nothing remains.

By the time she wandered up her driveway and into her house, a second wind of energy had burst through her. *There's still light out. I shouldn't waste it. I should get all of this—their bullshit—out of the house.*

Gracelessly, Rayne dragged the last bits of her parents' belongings to the foyer; her mother's perfumes and all of her expensive make up and nail polish. Her father's books and sports magazines. Everything that they'd ever owned and poured it into the last of the black trash bags she'd kept under the kitchen sink.

There's no point in me waiting, right?

Rayne had gone into the garage and pulled out all of the bags that she had tried to give to Mrs. Modie. *Bet you wish you'd taken them now, you old bitch.*

"What fire has been lit under your heels, cherub?" The House yawned in the creaking of the front door as she pushed it open.

"Just in the mood to purge, House. We won't keep anything else of theirs here anymore."

Slowly, Rayne began the work of dragging each bag through the lawn and down to the edge of her property where the mailbox and her trash can sat.

Though the effort rubbed the skin of her palms raw, even through her gloves, she did not stop. Bruises were already beginning to form in the curves of her fingers, likely to blister but she didn't care. She needed to get as many of these in here as she could and what didn't fit, she would allow to spill over into the grass.

The front door of her neighbour's house opened and Rayne tensed, keeping her back turned.

"Hello, dear," Mrs. Hamper called.

"Hi," Rayne shot back through gritted teeth.

"Lotta commotion round your way, huh?"

Rayne rolled her shoulder. "Suppose so."

"You sure are throwing quite a bit of stuff away over there. Your parents' things, I'm guessing?"

"Yup."

"I don't know why you'd want to throw any of that out," the old lady said. "Sure, you may think it's worthless now, but one day you're going to look back and wish that you had all of those things. They were your *parents.*"

At this Rayne turned, tossing the last of her parents' bullshit into the trash. "Fat chance of that ever happening. I already carry their blood within me and that alone is too much," she snapped, walking back up her driveway. "But since you're so concerned about my garbage, Mrs. Hamper, you're welcome to bury yourself in it and rummage around as much as you'd like. Imagine it will feel mighty comfortable for you."

Mrs. Hamper's mouth hung wide open, outrage contorting her sagging face into something hideous.

"And, matter of fact. Why don't you mind your own damn business from now on and I'll do you the favor of the same, huh?"

As the door closed, Rayne could practically hear Hawthorne's dark, liquid smooth chuckle on the wind. "*That's my girl.*"

Rayne did not know what to do with the small kernel of pride that came with their words.

CHAPTER TWENTY-FIVE
rayne

"You are fretting, beloved,** " The House purred, heat from the vents above blanketing her. "*You've been buzzing around all morning like a hummingbird in spring. What's gotten you so flustered?*"

Rayne leaned against the sink in her bathroom, back turned and her bare hands clutching porcelain. Even with the mirror fogged from her earlier shower, she didn't want to turn around. *I can't look at myself, not yet.*

She had scrubbed herself raw, undone every tangle in her thick hair, and shaved every bit of hair off of her body. Still, it didn't feel like enough. *I don't know that I'm enough. What if when they're human I look different? What if they see me like everyone else does?*

"Come now, cherub. You cannot hide from yourself and ignore me, you must pick one insult to bear me at a time."

Rayne sighed, her face crumpling into her hands. "I don't know what's wrong with me. It's just Hawthorne. They've seen me before. They know what I look like but—what if it's different, House?" Drawing a shaky breath in, she asked the question that she hadn't stopped thinking about since she'd woken up. "What if they're different?"

The House held its breath, exhaling in a warm huff of air against the top of her head. *"Get dressed, beloved. Come downstairs, make yourself some tea and we will talk."*

Outside snow trickled down in slow, lazy flakes. Rayne bundled herself up to stave off the chill, opting for a pair of black cargo pants over her thin tights and a second shirt under her hoodie. When she made it downstairs, she found the fireplace already burning and the cabinet where she kept her tea and coffee wide open. Once she'd set the kettle on the stove and her mug nearby, Rayne sat at the kitchen island and began braiding her damp hair.

"What did you want to talk about, House?"

"You do not need to go into the woods today, dear one."

"What?"

"Your wraith will meet you here but," The House paused. *"You need not let them in. We could spend this day fighting off the darkness, you and I. We need not involve ourselves with them at all."*

"No, House. I won't do that. I want to see Hawthorne today. I—care about them," Rayne said, her voice trailing off.

"Would rather that you didn't."

"Why?" she snapped. "Is your dislike of them so severe?"

The House shifted. *"It is not a matter of my taste, cherub. I think only of you."*

Rayne scoffed. "You still think they're dangerous? That they're going to eat me the first chance that they get?"

"I know it," The House answered. *"But no, that is not what ails me."*

Rayne sighed, pausing the meticulous braid she'd nearly finished. "Then what is?"

"There is—a world beyond this one, cherub. You have but peeked through the window. Once you have walked through that door—" The House paused, the fireplace crackling. *"You will never be able to close it."*

"I think we're well past that point—"

"No," The House hissed and despite the fire, the air around her was cold and biting. *"You know nothing of what lines look like after they have been*

crossed, but I fear that one day you will. And I can do nothing but watch you do it."

"House."

"Yes, Rayne. I am just a house but that is the thing about houses; we have been everything and nothing all at once. I was the trees in the forest, the dirt of this mountain, and I remember it all. I have seen what was and I know what we will be and I—"

Rayne placed her cheek against the cool counter. "Darling, House. You're fretting again. You know that you have as much of my heart that I can give. I want to savor what time there is left between you and I. With Hawthorne too."

"Leave me, if you must. Shatter what is left of my heart. But please, cherub, reconsider that wood. Reconsider them."

"No, House! I will not. They're the first person who ever looked at me like I wasn't an apology waiting to be uttered. Am I allowed nothing of my own?" Rayne snapped, slamming her balled fist down as she leapt from her seat.

Pain shot through her hand, jolting her out of her anger. She rubbed her smarting hands through her gloves, shame cooling what fire had burned within her only a moment ago. Rayne walked into the foyer to grab her boots from the coat closet by the door. "Listen, House. When I come home, I will feed you a bit of my hair. I saved some for you. I'll even bring you some sweet, sappy pine cones from out in the woods and feed them to you later. You'll smell so pretty, would you like that?"

The House sighed and the cold air gave way to its usual heat, like a pair of arms embracing her. *"Yes, dear one. I would like that very much."*

"Okay, I have no idea where the fuck I'm going."

The image of Hawthorne's tree hung high against the wall of her mind but the path to it was foreign to her. Still, her feet did not once stop their march through the dusting of snow on the ground. The scenery was not entirely unknown to her, she remembered the path of pine and holly trees still lush with greenery, the skeletons of maple and red pines. She remembered the small brook and the battered bridge that someone in town had made across it that had been around longer than she had been born. Even the hand painted signs and crucifixes that spoke of God's love like an omen.

Have you met your Saviour? He already knows you.

You will meet Him.

God is coming.

But past the graffitied boulders and hanging blue bottles from tree branches, the path bled into untouched land, and soon she was stepping over fallen branches and ducking through bushes. Rayne did not stop, she wasn't sure if she could anymore.

The clearing appeared out of nowhere, a circle of maple and red pine trees and toward the back of it, there it was; a tall hawthorn tree, reaching toward the sky with black bark.

Exactly like in her dreams.

Rayne headed into the center of it, not wanting to get too close but not wanting to risk staying away either.

"Hawthorne?" Rayne whispered, her voice barely above the delicate sound of the snow. "Are you here?"

From behind their tree, a man stepped calmly into the clearing. He was taller than any man Rayne had ever seen before, easily looming a foot over her. His skin was only a few shades darker than the snow and his curls were nearly as black as the bark of the tree behind him. He was wearing a simple white t-shirt, plaid jacket, jeans and hiking boots. It was a very un-Hawthorne outfit if she'd ever seen one.

The man did not immediately come to her nor did he smile, he merely watched her.

Doubt flooded in, rooting her in place. *Oh, fuck. I didn't bring a weapon. What if he's one of them mountain folk? Or one of those witch doctors that hasn't put on his skin yet?*

The man inhaled, closing his eyes. "Even in this form, your fear is the sweetest thing I've ever smelled." His voice was deep, soothing in its smoothness.

"H–Hawthorne?"

"Of course, little wolf. Who else would I be?" Their smile was too large, too other to look normal on their face but Rayne didn't hesitate before she launched herself at them.

The scent of dirt greeted her as Hawthorne caught her, pulling her flush against them. Their clothes were damp against her cheek and beneath the feeling of that was the sound of their heartbeat.

Rayne pulled back, startled, to stare up at them. The top of her head only just reaching the beginning of their sternum. "You're really alive... you have a heart beat."

They smirked down at her, exposing dangerously sharp canines. "You'll find out soon enough that I've got more than that."

Her face flooded with heat and she tucked her head back against them to keep them from seeing. It was more than their words that affected her, it was everything about their appearance; the dark dusting of stubble along their jaw, the sprinkling of freckles only just visible over their nose and along their cheekbones. Their eyes were most lethal of all, piercing and hazel like sunlight through a fading autumn leaf.

They're beautiful. When she pulled back again, there was dirt smudged against her cheek. *They're beautiful and covered in dirt.* "Were you rolling around in the snow or something?"

"Hm? Ah. No. The journey from the roots of my tree to the surface is not a simple one. I shook off as much as I was able."

"You were underground?"

"Quite. But at this point, I am used to dragging myself up here without assistance. I do not enjoy swallowing so much of the soil though."

Rayne shuttered at the thought of the world pressed so tightly around her and having to drag herself through the damp darkness. Her hand fell to the one at her waist and gently pried it off of her. "You could shower back at the house if you want. I can run into town and buy you some more oranges while you do.

Anything you want." Her fingers traced the calloused skin of their palms before carefully slipping into theirs. Hawthorne's large hands immediately latched onto hers, swallowing them whole and the sight of her entangled in another was not something that she had ever imagined seeing.

"Yes, I would like that."

Rayne moved to leave, to pull them along with her but they remained rooted in place, staring at her as if they did not recognize her. "Hawthorne?"

"Do you still not remember?"

Remember? Oh! "Oh, yeah. You'd asked me for orange soda last time. I won't forget it."

Hawthorne squeezed her hand, shaking their head. "No, Rayne, not that. *This.* This place—it doesn't—you don't—does anything look familiar to you?"

Nervous laughter fell from her before she could stifle it. "Of course, it's familiar. You've been trying to get me here since that first night. That's how I got here."

Their hand fell from hers, running through their hair. Now that she was closer to them, she saw that their curls were not black but instead a deep brown. Like the earth. "That is not what I meant, Rayne. You have been here before. *We* have been here before. Do you truly not remember?"

"I don't understand. I've never been here, I just... I saw it in my dreams. You showed it to me."

Hawthorne scoffed, turning away from her for a moment before they looked back. Their face, which she was used to not being able to read, was now flush with disbelief. "Yes but how did you know how to get here, Rayne? I did not show you the path. If you have not been here before, how did you manage not to get lost on the way here?"

Rayne's mouth opened but closed just as quickly as she wracked her mind for the answer. *I didn't really know the way here. I couldn't have. I just kept walking. Like—* "You called me here, didn't you? With your magic?"

They smiled bitterly. "I can only control what I can see. I could not have compelled you here unless I had you in my sights, and even then, my power is limited in this form."

I kept walking like my body already knew the way here. Rayne scanned the trees, the mountains in the distance and the dense forest that she had traversed to find her way here. The mountains were the architecture of the town and every curve of them was a distant relative to her now. But the forest was a different beast, foreign and comforting all at once. It was too easy to get lost in the wood.

"I don't understand," Rayne whispered, turning back to Hawthorne. "How could we have been here before? I've never known you before coming back here. We were strangers."

Hawthorne's expression softened into discomfort. "We have never been strangers, Rayne Dorne."

The finality in their voice sent a ripple of fear up her spine and a dull ache set behind her eyes.

"I don't understand," she repeated, her throat dry as bone.

"Let me show you." Hawthorne reached for her hand, palm upturned and open.

Rayne hesitated, looking down at their hand. Somewhere inside of her, she felt as though she was standing on some invisible precipice.

House's words sang through her mind: "***Once that door has been opened, it can never be closed again.***"

Before she could think better of it, she slid her hand into Hawthorne's and allowed them to lead her back toward the house.

Hawthorne was steadfast as they trekked back through the forest together, they moved as if the entire woods belonged solely to them. Rayne could only watch the back of their head, searching for the memories that they swore she had.

"***Tracking mud through my carpets again!***" The House cried as they entered. Hawthorne barely granted Rayne enough time to close and lock the door behind them before they were tugging her upstairs.

"Hawthorne, where are we going?" Rayne demanded, though she made no move to stop them or herself until Hawthorne made a left at the top of the stairs and led them toward *that* door. "No. Hawthorne, stop." She dug her heels into the carpet and they finally came to a stop.

"We have to go in there, Rayne. You will not understand unless we do."

Rayne shook her head, struggling to get enough air now. There was no air in that place. *If I go in there I'll choke. I can't, I can't!*

"Rayne—"

"You shall not strong arm her into getting your way, wraith. I would sooner drag you down into the earth of me than allow you to force her."

"I will never force her into anything," Hawthorne snarled, glaring up at the ceiling before their expression softened and they turned back to her. "Rayne, I will not ask you to do anything that you do not want to do. I am trying to help you understand. I know what you are scared of. But they're dead. They cannot hurt you any longer."

They're right, I know. My parents can't hurt me anymore. But—

"It will just be you and I in there, Rayne. Trust me."

Trust was a crooked, terrible thing that had always had a way of punishing her for giving in. The "friends" she'd made at school, the teachers that did little to step in, her parents, her brother. All of them until Hawthorne.

Swallowing the words that she couldn't manage around the dryness in her throat, Rayne nodded and gave Hawthorne her hand again.

Their thumb brushed over the back of her glove and they offered her a small smile before they turned back to the door and turned the knob to no avail.

"House," Hawthorne hissed. "Open the door. I know you have locked it, you menace."

"You can't—"

"House," Rayne managed. "Open the door. Please. I have to know."

The House sighed miserably and the door creaked open.

Her childhood bedroom.

The room smelled of her past, soft, blurred, and subdued. The way she had spent most of her time as a child. She recognized the scent of roses, the cheap potpourri that Rayne's grandmother used to love and had passed down to her.

Even with her boots on, she could feel the lush material of the salmon colored carpet and imagined it at her back as it used to be when she gazed up at the glow in the dark stars she'd snuck onto her ceiling. Her mother had been furious, screamed at her for ruining the value of the house. *'How am I ever going to be able to sell this house one day if all you do is mess up every room you're in?'*

Hawthorne did not flip the light switch and she pretended that it was because of the snow and the sun's light reflecting off of it that it bleached out all else and not because of how she could not handle it. Not yet.

Plastic ivy decorated the wall and draped down to her bedframe, roses wrapped around the bed frame. Pink roses, ribbons, and ballerina slippers were painted on the base of the walls and along the window frame. It was a beautiful room, a perfectly curated cage. Her parents gave her a perfect room, thinking that they could just lock her away in her ivory tower and that she would be fine.

Her favorite fairytale as a child had been Rapunzel; a girl locked away with nothing but the bare minimum to keep her sane.

She eyed the bookshelves that lined her walls, some of them so full that they had spilled over into little piles on the floor. Books had been the things that she lost herself in and the one thing that her parents had indulged her. Of course it was to keep her quiet but it had been a kindness even if only just.

The pain that had been gradually building behind her eyes was no longer a dull ache but a throbbing orb of pain. *I haven't gotten a headache like this in years.*

"Hawthorne," Rayne began. "Why are we in here?" Her hand had fallen out of theirs and wrapped around herself.

Hawthorne hardly fit in her room, the top of their head nearly brushing against the ceiling. They remained in place, close to her but not enough to impede on her space. "Your book of fairytales. Do you remember it?"

Rayne froze, blinking at them. *How the fuck do they know about those? Maybe I told them? Yeah, I had to have.* "Yes. Why?"

Hawthorne gestured to a box beside the bookshelf. "Find it."

She wanted to ask why but the sooner she did this, the sooner they could leave.

Glancing around the room, Rayne sought out her old bean bag chair that she had often used to kneel to protect her skin from the friction of the carpet. She found it shoved in the closet along with a dozen other of her most used toys. Clearly her mother had been in a rush to wash as much evidence of her joy as she could. Rayne ignored the brief but searing rage that bubbled at the thought and plopped the bean bag down, kneeling into it.

Carefully, she removed each item and there it was, its emerald green cover covered in a thin layer of dust, but she could still make out the small illustration of a wolf on the cover.

Her book of fairy tales.

These she had loved desperately, the dull, fraying ends of the paper were proof enough of this. Her fingers moved of their own accord, flipping through the pages. But it was the writing on one that caught her off guard. Rayne had always taken immaculate care of her books even as a clumsy child. She had never even so much as dog-eared a page, opting instead to use thin bookmarks that would not harm the spine. She couldn't think of a single reason as to why she would have felt the need to write in her book.

It was the tale of Little Red Riding Hood where she had written, circling the Wolf's head and drawing a little smile over his scowling muzzle. 'Mr. Wolf is much nicer than this.'

Mr. Wolf.

Who the fuck is that?

On the next page where the Wolf was beginning to devour Little Red Riding Hood, her younger self had again scrawled near the wolf's head and drawn a big smile over its maw. This time though, she'd gone out of her way to draw long, jagged teeth. '*Mr. Wolf would never eat me. If he tried, I'd eat him first.*'

I don't remember writing this. Rayne flipped through the rest of the book and every single page where a wolf was illustrated, there was a smile sketched over the wolves.

"What is this?" Her fingers trembled against the dusty pages and she clenched them into fists to keep Hawthorne from seeing.

"You tell me, Rayne. That is *your* book. Why did you write those things?" Hawthorne pressed and there was something in their voice, an emotion she didn't recognize in them. *I can't read their face like this.*

She snapped the book closed and tossed it across the room, nailing the closet door. "I don't fucking know! Why are we in here? *Why* are you doing this?"

"You might as well tell her now, wraith. No going back for any of us it would seem."

Might as well tell me? "House? Have you been hiding something from me?" Rayne asked, hating how pathetic the question sounded.

"Oh, cherub. It was not me. They—"

Hawthorne snarled, slamming their fist into the wall. "You will not interfere. Mind your business for once in your miserable existence."

The House sighed. **"*Terrible, terrible, terrible,*"** it muttered, its voice shrinking into the nothing.

"Hawthorne," Rayne snapped to draw their attention back to her. "What the fuck is going on?"

They rubbed their reddened knuckles. *Like they're nervous.*

"Where is your diary, Rayne?"

I did keep a diary, didn't I? How do they know that, how could they possibly know that? I never told them any of this. Rayne rose to her feet, shaking her head. "No. No more scavenger hunt. Tell me what is happening here."

"Rayne—"

"*Now.*"

Part of her expected them to laugh, to wrap her in shadows for daring to demand anything of them. Instead, they took a deep breath and answered her. "I know you, Rayne. I have known you since the moment you set foot in this town as I have known for the entirety of your life."

The headache screamed behind her eyes. "That's not true."

"It is," Hawthorne continued, too gently for her to bear. "Think for just a moment. I know you do not like to remember your childhood—"

"You don't know *anything* about my childhood!" she spat.

"Do I truly not seem familiar to you? When you look at me," Hawthorne swallowed. "Does nothing come to mind?"

Rayne's eyes drifted to them and she looked at Hawthorne, really looked at them. Tall, perfect, and unsettling all wrapped in one ethereal package. *I would have remembered seeing anyone like this, human, monster, or not.* She shook her head. "I couldn't have known you, Hawthorne. It's impossible."

"And yet, it is true all the same."

"Why are you doing this? Are you—fucking with me?"

Hawthorne scoffed though it was more animal than anything else. "No, I am not *'fucking'* with you."

"Then—"

Hawthorne strode across the room to the box of her belongings and grabbed her stuffed penguin. "This was your second favorite toy and you named him Pettigrew after that book your grandmother gave you for Christmas. You had a stuffed bat named Bartholomew but your mother threw it away after you got blood on it."

They moved to the bookshelf next, and keeping their attention on her, pulled a book. "You reread this book fourteen times when you were eleven years old. You loved the sapphire dragon and the ice queen most of all. You reread their parts in the book more than any others."

The tears that burned her eyes stung just as much as the headache tearing through her mind as she choked on the words that wouldn't come.

Hawthorne gestured to the opposite side of the room, to the window. "There, just under the window, your parents repainted where you drew a small castle in crayon. Your mother took all of your books away for a week and you cried so hard that you threw up."

Every memory slid into place; the stuffed bat she adored more than anything, the penguin that she came to love after its loss, the hours spent rereading her favorite novel, and the sound of her mother's voice when she'd caught Rayne doodling on the wall. All of it existed in the trenches of her youth, all of it except for Hawthorne.

"How do you know all of this?"

Hawthorne's expression shifted back into something she did not understand. "I saw it. And what I did not see, you told me."

"In my dreams, were you in my head? Did you go through my memories?"

"I am only able to enter a dream and shift the landscape of it. I can go no further than that."

"Are you lying to me?" she whispered.

Hawthorne moved closer to her. "You know I am not."

She shook her head, the tears beginning to drip off of her chin. "I don't—why don't I remember you, Hawthorne?"

They approached her carefully as if they could sense how close she was to bolting, how between the throbbing of her head and the tears smudging her vision, she was choking. Rayne stayed in place even as their large hands cupped her cheeks, thumbing the tears away. "You are crying. I recognize the action but I do not understand its meaning. It is not something that I can ever do," Hawthorne murmured, their eyes following the track of her tears as if they held the answer. "You cannot remember me because I took every memory of me that you had."

Rayne's brow furrowed. "Why would you do that? If I knew you all of my life, why would you take that knowledge from me?"

Hawthorne scoffed. "Because you asked me to. But it was only supposed to be one memory, one afternoon. I had never done it before and I took too much, I hurt you."

Because you asked me to.

The words dropped into her stomach, spreading into her chest. *They did something for me. But, I don't understand.* "Can you give them back then?"

A dark expression clouded Hawthorne's face. "I do not know how, and I will not risk harming your mind," they continued. "But, I think I can show you mine."

CHAPTER TWENTY-SIX
hawthorne

This was not how Hawthorne had imagined their reunion going. It was evident that her memory was gone, but they had assumed that once she saw them in the exact spot where they'd met, everything would fall into place.

I do not know where to go from here.

Like the first time that they'd played around with Rayne's memories, they had no idea what they were doing. Rayne had sat back down on her bean bag chair, eyeing them up and down. "So, what now? How are you going to show me?" She sniffed, rubbing the evidence of her tears from her cheeks.

Hawthorne knelt down so that they were nearly eye level with one another. "I have an idea but I do not know if it will work."

"You said that you did this before."

"Yes, but I was going in blind. I am still unsure of the way forward. I have never done this for anyone but you," Hawthorne explained, offering her their hand. "I believe that I can compel you to see what I see and share in my memories."

"Compel—like with your shadow things?" she asked, her hand hovering over theirs.

"Correct." Hawthorne kept their palm open to her, allowing her the space to make her choice. "I will do my best to keep the sensation from being... unpleasant."

Rayne tugged off her glove, discarding it behind her before slipping her hand into theirs. Hawthorne knew that she did not like the look or feel of her hands but they had never seen anything more beautiful than the marbled flesh and the different shades of scars that covered them. They brought it to their lips, closing their eyes at the feeling of her skin against theirs.

"Are you ready?"

"Yes," Rayne whispered. Though this form hindered their usual hearing and sight, they could still make out the rapid fire of her pulse beneath their thumb.

Human bodies were not designed for magic: whether it was their emotions or their excessive organs, little magic could live within them. There were some humans that had learned to wield it and to flow with the river of power.

But Hawthorne and their kind *were* the river.

When they were themself, they needed only to reach for their desire, but in this form, the magic needed to be conjured, ripped out at the root. Fire seared through their blood, nerve endings singing in discomfort as magic tore through them. Their fingers blackened, the capillaries and veins darkened to a deep purple beneath their pale flesh.

Rayne gasped, clutching their hand. "Hawthorne?"

"It is fine, Rayne. I am alright, magic simply looks different in this body," they replied, taking another deep breath. The magic ignited up their spine, through their throat and finally to the tip of their tongue. *There we go.* When they opened their eyes, the edges of their vision blurred and Rayne stared up at them with wide eyes.

I must be careful with the spell. "Your sight is tied to mine as long as your hand remains in place. You will see exactly as I see, in this realm and the next, in the present and the past."

The connection between them snapped into place and Rayne jolted. They brushed their thumb along the back of her hand to keep her with them. The memory of the night that they met her danced before their eyes.

The Solstice had been no different than any other. Only a few hours until midnight and I had eaten my fill of everything in sight. I did not venture into Bury tonight, truth be told, I was bored with my hunting there.

Superstitious old towns were fun but there was something special about watching the fear in a human's eyes that had never believed in anything and hearing them pray to a God that they had not believed in until their final moments.

My body was beginning to break down now, my hands already having gnarled back into claws and my skin melting back into shadows. I was done for the night and intended to sleep while I still had a body that could do so. I savored the unforgiving bite of the winter wind against my chapped human skin and the ache in my knees from walking so many miles in one day. It was in these small moments that I enjoyed the idea of being human but only then. I am what I am and I love that dearly.

My beautiful tree came into the few and I breathed in the bitter scent of its bark. Its branches were heavy with blood red rubies, as if it decorated itself to match my hunger. I loved my tree completely and it was so rare that I got to experience it in all its glory. **I will spend my last few hours sleeping under it, I think. That is the best way for me to end my Solstice.**

But as I moved closer to my tree, I saw a small, shivering bundle huddled under it. The bundle was brightly colored, an unnatural shade of pink and purple. **What creature would be foolish enough to come to my home on the Solstice?**

The bundle sneezed and I halted to a stop. **It is alive.** *I did not bother to hide my smile.* **It will not remain as such for much longer.**

When I knelt down to get a better look at the bundle, I realized that it was not some stupid animal but instead a stupid human child, trembling in the snow. Its bright colors were a puffy jacket, there were dark green mittens on its hands and matching pink boots on its small feet. The child had long hair, wispy with melting snow and braided back.

Hmm. Not what I expected but I will not waste such an easy meal. But I will frighten it first. One last taste of fear with my meal before I go back into the ground.

I ate anything that pleased me: men, women, children, animals, even spirits. It did not matter to me. If a creature was not strong enough to ward me off or lay me low then they did not deserve to live.

I knelt down on one knee and even then, I towered over the child. It would not be much of a meal on its own so I would have to do a thorough job in scaring it.

"Hello."

The child rolled onto its back and blinked its eyes open. Its dark skin was red with cold. "Why don't you come out from under there?" I asked, offering it my hand. Scaring children always worked better when I lured them into a false sense of security first. I had time. I could give the child the illusion of safety for a few minutes.

The child took my hand, grasping my finger as it pulled itself up. Looking at it now, I realized that it was a little girl. I could not fathom to guess her age, but she was younger than any other child I had ever seen this far into the forest.

I smiled at her and her eyes went wide. "What were you doing under my tree, child?"

"Are you a fairy?" the little girl asked, making no indication that she had heard a word I'd spoken.

The question was so ridiculous that I could not help the laugh that tore out of me and echoed through the trees. The idea of me as one of those wretches was much too amusing for me. "No, never that."

"What are you then?"

I thought a moment, tilting my head. "A wolf."

"You don't look like a wolf," she replied.

I shrugged. "Not all wolves look the same. Now, why are you here?" I asked again, glancing around. "Are your parents nearby?"

"No. I got lost. I was looking for fairies."

Curiosity licked at me just as furiously as my hunger. **How could a child make it this far into the wood unassisted?** *It was a strange thing, something new to me and I needed to know more to have the hunger sated. "You are alone then?"*

The little girl nodded. "Where's your coat?" she asked, pointing at the simple long sleeve shirt I had on. "Aren't you cold?"

"I do not get cold, little human. What is your name?" I asked.

"Rayne."

Once she had given me her name, I knew that some part of her had begun to trust me. As intoxicating as curiosity was, it could be short lived and already I could feel myself slipping back into my hunger. I cracked my neck, rolling my shoulders as I began to shift into more of my true self.

"Well then, Rayne, what do you say to us playing a little game? You run home and I—"

"I don't want to go home," Rayne said. Her shivering had begun anew.

I blinked. **Well, that is certainly new.** *"Why not?"*

"My Mama don't like me. My Papa neither. They're always mad at me."

"Why are you looking for fairies?" I inquired.

"I want to live with them. My Mam'maw said they take bad kids and I don't wanna go home."

In all of my years, all of the children I had eaten had almost always been for the same reason: they wandered too far from their parents and were not able to make it back to them before I found them. Some of them had been runaways, yes but usually they were teenagers. Never had I found a runaway child this young.

Something is wrong with this child, *I thought, looking her over again. There were scars all along her face and a bandage peeking out from her neck.* **She might be some changeling finally called home by her kin. I will not eat her and poison myself.**

I released her hand from mine before any more of her sickness could seep into me. She was small and weak, the cold would kill her before long. "Then I will not get in your way, little Rayne," I said, pointing toward the mountains in the far distance. "Your fairies reside in that direction."

She followed my finger and turned back to me, smiling and exposing a missing tooth. "Thanks. You're real nice." She turned and started her slow journey out of the clearing, every few steps, she would fall into the snow. There were no tears, no whining, nothing. When she fell, she righted herself on small, shaking legs and then started walking once more.

I watched, frowning at the pathetic little creature that would surely be dead before midnight, and a sensation settled in my stomach like a rock. It was unpleasant and pointed entirely at that foolish, strange human child. I did not like the idea of her dying in the snow like this despite my own desire to eat her only moments ago.

I do not know what compelled me, but I shed my human shell, shucking it like corn to shift into myself. I shook the remnants of blood and tissue from my fur before I trotted off after her. She had only just made it out of the clearing by the time I'd caught up to her. She did not scream or shrink away in fear when I approached, instead she ran her mittens through the fur on my side. "Hello, Mr. Wolf. Are you going to take me to the fairies?"

"Get on," I demanded, lowering myself to the ground so she could climb onto my back. "Hold on, I will not stop and come back for you if you fall."

Rayne struggled to hoist herself onto my back as she gripped my fur. I did not help her and she did not ask. After a few minutes, just as my patience was beginning to thin, she finally got herself onto my shoulders. I gave her no warning before darting off into the woods, huffing the air.

Like all humans, she was a cluster of smells knotted together: the bitter adhesive of her bandages, the peaches on her breath, the distant scent of juniper oil in her hair. I followed the thread of all of them as I sped through the forest until I found myself at the edge of it, two houses on the other side of the road.

"This is my house!" Rayne cried.

"Yes," I said, crouching down and shaking her off of me. "It is. Go home, child. Bad things happen to children out in the forest."

Rayne sat in the snow, her small lip trembling as she glared ahead at her home. "I don't want to go back."

"Then don't," I replied with a shrug. **It makes no difference to me what this child does. I have gotten her out of the forest. If she cannot make it ten feet to her own house then she is truly unfit to survive.**

I turned to leave but that feeling rushed into me again, knotting around my gut in discomfort. A quick glance over my shoulder and I saw that she was still sitting there, shivering in the cold despite her proximity to home. I should have left her I wanted to, but more than that I wanted to rid myself of the discomfort that came when she shivered so pathetically. With a sigh, I sat back on my haunches at her side.

"You will die out here, little human. Go back to your warm bed. Surely what awaits you inside cannot be worse than freezing to death," I said. I had never really spoken to a child like this, let alone a human one. I did not know how much thought or comprehension she was capable of. I could have been speaking to a wall for all that I knew.

"My Mama will be mad. The fairies won't."

I do not know what possessed me but I said: "If I promise to take you to the fairies tomorrow, will you go home tonight?"

Rayne looked up at me with those wide, frightening little animal eyes of hers and nodded. It did not make sense to me why I would say such a thing and tangle myself in a promise. **I will simply not return to this part of town. She will not be able to find me again.**

I shook the snow from my fur. "Off with you, then."

Rayne stood and threw her arms around me. I froze, a low snarl sounding from my throat in response. She pulled away before I could snap at her and she smiled up at me, seemingly unaffected. "Thank you, Mr. Wolf."

I snarled again, watching her toddle through the snow, up the salted driveway of her home, and to the front door. Something rooted me exactly where I was. I needed to see her enter the home so that I could be sure the feeling would go with her.

When Rayne finally made it to the front door, she stood on the tip of her toes in an attempt to reach the doorbell. Her mittened fingers almost brushed it but she was just too short to do it on her own. She did not ask me for assistance or call out to me, it was not as if I would help her anyhow.

She set her brow and slammed her small fists against the door nearly a dozen times until I could hear movement inside of the house. The door swung open and a beautiful woman peaked her head out. Her black, silken hair spilled over her shoulders as she clutched her robe tighter around herself against the chill. Her dark eyes settled on Rayne and her mouth immediately settled into a scowl. "What the hell is wrong with you, banging on the door like that? Do you have any idea what hour it is?" she snapped.

I had never disliked a human so quickly before.

"Sorry, Mama," Rayne murmured. "But I was-"

"I don't want to hear it. Get your ass in the house before your father finds out you weren't in bed." With that, she shuffled Rayne into the house and the door closed behind them. The discomfort did not follow with her.

"Pity," Rayne managed wetly, swallowing. Hawthorne opened their eyes and found her already watching them through a mess of tears drenching her face.

"What?"

"The feeling that you had when you looked at me. It was pity."

Pity.

Hawthorne had heard the word many times before but they had never had anything tangible to tie it to, nothing that could ground the meaning for them. *But now I know. When I feel that again, I will know that I am pitying something.*

"You were going to eat me," she whispered, another tear slipping down her cheek. They wanted to comfort her, to wipe it away but they could not break the connection between them without losing the magic.

"Yes, I was."

"And you didn't because you... pitied me."

"That, and I think I was curious. I had never seen a child so small all alone in the wood."

"Did you ever come back to take me to the fairies?"

"No," Hawthorne admitted. "You came to me. I did not think you would, nor how you did it, but you found your way back the next day."

They watched as a dozen expressions reflected across Rayne's face; there had been a time when they had known every iteration of her emotions, where they had been able to read her from across the room, and could predict every one of her storms before they hit. But Rayne was no longer that little girl.

"And you didn't eat me then either," Rayne said though she was not really looking at them.

Hawthorne knew enough about human emotions to know that they occasionally needed time to settle, to be felt, so they did not press Rayne to voice what was going on for her. "You kept finding me and I kept letting you. I... pitied you and I realized quickly that despite your family, you were very much alone. It was different from the way that I was. I had chosen it and you had not."

Rayne swallowed, opening and closing her mouth as if she was choking on what she wanted to say. "How long did—you didn't ever feel like *this* toward me when I was—?"

They nearly released her hands, their lips curling in disgust. "Gods above, Rayne, *no*. I did not think of you that way ever. You were a child, a delicate one at that and eventually, I wanted you to be safe," Hawthorne explained. "This—whatever it is I feel for you now is new, different."

"What do you feel for me now?"

"I don't know. You humans, you are born knowing exactly what your feelings are and how to feel them. My kind... we are not. Emotions are not natural for us. In a way, all of those years ago, we were both children. While you were experiencing life, I was learning what it felt like to seek a friend. I wanted you safe and happy, Rayne."

"Wanted?"

I do not know if I can talk about this yet, if I can tell her at this moment. The stillness that they often exuded did not translate into their human body, they worried the corner of their lip with their teeth and their fingers thrummed against the back of Rayne's hand. "I have another memory for you."

Rayne, caught in between the awkward stage of child and preteen sat curled in her bed. Her day fell into a rather rigorous schedule: wake up two hours before the school bus would come to shower and dress her wounds, school, homework, dinner, a bath to clean her wounds again and then, bed. This was one of those rare occasions where she had some time to herself, time away from her mother's scrutiny and the harshness of the world.

I watched from the closet as she clutched her book tighter to her chest so lost in the story that she was oblivious to all else in the world. The perfect time for me to frighten her. I creaked open the closet door behind her bed slowly and raked a claw down the wood paneling.

Instead of startling, she giggled. "You can't scare me, you know."

I very much could, but real fear was not something that I ever wanted to see on her face again. I slunk over to her bed, folding in on myself to fit on the edge of her bed. "No? Well, I will just have to try harder next time."

"I'm sorry that I couldn't come see you after school. I had a lot of homework to do and my mom wouldn't take her eyes off me."

"I figured as much, which is why I am here to visit you." I shrugged, stretching back. Her bed was much too small for me to even sit on, no matter how tiny I tried to make myself. I spilled onto the floor beside her to grant myself more room. "What are you reading today?"

I enjoyed books, they were the only human innovation that was worth its while. Every chance that I had, I would read as many as I could regardless of language or genre. I thought that in my time, I'd read nearly every book available. But I had never thought to include children's literature.

Rayne was a voracious reader. From what I knew of her life, she did not have any human friends or take part in any after school activities so most of her time was spent with her nose buried in a book.

"The Salt Chronicles. It's about a mermaid that lives alone on an island and she eats anyone that comes too close," Rayne said, handing the book to me, her finger between the pages so that she didn't lose her place. I was careful to use my finger to do the same as I inspected the book.

"And what about the faerie court book that you were reading yesterday?" I skimmed through, picking up tidbits of the story as I did.

"I finished it, of course!" Rayne sat up, swinging her legs off of the bed. "The librarian at my school said she never saw anyone work through books as quickly as I do."

"I believe that," I said as I handed it back to her, to which she then slid her red dragon bookmark in it and placed it down on the bed. "Well? Are you going to tell

me how it ended? Last I remember she had just discovered the curse placed on her family."

Rayne grinned at me, nothing lit her up more than talking about stories. *"Okay, so—"*

Behind me, I heard the unfortunately familiar sound of her mother's heavy footfall and the nauseating wave of her pear blossom and mint perfume. I held up my hand to silence her, though I was loath to do so. *"Your mother is coming."*

Rayne immediately began scrambling back into bed, hiding her book under her pillow, turning her back to the door and pulling her sheets over her head so that her mother wouldn't be able to see her face.

"Don't go," she whispered.

"Never. I'll be right here, just under your bed," I promised before slipping under the small crawlspace of her bed.

"Rayne?" Thelma thundered, clattering into her room like a summer storm. Rayne, in her rush to pretend to be asleep so that her mother would not attack her, had forgotten to turn off the light. It was such a small thing and it should have meant nothing. But in the Dorne household, everything Rayne did was under scrutiny.

"Dammit, Rayne, electricity isn't fucking free! You gonna pitch some money in to help out around here? Maybe get off your lazy ass and get a job?"

I could hear Rayne freeze in bed, even lessening her breath to keep her mother from noticing that she was awake. Playing possum was always the best move when faced with a predator. **Smart girl.**

"Thels," her father's voice called after his wife from the hallway. *"She's fucking twelve, she can't get a job yet."*

"We had jobs at her age," Thelma shot back. *"And we turned out fine. All she does is sit in her room and daydream and talk to her stupid imaginary friends. Did you see her test score today? She got a C, a fucking C!"*

"So what? She's trying and she can always retake the damn thing," Cassian replied evenly. I had come to learn that while her mother was a volatile, raging viper, Rayne's father was the more subdued one. There were days where he almost

seemed to defend his daughter. I could not be sure of it but there were moments where he seemed as if he loved Rayne.

I did not understand human emotions but I had a mother and while my father was not worth the dirt between my toes, no matter what I'd done, my mother had never once spoken to me like this.

Hatred had been a foreign concept to me until I met Thelma and Cassian Dorne.

"She shouldn't have to retake anything, what responsibility does she have? After everything we've done for her you'd think she'd want to impress us or do... something other than lay around in her room all day. You know, her pretty friend Cindy? Her mother told me that she's already out volunteering in her free time, straight As, up for best in class. I just—I wish that Rayne were better."

I swallowed the growl that was building in my throat and focused on the sound of Rayne's breathing above me, the tears that I could smell beginning to pick at her eyes. One day, I was going to kill Thelma Dorne and I was going to do it slowly.

Cassian sighed. "Well, there's nothing to be done about it now. You get the kid you get, even if you want to give them back."

"Parenting isn't supposed to be like this. We shouldn't have had her." Thelma sighed.

My hand moved, as if by instinct, under the blanket to reach for Rayne's hand. She caught it and clung to me for dear life.

"Nothing to be done about it now. It's not like we can just leave her—we'd get caught. Anyway, that's enough of that. Why don't we go downstairs and finish that movie? I don't have to be in the office until 3 tomorrow," her father said, clicking the light off in her room.

And just as quickly as they'd come, her parents had left but the damage had been done. All they did was damage her.

The moment that they were gone, I moved onto Rayne's bed, ignoring the discomfort as I sat cross-legged at her side. I did not let go of her hand and I did not move away from her as she cried against the pillow. I hated her tears for I knew that they only came when she was distressed.

"I hate when I cry," Rayne sniffed, burying her face against the fabric. "I feel like a baby."

"You are just a child," I said, patting the back of her hand. "But a very brave one. You are as much a wolf as I." It was the most honest thing I had ever said to her. Rayne, whether she realized it or not, was more resilient than most humans could ever hope to be.

She turned toward me, her face red and eyes bleary. "Really?"

"I only say what I mean, little wolf. You know this."

She smiled a little and I felt the tension in my chest loosen. The world did not seem right when she was upset. Rayne was the only companion that I had ever known, the only friend that I had ever had. Her happiness was of grave importance to me.

"I wish that I could live with you in the forest," Rayne whispered. This was not the first time she had expressed such a sentiment to me. It was a complicated desire for both her and myself. I did not stay in one place for very long. I liked to roam, save for during the Winter Solstice. Her living in the forest with me meant responsibility, a tether, and eventually a cage. As much as I cared about Rayne, I would suffer confinement for no one.

And, I did not want to be like everyone else in her life and abandon her.

"That would be nice, wouldn't it? But you still have your studies to focus on, don't you?" I asked, patting the top of her head. "And your plan to get your good grades and make your money so that you can go anywhere in the world. Or did you forget?" I teased.

Rayne laughed a little, wiping her running nose. "Nah, I remember. Mr. Wolf?"

"Yes, Rayne?"

"Will you stay with me until I fall asleep?"

I smoothed a damp strand of hair away from her cheek. "Of course. Shall I tell you a story? It's a rather good one and I can promise that you've never heard it before."

I knew a great deal of stories and I saved them for the bad days where Rayne needed to be reminded that there was still magic and beauty in the world.

She settled against me, resting her head on my knee. It never failed to amaze and confound me how deep her trust for me went. Human friendship was truly the strangest thing. "Once," *I began, clearing my throat.* "There was a girl who lived on the moon."

Emerging from the ocean of their memories with her was like a fresh burst of oxygen after being thrown in ice water.

"You saw that?" Rayne whispered. "You were around in the house with my parents?"

"Not always, but yes, I would come to visit you when I could. There were times, such as that where you could not come to see me."

"Were you there for all of it?"

Their expression darkened. "I was there for much of it. I bore witness to their treatment of you most of the time." They kissed her hand again, needing to feel her skin against their lips once more. "Watching you grow up and grow into yourself was a privilege, and I am grateful for the experience."

"Then why didn't you come with me when I left?" Rayne asked. "Why did you just leave me alone for all those years?"

"Why did *I* leave *you*?" Hawthorne hissed, something sharp cutting into their chest. "You are the one who left. You said nothing. One day you were there and then you were gone. I know that you could not remember details about our time together but you forgot *everything*. Me."

"I don't understand how that could have happened."

"You asked me to erase your memory. One day after school, close to your graduation, you came home crying, not like the other times. I had never seen you so upset and you begged me to erase that day for you."

Rayne's brow furrowed and she looked past them, biting down on her lip. "Why would I do that?"

"You never told me. You were inconsolable, and I just wanted to help you. I had never removed a memory before and I—I hurt you. You were bleeding and I did not know what else to do. I found your phone, called your human emergency services. When you came home from the hospital, I came to see you but you were frightened. I thought you may have been angry with me so I tried to give you space, kept an eye on you when I could. But when I came back from the forest one day, you were gone. You'd packed everything and left without a word."

"You could have followed me," Rayne whispered and fire ignited within them again. It was a thought they'd had time and time again, pulled between their desire to see her again and the indignation of her abandonment.

"I wanted to forget you!" Hawthorne hissed, dropping her hands. "I left Bury with no intention of ever coming back, save for my tree. But I was different after knowing you. I began to keep time. I'd never noted the passing of it, but suddenly I was aware of every moment. I thought of you so much and my chest was cold and empty every time that I did."

"You—you missed me," Rayne said, her gaze settled back on them, wide as the moon.

"Missed?" Hawthorne did not understand the meaning of the term.

"It's when you want to see someone badly but you can't. So you think of them instead. It's like an ache."

An ache. Yes. That was exactly what it had been like without her. "Yes, I *missed* you. You were the only companion I had ever had in my life. I liked having you around. I had grown used to you, and then without you I felt... "

"Lonely," Rayne finished. "You were lonely without me."

Lonely. That was what I was feeling. I do not ever want to feel it again. "Yes." Their voice came softer than they meant it to. "I missed you and it was maddening. But then that missing turned into a fire. I do not know the name for that sensation."

"Anger. You were angry at me for leaving, for forgetting you." Rayne was moving closer to them, leaning closer but they couldn't give in to her gravitational pull just yet or they'd never escape.

"Yes. And I wanted to see you again but I wanted to free myself from ever thinking about you again," Hawthorne continued. "I wanted to kill you but I wanted you to recognize me first, so that you would know it was *me*. I wanted to see the light going out of your eyes knowing that it was your wolf taking it from you. That's why I brought you here, Rayne."

Rayne pulled back, her nose scrunching. "My brother called me here. I came back for Callum, because he asked me to."

Hawthorne wanted to laugh at her naivety. How she could still cling onto the idea that anyone in her family had ever seen her for who she really was. Save for her grandmother, none of them had ever loved her. They smiled bitterly. "No, he didn't. That phone call was from me. I called you back here."

"No. You couldn't—how?"

"Mimicry is the easiest form of magic, little wolf. I need only hear a voice once to be able to conjure it again."

Rayne's brow furrowed and somehow, Hawthorne knew what she was going to ask them next, the question that they'd been hoping to avoid for just a little longer.

"Hawthorne, where is my brother?"

They sighed.

"I killed him."

CHAPTER TWENTY-SEVEN
rayne

I killed him.

Callum is dead. I'm the last Dorne.

Hawthorne remained silent, their hazel eyes remained unblocking, fixed fully on her, their expression blank. The splitting headache that had plagued her earlier had subsided, all of the pressure melting away to be replaced with the ocean of feelings threatening her now. Rayne did not know what she was feeling; she had always held onto the hope that she would see her brother again, that they might reunite without the tyranny of her parents.

"Why?"

"Your brother was not good to you," Hawthorne answered, monotone as ever.

"You don't get to decide that for me!" Rayne hissed.

"Do you want to know why I killed him?" Hawthorne asked, tilting their head toward her. "I will not tell you if you do not want to know."

"I—" She hesitated a moment. *I need to know.* "Yes."

"Your mother was diagnosed with some terminal illness, a type of cancer. She did not go into detail but she panicked and called your brother. He came back a few days later."

"No. My brother ran away when he was sixteen. He emancipated himself and my parents never heard from him again," Rayne corrected, and even to her own ears it sounded as if she were reading from a script.

"A lie. When he came home, they spoke about the estate and they were going to give him everything. They wanted to leave you with nothing because you 'abandoned the family'."

Abandoned the family. Rayne could hear her mother saying those exact words, spitting them at her like venom as she glared at Rayne with all the contempt in the world. As if Rayne alone was the sole cause of her mother's misery. Of course her parents hadn't planned on leaving her anything, of course it had nothing to do with the fact that she was second born and Callum was older.

No. It was strictly because she was herself. That alone was a crime in her family's eyes. "How do you know all of this?"

"They were gathered by the fire on the back porch. I heard all of it. I still would come by the house every once in a while to see if I could catch your scent again. I knew that it was the only way to get you back here and I," Hawthorne paused and swallowed before looking at her. "I didn't want them to hurt you again."

"You had no right."

Hawthorne nodded. "I did not."

"I *loved* my brother," Rayne said because it was true. She loved Callum and she had told him as much in their childhood so many times that the words jumbled together. *I love you, I love you, I love you, I love you.* The same way that Rayne had told her Mam'maw, and then she'd lost her.

Loving anyone was the quickest way to lose them, and even though the thing within her chest was dangerously close to bursting from all that she felt for Hawthorne, she couldn't admit it or she'd lose them again.

"I know you did, Rayne. Did he love you as well?" Hawthorne offered.

Their words were a dagger that she had no defense against.

Rayne stood abruptly, nearly falling back onto the cushion with how quickly she'd moved. "I need a minute."

Hawthorne cocked their head to the side, eyeing her curiously. "A minute to what?"

"It's an expression, Hawthorne. I need to think."

Amusement tugged the corners of their mouth. "And you need to move to think?"

She frowned. "No. Well, right now, yes." Rayne moved to leave the room and Hawthorne followed close behind her. "I told you that I needed to think," she snapped over her shoulder.

"Yes. You did not say that I could not come with you."

"Okay, well you can't. I'm trying to think about how I feel about the idea of you having killed my brother. You make thinking hard, you take up so much space in a room. Just by being there, shadow or human. You're just... *you.*"

Their arm snaked around her waist and caught her against the hallway wall. The scent of her rose soap wafted softly from their skin, mixing with their natural earthy depth and she leaned in closer, breathing them in. *They smell so fucking good, like a thunderstorm in spring, drenching the dirt.*

A wave of calm rushed over her the more she breathed them in, the closer that they remained to her.

Get a grip, dammit. They just told you that they murdered your family! She shook her head and began to pull away from them. "This is the exact opposite of space. I said I need a few minutes alone."

"I heard you," Hawthorne replied though they made no move to back away from her. "But I do not want any space between us ever again. If I had it my way, we would be just like this, all day."

The confession settled somewhere in her chest. She wanted more even though she knew that she shouldn't, that this thing between them was as rotten as she was. "It's healthy to—"

"Don't do that," Hawthorne snapped.

"Do what?"

"Do not put outside rules on this, on us. I do not care what is considered healthy by others. I care about what is healthy for you and I." They brushed a loose curl of hers behind her ear. "If you want me to leave you alone right now, then I will. Would you like me to?"

"No," came her immediate and treacherous response. "I want you to stay."

Hawthorne smiled at her and she was glad to be pinned against them and the wall, lest her knees give out on her. They were too good at charming her. "Then take your time to think, little wolf. I will not distract you nor will I leave you. Would you like to think out loud?"

"I—yeah, actually, I would," she mused and their smug grin was not lost on her. *Why didn't I think to do that?* Rayne pushed back against their chest, frowning. "You don't know everything about me, you know."

Hawthorne laughed and she wanted more of it, would lap it up off of the floor if she could. They were a thirst that she was not sure could ever be quenched. "I know everything there is to know about you, Rayne," they purred, lips feathering against the top of her head. "Now, stop trying to pick a fight with me to avoid thinking about everything I've told you."

Rayne blushed at being read so easily and hid her face against their chest, her hands resting at the small of their back. "I miss my brother," she admitted against the earth of their skin. "I miss how I imagined things could have been between him and I if he... "

"Did not hate you?" Hawthorne finished.

She pressed closer and they allowed her to do so, doing nothing more than moving the hand at her cheek to slide into her hair. "Yes, if he didn't hate me. If not even if he loved me but if he liked me at least a little. I may not have mattered to him but he mattered to me. He was still my brother."

"Yes, I understand," Hawthorne replied evenly, as patient with her as ever.

"You do?"

"I may not always enjoy my siblings but they are mine."

Rayne's head shot up. "You have siblings?"

"Yes. Three sisters. You are distracting yourself."

"My grandmother used to talk to us, well me mostly, when we were children and she'd tell us about kin-killers. Family murderers and what became of them.

I'm scared that will happen to me. That I'll start to change into something... *worse.*"

"You did not kill your family, Rayne," Hawthorne reminded her. "I did."

"But you did it because of me."

"And? What does that matter? I did what I wanted because I wanted to." They twirled one of her curls around a long finger. "You are dancing around this again."

They were right and she hated it. She hated how patient they were being with her and yet there was a part of her that craved it. No one had ever been patient with her before and she wanted more of it.

Rayne craved her beast's gentleness with a violence that should have frightened her.

"I don't think that I'm sad, and I think that I'm supposed to feel sad about it," Rayne said, her hands running up the muscles of Hawthorne's back. "I'm not angry. I feel... nothing about his death."

When Hawthorne remained silent, she continued, "I mean, I wasn't good enough to stay in his life as far as he was concerned. So why should his death stay in mine?"

Hawthorne smiled. "That makes perfect sense to me, Rayne."

Silence drifted between them, Hawthorne did not attempt to fill it. They merely did exactly as they promised and stayed close, their chest moving in time with hers. "My parents didn't both have heart attacks at the same time, did they?"

"Yes, they did. But make no mistake, I killed them. My only regret is that I could not have caused them more pain."

"How?"

"In their sleep. I kept them trapped there and then I gave them some very unpleasant dreams. Their rotten hearts couldn't take it, it would seem."

Rayne's heart was beating wildly in her chest. "And you did that for me?"

"And I'd do it again," they swore, searching her gaze.

"But why me?" she ventured, her mouth just a breath away from theirs.

They sighed with that hungry grin, their teeth brushing her lips. "Why *not* you?"

"You said that you were angry with me before, that you wanted to kill me. And now? What do you feel now?"

Their fingers ran through her curls, careful as ever, they didn't even so much as snag even once. "When I look at you, every ounce of me turns toward you. I cannot stay away from you. I would follow you anywhere. And you, I feel you in the earth of me."

Throat dry, knees trembling, Rayne knew what this meant. She'd read about it, heard it spoken of time and time again but never in her wildest dream could she ever dare to imagine that it would be felt *for her*.

"Do you—is it love? Do you love me, Hawthorne?"

Relief and recognition painted Hawthorne's face and they laughed a little before sweeping her up in their arms. "Yes! That is it exactly! I love you, Rayne. I think I have loved you since the moment you stepped foot back in this town."

She wanted to say it back, she had never known that love could be this big, all encompassing weight and yet so insular. What did she know of desire before Hawthorne? *Nothing, nothing at all.*

Rayne loved them as she would love nothing else in this world or the next. She would make no space in her thimble of a heart for anything other than her dear wolf.

She should have said the words back, told them all of this but instead she tucked them away, digging her claws into them over and over again as they replayed in her mind. *They love me, they love me!*

Hawthorne leaned down to kiss her and pull the words that she could not speak right out of her.

Their lips were so warm and they tasted of maple, like they carried the very forest in their blood. Hawthorne had been her first kiss in their normal form but that did little to prepare her for this. They towered over her, lifted her with their thick arms as if she was weightless. And still, they were just as gentle with her as they always had been. Mortal body or not, Hawthorne had single handedly done what none other had managed.

How long would they have this body? Can I let them let it go after the night is through?

"How long did you say that you have this body?" Rayne managed, breaking away from their sweltering kiss long enough to speak.

"Until the sun rises," they murmured, dragging their teeth against her neck, their tongue following suit. A shiver slid down her spine and went straight to her middle. "Think you'll be able to last that long?" they purred in her ear.

"Yes, but not in here. *My room*, not this one."

Once Rayne had become a teenager, closer to her freedom, she had done everything that she could to distance herself from her painful childhood. The first step in that had been moving out of her room and into Callum's. She had gutted it and made it completely her own, not the gilded cage her parents had given her, but something that was completely her own. That was where she wanted Hawthorne, not here in the dust of every agony she'd ever suffered.

Hawthorne did not set her down, instead they carried her down the hallway. They ducked into her room behind her and she leaned over their shoulder to close the door—the ridiculousness of the action only hitting her after. This was her house now, Hawthorne was hers, she didn't have to worry about anyone unwanted coming in.

"Can you put me down?"

Hawthorne groaned, burying their face in her shoulder before huffing indignantly.

"For just a few moments. How else will I get undressed?"

At this, Hawthorne raised a brow and lowered her back onto the ground. She slipped out of her shirt, exposing her velvet bralette underneath. Hawthorne's hazel eyes fell onto her chest. *Look at me like that forever.* Blushing, she turned her back to them. "Could you undo my braid, please, Hawthorne?"

Her hands pressed against her stomach and she chewed on her lower lip as she waited for them to move. *Mam'maw would throw a fit.* Hair was holy, it was the direct connection to the Creator and all of their ancestors. Her grandmother had always taught her to take pride in her hair and to only allow those that loved her to touch it. Before she'd died, Rayne's grandmother was the only person who'd ever touched her hair. After she'd died, Thelma had attempted but her touch was rough and often left Rayne crying. Since then, Rayne had never let anyone else touch a strand of her hair if it was unbraided.

The braid meant protection, working as a shield against spirits and negativity energies alike. There was a ritual to it, a proper way to do things and if Hawthorne truly was the missing thread in her life, the blank space between her memories, they would know this.

It's not a test, she thought. *Not really. I just want to be sure.*

"My hands are not clean," Hawthorne said from behind her, rubbing their hands against the thick material of their jeans. "I have no smoke to purify them. Are you sure you would still like for me to undo it?"

Not trusting herself to speak, she nodded. *It must be true, all of it. They have really known me all of my life.*

The floor creaked beneath them as they crossed the room and their presence blazed down at her back, like the setting sun. Gently, they removed her hair tie and she felt their fingers slide between the thickness of her curls as they unworked each section of her braid. They brought their fingers into her scalp, stroking through the thickest part of her hair and she sighed, leaning back against them. Her beast took slow, deliberate strokes through her hair, luxuriating in it.

One hand moved and she was startled to feel their thumb stroke her cheek, brushing away a tear that she hadn't realized had fallen. Rayne blinked open her eyes and looked up, meeting their gaze. Hawthorne was looking down at her with an affection that felt profane. "Why didn't you just tell me when I first came back?"

"I was angry with you. And I think that there was part of me that wanted you to remember on your own. To come looking for me."

"Do you think that I'll ever get them back?"

Hawthorne's expression shifted. "I think that if you have not remembered anything on your own after all that I have shared, I do not think you ever will," they admitted. "But, I will share all of my memories of our time together with you. It is not the same but neither of us will be alone in it any longer."

Neither of us will be alone.

"Take me to bed."

Hawthorne brushed their lips against the crown of her head and did exactly as she asked. Rayne was laid down into bed with all the tenderness of a body being put to rest, her beast sliding over her like dirt over a casket. Rayne pressed herself close to them and they nuzzled against her nose. She leaned forward, her mouth opening slightly before they claimed her lips.

The kiss was unlike anything else she had experienced. It was without their usual hunger and replaced with something so delicate that her hands began to shake.

Rayne pulled Hawthorne closer, her own fingers sliding into their dark curls and tugging them closer. *I will break you open and tear out the pearl of you.*

Their tongue flicked against her lip, teasing her but also, she recognized, asking her for more.

Her fingers tangled in their night sky of curls, their hands exploring her exposed arms and chest, not daring to go further down as she had not removed the rest of her clothes. Rayne pulled them down in the abyss of her dark bed sheets, drinking them in like wine.

She pulled away but she dug her fingers into their scalp, to keep them close before they could try to pull away. "Will you stay after?" she whispered into their ear. "Will you come back to me after your body is gone?"

"I never left," they said, smoothing a curl away from her forehead. "I will not endure any place where you are not. What about you?"

"What about me?"

"Will you stay? Or are you still so set on leaving me behind?"

"I could not leave you again." Rayne's fingers slid up their stomach to their chest, stopping where the temporary heart beat its refrain. She never noticed how magical heartbeats were before she heard theirs. She could literally hear the sound of their body keeping them alive. "I never thought I'd like the sound of a heartbeat so much," she said more to herself than to them.

"It's yours," Hawthorne declared, grasping her face between their hands and kissing her as a man starved. Their lips move from hers to the column of her neck, sharp teeth brushing against the sensitive skin there. "Now that you have it, what will you give me in exchange?"

"Anything," she whispered, arching into their touch.

"Surely you can do better than that, little wolf," they said as they ran their long tongue down her collarbone.

"Whatever you want." Her nails dug into their skin and Hawthorne let out a growl that coalesced in her core.

"Still haven't learned, have you?" They pried her hands from them and pinned them over her head. "Offering yourself up on a platter to any hungry thing?"

"Just you," she admitted, batting her lashes up at them. "You are the only hungry thing I want to be eaten by."

They held her gaze, a flame to a wick. "I want you to stay here. In this home, with me. Let me be the ghost in the halls while you sleep, let me claw at your doors and pull you into every nightmare you've ever had. Let me give you the world."

Yes. Haunt me. Take me into the dark with you. That was all she had ever wanted, was to be wanted by someone that she cared about. For someone to look for her, to chase her, *love* her.

She moved the dark curtain of their curls from their face and those starless eyes were already staring back at her. Her thumb traced over their cheek and the constellations of freckles that she found there. *How beautiful you are. Has anyone ever told you?* It was a terrible power that she liked to think that they would wield as a dagger against the ugliness of the world.

"Rayne," Hawthorne whispered, their voice trembling and she realized that she had simply been staring at them. "Your answer? I need to hear it. Will you stay with me?"

"Yes, I will stay here with you."

Hawthorne smiled and she was sure that light of it could combat that of the sun. They laughed against her ship-wrecked skin and Rayne wondered where it was that their laugh originated from. The sound of fallen leaves scraping against asphalt or the great shuttering of a pine tree as it collapsed onto the forest floor?

What I wouldn't give to hear it every second of every day.

"What would you have done if I had refused?"

Hawthorne chuckled once more as they grasped her hand and pressed it to their lips. "Follow you to the ends of the earth," they replied, their tongue running along her skin as they pressed a kiss to her inner wrist. She giggled but they fixed her with a look that told her the severity of which they spoke, pinning her with their lethal weapon of a gaze. "As I said, I will not tolerate any place devoid of you."

Rayne worried her lip with her teeth. "But what about when I die?"

Hawthorne tugged her closer, their practiced hands moving her with ease. She could not help but marvel at the lightness of their touch even in this form.

How was it that no one in all of her life had ever handled her with such gentleness?

"When you die," they began, eyes tracing the outline of her full lips. "I will be the one to put you in the ground. I will follow you into everything that comes next. You need only wait for me."

Their fingers traced down between her breasts and she shivered. In response, her nails raked up their back.

She would not go gently into this, and though her wolf regarded her delicately, she wanted to leave her scars on this creature that had marked her so deeply.

But underneath it all there lay that fear of being seen, of being known so completely by another that froze her in her tracks. She had regarded herself as a secret for so long with her body acting as her own private punishment that she realized she did not know how to be with someone.

I'll learn. I want to be with them. Only ever them.

But despite this knowledge, the fear cemented within her. Who would she be when she belonged to another? Would everything that she struggled with now belong to them? Would Hawthorne end up tangled in the web of things that she couldn't give voice to?

And everything that she was sure Hawthorne kept tucked under their tongue like a razorblade, would that belong to her now too? As she lay with them, half naked and thinking, Hawthorne remained silent, brushing their thumb absently over her hip. Waiting.

As much as her monster threatened her, pressed their teeth to every tender spot she had, they never forced her. Never made her do anything against her will.

She wanted to work this out on her own but shame at her own lack of understanding when it came to others just wasn't there. There was a wall there, a desert that she couldn't cross on her own.

"I don't know how to do this," she said finally and her entire body tensed despite the tender embrace of her monster. "I don't know how to make space for you, to let you see... my body."

"Tell me what you're afraid I will see."

"I'm not pretty," she blurted, sliding back into the dark pool of self hatred.

"I did not ask you what you thought about yourself, Rayne," Hawthorne snapped. "I asked you what you thought I was going to see when I looked at your body. *Explain* it to me."

"I am... afraid that you'll see all of the scars that I have. Not just the fresh ones but the old ones that didn't heal right or just don't look good." Her hands wrung themselves of their own accord and her monster's hands slid over hers.

"And what if I like what I see?"

Rayne shook her head. "Why would you?"

"That is not the question," they said with that easy grin of theirs. "The question is what if I like what I see? What if your scars remind me of angry ocean waves or the bark of my favorite tree? What if they are beautiful to me, Rayne? What then?"

The hungry thing inside of her howled in delight, desperate with the desire to be desired. Rayne bit her lip. "What if you don't?"

"Only one way to find out, and that's on you to decide." They shrugged.

Rayne took a deep breath and slipped out of bed.

CHAPTER TWENTY-EIGHT
rayne

*T*here's *no going back now—no way to make them unsee you and no way for
you to unlove them either.*

"Can you turn around?" she asked over the screaming fears within her mind.
"I'll tell you when I'm ready, okay?"

Hawthorne sat up. "Are you sure?"

Rayne nodded, not trusting herself to speak just yet. She was not brave, and
Hawthorne robbed her of what little courage she had managed to scrounge
together.

"You do not have to do this, Rayne," Hawthorne continued as they turned
their back to her as she began to undress. "As much as I want to see you, I will
not do it for the sake of sacrificing your comfort. This is not some test to pass."

Her heart swelled; every moment that she thought she could not love her
beast more, they proved her wrong, and she fell deeper into their depths.

"If I don't do this now, I don't think I ever will," she said, a nervous laugh
bubbling out of her before she could stop it. She reached behind her to undo
the hooks of her bralette. "Could you—?"

They were behind her in a moment, their chest pressed against the curve of
her back and their cock flush against her ass. Heat bloomed in her cheeks, and
her heart thrummed away in her chest. Without a word, Hawthorne unclasped

the hooks, and her bra fell away. She stilled, waiting for them to move away from her, to say something, but instead they both stood utterly still. She watched their reflection in her vanity mirror, and they stared at her back, completely transfixed.

Finally, they cleared their throat. "May I?"

She nodded, not trusting herself to speak. "You have a beauty mark," they marveled, brushing their thumb over her left shoulder, just between her upper shoulder blades. "Just here." They leaned down and pressed a kiss to it.

Rayne wasn't sure if she was breathing.

"And another here." Their thumb moved to her lower back, at the curve of her spine, and pressed another kiss there. Soon, they were kissing every bit of exposed skin they could reach.

"Can I undress you the rest of the way?"

"Yes," she answered before her brain could rebel against it.

"Turn to me."

Rayne turned to face Hawthorne just as they knelt before her, staring up at her with an expression that had tears stinging her eyes. *Why does this hurt? Why does it feel like a stab through my chest, like a blade?*

Hawthorne was not simply looking at her; they were seeing her. All of her. She had to resist the urge to cover her breasts with her hands, to hide from them. They had borne themselves to her, body and soul, and now, it was her turn.

She was down to her leggings and her thick, black thigh-highs. She watched as their eyes devoured her chest, her dark, peaked nipples, and the softness of her stomach. She could only think of the scars that littered her shipwrecked skin, the stretch marks at her hips.

Do I look as though I've been chewed up and spit out by the world?

Hawthorne leaned forward to rest their forehead against her stomach, wrapping their arms around her waist. "You're so beautiful, Rayne," they whispered against her skin. "I have never seen anyone or anything half as lovely as this."

She wanted to ask them if they were sure if they meant it, but they had moved. Their tongue found her nipples, and she believed them. With their other hand, they worked her nipple between their two fingers. "I am never going to let you go. No one else is ever going to have the right to lay eyes on you. You're mine, aren't you, pretty girl?"

"Yes," Rayne moaned, her fingers sliding into their hair.

"I am going to ruin you, Rayne. I'm going to fuck you so good that you're never going to stop craving my cock. You're going to beg me for it all year long and thank me so prettily when you get it," they murmured against her skin.

She wanted to crawl inside of their words, to do exactly what they asked of her. She wanted to be kept; she wanted Hawthorne to lull her into their waiting arms.

They paused their ministrations with one nipple, still running their tongue along her other as they eased her out of her leggings and her thick socks, kissing their way down as they did.

Rayne was almost completely naked before them, save for her panties. No one except her family had ever seen the pink scars that spotted her legs, darkest around her knees and calves. She took a step back, but Hawthorne held fast, keeping her right where she was.

"Don't run from me, Rayne. I told you already, you're beautiful."

Tears stung her eyes as she trembled under their touch, her nerves gripping her by the throat.

"Not yet," they crooned, reaching up to wipe away a stray tear and bring it to their lips. "Your tears taste so sweet. And you're going to shed more of them for me, but only when my cock is inside of you. Understood?"

She nodded, sniffling.

"Say 'Yes, Hawthorne,'" they crooned.

"Yes, Hawthorne."

They grinned. "Good girl. Now, open your legs for me."

Rayne obeyed, albeit a little uneasily at first. Hawthorne moved down from her nipples to tuck their face between her legs, kissing their way down as they did. They slid their tongue under her panties, and with one swift tug, they ripped them away from her, exposing her completely.

Hawthorne swore and breathed in her scent as if she were the most intoxicating thing they'd ever smelled. "You're going to take my cock, Rayne. But not before you cum on my tongue."

She expected Hawthorne to tease her the way that they always had before but they wasted no time flattening their tongue against her clit and going at her as if they were starved. Her thighs quivered with each movement of their wicked tongue, and their other hand braced her ass to keep her on her feet.

"You taste even better than I imagined," they moaned against her. "How am I ever supposed to let you leave this bedroom?"

Hawthorne's words pulled her in and lulled her into a cocoon of pleasure just as much as their tongue did. She tugged on their horns and swore. "Fuck, Hawth, I can't—"

"That's right, beautiful. Say my name." Hawthorne purred against her; the feeling of their voice vibrating against her was enough to send shivers down her spine again. They lifted her and plopped her down on her bed. Before she could even think to respond, their tongue was between her thighs once more.

Rayne dug her nails into their scalp as her orgasm ripped through her, and Hawthorne groaned against her.

She melted into the sheets; her limbs were soft and relaxed. Hawthorne nipped her thigh and smirked up at her. Their body had changed again; their pupils were blown out and so large that they devoured the iris of their eyes, and their teeth had begun to change shape. Sharper. "You should know that I am nowhere near done with you."

She hooked her legs over their shoulders. Her beast slid a finger inside of her, and her back bowed as their mouth pressed into her again. Rayne felt untethered, floating through an ocean of pleasure she had never imagined experiencing. She dug her nails into their skin while Hawthorne's free hand balled the sheets behind her in their fists.

She was hungry and selfish and wanting, but so too was her wolf. They gave as much as they took, but she would take more. She would *not* allow herself to be sated.

She loved them, and she would inflict that love upon them. Her adoration would be nothing less than a plague.

Hawthorne did not allow her a moment's respite as they pushed her to the edge over and over again until their name became a prayer on her lips.

At some point, Hawthorne plopped down beside her on the bed, licking their lips like a cat and tucking her against them in one swift motion. Rayne allowed herself to be gathered, something she was begrudgingly growing quite fond of.

Still, she had not gotten used to the firmness of their body as she curled against them, the softness of the dark hair on their chest, the scent of damp earth that clung to their skin.

A dozen thoughts raced through her mind, and she wished that she could find the power to voice them all.

I will carve a space within myself for you.

Loving you is an aching wilderness.

But then Hawthorne's hand smoothed over her hip, gripping it possessively for a moment before their thumb idly caressed it. She didn't have to explain herself; she didn't even need to speak if she didn't want to. She could lie beside them, and the world passed them both by.

"Where did you bury my brother?" Rayne inquired, the thought only just dawning on her.

Hawthorne chuckled. "You've just spent the last half an hour screaming my name, and now you want to know where your dead brother is?"

She frowned. "I only just thought of it."

"An odd time to do so."

"Are *you* calling me weird *again*?"

They nuzzled her shoulder, and she struggled to maintain her irritation with them. "Very much so. An odd little creature."

"Just tell me," Rayne huffed.

"I ate him," Hawthorne replied. "What's left of him is buried in the backyard. Beneath the pine tree."

The knowledge settled within her, but no emotion accompanied it. *My brother is dead and I don't care. I really do not care.* She pressed her face against

Hawthorne's shoulder, a small, giddy giggle leaving her throat. It felt like freedom.

"Are you sore?" they asked, leaning in to steal a kiss from her. She shook her head. "Use your words for me, gorgeous," they purred.

"No, I'm not sore."

"Good." Their hands coasted over her hips and dug into the thickness of her thighs while remaining mindful of her delicate skin. "I told you that you had my heart, Rayne, and I meant it. But it is not the only thing that I want to give you."

"Like what?"

"What else do you want, Rayne? You're half full of desires, and yet I know so few of them."

"Wanting is a private terror," she retorted by way of hiding.

"*I* am your terror," Hawthorne sighed with a smirk. "Tell me."

Rayne closed her eyes and allowed herself a moment to sit with the ache in her gut, that pointed, uncontented thing that had never once ceased its howling. *What's your name? What will fill you?*

She thought back to her youngest self, the little girl that she had seen wandering in the snow through Hawthorne's memories. She had been so small, so weak, and even now, fully grown, she was still just as fragile as she had been then.

Who would I be if I were stronger? "I want power," Rayne declared.

"Name the desire fully. I know there is more in you than that," Hawthorne said.

"I want to stop being so frightened of everything and everyone," she continued and then abruptly closed it.

"Do not make me pull it from you, Rayne. Speak freely."

Rayne pinched her eyes closed, unable to stomach the expression on Hawthorne's face when they heard every desire in her terrible heart.

"I want to be terrifying. I want never to see pity reflected in the eyes of another. And if that means that I must tear out those eyes, then I want that too. I do not want to be this delicate, slip of a flower. I know you cannot take this away, but forge me into a dagger. I never want to give my power away again. Unmake me."

Hawthorne kissed her cheek, their foreheads falling together. "There you are. And what about the town?"

Rayne peered an eye open. "What about it?"

"They've treated you like trash. Mocked you, berated you, shunned you."

She swallowed, nodding. "Yes."

"Now what will you do about it?"

I could do something about it. I wouldn't have to be helpless anymore. "What can I do?"

Hawthorne smiled, their grin as wide and inhuman as ever. "Whatever you want. They called you a monster. Why not show them what true monstrosity is?"

"Cherub, you need not change yourself for them. For anyone," The House whispered, the wall beside her bed shifting. **"Stay as you are, beloved. You have always been worthy of love."**

"House," Rayne began, looking up at the ceiling. "Did you know who Hawthorne was to me? That they were Mr. Wolf?"

The roof shuttered with House's fretting. **"It is much more complicated than a simple question of knowledge, cherub. There is so much that you cannot see, even they in their age cannot see it. I have only—"**

"*Did* you know?"

The House sighed. **"The moment you ran from your wicked parents and me, I kicked them from my bones and would not allow them reentry until you came back. Until you remembered them of your own volition and could make the choice fully. I have known them, yes but—"**

"You can't demonize Hawthorne and in the same breath admit to lying to me over the last few weeks," Rayne snapped. "You took the choice from me. You won't take this one too."

The House wailed along with the wind whipping against the windows.

Do not listen to the House.

"The note," she chirped, drawing Hawthorne's attention back to her. "Did you write it?"

Hawthorne's head tilted. "No, I did not."

They told me that their nature would never change. If they're a spirit and spirits never give more than offered, then I have to ask them better questions.

"Did you have something to do with my brother writing it?"

Hawthorne grinned, something like pride dancing across their expression. "That I did."

Were they warning me or luring me?

Hawthorne had never hidden their desire to devour her; they spoke openly of their brutal wants without an ounce of shame. *I'm not even sure if they're capable of feeling shame.*

They were a callous thing, viscous as they were ravenous. And yet, they had never hurt her, even in her dreams. When they tore her apart, it was at her own request. This monster—her monster—cared for her. Here they were offering her power, retribution if she chose. "Can you really do what I asked?"

Hawthorne offered her their hand, and magnetized to them, she slipped her hand into theirs. "I have only an idea, but I believe so. When I took your memory, I had never done such a thing before. Does that lessen your trust in me?"

Rayne shook her head. "No. What do we do?"

"I will give you my blood while I have this body, and you will give me yours."

"I thought your kind didn't give?"

"We do not, and that is why this may be successful. It is not in our nature, nor is it in that of humans, to have true magic at their fingertips," Hawthorne explained, fixated on Rayne's hand, though she did not feel the urge to recoil. "Something surely must come of this. I will not shrink away from it. Will you?"

"No."

No more hiding. Not if I can help it.

Hawthorne pulled her closer, settling her between their legs, their cock pulsing to life against her thigh. "We will be the Great Snake devouring its tail."

To devour and be devoured in return. Rayne kissed them, her fingers sliding into their hair and she kissed them as if they might never do it again. Hawthorne responded in kind, pulling the breath from her. Sucking their bottom lip between her teeth, she bit down as hard as she could until she felt flesh split.

Thick, syrupy blood oozed against her tongue as sweet as it was bitter; like syrup against metal. Hawthorne snapped back, their finger moving against the punctured seam of their lip. Blood beaded and streamed down their chin, and when they wiped at it, their hand came back black. They looked down at their hand, marveling at their own blood.

Maybe they haven't. Am I really the first to wound you? Rayne thought, licking the blood from her own lips.

Hawthorne looked at her, and there was no denying what she saw there: the unrestrained desire *for her.* They captured her lips with their own, pressing her down further into the mattress. "You will have to draw more blood from me than that, little wolf. Are you so eager to sink your teeth into me?"

"Yes," she breathed, bucking her hips against their thigh.

They chuckled. "Then you'll need to wait just a little longer. I will go first." Hawthorne swept the hair from her face. "But I want to see all of you while I do."

Hawthorne trailed a series of kisses against her skin, down her neck and between her breasts, down the line of her stomach. They avoided the tiny patches of unscarred skin and instead sought the marred, ugliest bits of her. "Can I leave a mark on you, Rayne?"

Fire made a home in her blood, singing in her veins. "Please."

"Where shall I leave it then?" Hawthorne asked, seemingly more to themself than her. "Your pretty stomach? You seemed to love when I tore into it in your dream," they purred and she felt their voice all the way down to her bones. Hawthorne moved to her hips, sliding their tongue along the rise of her left hip bone. "No, right here. Over this birthmark. It's like a little star."

"Hawthorne, please."

"Mm. I could get used to hearing my name on your lips like that. Are you ready?"

"If you don't bite me right now, I'm going to kick you in—"

Pain burst to life at her hip as their teeth dug deep into her soft flesh, the hazel in their eyes darkened until it was nearly black, the shape of their mouth shifting. Blood pooled along her side and soaked the sheets. Beneath the sting, pleasure, feather light and nearly hidden, vibrated through her.

The moan that worked its way out of her was foreign, the voice of another woman, wanton and more animal than anything else. Hawthorne's tongue smoothed over the wound, lapping at her blood. "I am glad that I did not eat you before," Hawthorne grit out, the humanity in their voice long gone. "I would have swallowed you down in one bite and regretted not getting to savor the taste." Their entire mouth was smeared scarlet, running their tongue along their lips.

"I would have made sure to give you indigestion. Come here."

Hawthorne returned to their place above her, and she welcomed them with open, greedy arms. She tasted herself—her blood on their lips, licking it as her hands groped every inch of their body that she could. The feel of them was too much for her and not enough at the same time.

The language of bodies was not one that Rayne would ever consider herself fluent in, and yet she desperately wanted to learn. Hawthorne's cock brushed against the soft skin of her thigh, and she ground back against them.

"I was not as careful as I should have been last time we were intimate," Hawthorne said in her ear. "It was your first time, and I was inconsiderate. I will not make the same mistake this time."

Rayne blushed. *It's like they can read my mind; they always know what I'm thinking about.* "I—okay."

Hawthorne reached between them, grabbing their cock and aligning it with her entrance, but making no further move forward. "I will go slowly," they said against the shell of her ear. "At least, until you beg me for more."

She opened her mouth, prepared to poke a hole in their cockiness when they edged inside of her, silencing her with a moan. Rayne wrapped her arms around their neck, her nails digging into their pale skin. Her breath caught in her throat, and she hid her face against their shoulder. Their lips stayed at her ear, murmuring words of encouragement that liquified her spine.

"There you go, just like that. Fuck, you feel so good, Rayne."

The burn of them stretching her lasted only a few moments before giving way to pleasure. Her heels locked around their waist, trying to usher herself nearer, to push them deeper. She would have begged, would have cried for them to move, but her beast took mercy on her.

Friction had never felt so good, so perfect against her skin, and each thrust sent her closer and closer to that wicked edge. Hawthorne's hand returned between them, and their thumb found the sensitive bundle of nerves, their thumb working her clit in slow, agonizing circles.

Rayne's head fell back against the pillow. "Fuck, Hawth! Right there. Oh, fuck." Her pleasure crested, and as the weight of it rushed against her, she bit into Hawthorne's shoulder as hard as she could. Hawthorne cried out as they spilled inside of her, chasing her orgasm a moment after her.

She panted against their skin, trying to catch her breath, but the heat from her orgasm didn't fade; it traveled from her center, through her hip, and radiated up her body. Rayne winced, warmth giving way to an inferno, and she pushed at Hawthorne.

"What is wrong?" Hawthorne inquired, slipping out of her and moving away from her. "Did I hurt you?"

"Everything's burning. My skin, my veins, my—" Her gasp cut off the rest of her sentence. *Holy shit.* The skin where Hawthorne had dug their teeth into her was raised, raw, and purple. Her veins darkened, blackening as whatever Hawthorne had given her traveled through her bloodstream like venom.

Hawthorne's eyes were wide, their mouth hung open. Rayne peeled herself out of bed, stumbling into her bathroom. The fire shifted form, no longer burning but singing, dancing inside of her. Rayne grasped the edge of the sink, trembling with the enormity of all that was working its way into her. She heaved into the sink, her stomach empty and full of magic at the same time.

"Rayne?" Hawthorne appeared at the door, mindful of her space while remaining near. "What is happening? Tell me what you are feeling."

"I don't know. It doesn't hurt, but it doesn't feel good either," she replied, her head hung as she heaved again. She looked up, meaning to turn to Hawthorne, but she caught her reflection in the mirror and froze, transfixed by what stared back at her.

Is that me?

Her skin remained as it always had, still covered in her scars, but now, beneath it, black marks, like spiders' legs, had worked their way into it. Every capillary and vein had been filled with black roots that reached down deep into the core of her.

Like a tree.

'*The earth of me,*' Hawthorne had said. Hawthorne's blood was inside of *her* now.

The eyes that looked back at her were not the ones she had been looking into her entire life. Now they gleamed like stars on a winter's night, distant and dark. Her canines felt just a touch sharper, running her tongue along them, she was sure that she would draw her own blood if she weren't careful.

Her body was still shaky, but the nausea was slipping away, replaced with a quiet certainty. *I look different. Not beautiful—never that—but maybe something on the other side of it.*

"I can hear you," Hawthorne whispered, startling her.

"Hear what?" Rayne asked.

"Your thoughts," Hawthorne replied. "I heard what you just thought right now. That you looked different, something on the other side of beautiful."

Rayne whirled to face them, her heart hammering in her chest. "Can I hear you too?"

Hawthorne spilled into her mind like milk into coffee, seeping even further into her. *I am not sure. Can you hear me, little wolf?*

She laughed, breathless. "Yeah, yeah, I can."

Hawthorne grinned wildly. "I told you. There is no space between us now."

Hours later, she and Hawthorne had barely moved from the bed. She finally managed to pry herself away for a few moments while Hawthorne went downstairs to grab her a glass of water. There was something else she had to do.

She had taken a few minutes in the bathroom to gather herself before she snuck back out into her room to grab her cellphone. Rayne knelt to snatch it from the pile of clothes on the floor, as she did, she felt a sharp bite of pain at the rise of her ass. She yelped and looked over her shoulder to see her monster at the door with a mischievous smirk on its handsome face. "Come back over here."

"Not yet. I've got to make a phone call."

"Now?"

"It will only take a few minutes. Five."

Hawthorne pouted their lower lip, huffing. "Fine. But I *will* count, and I will drag you back into this bed."

They waved a shadow tendril at her lazily, and she swatted it away with a blush, scurrying into the bathroom. Being so openly desired was new but not unwelcome. She just felt like a baby deer taking its first steps out into the world instead of a grown woman entering what was her first serious relationship.

Once in the bathroom, she partially closed the door, not for want of keeping Hawthorne out but so their reflection wouldn't catch in the mirror and distract her from her task.

Soft, hazy afternoon light spilled through the window over the shower and bleached the walls with winter light, a snowstorm blew. Inside, the heat radiated, giving her home a cozy, safe feeling. *I never thought that I would feel safe in this hellhole. I don't want to leave.*

Rayne dialed the number that she had been given. "Hello?" Came Persimmon's voice, hesitant, uncertain. "Rayne, is this you?"

"Oh, uh. Yeah, it's me."

"Oh! Wow, okay. Sorry, I didn't really expect you ever to call. Talking doesn't always seem to be your thing."

Guilt reared its ugly head. Persimmon was right, talking wasn't really her thing. Unless she was talking to Hawthorne. Rayne shook the feeling away. *If*

Persimmon didn't want to pick up the phone, she didn't have to. I have nothing to feel guilty about.

That's my girl. You do not owe anyone an apology for existing, Hawthorne purred into her mind, and she smiled, the tiniest seed of pride taking root in her chest.

"I wanted to talk to you. I can call back later if now isn't a great time for you?"

"Nah, now is as good a time as any. I've got all these dishes to do, so it will be nice to have some company. What's up?"

Rayne took a deep breath, pinching her eyes shut. "I—I'm not leaving Bury. I'm going to stay here, in town... in this house."

Persimmon screamed so loud that Rayne nearly dropped her phone. "Seriously? Like for real, you're sure?"

"Yeah, I'm sure," she answered, regaining her grip on the phone.

"This is huge! We should celebrate! I can make dinner and we can drink wine and paint over that ugly wallpaper you said you hated. Ooh, we can even—"

"So, you aren't mad? I know that I said I was going to sell you the house. But things changed. I would understand if you were angry with me."

Persimmon's bright laughter sounded on the other end of the line. "Not at all. I was hoping you'd stay, change your mind. Manifestation for the win!"

In the mirror, she caught her monster's shadows slithering along the floor and wrapping around her leg and her waist. The grip remained chaste, gentle, soothing. Her gaze drifted to her reflection once more, and slowly, a smile found its way to her face.

"I gotta ask though; what changed your mind? You've done nothing but tell me how much you hate this town since the day we met. What happened?"

Hawthorne rose from the bed and slid behind her. They hardly fit in the bathroom, but somehow, they fit perfectly around her, their arms locking around her waist. "It was a lot of things and I—I met someone."

Her beast chuckled against her skin, nuzzling her hair and kissing their way down the column of her neck.

"Wait—what? Did you meet some dreamboat guy while you were packing up all your shit?"

Rayne smirked as Hawthorne nipped at her shoulder. "Something like that. But if I'm honest..." She caught her reflection in the mirror. "This town doesn't deserve to get rid of me that easily."

INTERLUDE:
CHAPTER TWENTY-NINE

rayne

Rayne couldn't decipher what time it was; all she knew was that the sun had begun to set, and her monster was in her kitchen, feeding her after making her orgasm so many times that she had nearly forgotten her name.

Hawthorne stood with their back to her, naked and humming as they flipped pancakes on the stove. Along their back, beneath the angry scratches she'd clawed into them, a constellation of freckles showed back at her.

God, they're so beautiful.

"I am glad that you are finally noticing," Hawthorne answered, winking at her over their shoulder.

Rayne sank into the couch, pulling the throw blanket over her with a groan. "I don't know if I like the idea of you hearing every thought."

Hawthorne laughed over the crackling wood from the fireplace. "No? I'm quite fond of it," they said. "But, if you would like space, we can work out how to construct walls between the connections. For the moments you would rather keep private."

Rayne peeked over the blanket at them. "I would like that. But not always, just sometimes."

"I understand. I have my own moments where I must come back to myself. I am mine before I can ever be yours."

"You understand yourself so well," Rayne marveled. "The way that you talk about yourself, it's so... good."

The stove sizzled as Hawthorne flipped the final pancake. "I have had a very long time to know myself. I am older than this town, than most mortal things." Hawthorne plopped the last pancake into the stack on the plate beside the stove, reached into one of the cabinets to grab syrup and utensils, and brought the plate to her. "If this is not enough, I can make you an omelet or whatever else you'd like."

Rayne sat up, crossing her legs and allowing the blanket to fall to her waist. Hawthorne made no move to hide their gaze on her chest. "Aren't you hungry? You've only had oranges today."

The kitchen island was a graveyard of orange peels, Hawthorne having torn through them. "I have your mediocre prepackaged meat thawing in the sink. I will cook us dinner before I return to the forest."

"How long will it take you to come back?" Rayne asked around a mouthful of steaming, syrup-soaked pancake. "These are good. You're really good at making food."

They smirked. "Not long. An hour at most. Becoming is slow, but shedding is simple. I will try to return to you as quickly as I can."

Rayne flashed them a shy smile, then looked away. *They want to come back to me. Me.*

Hawthorne froze with tension, a growl unlike any she had ever heard from them before nearly shook the house with its force. "Someone is here. I can hear the engine of their car. They've pulled into the driveway."

"Oh, maybe it's Persimmon?" Rayne said after swallowing another mouthful of food. "She could be coming by to grab some of the paperwork from when she was going to buy the house."

Hawthorne shook their head. "No, this is someone else. I have never caught their scent before; they are not from Bury."

House hissed, shifting in displeasure. *"Oh, I dislike her, cherub. I dislike her very much. Bitter as rotten lemons and as harsh as sea salt. Oh, dearest, make her leave!"*

Her? If it wasn't Persimmon and she wasn't from town, then who the fuck is she?

"I do not know," Hawthorne said, taking her plate from her. "I will put this in the microwave so it does not get cold. Answer the door, I will be here." The doorbell rang a second later.

Just as she opened her mouth to protest, whoever she was, knocked loudly at the front door. Hawthorne melted into the shadows of the house just as easily as they did when they did not inhabit their human form.

As she stood, she realized that she was still completely naked. *Fuck.* Rayne wrapped the blanket tightly around herself. Stomping up to the door, Rayne unlocked it and swung it open. Whoever had dared interrupt them had better have something damned interesting to say to justify it.

Juniper stood opposite her, thick, dark hair wind-swept and snow-capped, chapped lips set in a hard line. Rayne shivered with the gust of winter air that followed Juniper.

Her cousin's dark eyes fell to the throw blanket covering Rayne's skin, her bare feet, and then back up to her eyes. "Not exactly appropriate for the weather."

Rayne blinked. *That's because I'm in my house, enjoying my fireplace. I can wear and do whatever the fuck I want.* But her words stumbled over one another, knotting in her throat. "June. What are you doing here?" she managed lamely.

"Are you going to let me in, or are we both going just to stand here and freeze?" Juniper snapped.

Rayne stepped aside, shrinking against the door as she did so.

Juniper pushed past her, the snow on her boots already beginning to melt as she stepped into the warm cocoon of their home. She tossed her damp gloves on the floor along with her jacket, her gaze focused on the stairwell. "Callum?" she called. "Cal, are you here?"

Callum. Of course, this is about him.

"He's not here," Rayne said, closing the door softly behind her. "I told you that last time we spoke. I haven't seen him."

"See, that's the problem, Rainy," Juniper continued, narrowing dark eyes at Rayne. "No one has heard from or seen Callum in weeks. Not his job, his girlfriend, his friends. No one. It's like he's just disappeared."

Rayne's mouth opened and closed as she searched for something to soothe her cousin, a pretty, believable lie. None came. "What's that got to do with me?"

"You—"

"Who's that at the door, baby?" Hawthorne called from the kitchen before they stalked into the foyer. It sounded like them but different; their voice was more human, and their near-perfect pronunciation of each syllable lulled into something lazier. They had changed into a pair of black boxers, and their long-sleeved, plaid shirt hung open, exposing their bare chest.

They were nothing short of devastating.

Juniper turned to Hawthorne, brow raised. "Who the hell are you?"

Hawthorne sidled up beside Rayne, wrapping an arm around her waist. "I'm her husband," they purred, leaning down to kiss the top of Rayne's head. "So, who the *fuck* are you?"

Husband. Husband. Husband.

Rayne's mind struggled to wrap around the idea of Hawthorne being her life partner, not for lack of desire, but because she had never even considered it was an option they would explore, *least of all with me.*

The shock of it silenced her, though she smiled and nodded in agreement with them. *Husband? That's rather gendered.* She thought in their direction. *I thought you didn't like labels like that.*

I like the sound of it when it comes to you. And a husband is a role. I was going to refer to myself as your wife, but husband sounds much better, they replied, billowing into her mind like smoke. *Do you not like it?*

Rayne didn't like it, she realized. She loved it. The idea of Hawthorne as her husband and her as their wife was a secret and terrible want because she hadn't realized that it was there. But now, with it presented to her, she clutched at it with greedy hands.

I love it.

"Husband?" Juniper echoed, the shock evident on her face as she looked between them. "Married, you? When?"

"We've been married for a year today, actually," Hawthorne answered, and she nodded again, leaning closer to them. "We were actually in the middle of celebrating our anniversary before you chose to interrupt. I'll ask again, *stranger,* who are you?"

Juniper looked at Rayne expectantly, but when no introduction came, she cleared her throat. "I'm Rayne's cousin, Juniper."

"Nice to meet you, June," Hawthorne said, seemingly tasting her name on the edge of their tongue.

"Juniper. Only my family calls me June."

Hawthorne tilted their head with a smile sharp enough to cut glass. "We are family now, silly."

Juniper swallowed, remaining silent though her eyes slid to Rayne. "We need to talk. *Now.* Privately."

Would you like me to go? Hawthorne asked down the thread between them.

Yes, but I want you to listen. She'll keep bitching unless she gets what she wants.

Hawthorne leaned down to kiss the top of Rayne's head once more, though they remained focused on Juniper. "Of course. I'll be right upstairs if you need me."

They weren't even halfway up the stairs before Juniper had snatched Rayne by the hand and pulled her into the living room. Rayne winced at the friction. Even with the magic Hawthorne had gifted her, her skin was still just as fragile as it had been before.

"How long have you known your husband?" Juniper hissed, lower than the roar of the fire. "Truly?"

"I—it's been a year. We've been together for a year," Rayne stammered.

"And you didn't tell anyone? You didn't invite me or even Callum to the wedding?"

"Callum didn't deem me worthy of pursuing a relationship with, in case you forgot," Rayne bit back. "He was the one who left. If he wanted to reach out, he could have."

Even with the knowledge that her brother was dead and rotting in the garden, she wished that Juniper could offer her something different, just an ounce of proof that her brother had cared about her, even distantly.

Instead, Juniper sighed, rubbing the bridge of her nose. "Whether you like it or not, we're family. It's our job to look after one another, which is what I am trying to do now. Something happened to Callum."

"Like what?"

"I don't know!" Juniper exclaimed, throwing her hands up. "But something isn't right. He would never just abandon his life. Especially without saying something to me."

"Since you're such a fucking expert on him, then, I don't know why the fuck you're here in *my* house, in *my* face. Go find him if you know where he is," Rayne snapped with more force than she realized.

Juniper froze, staring at Rayne blankly but slowly, fury filtered in. "Rayne Cidney-Marie Dorne," Juniper fumed. "Have you lost your God-given mind? I am here looking for your brother, and all you can do is cuss at me?"

An apology rose and died on her tongue. *I didn't do anything wrong. I have no reason to apologize.*

That's right, baby. No one can make you small unless you let them, Hawthorne's voice caressed her as tenderly as they would have.

"And furthermore," Juniper continued, gesturing behind her to the couch and the rest of the living room. "This is not your house. Your parents left this place for Callum. What makes you think that he would ever leave it to you?"

"I–I don't know. I only found out when I went to the county clerk's office—"

"No," Juniper shook her head. "That doesn't add up. I don't believe you. I think you're lying. I think you know about what really happened to Cal."

Rayne stepped back, her blanket nearly slipping, and she clutched it tighter around her. "I don't know anything more than you do—"

"You're a liar, Rayne!" Juniper pushed against Rayne's shoulders, and she stumbled backwards.

Did she just touch you? Hawthorne demanded.

"I think that you and your '*husband*'," Juniper emphasized the word with air quotations, "lured Callum here once you found out that your parents didn't leave you anything, and you killed him."

Juniper was getting dangerously closer to the truth with every word that she spoke and Rayne's heart rate spiked with every passing moment. Her mind scrambled for a defense, for something believable, but Juniper's shrill voice was making any logical thought impossible.

"You've always been a conniving little bitch. I remember how you looked at your mother when we were younger, like you couldn't wait for her to drop dead," Juniper continued. "How can I be sure that you didn't kill them either? Everything has worked out so perfectly for you. Half of our family is dead, and you're always right at the center of it."

Hold on, Rayne. I'm coming.

"Even your grandma, Adele. You were the last person who saw her. Who's to say that you didn't kill her—"

"*Shut up!*"

Rayne's voice cut through Juniper's raving, sharper and with the same gravel that she had heard in Hawthorne's when they were a shadow. Her throat burned, and a shadow in the form of a blade shot out and ripped through Juniper.

The skin at her cousin's throat split, exposing the pink and muscle and viscera beneath it, blood cascading down her neck and soaking her shirt. Juniper's hand flew to her throat to stifle the bleeding, her finger squelching as they opened and closed in a desperate attempt to keep from bleeding out.

Juniper's face was contorted in shock and pain. Rayne could see her own reflection shining back at her in her cousin's teary, dark eyes as Juniper collapsed to the ground, gasping for air.

"Oh." Hawthorne cocked their head to the side as they approached to get a better look at Juniper. "You handled it yourself. Hmm, appears as though you missed an artery."

Blood drenched the carpet, soaking Rayne's bare feet. "I didn't mean to. I don't know how I did—Hawth, what do I do? She's bleeding." She shuffled away from the mess and closer to Hawthorne, their arm wrapping lazily around her.

"She's dying."

"Don't say that!" she shot back.

Hawthorne sniffed the air. "She is. I can smell it on her. Won't be long, a few minutes, maybe ten, fifteen at most." They patted her shoulder. "I had better get her outside."

"Outside?" Rayne gawked at them. "Hawth, we have to get her to a hospital."

Hawthorne chuckled as Juniper continued to gurgle at their feet. "And then what? What will you tell the doctors? That you found her with her throat slit, bleeding out in your living room? Or that you lost your temper and your magic nearly cleaved her neck in two?"

It was not their laughter that had irritation prickling along her spine, but the fact that they were right. She couldn't take Juniper anywhere without looking exceedingly guilty. "Okay, so then what do we do?"

"We need to get her outside before she dies in the house," Hawthorne replied with a yawn, moving their arm away from Rayne to roll up their sleeves. "Otherwise, we will be stuck with your bitch of a cousin for the rest of our lives."

Rayne blinked, her mind struggling to catch up to what Hawthorne had said as they knelt to haul Juniper over their shoulder. "I don't understand."

"Don't listen to them, cherub. Your wraith is full of lies and flesh. Leave your bleeding cousin where she lies. All will be well," The House crooned.

Hawthorne rolled their eyes, moving toward the back door and sliding it open. "The House is just trying not to lose out on a meal. Anyone who dies in here will be fodder for it, and their soul will be trapped here indefinitely. Why do you think I killed your brother in the garden?"

The House wailed, *"Oh, you are truly the cruelest creature there ever was! Am I to starve while you and our cherub feast so readily? What have I ever done to deserve such agony?"*

Rayne remembered what Hawthorne had warned her of all those weeks ago, of how the House would eat her if she let it. *They hadn't been lying; they really were trying to warn me. But what about my parents?*

"It was complicated, but I assure you, little wolf, their souls are long gone."

Hawthorne tossed Juniper across the backyard, her body bouncing against the snow-covered ground with a thud that made Rayne wince. She moved to follow after them, but Hawthorne stood in her way. "In just a blanket? I may not feel the cold, but you do. A jacket and shoes at least, Rayne," they said, nodding toward the coat closet.

Rayne looked past them at the dark mass of Juniper, the shaky rise and fall of her chest.

Hawthorne scoffed and pulled off their flannel, tucking it around her shoulders. "Button it. I am getting you shoes." They brushed past her toward the coat closet by the door.

"But, you said she's dying? Shouldn't we hurry?" Rayne asked, her finger trembling as she fumbled with the buttons.

"It is not as if she is going somewhere," Hawthorne called over their shoulder. "The important thing is that she is not inside." They returned with her puffy winter coat and their hiking boots that they'd arrived in. Wordlessly, they knelt before her and eased her feet into their shoes, securing the laces.

"There's no way I'm going to be able to walk in these. They're like ships on my feet."

Hawthorne tucked her jacket under their arm while they picked up where she'd left off with her buttoning and then held out the coat for her so that she could slip her arms into it. "You won't be. It's just to keep your feet from touching the snow."

"But—"

They hooked an arm under her thighs and scooped her up, pulling her against them as they stepped out into the cold. She shivered as the winter wind, heavy with snow, whipped against her cheeks. Though Hawthorne said nothing, she caught a glimpse of their self-satisfied smirk, and she pushed against their shoulder. "You're such an asshole."

"Undoubtedly."

Rayne nestled closer to them, her cheek against their bare shoulder. "It's nice having you here like this, even when you're a jerk. I wish you could stay. I wish I could be your wife here. For real."

"And you cannot be?"

"I mean, it's kind of hard to have a spouse that's only corporeal once a year."

Hawthorne made a thoughtful sound in their throat as they approached Juniper, placing Rayne down in the snow beside her body. Her blood seeped into the snow, slowly pooling around her.

Death was not unknown to Rayne; he had claimed her grandmother at such a young age that the understanding of mortality was thrust upon her before she even had a true sense of life. But never had she ever *watched* someone die.

Still, shouldn't I feel something for Juniper? She is still my cousin, and I never wanted her dead. I mean, not really.

Like most of her family, Juniper had tolerated Rayne and had taken every chance she could to speak down to her. To remind her of the dozen ways in which she wasn't good enough, in which Rayne was nothing but a leech.

"Should we bury her?" Rayne asked, wrapping her arms around her waist.

"Hm, not yet. Still a bit of life in her. Best if we let her die above ground. We cannot risk her seeping into the soil."

"Doesn't her blood make you hungry? You said it had a kind of hold over you before."

"*Your blood,* Rayne. But you are correct that its scent is typically enticing. Not as much in this body."

The sky bled a dusty pink as the sun dipped lower, and her time with Hawthorne was ticking away. Rayne worried her bottom lip with her teeth. "Have you ever tried to stay in that body after the Solstice?"

Hawthorne's brow furrowed. "Return to this body after my allotted time," they repeated, tasting the idea. "No. I have not. I am not sure either way as to whether or not it can be done."

"If you could, what would you need?"

Hawthorne made that same thoughtful noise once more. "It takes a great deal of energy to sustain this form. Food helps, but I would need more."

"More?" Rayne moved closer to them, ignoring the wet gurgles from her dying cousin.

"Yes. An offering, perhaps."

Offering.

Of course. Hawthorne was a god, or something close to it; it made sense that, like any proper deity, they would have demands to be met. But what kind of god were they, and what would sustain them?

"Where are you from originally? Not Bury." Their English was nearly perfect, practiced and, beneath that, unnatural.

"No," Hawthorne replied with a tight smile. "Not Bury. The names have changed, but the Far East, a place where the winters were long and summer rarely came. You are getting at something?"

Rayne nodded. "You were... a god once, or at least, the humans treated you like that. What did they give you? Surely they must have made offerings?"

"Blood, mostly, and sometimes violence in my name as an act of assuaging me. To keep their town and their livestock safe. I spared them once or twice. It was beautiful. But it served a purpose; the more sacrifices that were made in my name, the easier it became for me to exert my will in this world."

Juniper choked, letting out another wet, desperate breath. Rayne stared down at her, Hawthorne following her gaze. "And if I gave her to you?" she asked, her voice barely above the wind. "I already killed her so I could offer her to you then, couldn't I?"

Hawthorne looked at her for a long moment, their expression melting despite the cold. "Yes, Rayne. You could."

Her stomach fluttered, her pulse quickening as heat radiated between them. "Tell me how."

Hawthorne crooked a finger at her, and when she stepped closer, they gestured to the ground. "Kneel."

"But I don't have a cushion or—"

"Use her."

Rayne glanced down at Juniper. There was part of her that hesitated, that recognized the callousness of using her victim like a piece of furniture as she prepared to offer her to a god. There was that part of her, but it was small, and her chest was filled with emotions so immense.

Rayne knelt, using the meat of Juniper's thighs as a cushion for her knees against the rough, cold ground. Hawthorne stepped closer, their fingers brushing against the line of her jaw and coming to rest at her chin. Her attention caught on the outline of their cock through their boxers, and she had to bite her lip to keep from moaning.

"My eyes are up here," Hawthorne smirked, their thumb teasing along the seam of her lip. "Tell me what you're offering me, Rayne Dorne."

"Her soul, her body, whatever of hers you want to eat."

"Tell me why."

"I want you to have a body, Hawthorne. By any means necessary," Rayne confessed to her monster. The wind whipped between them, and then silence, even Juniper's heavy breaths slowed, everything quieting down for the two of them. "I don't care who or what needs to fall for that to happen."

Hawthorne knelt so that the pair of them were nearly eye level, towering over her even at this height. They leaned forward to kiss her forehead. "And I will do whatever I need to for that to happen as well, Rayne."

Their attention fell to Juniper. In the fading light, she saw their canines sharpening with the rest of their teeth, their jaw snapping as it unhinged. Rayne sat back in the snow as she watched Hawthorne tear into what was left of Juniper Stern.

Over the crunching of bone and the slick sound of flesh and blood squelching between teeth, Rayne giggled.

PART TWO
spring

CHAPTER THIRTY
hawthorne

H ours had passed, and Hawthorne had not once stopped watching her, unable to tear their eyes away from the woman that they had just claimed as their *wife*. The woman that they had tied themselves to for eternity.

Rayne slipped past them into the kitchen, and with her, the scent of pear blossoms and pollen trailed behind her. Her cheeks still flushed from laughter, from the promises they'd folded into her lips, her wrists, and the beauty marks that kissed her cheeks. Dirt from the bottom of her bare feet tracked into the house behind her, and they smiled down at it. As they had sworn their lives to each other, she had kicked off her shoes and dug her toes deep into the spring soil as if she wanted to awaken the very earth below them, so that it would not miss out on their love.

The dress she wore, she had made herself, along with the suit Hawthorne had worn for all of ten minutes, and then peeled off. Rayne's dress had been snow white, and she'd sewn dozens of black butterflies into the fabric. She had been spending more time with Persimmon and she had been teaching Rayne how to sew. Hawthorne was not one for human fashion, but her dress might have been the most beautiful dress that they had ever seen.

Another thing I hadn't known about her, but now I will never forget.

"Okay!" Persimmon said with a flourish as she placed the final porcelain dish down on their kitchen counter. "I've cooked you enough food and baked you enough sweets to last you both the weekend as long as Hayden doesn't inhale half of them."

Hayden.

It was the human name that Rayne had chosen for them, as they had both agreed that their name would attract more attention than either of them was looking for. Hawthorne did not mind. It was simply another title, a mask amongst the many that they kept at their disposal.

They liked Persimmon as far as humans went. She lacked many of the traits that Hawthorne found bothersome in other mortals, but more than that, she was kind to Rayne. Hawthorne was not an expert on human emotions, but if they had to make a guess, Persimmon would say that Persimmon cared about Rayne. Might have even loved her.

Rayne did not have enough people like that in her life.

Hawthorne glanced over at their wife to find her already watching them. She tucked a stray curl behind her ear and flashed them a small private smile. "Thanks, Persi," Rayne said without looking at the other woman.

"Yes," Hawthorne replied, nodding in agreement. "You are quite appreciated around here."

Persimmon's expression fell, her brow furrowing as she assessed Hawthorne. *She looks at me this way frequently. I do not know what it means.* Insecurity was not something that Hawthorne was wired for, but curiosity sparked to life every time they saw that same expression on her face.

It lasted only a moment, as it always did before her usual pleasant smile returned.

Persimmon waved a dismissive hand, the scent of pear and orange liqueur floating on her breath. "Don't thank me. It's the least I can do since you both refuse to allow me to get you a proper wedding present," she said pointedly, glaring at Rayne. "Just promise that you will please text me if you need something, okay? I will get it for you. This is your honeymoon, so you shouldn't be worried about anything other than one another."

They smirked. *As if I could care about anyone other than her.* Still, the gesture was not lost on them.

"Yes," Rayne offered, timid. "I promise."

"Perfect. So, what are your plans for the honeymoon?" Persimmon asked. Hawthorne raised a brow and cast a weighted glance at Rayne, winking. "No, I mean aside from *that.* Are you guys going anywhere?"

Hawthorne could sense Rayne's panic before her pulse even began to quicken. They slid to her side, wrapping an arm lazily around her waist. "We might just go to the next town over for a few drinks, maybe to dance a little, and then we won't be leaving the house much for the next few days."

"Next town over? Ambrosia Hill, really? Nothing but a bunch of yuppies and college kids that way."

Rayne glanced at them, and Hawthorne smiled at Persimmon, not too much, though; they were well aware that their true nature could easily seep through this one if they were not mindful. "I don't mind them. And Rayne has never really been to a bar before, so we figured now might be the time to do so."

Persimmon's face fell into that familiar expression before she looked to Rayne.

"Yup. Weird, I know, but—I mean, it's our honeymoon, so..."

Her friend's expression softened at that. "Yeah, you're right. To each their own," Persimmon threw another look Hawthorne's way before she clapped her hands together. "Well. Let me get out of your hair and get home before it gets dark."

"Thank you, Persimmon. Get home safe," Hawthorne called after her, mimicking what they had heard many a human say to one another when one of them was making a journey back to their house. Persimmon waved another dismissive hand over her shoulder as the front door clicked shut behind her.

Outside, the sky had burned, searing into a haze of scarlet and purple as the sun set. They could not help but note that, even in its final breaths, the light suited their wife perfectly. Hawthorne detested spring and loathed summer, but seeing Rayne covered in flowers, pollen, and artificial butterflies, it gave them a temporary appreciation for the season.

As soon as the door closed, Rayne frowned up at them, scrunching her nose at them the way that told them she was annoyed. "Why'd you tell her that we were going to a bar?"

"It was the first place that came to mind. And they are the easiest place to hunt." Hawthorne replied as they reached up to allow their fingers to coast through her curls.

"You need to hunt tonight?" she asked, her eyes sliding closed at the contact. "When was the last one?"

"About two weeks ago," they replied. "But tonight is the Spring Solstice, so perhaps any offerings made tonight will hold more significance than the others."

Rayne groaned, tucking herself under their arm. "I don't want to leave the house."

Hawthorne chuckled, rubbing a hand up and down her spine. "You do not have to. You could wait for me, and I can drag the bodies here, and then you need only come out back and do your part."

She groaned again, louder. "I don't want you to leave me either."

"Ah, it seems we've reached an impasse then, little wolf. Whatever shall we do?" they teased against the shell of her ear.

Rayne huffed and peeked out from under their arm. "Do you really need to hunt tonight?"

Hawthorne stretched their fingers, watching the trembling digits for a moment before returning their hand to her back. "I could hold out another day or two if need be, but my control of this body would lessen with each passing hour. Eventually, it will begin to rot."

They had both experienced that firsthand after Juniper's death. Though Hawthorne had felt no actual pain, the process of entropy itself had been uncomfortable. *I almost pity humans. It must be a special kind of torment to feel your body slowly becoming a corpse while you still occupy it.*

Rayne shivered against them, and with the door of her mind wide open to them, they could see her relieving the unpleasant memory.

Hawthorne leaned down to nuzzle against the top of her head. "I do not plan on letting you out of our bedroom anytime soon. Which is why I think it best we do this now rather than later. We'll head to the next town over."

Rayne's exasperation was tangible and too cute for them to hold against her. She pouted up at them. "Fine. I'll go change."

There were many ways to hunt, and Hawthorne was a master at all of them. Their centuries spent above ground with humans had taught them a great deal.

The most illuminating of all was that beauty was a particular kind of poison that nearly all humans would succumb to in the right conditions. Hawthorne held no illusions about its human shell; it was deadly because of how it was perceived, the attention it garnered.

Hawthorne brandished it like a weapon.

So when they stepped into *Road's End,* and nearly every head turned in their direction, they did not shy away from the attention. But they did shield Rayne from it, keeping her folded at their side.

Where beauty was a slow-acting poison, a perceived lack of it was blunt force trauma, an attack that the outside world would never stop. Attention had never been kind to her.

As they moved across the room to a booth along the far end of the wall, Hawthorne took in the bodies in the room, a dozen scents co-mingling in an ocean of stories. The sickly sweet sear of someone's blood that was heavy with disease, the oily burn of sweat from an unwashed body, the medicinal sting of someone's dandruff shampoo. Even in this form, Hawthorne could smell it all, but they did not hunt by scent alone when they were like this.

Rayne scooted into the booth, nestled in her band hoodie and scarf, her ear muffs protecting the delicate skin there from the cold. Bury's springs were traps; warm during the day and pleasant enough, but frigid at night. She was pouting so profoundly that it looked as though they'd forced her here. But Hawthorne knew better now; they'd been learning their wife over the last few months, and they had come to understand her body language.

She wants my attention, Hawthorne mused to themself, careful to keep the thought behind the thin barrier separating their minds. "Such a little trooper you are," they teased.

"I *am* suffering."

"Oh, I know." Hawthorne laughed, fishing their stolen wallet from the back pocket of their jeans. They carried no ID of their own or credit cards; they solely kept the thing for cash that they picked off of their victims. "You know, this place has cheese fries."

Rayne narrowed her dark eyes at them. "Are they good?"

Knew that would work. Cheese-covered potato sticks or 'French fries' as she and the other humans insisted on calling them, were one of Rayne's favorite foods and could pull her out of even the most sour of moods. Hawthorne slid their wallet across the table to her. "Only one way to find out."

"I've got my own money." She frowned.

"I know you do, and I'll snatch it from you until we get home if you try to use it here." Hawthorne leaned over to kiss her forehead. "You order, and I'm going to go do my rounds."

Rayne huffed but leaned into their kiss anyway.

Hawthorne pulled away from her and made their way to the bar, taking another look around the room for any potential weak links. Typically, they enjoyed the whole process of selecting whoever they wanted and taking time, but tonight, they wanted to get home and drag Rayne to bed as soon as possible. They would have to be quick.

They leaned their elbows on the bar, smiling at the woman behind it. "Hey, there."

She blinked and then returned the gesture. "Hey. What'll it be?"

Hawthorne did not care for liquor, but they recognized that it was expected of them to partake, especially in a place such as this. "Dealer's choice."

She laughed a little to herself. "You sure? That's a lot of trust to put in a stranger."

They smirked. "Guess I'm just a trusting person."

Hawthorne smelled him before they saw him; the lightest touch of cologne, something aquatic, beneath that the thick tar of nicotine and fresh air tangled in his hair that sang of a dozen places; none of them here.

The man sat beside him, a slight tremble to his shorter, stockier form, and he licked his lips nervously.

Ah. Must be his first time. And he doesn't smell as though he's from around here.

"Hey," the man said, looking ahead as if he was too terrified to look at Hawthorne directly.

"Hey," Hawthorne replied, sitting back in an attempt to make the man feel at ease. "First time here, huh?"

"Yeah, I'm just passing through," the man finally said, turning to them. He had a soft face, gentle eyes, and a pleasant smile. "I'm Cyrus."

Hawthorne extended their hand out to him. "Hayden. Nice to meet you."

The moment that their skin touched his, Hawthorne decided that they were going to make a meal of Cyrus.

Food acquired, Hawthorne thought to Rayne.

What's the game? she answered, unbothered.

Honeypot.

Got it. Don't take too long.

I won't. I'm probably going to have to make the first move and kiss him. Is that alright with you? Hawthorne bore no interest in anyone other than Rayne, but in games such as this, there was a certain level of physicality that could not be avoided. They would do everything in their power to avoid it though at the slightest inclination that it would upset their wife.

They caught her shrug in the mirror along the wall as she sipped at the water the waiter had brought out to her. *He's going to be dead soon, and I'm your wife, so what should I care?*

Gods, she was perfect.

Order your cheesefries to go, baby. This will be quick.

"So, Cyrus," Hawthorne said, clearing their throat and pretending not to notice the shiver the man let out. "You said you're passing through. Where are you heading?"

"New York," he said, sipping his old-fashioned. Hawthorne watched Cyrus bring the drink to his lips, allowing their attention to linger on his mouth. Cyrus swallowed, his cheeks flushing.

"New York. You're a bit far from home, aren't you?" Hawthorne rested their elbow on the table, their cheek against the heel of their palm. "What brought you out?"

"Work. I landed in Ohio, but I've got a big work thing in New York." Cyrus shrugged.

"Really? Why land in Ohio but then drive to New York?" Hawthorne laughed.

"Part of the job. Scouting locations, but I don't want to talk about work."

"Alright," Hawthorne said, smirking at him and leaning closer. "What did you want to talk about then?"

Cyrus nearly choked, sputtering on his drink just as the bartender brought over Hawthorne's drink. The smell of gin burned their nose, and it took everything in them not to sneer. They preferred whiskey if and when they did drink. If Rayne had food in her system, they might have given it to her since she was such a fan.

"On the house," she said, taking her sweet time removing her hand from their vicinity.

"Oh, wow. Are you sure?" Hawthorne asked, feigning modesty.

"Yup. You enjoy, handsome."

"Thank you, lovely," they replied, bringing the gin-heavy drink to their lips and trying not to spit it out as they swallowed it down.

"You smoke, Cyrus?" Hawthorne inquired, reaching into their back pocket to pull out a pack of cigarettes, though the stink of nicotine under Cyrus' pleasant scent already told them everything that they needed to know.

"Yeah, sometimes."

"Come out back with me." It wasn't a request, and as expected, Cyrus was on his feet immediately.

Outside was a small patio with rundown tables and umbrellas and an outside heater that no one had bothered to turn on. A few ashtrays littered the tables, half-filled with water and old cigarette butts. The door creaked closed behind them, and then it was just the two of them in the cold, under a red floodlight.

Hawthorne angled themself away from the light as best they could, lest their eyes catch it and alert Cyrus that something was off.

"You seem nervous," Hawthorne said, offering Cyrus a cigarette and their cheap lighter. "Am I that intimidating?"

Cyrus laughed nervously, though his hands shook as he ignited the end of his cigarette. "No, no. It's not you. I just—I don't normally pick people up in bars like this."

Hawthorne raised a brow and then, remembering that they were supposed to be smoking as well, mirrored Cyrus. "Are you trying to pick me up?"

Even under the bright red floodlights, Hawthorne could see how red Cyrus' face had gone. "I—well—you—"

"No need to be nervous, I don't bite or anything like that," Hawthorne chuckled, exhaling a thick cloud of smoke. "Unless you ask very nicely."

"I can *definitely* do that."

A little compelling may hurry this along. A glance above them revealed two cameras, one behind each floodlight. They swallowed down a growl of irritation. *I loathe technology. I suppose that I will have to go about this the old-fashioned way.*

"Cyrus," Hawthorne said again, tapping the ash from their cigarette onto the ground. "You didn't answer my question. Are you trying to pick me up, yes or no?"

He swallowed, nodding. "Yes."

"See?" Hawthorne flicked their cigarette into the rainwater-filled ashtrays all along the low wall behind them. "That wasn't so hard now, was it?"

They closed the small distance between them. They stopped just before they could touch, their bodies dangerously close to one another. "Can I touch you?"

"Yes." Came Cyrus' immediate response.

Hawthorne pulled Cyrus closer by the buckle of his jeans, grinning that wicked little grin of theirs. "Consider me thoroughly interested. But I've got a wife, and while she likes to keep to herself, she enjoys watching. Is that a dealbreaker for you?"

Hawthorne had spent years hunting alone, but now, with Rayne, the rhythm of that dance had changed. They found that the people they hunted were often lured into a sense of security when they saw Hawthorne had a woman with them. Strange to them, really, as Rayne was just as much a predator as they were.

"A wife? Oh." Cyrus bit his lip, and Hawthorne remained still, allowing him a moment to process.

He's not moving away. Good.

"I've never done that before," Cyrus said after a moment.

"Okay."

"But, no. It's not a dealbreaker."

Hawthorne smiled, barely resisting the urge to lick their lips. "Perfect. Can I kiss you?"

"Please."

Hawthorne, pleased with themself, caught his cheek in their hand before pulling him into a slow, deliberate kiss. The usual friction of kissing someone that was not their wife ground against their nerves. Before their union, Hawthorne had never given a second thought to kissing humans, but now, they did so only just enough to entice, and pushed the wrongness of it away.

My fries are going to get cold, and so am I, Rayne huffed into their mind, and they broke the kiss to keep from laughing at the irritation in her voice.

Soon, baby. Let me warm you up, try to think of me with my hands between—

Don't flirt with me when you're kissing someone else, or I'll lock you out of the house. They could feel the flutter of affection and sting of her desire along the magic between them.

Hawthorne kissed Cyrus again, their fingers sliding into his hair as their tongue teased against his lower lip. He pushed Hawthorne back against the wall of the building, but just as quickly as their back hit the wall, they switched their position, caging him in.

They pulled away enough to speak. "I like to stay in control. Problem?"

"No, uh, not at all," Cyrus answered, his lips already swollen and his breath coming a little shorter.

Hawthorne didn't respond, just pressed him back against the wall and kissed the breath right out of him. They were everywhere at once, seeping in like the setting sun; their fingers at his hips, their teeth nibbling at his lips, and the bulge of their cock against his thigh. He reached the zipper of Hawthorne's fly and they pulled away immediately.

"Not here," Hawthorne said as they had dozens of times before. "Come back to our place."

"I have a hotel—" Cyrus began.

"We have a guestroom at our place. You can leave in the morning or after if you want." Hawthorne said, licking the taste of him off their lips.

"How far?"

"Just up the way, about twenty minutes max."

"Alright, yeah. Let's go."

"Sure, just gotta grab my wife from inside."

Cyrus froze. "She's here?"

Hawthorne tilted their head. "Of course. I'd never be here without her," they replied, more honestly than they intended. "Is that a problem?"

Cyrus shook his head. "No, I just wasn't expecting to meet her so soon."

"You'll like her," Hawthorne lied. "She bites."

Hawthorne winked at him before he could read too much into their words, and held the door open for him back into the bar.

Rayne was sipping the remaining half of what they assumed to be a root beer, her cheese fries all but gone, and her mood brighter. They could tell by the way that her legs swung under the table.

Gods, she's cute.

They hid the thought to keep her chronic bashfulness from glaring to the surface. She smiled at them when she noticed their approach, and they nearly tripped over their feet.

"Hi, honey," Rayne said, tilting her chin up and pursing her lips. "You kept me waiting."

Hawthorne knelt to nip at her lip before stealing a kiss. "Sorry, love. Won't happen again."

They both made an active effort to avoid using any of their usual pet names for one another; those aspects of their relationship were not up for performance, regardless of how long their audience would live to see it.

"It better not," she huffed. If it hadn't been for the shift in her attention, they might have done something about the attitude she'd been wielding all night. "Who's your friend?"

"Hey. I'm Cyrus." He lifted his hand to wave at her.

Rayne did not return his smile; she glanced him over before reaching for her soda and draining the remains of it. "I'm Rayne. You coming home with us?"

"Oh, uh, yeah. And you're cool with that, right?"

She rolled her eyes, sliding out of the booth and pulling on her jacket. She reached into her jacket pocket, pulling out Hawthorne's wallet, and left a hefty pile of cash without bothering to look at the cost of her food. "You wouldn't be here if I weren't. We going or not?"

Cyrus blinked after her, looking back at Hawthorne, but they only shrugged. "Best not to keep the lady waiting."

Rayne was already half out the door, Hawthorne trailing lazily behind her. Over their shoulder, they noticed the slowing of Cyrus's pace, the consideration of his situation finally seeming to hit him.

Sometimes the prey caught twinges of the game's true intent before it completed. They raised a brow and stopped. "You alright?"

Cyrus swallowed, nodding. "Yeah, yeah, I'm fine. I don't know. I may have psyched myself out a little bit," He padded over to Hawthorne. "I just haven't done this before, so my nerves are doing the talking."

Hawthorne grinned. "Happens to the best of us."

CHAPTER THIRTY-ONE

rayne

Outside, the air was frigid even for spring, and Rayne shifted closer to Hawthorne, their arm automatically pulling her into their heat.

"Aren't you cold?" Cyrus asked, rubbing his hands up and down his arms. He was in nothing but a sweater and a barely there hoodie. It was all too easy to make him for a tourist.

Hawthorne was much better at pretending to be human than she had initially expected, but there were still moments where their otherness was on display for all to see. Currently, they were wearing a thin, long-sleeved shirt and hadn't even so much as shivered.

"No. I prefer this weather. I've been places much colder than this," Hawthorne replied easily.

"Not me. Where are you guys parked?" Cyrus asked with a shiver.

Hawthorne gestured toward the open field and the black thicket behind it. "We live just on the other side, so we typically walk. Do you mind?"

Around this point in the game, people usually sensed something was wrong: either they had spent too long looking at Hawthorne and had begun to notice the cracks in their performance, or the dread started to set in.

Rayne liked to watch their faces, the expressions that played across their features as they warred with themselves. She had never felt so comfortable watching people before, but now, it hardly mattered.

"No," Cyrus said finally. "It's fine. Lead the way."

Hawthorne's hands caught hers at her side, interlocking with hers. Her finger had healed much quicker than she had anticipated; the red tattoo branded into her middle finger had lost its previous sting. Last night, she and Hawthorne had sat before one another, tattooing their wedding bands into one another's skin.

Their blood mixed into the ink, their vows woven into a spell, and then etched into the other's skin.

Hawthorne had been so terribly delicate, and it never failed to amaze her how her beast was capable of such gentleness. They'd used their claw to tattoo her, unable to bear the thought of a foreign object digging into her skin.

"If it is to hurt, then it should be a pain you choose, a hand that cherishes you."

Tattooing Hawthorne had been difficult, every needle snapping the second it came into contact with their skin. In the end, Rayne had needed to use one of their claws to leave her mark on them. She had thought it would have felt silly, perched on their lap while she shakily outlined their wedding ring, but it had been one of the most beautiful moments of her life. Intimate nearly to the point of pain.

Her temple itched with Hawthorne's presence feathering into her thoughts, and she fought the smile tugging at the corner of her lips.

"So how did you two meet?" Cyrus inquired, slicing through the moment of quiet that had wrapped around them.

She and her husband looked at one another, and Hawthorne nodded. *Your turn.*

Rayne glanced Cyrus' way and shrugged. "We grew up together. Met when we were children."

Hawthorne raised a brow. *That's a new one.*

It's all I could think of. It's not exactly like it's a lie.

It is certainly not as true as it could be, either. they remarked, amusement heavy in their voice, and she resisted the urge to roll her eyes. It wasn't exactly as if it mattered what they told people, and she knew Hawthorne knew that better than anyone. They were just in one of their prodding moods.

"How about you?" Hawthorne asked Cyrus, bright and cheery as any human might have been. "Anyone missing you back home?"

A pause before he shook his head. "No. Not really."

"No? Their loss then," Hawthorne answered.

Rayne pressed closer to Hawthorne, and they gave her hand a gentle squeeze. She didn't like it when they went after people who were alone in the world. It felt too cruel.

Rayne preferred that they go after people with large families, wives, husbands, children, and siblings. Those that they killed with families would be mourned, would leave an impression on those they left behind for the rest of their lives.

But who would remember the lonely?

Don't draw it out with him, Rayne thought, tugging lightly on their hand. Gently. *Please?*

She didn't like to ask Hawthorne for things like this, they were who they were and she did not desire to change them, but their heart was not human. Outside of their relationship, Rayne didn't think that they had ever experienced compassion.

If they even *could.* She may kill for them, with them, but she was still human, and there were some atrocities that her soul could not bear.

Hawthorne frowned slightly. *It upsets you that he is without anyone to miss him.*

Yes, she thought back. *I know you say fate is cruel, but we do not have to be. Just this once?*

Just this once, Hawthorne replied, bringing her hand to their lips for a moment before the final act of their little play came to a close.

Hawthorne waited until the three of them had stepped into the forest to say their lines.

"Jeez, it's colder than I thought!" they said, rubbing their hands up and down her shoulders in a faux attempt to warm her up. "Love, do you want me to run ahead and get the heat going for us?"

"Yes, please," Rayne said, shivering. "Turn it up as high as it goes."

"Yes, ma'am," they purred, turning Rayne's face toward theirs and kissing her for a moment before their attention fell to Cyrus. "That's alright with you?"

"Uh, yeah. How much further away is the house exactly?" Cyrus inquired, squinting into the darkness for lights he would never see.

"Five minutes that way," Hawthorne replied, pointing off in a random direction. "Trees make it a bit harder to see, but once you do, you can't miss it."

"Oh. Okay."

Hawthorne stole a final kiss from Rayne, and then they were gone, jogging off into the forest much faster than any human should have been able to. She doubted Cyrus would have noticed, and at this point, it hardly mattered.

"Come on," Rayne nodded off in the direction Hawthorne had pointed. "Let's get out of the cold."

Neither of them spoke as they walked and the silence between them pricked at her nerves. Even though Hawthorne had only been gone for a few minutes, she wished that they were back. Conversation flowed with them.

"So, Rayne."

"Yeah?" she sighed, set on keeping her attention ahead of her.

"Do you always just watch when it comes to... stuff like this?" Cyrus asked.

Oh, yeah. He still thinks that this is about sex.

"Not always." She shrugged. "Sometimes I... play too."

"And, you like it?"

"I like it just fine," Rayne replied. "More than you will even."

"You said that you like to play... do you mean games or... ?"

The hairs on the back of her neck rose, gooseflesh pimpling her skin, and she sighed in relief. Behind her, the air dipped, so cold that it was nearly biting, and then warmth, prickling against the back of her neck.

Rayne stopped walking, stepping back into the shadows that curled around her like smoke, tangling in her hair. "Cyrus," she called. "You should run."

Cyrus turned, finally realizing that she was further behind than he thought. "Why would I—" He froze midsentence, mouth hung open, and his eyes fixed just above her to where she knew Hawthorne loomed.

Sometimes their victims screamed, sometimes they begged or stumbled back in terror as their mind struggled to catch up.

Cyrus ran.

When Hawthorne darted after him, it was silent, the wind cutting through the grass. Rayne remained still, squinting through the darkness and moonlight to follow the shape of her monster.

In the distance, she heard the moment of impact and Cyrus' terrified screams. Rayne had learned not to concern herself with the noise; it never mattered how loud or for how long they screamed, no one came. Ambrosia Hill may not have been Bury, but around here, most people knew the most important rule: never listen to anything that happens in the woods once the sun goes down.

Even if anyone suspected someone was being mauled to death in the forest, none of them would venture in to see what all the commotion was about.

"*Come here, baby*," Hawthorne's voice was a blade dragged against stone, all pretenses of their humanity long gone. The magic between them hummed to life; neither of them had been sure if it was the blood Hawthorne had given her or some grander design, but when one of them called for the other, they could feel it.

Not a tug, just some inner compass that knew where their true north was.

Rayne ducked deeper into the forest, her legs and her magic leading her closer and closer to Hawthorne.

Running water harmonized with Cyrus' screaming, and she found them both down by the river's edge. Cyrus lay on his back, his right ankle twisted at an unnerving angle, his left arm nothing but a shredded stump, blood drenching the rocks beneath him.

Hawthorne sat nearby, Cyrus' arm between their large paws, their claws scrapping against the rocks with every movement. They bit into the flesh and pulled back, muscle snapping with it.

"You said you would be quick." Rayne sighed, gesturing to the arm.

"*That* was my intention," Hawthorne replied around a mouthful. "*This* was an accident."

Rayne sighed and closed her eyes, willing steel into her bones for what she was going to have to do. This part never got easier. She turned on her heel and approached Cyrus.

He attempted to scramble away from her, kicking against the ground with his good foot. "Stay away from me!"

"Shh, shh. I know, fighting makes it easier for you." Her fingers brushed the switchblade in her pocket, flicking it open. "But I promise that the calmer you are, the cleaner of a cut I can make."

Rayne stepped over him, and Cyrus attempted to kick her ankle out from under her, and she smiled despite herself. *I like it when they fight. So much better than when they beg.* Unlike her husband, she was not immune to the pleas of those whom they killed. Sometimes she cried with them as the light fled their eyes, other times she would turn her face away in their final moments, desperate to see anything else.

There was guilt at times, disgust at others, but no matter which emotions rose within her, none could stay her hand.

Grunting, she sat square on Cyrus' chest to still his thrashing, her thighs locking around his torso. Rayne didn't want to drag this out longer than necessary, but he was doing little to help either of them.

"Stay still!" she hissed, jabbing her opposing elbow into him while she attempted to go for his jugular. Hawthorne had shown her the easiest places for quick kills, but she lacked their supernatural strength, and more often than not, found herself physically overwhelmed. "Hawthorne."

They swept behind her, careful not to touch her or Cyrus. They had both learned the hard way that offerings needed to remain free of Hawthorne's influence for them to have any effect.

"You have this, Rayne," they urged, and though she could not see them, the smirk that accompanied their following words ignited something indignant within her. "Are you really going to let some half-dead thing get the better of you?"

She swore and drove the knife into the side of Cyrus's neck, wedging it deeper even as the blood loosened her grip on the blade. "Hawthorne, I offer you this life in exchange for your continued physical presence at my side."

Something warm and wet slid along the collar of her neck, startling a moan out of her from the familiar sensation.

"I accept your offering, Rayne Dorne."

"Are you upset with me?"

Sticky with still drying blood drenching their clothes and chin and matting their curls, Hawthorne was still the most beautiful thing that Rayne had ever seen. Moonlight dripped through the pines, hitting their pale skin just right.

The walk home after a hunt was always a bit uncomfortable for her. They left no evidence of their presence in the forest, which meant trekking miles through the forest, covered in blood and viscera, until they were home and Hawthorne could properly clean everything.

Rayne smiled a bit, shaking her head and reaching her own bloody hand out for them to take. "No, Hawthorne. I'm not upset with you."

They nodded, their fingers tapping against her knuckles absently as they slowed to keep pace with her. "But you are upset."

Rayne shrugged, but catching a glimpse of their raised brow, she ventured for a better answer. "Upset isn't the right word. I really hate when we have to hurt someone who's alone."

"You have mentioned this to me before, but I do not understand what it is about it that you dislike so."

She chewed on her lower lip. "It's not fair, and I know you say that fairness is fake and all of that, and maybe you're right. But it makes me feel guilty to play any part in that."

"Guilt," Hawthorne repeated with their perfect enunciation, tasting the word.

Rayne understood that they knew the words and their definitions, but lacked the experience with them to ground that knowledge in anything.

"It feels like stepping into a pit of tar or being caught in a spider's web; it's hard to untangle yourself from it. You're trapped in something unpleasant except you're the spider and the tar."

Hawthorne's brow furrowed in thought, no doubt mulling over what those sensations would feel like in their own body. "I see," they said after a few moments. "That sounds uncomfortable, and I do not want you to feel that way. What if you select the next one we go after? Then you can find one with a family."

Rayne nodded up at them. "I think that might be easier for me. Thank you."

Hawthorne brought her hand to their lips and kissed it, dried blood and all.

When they finally arrived home, it was a little after midnight, and most of Bury was asleep. Still, they were both mindful to never be seen on their walks back, to always come through the forest and go through the back door on the patio.

"House," Hawthorne called, slipping out of their bloodied boots and tapping their hand against the glass of the door. "Warm yourself for her. She needs to change."

The House huffed, but inside, Rayne could hear the crackling of the fire sparking to life. *"You speak to me as if it is your blood rooted in my floorboards,"* It snapped. *"She is both my mother and my child, and I bear you only for her sake."*

Hawthorne chuckled, peeling off their pants and shirt until they were entirely bare for the biting early spring air. Their body, whether borrowed or crafted by their own magic, was perfect. Standing at nearly a foot taller than her, they often had to duck through doorways to avoid hitting their head. Their muscles were defined, but not in the way of someone who cared for aesthetics, but in the way of someone who cared for their own strength. Dark hair and silver hair peppered their abdomen, all the way down to their—

"You're admiring me rather loudly," Hawthorne remarked, voice dripping with amusement. "Let's save that for once we're inside, hmm?"

Embarrassment flooded her system, but its shape was different from what she was used to; the shame never arrived on its back. Hawthorne *saw* her. Rayne nodded, unzipping herself out of her jacket and freeing herself from the rest of her clothes. Once they were both bare, Hawthorne gathered both of their clothes in their arms and opened the door for her.

The room vibrated with warmth, and Rayne released a breath she didn't realize that she'd been holding. Hawthorne closed the door behind them with their foot and carefully carried all of their soiled clothes through the living room and down the hall toward the guest room and garage door.

It was some primal urge, Rayne reasoned, the compulsion to clean their clothes, body, and her as thoroughly as possible after hunting. Hawthorne did not fear being caught, and they did not acknowledge or accept human authorities.

It may be to keep some larger predator from catching wind of either of their scents and coming after them.

Rayne shivered, pulling her arms around herself as she listened to Hawthorne shuffle around the garage.

Movement in her peripheral vision caught her attention, and she looked over her shoulder into the backyard's darkness. Just at the edge of it, a small, white rabbit sat.

I've never seen a rabbit like that before. Rayne squinted to get a better look at it. *Strange that it would come out so soon after Hawthorne was just out there.*

In her time with Hawthorne, Rayne had come to find that it was rare for smaller animals to remain in their vicinity, sensing the danger. *But this one is just sitting there.*

The thing turned and darted back into the bush just as the door to the garage opened.

Well, there goes that.

"I'll clean everything else later. For now, let's get this rotting blood off of us," Hawthorne said as they stepped back into the living room, offering their hand. Rayne let them lead her upstairs and into their shared bedroom.

She hadn't been able to grapple with the thought of converting her parents' old bedroom into theirs, nor did she want to spend another moment in her childhood room, so she and Hawthorne kept the room she had had as a teenager. It was a tight fit with the two of them, but Rayne would never complain about being closer to her husband.

"Did you get hurt at all?" Hawthorne asked, turning her palms over to inspect her skin. While the magic had certainly made her skin tougher, it still wasn't as durable as she would like. And while she got hurt less, the danger always remained.

"I don't think so. Maybe the back of my knee when I was trying to hold him down—"

"Let me see," Hawthorne pulled her into the bathroom, grabbed a towel, and flipped the toilet lid down. "Sit."

Once she did, their fingers ghosted along her legs, from her thighs down to her knees, and she winced at the tender prick of discomfort as their thumb brushed the back of her right knee. Hawthorne nodded and kissed her knee. "The beginning of a blister, it would seem. I'll take care of it after."

Rayne only nodded, chewing her lip while she watched them move about the bathroom and start the shower. She never asked Hawthorne for anything; she never had to. Their attention remained fixed on her as if she were the sole axis of the universe. This level of care was above anything that she had ever experienced.

The *only* care since her grandmother had passed.

Steam from the shower spilled into the room, breathing fog against the mirror and windows and curling, loosening Hawthorne's curls until they were a dark halo around their head.

I love them so much.

Rayne kept the thought to herself, tucking it away from Hawthorne's reach as she stepped into the shower with them. They pulled her close, and she rested her cheek against their chest.

Love was a dangerous game for her, a gamble in which she always lost. Anything Rayne had laid claim to and offered her heart, shattered in front of her. Her Ma'maw. *How many times had I said 'I love you' to her, sang it like some song every chance I got?* Seven years. That was all Rayne's love had awarded her before Adele was gone. Then there had been her brother. Every time she saw him, she reminded him of how much she loved him.

Then she'd never seen him again.

Her parents had never earned the words from her, and they'd lived long and healthy lives until Hawthorne had come along.

If her love were a curse, some poisoned dagger, she would keep it away from those to whom it belonged.

Below her, the water bled brown and deep red, circling the drain. She pulled herself closer to Hawthorne, her nails digging into their skin.

I will not lose Hawthorne, too.

Spring entered the town with a whisper, but now it announced itself with an uproar of life. Bugs, blossoming flowers, sunlight, and steadily longer days were here before she had thoroughly prepared. Rayne disliked the warmer weather as it often meant more humidity, making life with her skin condition even more uncomfortable than it already was.

Hazy fog painted the early morning grey and pink, the sun's light peering through it and mixing with the sunrise.

Rayne stifled a yawn while she felt around in her purse for the keys to the old building, *her* old building now.

It had been *Timeless Thrift* owned by Melinda Modie and her husband, but after Hawthorne had killed Melinda, they'd gone back a few weeks later for her husband. When the building had gone up for sale, Rayne hadn't realized how much she had wanted it until the opportunity arose for her to have it.

Since the sale of her house had fallen through, Rayne only had her savings to fall back on when she'd taken some paid time off at work. Most of her money was in the cash box she kept in her old apartment with Trisha. Rayne had been prepared to make the drive back to the city to collect all her things, but Hawthorne reminded her of how much easier her life was.

A quick video call and a little bit of their magic, and Trisha had everything express-mailed to her.

Hawthorne had ended up paying most of the down payment; they had not been lying when they told her they had money. Years' worth of killing and collecting cash that they rarely spent had left them flush with it.

For the first time in her life, Rayne owned something that no one could taint. House, as much as she loved it, would always carry the memory of her childhood, and her old apartment had been okay, but living with a roommate had sucked.

Timeless Thrift was hers, even if she didn't know what to do with it yet.

Finally, fishing her keys from her purse, Rayne unlocked the door and stepped inside, tossing her bag onto the floor as she did so. She felt along the wall until she found the light switch and flicked it on. *I still need to get used to the layout of this place.*

It had only belonged to her for a few weeks, but she and Hawthorne had already begun gutting it and moving furniture around. Hawthorne did not care much for decorating, but they were fantastic at moving heavy items around and could be bribed to do most anything that they deemed annoying with the promise of an orange or two.

Fluorescent lights hummed above her, flickering slightly before settling. Rayne paced the floor slowly.

Okay, so we took all of the garbage off that back wall. I think we just have to paint it now. Should it be black like the rest, or maybe an accent wall?

Rayne startled with the sound of a bell cutting through the quiet, the bell hanging over the front door that rang whenever it was opened or closed.

"We're not—oh, hey, Persimmon."

Persimmon held two paper cups of steaming coffee in her hands, raising them slightly above her head as if to shield herself. "I come in peace, I promise. I even brought coffee."

Rayne smiled and waved Persimmon deeper into the store. *She always makes it easier to feel like a person.* "Thank you. You didn't have to do that."

Persimmon shrugged, sliding the cup into Rayne's hand. "I was in town, and I saw your car out front." She looked around. "I brought one for Hayden, too. Are they here?"

"No, they're working first shift today." The lie was practiced and easy, but it didn't stop the guilt she felt for not being able to tell Persimmon the truth.

The truth was that Hawthorne was at home, passed out in their bed, where they would most likely remain until late tonight. Though they didn't need to sleep every night, they had discovered that sleeping deeply once every few weeks while they were in their human body made things more comfortable for them.

"Oh, got it," Persimmon replied. The slight shift in her tone immediately tore at the age-old scar of Rayne's uncomfortable interactions with others. *Was that the wrong thing to say?* "What did you say that they did for work again?"

"Park Ranger," Rayne answered, taking a sip of her coffee. *Milk, honey, and sugar. She must have been paying attention all those times that I made coffee at her place.* "They get weird hours."

Persimmon's lip quirked, frowning for a moment before her easy expression returned. "Makes sense. I'll give this to you then, no need for it to go to waste. I didn't know how they would take it, so it's just an espresso."

"They'll like it. Thank you."

"So," Persimmon gestured toward the freshly painted wall. "This place is coming along pretty well, huh? Love the new look. Know what you're gonna do with it yet?"

Rayne shook her head. "No, not really. I guess—I don't know, I didn't want to rush. I just wanted to breathe, to give myself time to figure it out." It was more personal than she had gotten with anyone other than Hawthorne, and even though she knew Persimmon didn't seem to mind listening to her, she couldn't shake that fear. "Maybe that's a little ridiculous."

"Not at all, Ray. It's your prerogative what you want to do. I was just curious."

Persimmon didn't stay for long but offered her assistance with any renovations that she and Hayden were working on, reminding Rayne that she was used
to handiwork. It was nice to have the help, and Rayne appreciated Persimmon's
kindness. An idea struck Rayne just as Persimmon was leaving. "Hey, Pers?
Would you be open to painting something for me, like, here I mean?"

"A mural?"

"Yeah." The inside of Persimmon's home was gorgeous, covered in her art-
work, and Rayne wanted a fragment of that for herself. "I'd pay you."

Persimmon scoffed. "Like I'd let you." She winked. "I'd love to paint something for you sometime, Ray. Consider it a wedding present." She waved at
Rayne over her shoulder at her before heading out.

*If I were braver, I'd ask her if we were friends. If that's what this means, why
does she stay?*

When the bell above the door rang again, Rayne was in the middle of drinking Hawthorne's long, cold coffee, mopping the tile floor in the back of the
store. "Did you bring more coffee?" Rayne called over her shoulder as she leaned
the mop against the wall, rolling her sleeves back down.

"I'm afraid not," a male voice called back.

Tensing, Rayne stepped out from the back of the store to see Pastor Creary
standing in the center of her store, his arms tightly at his side. When their eyes
met, he blinked and took a step back.

She bit back a smile. Before her deal with Hawthorne, the distance others
set between her had hurt, but now it was a reminder that she wasn't like them.
Didn't want to be.

"As you can see," Rayne gestured around them. "We're in the middle of
renovations. But you're welcome to come back when we're up and running."

"I can see that, yes. But I came to talk to you, Rayne."

"Did you? Well, what can I do for you, *pastor*?"

His back straightened at the question. "You haven't been coming to church."

Rayne scoffed. "Not since I was nineteen. That news or something?"

"You haven't been coming to church," he repeated before pressing on, "And
something is wrong with the forest. The spirits there are angry, and God, well,

He might be punishing us for something." When Rayne did not answer, he spoke more slowly, more quietly. "There have been too many disappearances, too many deaths for this to be something natural."

"What exactly has that got to do with me?" Rayne asked, crossing her arms to hide the trembling of her hand.

Tobias Creary was no different from anyone else in Bury; he believed in God and the Devil and everything in between. The Devil was just as real as the voices from the souls trapped in the mines.

"I've been asking people to come to services once a week, cleanse their sins, and pray for each other. We're stronger together."

Rayne shrugged. "I got my own form of prayer, things my Ma'amaw taught me. If I need cleansing, I've got it covered."

No amount of smoke or holy water can cleanse what I've done.

Still, she clung to her old ways, the only remaining tether she had to her grandmother and her culture.

"Your grandma kept with the church."

"That's her prerogative."

"She might have been a bit unconventional, but she was a God fearing woman—"

"What would *you* know about her?" Rayne hissed, the burn of Hawthorne's magic rising with her anger. "I know you think you're doing me a favor, but coming into my space and telling me all that I *should* be doing sure as hell isn't."

Pastor Creary exhaled through his nose, rubbing the bridge of it with his fingers. "I'm worried about you, Rayne. We all are. You're spending all your time cooped up in that house where your folks passed... it's not good for you. You should let your community help you."

We. Community.

Where had that "community" been her entire life? Those same people who were feigning concern now were the same people who had whispered and giggled when she walked by, mocked her heavy bandages as a child, and kept her separated as if she were contagious.

None of them cared about her; they never had.

"I'm fine," Rayne ground out.

Pastor Creary's lips set in a tight line before he spoke again. "Heard you got married."

Rayne shrugged. "Heard right."

"Where you'd have your ceremony? Certainly wasn't in town."

Her hands clenched into fists at her side. "We had a private ceremony out of town. Not that it's any of your business. Now, if this interview is over, I'd appreciate you getting off my property now."

He sighed. "Alright, Rayne. But do me a favor? Bring your husband down to the Church, if he ain't from around here, he should get cleansed proper. Or at least come down and meet everyone."

Rayne refused to answer, glaring at him until he took the hint and left, the bell ringing behind him.

"Fuck you," she said once he was gone. "I don't owe you shit. And I promise that the last thing you want is to meet *my* husband."

Coming home to someone was not something that Rayne had ever expected would be in her future, but now, sitting between Hawthorne's legs in front of the fireplace, a mug of tea warm between her palms, she could not imagine being anywhere else.

The night was cold, and the House was slow to heat, so despite the roaring heating system around them, it was still a little chillier than expected. The two of them sat nestled in the bramble of blankets to keep Rayne comfortable.

"How was your day?" Hawthorne murmured against the shell of her ear, nuzzling into her hair.

"It was pretty good. I got a lot done at the store, which was nice," Rayne replied, leaning back against their chest. "Persimmon came by, she brought coffee for you and me."

"That is a sweet gesture on her part."

"Mhm. I asked her to paint a mural for me in the store. I don't know of what yet, but something will come to me," Rayne said before taking a sip of her tea. "How about yours? Did you get enough sleep?"

Hawthorne kissed their way down the column of her neck. "Yes, I did. It is inconvenient to have to do so, but at least it is only once or twice a month."

"There are so many rules in your world," Rayne mused, watching the steam rise from her tea. "All the magic. I thought things would be simpler."

"Things are very simple, and that's what makes them so difficult," Hawthorne answered.

Rayne resisted the urge to roll her eyes. She adored her husband and found them more fascinating than she cared to admit, but they, like House, had a particular way of speaking in riddles. "You say things like that all the time, but then you never explain what they mean."

Hawthorne chuckled in her ear. "You know what you need to do for an explanation, little wolf. Ask."

"What do you mean when you say that?"

"What I mean is that with magic, with conjuring, the world is your oyster. If you have the power and the capability, you can do anything. But there will *always* be a cost," Hawthorne explained. "I can have this human shell for a cost, but even then, to remain in it, there are dues to be paid. Rest, food, discomfort."

Rayne frowned, turning to look up at them. "Is it like that with everything? Even the spells you do daily?"

"No. I exist in magic; it is in my blood. There are things that I can do that are as easy as drawing breath to me."

Rayne looked down at her hands, the memory of how Hawthorne's black blood had pulsed through her veins, darkening them. Though the magic was still within her, the appearance of their blood had faded. "Can I do those things?"

Hawthorne raised a brow, glancing down at her. "Truthfully, I do not know," they answered. "I have never heard of anyone doing what we have done. So your abilities are a mystery to me. All I know is that magic can never make a home in you."

"Because I'm human?"

"Yes. Magic is not... *natural for you,* and so even when you manage to capture it, it will fight against you. You will have to learn how to control it."

Rayne thought back to Juniper, the rage that had consumed her the moment Juniper had mentioned her grandmother, and then the magic that had split out of her without warning. "I still don't know how I did that to June."

"Neither do I. But some part of you has taken to the magic. I do not know that I can teach you anything, but perhaps I can guide you, if nothing else."

"I—" Rayne could practically hear Hawthorne's smooth voice in her ear, praising her when she impressed them and chiding her when they thought she could do better. It shouldn't have been so arousing to her, but the way that Hawthorne spoke to her drove her treacherous body wild. "I would like that."

"Of course you would," Hawthorne whispered, amused and nipping at her ear.

"Could we try today?" she asked, nuzzling closer to them.

"Hm. What's your pain level today?" they asked. "Are you sore from everything you were doing at the store earlier?"

I don't know that I'll ever get used to this. Hawthorne understood her body and her disease better than she did sometimes. They could tell when something was too much or becoming painful; they went out of their way to make sure that she was always comfortable and protected from any excess friction. Walking was fine, but sometimes, if she spent too long on her feet, her feet would blister or bleed. It was one of the many reasons she wanted to find a career she could do remotely, without the pressure of performing strenuous tasks daily.

"About a five out of ten," Rayne replied with a shrug. Three was about her typical range; it was rare for her to have days with less pain than that, but when she did, she always took advantage of it. Once her pain levels reached about a seven out of ten, Rayne needed to take an ibuprofen and lie down until she was at a tolerable level once more. "And I'm not sore, but my feet may just need a break."

"Then no, baby. Your body has had enough for the day. We'll see how you feel tomorrow, and if you're feeling better, then we will."

Rayne pouted, but it was more to protect her dignity. She would never tell them how much it meant to her that they cared enough to look out for her. Hawthorne's arms tightened around her, pulling her closer. Their lips painted a trail down from her neck down her spine, and her frustration with them quickly dissipated.

Around them, The House shivered, creaking, trembling despite the windless night.

CHAPTER THIRTY-TWO
hawthorne

Hawthorne couldn't pinpoint the exact moment that the realization hit them, but the town of Bury was beginning to change. More specifically, it was starting to change for Rayne.

They were all too familiar with how people in town had looked at her throughout her life, irritated and occasionally disgusted. But now, when they looked at her, the thick scent of fear followed. Whispers floated in the air like ash, and though Rayne may have missed them, Hawthorne did not.

"Something ain't right with that girl. Look at her eyes."

"It's witchcraft, pure and simple."

"That man ain't normal. No soul."

"The Dorne girl sold her soul to the Devil."

Hawthorne paid no mind to what the locals said about them, but the way that the other humans in town looked at Rayne was all too familiar for them. In their time, Hawthorne had seen mankind through the ages, and if there was one thing they had learned, it was that when terrified humans banded together, they were capable of true savagery.

I do not know if I should bring this up to her. She worries about so much as it is. But then, what does she have to worry about? So long as I am here, no one will get close enough to even dream of harming her.

"I was thinking that we could work on some stuff in the shop for a few hours and then call it early for the day? I've got work for a client tomorrow, and it's probably going to take up most of my day," Rayne said, shifting her eyes from the road to Hawthorne. "I want to spend time with you before then."

Hawthorne kicked their boots up on the dashboard. "I am more than content with that plan," they replied. "I appreciate that you enjoy your job, but you do not have to work if you do not want to. I have enough money for you to pay for anything you'd like."

Rayne's brow furrowed. "You can't have *that* much money saved up from murdering people?"

Hawthorne shrugged. "It is not as if I have had much to spend it on."

"Where do you even keep it?"

At this, Hawthorne remained silent, grinning at Rayne, knowing that it would pluck at her nerves. She was so easy to irritate, and they enjoyed how annoyance looked on her.

The only hardware store in Bury sat on the edge of downtown, a rundown corner store whose signage hadn't been updated in at least fifty years. Since her acquisition of the store, Rayne had been spending most of her money here. Hawthorne hardly cared for it, but they accompanied her every time now since having mentioned that the shop owner continually was condescending to her. Apparently, in his opinion, women could not be trusted to manage anything other than homemaking.

He had voiced no such thoughts since Hawthorne had made their presence known.

Once Rayne parked the car, Hawthorne hopped out to open the door for her on her side. Rayne murmured her thanks, her cheeks flushing with that pretty shade of pink Hawthorne would never stop chasing.

The bell above the door announced their entrance, and Hawthorne ducked inside behind Rayne. The shop owner—Hoffman or something of the like—stopped mid-conversation and stared at Rayne. The man he had been speaking to Hawthorne recognized all too well: Len.

Len's expression fell the moment that he laid eyes on Rayne, his thin lips setting into a tense frown.

"Hey, Mr. Hoffman," Rayne said with more politeness than anyone in this town deserved as far as Hawthorne was concerned.

Mr. Hoffman, an elderly man with white, wispy hair and a stained, pale-yellow shirt, nodded from behind the checkout counter. "Rayne. Nice to see you again."

Liar. Hawthorne could hear the way the old fool's struggling heart picked up when he looked at her.

He looked at Hawthorne and opened his mouth, but quickly shut it. No one in the town seemed to know how to respond to them. They quite liked it that way.

Hawthorne smiled, wide and unnatural, and Mr. Hoffman winced while Len's eyes narrowed.

Rayne ducked down the nearest aisle, keeping her attention anywhere but on Len.

There was something that happened between the two of them; Hawthorne could tell from the way Rayne reacted whenever he was near her. It was different than how she responded to most of the town. Something about Len made her uncomfortable, *scared* her, and Hawthorne hated it.

They had tried to bring it up to her a few times in an attempt to get to the bottom of it, but every time she danced away from the subject or told them that she didn't want to talk about it. They had offered to rid her of him, but Rayne had been adamant that they didn't; she'd said that everyone in the town would immediately suspect her. While Hawthorne respected it, they did not like it.

I will kill that man one day.

"What are we here for?" Hawthorne asked, pulling Rayne's attention back to them.

"More screws for the shelves we made, mostly. And I think we're going to have to double check the plumbing, but that's for another day," Rayne answered. "Today, we just need lots of screws and nails."

Hawthorne trailed slowly behind Rayne, largely content to watch her flit about the store as she grabbed what she needed. *She is truly the most fascinating woman I have ever known.*

Despite her fragile body, she was resourceful and taught herself to do most things she needed. A habit born from her childhood, they knew but none less astounding to them.

When Rayne finally finished and stepped up to the checkout counter, Hawthorne angled their body so that Len couldn't look at Rayne, stepping between them both.

"I didn't catch your name, stranger," Len said, leaning his elbow against the counter in an attempt to seem at ease, but Hawthorne could smell the tension rippling through the man.

Hawthorne turned their head toward Len slowly, staring down at him. Len was a large man, well over six feet and bulky. "That's because I didn't offer it."

Len smiled, though it didn't reach his eyes. "You must not be from around here."

"I'm not."

"Well, in these parts, we take care of one another. We're all kinfolk, but that starts with getting to know one another," Len offered his hand. "I'm Len Kappler. Ole' Rainy over there probably told you all about me."

From the corner of their eye, they caught the tightening of Rayne's shoulders at the use of the nickname. Hawthorne bit down the growl bubbling at the back of their throat. They looked down at Len's hand and then back up at him. "Can't say that she did." They grabbed Len's hand and shook it, squeezing hard. "Hayden."

Len inhaled sharply, and Hawthorne drank in his discomfort. "You—uh—got a last name, Hayden?"

"Dorne."

"You took her name?"

Hawthorne released his hand. "Rather inquisitive, aren't we?"

Len pulled his hand back, holding it against his stomach. "Just making conversation. What'd you do for work? Can't say I've seen you around town."

"Park Ranger, about thirty minutes up the way," Hawthorne replied, nodding behind Len.

"In Ambrosia Hill?" Len asked, brows raised.

"That'd be the place."

Eyes narrowed, Len nodded. "Huh. I've got some friends who are rangers that way. I'll have to tell em' that I met you."

Interesting.

There was something more to Len's questions; Hawthorne could feel his true intent shifting just beneath the oily surface of his words.

Perhaps he can sense that I am not as human as my skin would make me appear.

It would not matter in the long run, as no one human here could know what they were. There was no English name for what they were, but it was not themself that they were concerned with.

Rayne.

Even though their magic flooded her veins, she was still human and a fragile one at that.

She could get hurt.

Hawth, can we leave now, please? her voice whispered in their mind, breaking the apparent staring contest they'd been in with Len.

Yeah, baby. Let's get out of here.

"Well, it was an... experience meeting you," Hawthorne said, reaching behind them for Rayne's hand. "Be seeing you."

Sweat, mud, nicotine and cheap beer—even from their place in the garage, Hawthorne could smell the small gaggle of humans on their way up the hill toward the House.

Switching off the hose they'd been using to rinse the blood off their boots, they threw down a towel to catch the bit of runoff there'd been and stepped back inside. The two of them had gone on another hunt last night, and as usual, they handled all of the cleanup.

Rayne's nose wasn't as keen as theirs, and her eyesight was not as good, so they ensured that they got rid of any evidence of their kills.

I had done nothing different yesterday than I do every time we kill, they thought. *Whatever they're coming up here for, it can't be that.*

"Baby," Hawthorne called, wiping their hands on their shirt. "Where are you?"

Rayne poked her head out from the living room. "Right here. What's wrong?"

Hawthorne closed the door behind them, locking it. "Nothing's wrong. But you should know, some humans—men mostly—are on their way up here."

Rayne froze. "Here? But why?"

"I don't know, but that's what we're gonna find out."

"How?"

"When they come knocking, and they most certainly will, answer the door and see what they're on about."

Almost instantly, Rayne was chewing on her lower lip. "Okay. But what if they break in?"

Hawthorne raised a thick brow and closed the distance between them, kneeling in front of her on the couch. "You think I'd let anyone hurt you, let alone set foot in this house?"

She shrugged, and they kissed her nose, earning a small smile from her. "You'll be fine, Rayne. This is solely so we can see what's going on in the town when neither of us is there."

Hushed voices and the glow of cellphones flickered in the darkness and flashed in front of the window. Not even a moment later, a demanding knock pounded at the door. "Go on, little wolf," Hawthorne encouraged, nudging her toward the door. "I'll be right here."

Rayne nodded and slowly made her way to the front door.

"You're rather quiet about all this," Hawthorne said to the House as they stood, brushing their fingers along the wall. "Don't you have some biting remark or anxious whining to be doing?"

House scoffed. *"Since when have either of you ever listened to me?"*

The House has been terribly morose all spring. Perhaps Rayne and I haven't been giving it as much attention as we should be. We have been rather wrapped in one another.

"Open up, Dorne!" One of them called just as Rayne pushed open the front door.

Outside, a group of five men, only one of whom Hawthorne recognized as Len, stood, some of them swaying on their feet. *Drunk.*

"Uh—can I help y'all?"

"We're trying to help *you!*" one of them slurred.

"By doing all this hootin' and hollerin' on my front yard?"

Len took a step forward, and Rayne stepped back, further into the House. Hawthorne moved closer to her but stayed on the opposite side so that none of the men could see them yet.

"We are trying to help you, Dorne. Trying to save you from that... *thing* you married."

There it was.

"*Thing?*" Rayne bristled, gripping the doorknob as she stepped fully out onto the front porch, their magic licking at her heels. Hawthorne tilted their head to get a better look at her shadow, which shook and frayed around the edges, the air sweet with the scent of conjuring. "I'd appreciate it if you watched your fucking mouths when it comes to what you say about my husband."

She's conjuring without meaning to, they thought. *The magic seems tied to her emotions somehow. How strange.*

But as quickly as it had come, it disappeared, and her shadow molded back into its normal shape. *She can't sustain it for long. So even though it comes quickly, it leaves just so.*

"Ain't no *man,*" Len spat back. "He's a haint. He's a sk—one of them flesh wearers."

Hawthorne was not as familiar with Bury superstitions and could not imagine why Len did not finish his statement.

"That's a heavy accusation to be making," Rayne snapped, hands falling to her hips. "Especially when you don't have a lick of proof, just the stench of beer. Now, can you get off my land before I call the sheriff?"

"Where'd he come from?" one of the other men called out, waving a lit cigarette at Rayne as ash fell onto the lawn.

"Yeah," another man chimed. "I don't recollect seeing any new cars coming up this way. Nothing. He's just here one day."

"He doesn't have a last name, that's why he's hiding behind yours! Where'd he come from, *really*? Cus I think he came from the wood, down the other side of the holler. No man's land."

"You're all fucking drunk."

Len climbed another step onto the porch toward Rayne. "This is a God-fearing town, Rayne, and now something evil is walking among us. It's got to go."

Rayne scoffed. "I'm closing the door now. Y'all got until the count of ten before I come back out here with a shotgun."

It was an empty threat, of course. Hawthorne knew that guns made their wife nervous, and she made it a point not to keep any in the house. *She will never need one as long as she has me.*

"You little fool, we're trying to save your sorry soul!" Len stepped too close to Rayne's space, crowding her. "We'll do it by any means—"

"Now, what on Earth would possess any of you to come knocking on my front door?" Hawthorne asked, finally stepping into the doorway. Rayne melted into their side, and they wrapped their arm around her. "And start yelling at my wife?"

Len's posse took a collective inhale, stepping back until they were at the edge of the lawn. Len fell back with them, stumbling down the stairs.

"Well?" Hawthorne asked, cupping their free hand over their ear. "What have you got to say? Come on, speak up. You were all so loud before." *Please, give me a reason to nourish the soil with your blood, human. There is nothing that would bring me more pleasure at the moment.*

"We... just came to talk to Rayne. We didn't mean any harm," he mumbled. *Coward. But then again, men like you always are.*

"I suppose then, as long as you make yourselves scarce, we don't have a problem. But I had better not ever catch wind of any of you talking to her like that. Otherwise, you will have *nothing* but problems with me. Now, leave."

None of them wasted any time in their departure, and Hawthorne watched the last of the light from their phones get swallowed up by the darkness before they closed and locked the door.

Rayne launched herself at them immediately, clinging in a way that wasn't like her. Hawthorne rubbed soft circles into her back, tilting their head down to get a better look at her. "Hey. What's wrong?"

"I don't like that they know about you," she murmured. "Even if they're not completely correct about everything, they know enough."

"So?"

Rayne pulled her head from their chest, blinking up at them. "So? What do you mean by that? Hawth, they *know* you're not human."

"And what exactly are they going to do about it?" Hawthorne smirked. "No human weapon can harm me, even if I am in this body. I will return to my true form."

"So, you can't die?"

Hawthorne chuckled, kissing her forehead. "All things die. Some take longer than others. So while my death will come eventually, it will not be at the hand of any human."

Rayne relaxed into them a little. "That's good to know." She pursed her lips for a moment before speaking again. "What will you do once I've died? Since you're going to be alive for so much longer than I'll be."

Hawthorne frowned; it was not a thought that they liked to entertain, though they already knew the answer. "I told you once before, Rayne," they said against her hair. "I will not remain anywhere without you. When your time has come, I will follow you."

Now that Hawthorne had experienced life with Rayne, no version of them could return to how things were before her.

Death was something that their kind could choose before it came; it was a simple decision that many spirits made after being alive for too long to find anything entertaining anymore.

But Hawthorne was not like them now, and they never would be again.

I may be the only spirit who will die for love.

CHAPTER THIRTY-THREE
rayne

D *ammit, I hate running late!*

Rayne tore through the town, nearly blowing past a stop sign in her rush to get to her shop. One of her least favorite clients had made a nuisance of himself by insisting on personally sitting down over the phone to double-check all of her work.

"Like I can't fucking do math," Rayne grumbled as she brought the car to a stop at the next red light. "My numbers *always* check out."

Rayne sighed, rolling her shoulders and cracking her neck. *I swear I've been catching every damn red light in existence.*

Movement across the street caught her attention. Out of an overgrown bush along the sidewalk, just beneath a streetlight, a white rabbit slowly hopped out. Its eyes were scarlet red and set straight on her car. *Another one? Or maybe it's that same rabbit from before.*

The little creature did not sniff the air or move to chew on any of the leaves surrounding it; instead, it sat perfectly still and stared at her dead on.

"What a weird little bunny," Rayne whispered.

Above her, the light shifted from red to green, and she drove slowly, creeping past the rabbit as she drove by. But unlike the last time when it had run, this time it stayed put, its head following her car as she moved past it. In her rearview, the thing still hadn't moved. It sat frozen and staring at her like some marble statue.

I've never seen a rabbit do that before.

When Rayne finally arrived at the store, Persimmon was standing out front, leaning her back against the door while she scrolled on her phone. At her feet, a neon yellow suitcase sat.

"Shit!"

Rayne slammed her car into park and scrambled out of the seat as fast as she could.

Persimmon looked up from her phone and smiled, waving.

"Persimmon, I'm so sorry that I'm late," Rayne rasped, fidgeting with her keys until she found the ones for the front door. "I had a client hold me up. I can pay you extra for the wait, I don't want you to think that I don't respect your time."

Persimmon scoffed, rolling her eyes. "I don't think that, Ray, and you don't have to apologize. It's not like you're holding me up. I cleared my whole schedule for this."

"Oh. Okay. Thank you," Rayne murmured, lowering her eyes.

"Yeah, yeah. Are you gonna let me in or what?" she teased, knocking lightly into Rayne's shoulder but not hard enough to hurt her.

I really don't know what I did to deserve someone like her in my life.

"A white rabbit, huh?" Persimmon asked over the music blasting from Rayne's old pink and white CD player, rubbing her hands on the old, tattered towel she'd brought with her. "I can't say that I've ever seen one of those around here."

"That's what I was thinking. It's just so *weird*," Rayne answered, her head buried under one of the shelves of expanded counter space she and Hawthorne had built together.

"You really do have an interesting taste in music," Persimmon called.

WiFi was hit or miss in this part of the state, and with Rayne's luck, her store just so happened to be in a dead zone, so she'd had to improvise.

My store.

Her wedding present from Hawthorne. It didn't matter how many times she said it; she never got used to the idea that someone could love her enough to marry her, to try and give her everything that she'd ever wanted.

"Interesting," Rayne repeated, poking her head out from the counter and standing to admire her work. "Is that a good thing?"

"Yeah, of course. Very goth, spooky, all of that," Persimmon replied, without looking up from her work. "I wouldn't have said anything if I didn't like it. Wanna come see what I'm painting?"

Instead of answering her, Rayne stepped out from behind the workstation she'd set up for herself and approached Persimmon's. Around her sat a dozen different paints and paintbrushes, along with several sketches. But it was her work on the wall that captivated Rayne.

Persimmon had painted the beginnings of a coyote in the grass, surrounded by hawthorn and cornflowers. Its face, animal as it was, held a particular quiet joy Rayne had never seen depicted this way, and its gaze was toward the horizon, a nebulous shape Persimmon had yet to complete.

"Do you like it?" Persimmon inquired, watching Rayne.

It was perfect, more than Persimmon could ever understand.

Rayne had not yet spoken the name aloud, even to Hawthorne, but she had decided to call the shop *Fairy Hill*, a stark contrast between the other sensible shop names around town.

In the memories Hawthorne had shared with her, there was a book that they'd read together of the same name about a place beneath a great hill, a portal to another world.

That's what this place is to me, another world. One that I'm building.

Everyone in town was only going to think less of her now, sure that she was aligned with unnatural forces in the world, but why run from it? Rayne had spent her whole life running from what made her different, trying to force herself into tiny pieces in the hopes that she might finally fit into one of the boxes laid out for her. She was not like anyone else in this town, and she never would be, so why pretend?

It didn't matter if the rest of Bury never set foot in her shop; unlike the rest of them, Rayne had lived outside of this town. She remembered that there was an entire world beyond it, so she focused all her attention on selling and promoting her shop online.

Fuck Bury. I will live and thrive here out of spite. Watch my joy, motherfuckers.

"Yeah," Rayne said, nodding and wiping at her eyes. "Yeah, I really do."

Persimmon beamed at her. "Okay, good. Because I was going in totally blind here and just feeling it out as I go."

"You did great," Rayne answered, stepping back to admire it further. "Why a coyote?"

Persimmon shrugged, turning away from Rayne. "I've always loved them. They're so resilient, you know? They're scavengers. There's nowhere that you can place them where they wouldn't find a way to make a life for themselves."

From the corner of her eye, Rayne watched Persimmon admire her work. *I know so little about her,* she thought. *I haven't really asked. She's always been so inquisitive about me and my life... I guess I was just scared to overstep. But now? Well, I'm still scared to do that, but I think I can trust her. We can trust each other.*

"Hey, Pers—"

The bell above the front door chimed, and both she and Persimmon turned to face it.

Rayne froze, the smile that had been on her face only a few moments before wiped away instantly as she stood staring at Len Kappler.

For a moment, she was sixteen again, alone behind the rows of sweet corn while his mocking laughter floated on the wind. She was eleven, locked in the bathroom of their elementary school by Len's girlfriend while the rest of her peers left for the bus. She was nine, hiding between the library bookshelves while Len and his friends circled, threatening to throw her down the stairs.

For a moment, she was afraid of him. But only a moment. All of those versions of her were dead and gone, and she was tired of being scared of him. "Get out," she spat. "Now."

Len smiled at her with the same kilowatt grin he always had; cold, mocking. His hand flew to his heart dramatically, and he pouted. "That's not very nice, Rayne. I came here to try to have a heart-to-heart with you."

"Funny, I always imagined that you had a jar of piss where your heart was supposed to be."

Persimmon looked between them, confusion clearly written across her face. Len frowned at Rayne, but instead of responding to her, he turned to Persimmon.

"Hey, Pers, didn't expect to see you here. Everything alright with you on the farm?"

Persimmon nodded. "Uh, yeah. Everything's good."

"That's good, I'm glad to hear it. Do you mind giving Rainy girl and me a moment?" he asked, gesturing toward the door. "It's really important we talk, and it's, well, it's kind of private."

Persimmon turned to Rayne, brow raised, and though she said nothing, Rayne could read her expression clearly: *Do you really want to be alone with this guy?*

Rayne nodded. "It's okay. We *should* talk."

"Alright, well, I'll be in the back then." Persimmon-eyed Len once more before she headed deeper into the store.

Only when Rayne heard the door close did she speak. "This had better be—"
"I know."

Rayne scoffed. "Can't imagine there's much that you do."

"I *know*," Len repeated, low. "You and your... demon. It's been you, all of it."

Shit. This is not what I was expecting. Part of her had been hoping that the night they'd come up the hill was nothing more than liquor and spite swirling in their veins; she hadn't thought that they would keep up with it once they were sober.

I should call Hawthorne, Rayne thought, preparing to reach for the magic between them. No, that's not fair to them. *Len is my problem. I can handle him.*

"All of what?" Rayne asked, jutting her chin out. "If you're going to make accusations, speak plainly."

"All the deaths. The Modies. The way you got this place so easily."

Rayne laughed, incredulous. "Me? You think I'm capable of killing anyone? I can barely walk a mile without my feet bleeding. You think I could murder a bunch of people and not be in a full body cast?"

"No, not you," Len snapped, stepping too close, and Rayne felt behind her for anything sharp, anything that she could use as a weapon if she had to. "The demon. I'm not the only one who's noticed either. Pastor Creary, half of the town is sure you sold your soul."

Her bitter laughter came again. *Figures that I spend my whole life trying to fit in, hoping for someone in this town to see me as I am, finally, and they only bother to look after me as magic has had its way with me.*

"What'd you sell your soul for, Dorne? Money, power?"

"If I ever did sell my soul it sure as shit would be for something more substantial than either of those things."

"You can still be saved. Pastor said so. You've just got to come down to the church, repent, get right with God."

Rayne faltered, her lower lip trembling at his words. *My Ma'maaw would have said the same thing if she could see me now, if she knew half of what I'd done.*

If there was a Heaven, her grandmother was there just as surely as if there was a Hell, Rayne would never see her again.

What would her grandmother say if she could see her now, tethered to some eldritch god and killing good folk in their name?

But would she forgive me if she knew I was doing it for love? That I, of all people, had someone who truly loved me?

Rayne shook her head, regaining her focus. *The last place I'm gonna start worrying about any of that is in front of fucking Len Kappler.*

"What's between God and me ain't no one else's business," She retorted. "Now, if you're done spouting nonsense at me, I'd appreciate it if you got on."

Len sighed, rubbing his hand over his mouth before he turned back to her. "If you won't get right, then... you gotta go."

Rayne blinked. "Excuse me?"

"You and your demon. Both of you."

Rage licked at her spine, and her hands balled into fists at her side. "I'm not going anywhere. My family's been here just as long as anyone else's; they're buried here, part of this land. I will *not* be chased out."

"What makes you think that you've got a choice?" Len snatched her arm so quickly that she didn't even have a chance to process that he was touching her until white, hot stabs of pain licked at her nerves. She could feel her skin tearing under his rough grasp.

She forced her steel-toed boot into his shin as hard as she could manage, and he hissed in pain. "You fucking bitch!" he snarled at her. Rayne stumbled back over one of the empty boxes, biting down on her lip to keep from crying out at the sharp corner that had bitten into her skin.

Len had doubled over, hand flying to his shin, and for a moment, both of them were on the floor, glaring daggers at one another.

"Fine," he grunted, staggering to his feet. "I didn't want to have to hurt you again, Dorne, but—"

Rayne hadn't heard the door to the back open, but Persimmon was at her side, hand at something at her hip. "Len, you better step the fuck back." She cast a glance down at Rayne before returning her attention to Len. "You alright, Ray?"

"Yeah. It's... I'm fine." Rayne grumbled. *Someone else is stepping in to save me again. I don't need it. I shouldn't need it.*

"Pers," Len balked, looking between them and gesturing down at Rayne. "This doesn't involve you. You *need* to stay away from her, trust me."

"And you *need* to get your sorry ass up outta here."

Rayne moved to her feet, hissing in discomfort. Beneath her gloves, she could feel her wrists getting sticky with blood. The scar at her hip most likely freshly torn open again. *Fucking great.*

Len scoffed. "Or what, Pers?"

Persimmon moved the hem of her sweater, flashing the holster at her side.

Well, shit. Persimmon really is Bury through and through now.

Rayne loathed guns, but she didn't know a soul in Bury who didn't keep at least one somewhere on their property. She had never planned on staying, so she'd never even considered getting one, and then when she did finally stay, Hawthorne was at her side.

"Don't defend her! Do you even know *what* she is, what she and her demon man have done?"

"All I know is that she's one of mine and I don't take kindly to people who come after me and mine."

Rayne froze, staring at Persimmon with her mouth agape. No one had ever claimed her save for her grandmother and Hawthorne.

Len shook his head. "Don't do this, Pers. I ain't got no gripe with you, no one does. You belong in this town. Don't throw that away for *her*."

Persimmon's fingers gripped the gun at her hip. "You've got fifteen seconds, Len. Don't make me start counting."

The chance for her to do so never came. The shop door opened, and in a flurry of movement, Len was knocked to the ground by a shadow. He didn't even have enough time to scream before a clawed hand squeezed his throat. Darkness spilled around them, tangling around Len's limbs in a vice grip. Shadows sharp as razors drew across Len's face toward his eyes. He struggled, attempting to kick and fight his way out from under the monster on top of him. Beneath them, Len was sobbing, trying to beg with what could have been his last breaths. The sharp scent of urine hit the air, and if it were any other day, she might have laughed.

He was terrified and pathetic, and the sight of him so helpless, tears spilling down his cheeks, warmed her in a way she had never anticipated. If anyone deserved to be torn apart by her husband, it was him.

A gasp to Rayne's left drew her back to reality. She and Hawthorne were not alone in this violence. Persimmon stood beside her, wide-eyed and rooted in place. Len deserved to die, and he deserved for it to be slow, but Persimmon didn't deserve to *see* it. She hadn't asked to get caught up in this mess.

Hawthorne, that's enough. Persimmon is still here. Finish this later.

She was met with static on the other end, their mind a burning haze of nothing. No thoughts, just a fire of emotion. *Anger. They're angry. I didn't know that they could feel anger.*

"Hawthorne!"

They inclined their head toward her a moment before their jaw opened, unhinging wide enough that they could fit half of Len into their mouth if they desired. Instead, they breathed a single word: "Leave."

Len wasted no time in scrambling to his feet and flying through the front door like a bat out of hell, and as she watched him go, a sinking feeling settled in her stomach.

The feeling that she had misstepped somehow.

The shadows dissolved, leaving only Hawthorne's human form behind. Their forearms and neck were still splattered in darkness, and their eyes two black pits. They moved to her, sweeping her hair from her face. "I could smell your blood all the way from the house."

"I'm okay," she said, patting their chest. "I've been hurt worse." Hawthorne frowned at this.

Persimmon knelt with her back to Rayne, throwing all her painting supplies into her suitcase with little care for where they ended up.

How am I going to explain any of this to her?

"Pers," Rayne began as she stepped out of Hawthorne's orbit, approaching her slowly. Persimmon tensed. "Thank you for—"

"I need to leave. That was a lot and I—I need to go," Persimmon said, looking everywhere but at Rayne.

"Okay. Are you alright? You didn't get hurt—"

"I'm fine, Rayne!" she snapped, slamming her suitcase closed as she rose to her feet. She took a deep, shaky breath. "I'm fine. I need to get out of here."

Rayne watched her friend leave, all but running toward the door. *Friend.* They *were* friends. She hadn't realized it before today, before Persimmon had stood between her and a man set on hurting her. Before Persimmon had chosen her.

Outside of Hawthorne, Rayne never had a friend, and even then, she could only watch her memories through Hawthorne's eyes. She didn't remember what friendship looked like, but if she had, she might have seen that Persimmon had been that to her all along.

I need her to know that I appreciate her, and I should apologize for being so foolish and for not telling her about Hawthorne sooner. She is a friend, the best one I've ever had, and I—she should know.

"Persimmon, wait!" Rayne called. She followed her out of the store and into the parking lot. Persimmon slowed but didn't stop, didn't turn to look at her. "I'm sorry. About not telling you. I didn't mean for you to find out this way."

Persimmon scoffed. "Did you mean for me to find out at all?"

Rayne hesitated. "I–I thought about telling you, but I was scared. I didn't know what you'd think of me."

At this, Persimmon stopped entirely, whirling on Rayne. "You didn't have to tell me anything, Rayne. I *knew.*"

"W-What?"

Persimmon shook her head and gestured toward the shop. "From the first moment you introduced me to *Hayden*, I knew that they weren't human. I knew that they were... whatever they are. The signs were there in every move that they made. I've always known."

Rayne searched for the words, her mind scrambling for memories of Persimmon and Hawthorne's interactions, if there had been anything, a moment where Hawthorne's otherness bled through.

"And I didn't even care. I just kept hoping that you would tell me, that you would trust me enough to let me in." Persimmon looked at Rayne, and as terrible as Rayne could be with reading people, she recognized the hurt looking back at her. "I've never had a friend like you before, Ray. I let you bleed into every aspect of my life, and all I wanted was for you to trust me. But you didn't, you don't, and maybe—maybe you never will."

Panic locked her throat. *Wait, no. That's not it.*

"I'm sorry that it took me *threatening* to gun someone down for you to think I'm trustworthy enough to be your friend."

"No, Pers, that's not—"

"I need space, Ray," Persimmon sighed, turning away from her. "I care about you, I just... I need some time to breathe. To figure out where I stand with everything."

Not trusting herself enough to speak, Rayne nodded, stepping back and out of Persimmon's way.

She watched as Persimmon tossed her bags into the bed of her truck, backed out of the parking lot, and sped toward the mountains.

Hawthorne hadn't spoken a word to her or even thought anything her way since they'd left the store together. They knelt before Rayne, carefully blotting the water from her wrist to get a better look at the cut there. Showering had been too painful, so she'd opted for a bath instead. Once she'd stepped out, Hawthorne was already waiting for her with her black floral bag of medical supplies.

They'd nudged her toward the bed without a word and set to cleaning her wounds.

Rayne pretended to be too focused on braiding her hair to notice their silence, her fingers sliding through the damp curls at her back a welcome relief from the guilt nipping at her heels.

"Why didn't you call for me?" Hawthorne asked as they unzipped the bag, not looking at her.

"I—I didn't want to bother you. Len is my problem, and you shouldn't have to clean up after me," Rayne mumbled.

"Bother me?" Hawthorne repeated. "How would your well-being *bother* me?"

"I was okay. It wasn't bad," Rayne answered, and it sounded weak even to her.

"Yes, but it could have been. What would have happened if Persimmon had not been there or if I had not been close enough to smell your blood when I did?"

Rayne finished her braid and balled her free hand into her lap, staring down at the floor. *Am I really that weak? Does everyone always need to step in and save me?*

Hawthorne sighed and placed the bag down, slipped their hand into her lap, palm up in silent offering. Rayne didn't look at them as she took it, fearing that she would see anger or hurt on their face as she had seen on Persimmon's.

"Rayne. I do not want you to think that I believe you are incompetent or that I do not trust you. I do. But you are precious to me." Their thumb traced along the back of her hand. "I cannot handle the idea of you getting hurt. I need you to trust that I care about you and that it is because of that care that I offer my assistance. You are too stubborn to be weak, little wolf."

Rayne pouted to hide the smile that threatened to give her away.

"This marriage that we have is a partnership, is it not?" Hawthorne asked, and when she nodded continued. "That means we share all. If someone threatens you, they make the same threat to me. There is no world in which I allow that to stand. Do you get what I am saying, Rayne?"

"I get you," Rayne replied, squeezing their hand. "I'm sorry that I didn't call you."

Hawthorne brought her hand to their lips. "I forgive you. Now, let me tend to your hand. I want to leave for the forest before dark."

"Leave?" Rayne asked. "Where are you going?"

"I need to hunt. Our run-in with that man left me hungry, and that will need to be sated if we are going to handle him properly. I cannot think straight."

Handle him. "We're going to kill him?"

Hawthorne's brow furrowed in confusion. "Of course. He made you bleed," they said as if it were the easiest conclusion in the world. "But you said that people in the town would assume you were behind it. So, we will need to make it look as though it could not have ever been you. So, once I have returned, we will plan. I should be back before dawn."

Later, after Hawthorne had left for the woods and Rayne was alone, it hit her how quiet the House had been.

"House?" Rayne called after locking the front door and heading back up-stairs, her fingers tracing idly along the wall. "Are you sleeping?"

The House shifted, the floorboards creaking like old bones. *"No, dear cherub. Rest is not the same for you and me."*

"You've been so quiet today. Are you upset?"

The House paused, shifting again. *"Emotions find their way into my bones like dry rot, I fear,"* it sighed. *"Come, lie in bed, and I will warm myself for you."*

It didn't really answer me, she thought, heading into her room. It had been a long day and exhaustion was beginning to pull at her.

Once she was in her bed, the sheets pulled up to her shoulders, the heat kicked on, humming as if the House itself was singing to her. The temperatures never made sense to her; it could be the middle of winter, and House would be sweltering or the dead of summer, and the House a tundra. As a child, it had baffled her, but now, she was beginning to understand that the House's emotions were more tied to the temperature than it wanted to admit.

"Do you know that I was not born loving you, cherub?" The House asked. "Yes, you are my creator, but love was not something I began with."

"You never told me that."

"No? Forgive me, age and dust play tricks on my mind," The House said, the windows stressed like a humorless laugh. *"You were small, so small. One night, there was a terrible thunderstorm. You hated thunder, do you remember that? The rain was terrible, battering away at my roof, lightning striking the trees around me, threatening to come crashing down into my guts. But I was so strong, not even a leak made it into the whole me for how well I cradled you all."*

Rayne could not recollect this night in which House was describing, but she could see it all the same, a younger, more timid version of her curled quietly in the dark while a storm raged on.

"Your family—an ungrateful bunch, did not even acknowledge my strength, my good work. They thought I'd crumble into nothing and hid in the basement as if the dirt could shield them better than me! But you, my dearest cherub, sat at the top of the stairs, clinging to me. You pressed your little lips to the banister and said, 'Thank you, brave House.' I knew then that I would love you until Skyfall."

Her eyes misted at the memory of a girl she would never know, a self gone, but mainly at the House that had loved her more stubbornly than anyone else.

"I love you, House. I always will," she whispered.

"Yes," The House repeated. *"Until Skyfall."*

Sleep crept over her quietly, snatching her from the waking world. But when Rayne awoke, it was not to her husband's return but to the stinging scent of burning plastic, smoldering wood, and the acrid stench of searing flesh.

When Rayne opened her eyes, she saw fire.

CHAPTER THIRTY-FOUR
rayne

Her eyes, still heavy and blurred with sleep, could make out the shape of flames dancing against the darkness through her window. Too close but far enough that she realised it was not her house on fire or the forest, but something on the mountain.

Something close.

Sirens screamed in the distance, growing closer with every passing second. "House, can you see what's burning?" Rayne asked, scrambling out of bed and rummaging around in the dark for socks. The House was still, silent save for her fumbling.

"House!" she snapped. "Answer me, damn it! What's burning?"

Softly, barely a whisper came its response, *"I'm sorry, cherub."*

Rayne let out a huff of frustration, pushing out of her room and down the stairs to shove into her boots. The world outside had morphed into something she hardly recognized; the sky was a bloodied red, dark smoke scabbing it. Ash tainted the air, stinging her eyes and burning her lungs.

Up the way, Rayne could make out the small frame of Mrs. Hamper, outside on her front porch, arms wrapped tightly around herself as she stared down the hill, past Rayne.

Rayne lifted her hand to her eyes, squinting down the mountain to get a better look at what was on fire. It was not the trees, a car, or anything so small; instead, it was a house.

Persimmon's house.

Rayne nearly stumbled over the front steps of the porch in her rush, racing down the dirt path. Around her, the forest was silent save for the howl of sirens, the roaring of the flames, and the rocks kicked up from underfoot.

Please be outside when I get there, Pers, Rayne begged. *Please be okay.*

Her house may have been on fire, but that didn't mean anything. Persimmon was too bright, too strong to get caught up in a house fire. She spent her days working the land and her nights capturing the beauty of the world with her paintings. *She isn't the type of person that this can happen to.*

Her house might be unsalvageable for the time being, but it would be okay. There was plenty of room inside the House, a whole guestroom and bathroom downstairs that Persimmon could stay in for as long as she wanted. *She can stay with us until she gets back on her feet. It's okay. She's okay.*

A firetruck sat perched in front of the fork of the road that led directly to Persimmon's house. Rayne cut through the trees, covering her mouth with her hand to keep from inhaling more smoke.

Persimmon's garden was burning.

A small crowd had formed in front of the smoldering ashes of Persimmon's home, far enough away so as not to hinder the firefighters as they continued to put out the last of the flames.

How long was everything on fire? Why hadn't I woken up? Why didn't House say anything?

The small grove Persimmon had on her farm was dead, nothing remained but a charred field of ash. The house was all but gone, nothing but a blackened skeleton that reeked of burning wood and seared lemons. Everything was gone.

But where was *she*?

Rayne pushed through the group as she searched for a familiar head of tangerine colored hair in the crowd. "Persimmon?" The voice that fell from her lips hardly sounded like her own, ragged and dry. "Persimmon!"

"Get back, ma'am!" A firefighter shouldered her further into the crowd, farther from the house.

Rayne pushed her way back, grabbing at the thick material of his gear. "There was a woman inside this house, Persimmon. Where is she?"

Even through the thick mask they wore, Rayne could see their eyes, how they looked past her. They didn't answer her, but when she turned, following their attention, they didn't need to.

She watched as two firemen carried a white tarp between them, something was wrapped up in it, shielded from prying eyes. Rayne found herself moving toward them, pulled like the tide to a truth she couldn't bear.

"Easy there, Dorne," Officer Creed stepped between her path. "Don't go doing that. You've got to stay over here."

"Who is that?" Rayne rasped.

"You know I can't tell—"

"Who is it?" someone shouted, a voice that sounded dangerously close to her own.

Brian exhaled through his nose, looking over his shoulder and then back at Rayne.

"Were y'all close? You and the Jaxson girl? You know if she's got family around here, someone I could call?"

Rayne's stomach churned, bile rose and fell in her throat. "No."

It wasn't an answer, but Brian nodded like it was, like she was capable of conversation as the world slipped out from under her feet. The weight of everything around her became too much to bear: the flashing lights of the firetruck, the scent of burning, the smoke that seared her lungs and pricked at her eyes like needles.

He took off his cap and scratched his head. "Yeah, I figured. Good, you're here though. I was headed your way too."

"My way?" Rayne repeated, her eyes fixed on the white tarp, which looked so wrong on Persimmon's front lawn.

"Your shop down on Main? Yeah, there was—a fire, electrical, they said. Barely anything left," Brian shook his head. "Real shame most of it's gone. But

it's a good thing ole Lenny boy was there. Caught things before they got too
bad."

Fire. My shop. Electrical fire. Len.

Len. Len. **Len.**

"What caused the fire?" Rayne heard herself ask.

Brian raised a brow. "I just said it was electric—"

"No, not for the shop. The house. Persimmon. What happened?"

Brian shrugged. "Too early to say. Fire department has to report back to us
what—"

He was speaking, Rayne knew, but her ability to hear him faded, drowned
out by the static behind her eyes.

*'I hope I've never got to deal with any kind of fire. He's the last person I'd want
saving me.'*

Persimmon had joked about Len as a fireman when they'd first met. *Like she'd
known, even then, that he was capable of doing something horrible. Something
like... like burning her house to the ground.*

Rayne stepped back away from the crowd, away from the body of her friend
and the dying fire.

He did this.

Persimmon, who Rayne had never heard utter an untrue or unkind word
about anyone, who had an easier smile and even easier laughter. She'd built a
life for herself she'd loved, and now it was gone.

For what?

At the edge of the forest, its fur pristine and whiter than bone, the rabbit sat
perfectly still. Unmoved and unbothered by the fraying world around it, all of
its attention remained on Rayne.

She stared back as if the stupid thing held any answers for her.

Without anything to stop her, she began the long walk into town.

With every step that Rayne took, she felt herself fraying, splitting into something that she could not name. Her eyes were drier than they had ever been, and her mind was a dull haze of nothing. Her body was numb, sensationless, and without the sound of her own footsteps, she would not have even been aware that she was walking.

Shadows dripped from her fingertips, pooling around her and snaking back up her legs, her arms, grabbing, snatching hands. Her vision vignetted, swallowed by shadows. Her husband's blood thrashed through her veins, feeding into the anger that choked her as tightly as the hands around her throat.

Rayne did not know where her body and her borrowed magic were taking her, but she did not resist the current of it until it splashed her against a door. Her hands flew in front of her face to shield herself from the force as she was pushed through.

Her vision returned gradually, shadow giving way to low light and candle glow. Chest heaving with effort, she spun, taking in her surroundings. High ceilings, chipping white paint over rotting wood, the scent of melting wax. *Church.* "What—why the fuck am I here?"

"I knew you'd find me," Rayne bristled at his voice, every hair on end as Len stepped out from the baptistery room, hair damp. He was dressed in all white, not even a smudge on him. Around his throat, black and purple bruising darkened his skin from where Hawthorne had nearly crushed his windpipe, an extended cut along his right cheek.

"I didn't think it'd be so soon, but I guess I've got a habit of underestimating you," he continued, around a mirthless laugh. "And yet, here you are."

"You killed her!" Rayne hissed. "You fucking *murdered* her, then you just came here like she was some sin to be washed away. She was innocent. She didn't do anything to hurt anybody!"

"And what about those people you and your demon killed? Did they ever hurt anyone?"

Rayne stilled.

"All those people you cut down," Len continued, pointing behind her. "Did you ever think about who they might have been?"

I—I did. But I didn't care. I knew we were killing innocent people, maybe even good ones, but it didn't matter. It was for Hawthorne.

How many times had Rayne joyfully led someone to their doom only to go home and bathe herself in juniper and cedar smoke to keep those unhappy spirits from remaining near?

Too many to count.

Her Mam'maw had told her once that to kill another was to cleave one's soul into fragments that could never be repaired save for the Creator's touch.

How many people did I kill?

Too many to count.

"I didn't want to hurt Pers," Len said softly, frowning. "She was part of this town, part of this community, and she—she'll be missed. Unlike you. No one is going to dare speak your name long after you've disappeared."

"No. You don't get to stand there and act sorry for something you did. Just tell me why, what was worth her life?" Rayne demanded.

Candlelight caught in Len's eyes, misty and filled with unadulterated vitriol. "Couldn't get to you. Didn't want to risk your demon again. If you didn't have her or your little shop, figured you'd skip town."

Rayne took a step back as the weight of his words settled over her. Persimmon had died because of her, her life reduced to nothing more than a message to be delivered.

Those flames were meant for me.

The air in the room thinned, her ragged lungs unable to get enough of it as she attempted to breathe in a world that was closing in on her.

"You stand here, lecturing me about right and wrong like you aren't covered in blood, fresh off of killing some poor bastard." Len scowled.

Blood? I'm not—

Lifting her hands, she found them soaked in dried blood. Bits of skin and hair caught between her fingers and under her fingernails.

Whose blood is this?

A montage of images flashed before her eyes: a creature shaped like her following a trail, sweeping into a house, crawling up carpeted stairs into a bedroom.

Pictures of Len along the walls, grinning beside a woman holding a baby, a toddler at her side. Eyes wide in surprise and then dull. Skin separating from muscle, intestines squelching under her heel, bones snapping.

Her fingers shredding into a pile of skin and organs.

I must have killed—but why don't I remember?

"Do you have a family, Len?" Rayne inquired. Police sirens sounded distantly behind them. Rayne laughed despite herself. *Here I am, all torn up about random innocent people I've helped my husband kill, but now, after apparently having killed Len's, I couldn't care less. I don't even know their names.* "Or, *did* you have a family?"

Disgust contorted Len's face into something ugly—had he always been so hideous?

"Don't you dare talk about my family, bitch!" he snarled, his hand fumbled at his side, and from his hip, he pulled a gun. He cocked it, pointing it dead at her. "Fuck a warning shot. Go back to hell."

"Bet a fiddle of gold against your soul that you'll get there before me," Rayne said, smirking down the barrel of his gun.

"Wha—"

This time when shadow took all Rayne had, she dove headfirst into the darkness, gunfire acting as the soundtrack to her descent.

CHAPTER THIRTY-FIVE
hawthorne

Their neck snapped back into place with a resounding crack, the forest swallowing the sound of their shift. Returning to their human bodies was always a bit uncomfortable, though they were beginning to get used to it. *With how much time I spend in it, I should be.*

Hawthorne had shed their mortal skin and ventured deep into the nearby forests until the scent of humans burned away as paper to flame. For a few hours, they forgot about the never-ending screech of mortals and their electricity, the unyielding stench of their flesh as it rotted around them, every day they spent alive another day closer to the grave.

They forgot the humans and remembered themself.

I could leave as I once did. The world is vast, and there are places yet tainted by human hands, true perfection.

Almost.

Nothing could ever truly be perfect without their wife at their side. Even now, she was drawing them back into her orbit simply by existing. They had spent too long away from her, and now that they had remembered themself, they craved her.

Hawthorne did not announce their return, as it was not their kind's nature to make themselves known unless called for, so they did not feel the need to tell her they were coming home to her. *It is not as though she can get away from me. I will find her regardless of where she is.*

It hit them as soon as they were within the forest limits of Bury: the scent of blood, ash, and the acrid stench of burning flesh. Beneath those, the crisp burn of raw magic.

Something must have crept into the town while I was away, they thought, pushing their way through the thicket. *Figures that a lesser being would take advantage of my absence. Let them feast if they must.*

Almond, followed faintly by rose, came next, and Hawthorne froze. *Rayne.*

The town still lay a few miles ahead of them, barely visible, and though dawn was nearing, it was still too dark for Rayne to be alone in the forest without them. She wouldn't have wandered this deep on her own unless she was looking for something or—

Hawthorne darted off after her smell, trailing her. *Rayne, where are you?*

The thought was met with resistance, the other end of their connection going taut and then silence. They could still feel her humming at the base of their skull, even if she was quiet. *Trying to hide.*

A dozen scenarios bloomed to life in their mind of what could be ailing her, why she would try to shield herself from them, and none of them kept their accursed human pulse from racing.

Her scent finally coalesced by the river, and they broke through the trees, skidding to halt in the stony dirt. "Rayne."

Her back answered them, her face turned toward the river, and every muscle in her body tensed. Her hands and legs were drenched in blood that wasn't her own. Hawthorne sniffed the air. *It's that Len man. A woman, two other scents I don't know, but I can smell Bury on them.*

Rayne had killed with them before, but everything about her posture was wrong; even her breathing wasn't right. Nothing about her demeanor was right.

"Rayne," Hawthorne tried again, approaching her slowly. "What's going on?"

She finally turned to them, her face covered in ash. "He killed her," she croaked, her voice hoarse and raw.

"Who, baby?"

"Persimmon. She's dead," Rayne continued, the hands at her side beginning to quake. "She's dead, and they killed her to scare me. To get us to leave. She's dead, and it's my fault."

"Why didn't you call me?" Hawthorne asked. "You said that you would—"

"I'm sorry."

Hawthorne could feel that she was going down before her feet gave way beneath her, and they stepped in to catch her, following her down into the dirt. She clutched at their shirt, her hands fisting into the fabric greedily. "It's okay, Rayne, you're okay."

Rayne shook her head, her eyes filling with fresh tears. "She never did anything to them, to *anyone*. And he still killed her. They—they had to die."

It was a shame that Persimmon had been killed; Hawthorne had been fond of her as far as humans outside of Rayne went. But they could not grieve.

They were incapable of tears, of sorrow. It was something that they could never join her in.

Hawthorne held her tighter, brushing their hand through her dust-matted curls. "How did you kill them?"

Rayne was covered in blood, her hands sticky with it, so it would have made sense for her to have done it with her bare hands, but then why did the air sing of spells?

She looked up at them, shaking like a skeleton leaf in their arms. "I—" Rayne looked past them, further down the riverbank. Hawthorne followed her gaze to the hulking mass of red and pink flesh, hulled from the bone. Muscles and tendons decorated the shoreline.

Whoever that had been, their little wolf had certainly seen to their suffering.

Hawthorne's attention returned to their wife, their brow furrowing. *She is not physically strong enough for any of that. Her own flesh would have torn, and yet there is not even a scratch on her.*

Anger streaked across her face. "I thought if—it felt good, but it wasn't enough," she whispered. "Nothing will ever be enough."

Hawthorne looked again at the mutilated mass, the large, clunky cuts. *Like when she killed her cousin.*

I have never seen magic used this way before.

Magic was not typically woven from a place of emotion; it was crafted from necessity, sometimes for sport, but the language of feelings did not translate into it. And yet, Rayne had forged a weapon of it not once but twice. It was clumsy and ill-conceived spellwork, yes, but it was more than a human should have been able to do.

Did I make a mistake in granting her such power?

"Come on, little wolf," Hawthorne said, smoothing her hair from her face, looking away from the mess she'd made. The scavengers of the forest would make quick work of the body. "Let's get you home."

The House was eerily silent upon their return, not even asking what had happened to Rayne and why she was drenched in blood that was not her own.

I will speak with it later. I know it has something to tell me.

Hawthorne had carried Rayne home and up the stairs to the master bedroom, where the only bathtub in the house lay. They ran her a warm bath, filled it with what bubble solution and oils that they could find. They had little idea of what they were doing, and if

Rayne minded, she did not make mention of it. Rayne did little of anything, naked and sitting on the edge of the tub with her arms curled around herself, staring at her own reflection in the water.

What they knew of grief was that it was a strange and furious beast, difficult to understand and tame. *I do not think that I can do that for her. But I will hold her while she battles it.*

Hawthorne did not like to put spells on Rayne without her consent, but they *hated* the way that she was looking at herself, how she seemed to be shrinking in front of them. *It will be one spell for only tonight. I will apologize for it in a few days when she has righted herself.*

Shadows seeped from their spine, spilling onto the floor and wrapped around Rayne's ankle. By the time she realized what they were doing, they had already had hold of her.

"You feel at ease, Rayne. You have never felt more comfortable than you do right now," Hawthorne whispered their honeyed words in her ear.

Rayne's shoulders dropped, and she sagged against them, nodding. "Okay."

"You are going to enjoy your bath. You will not think of Persimmon or anything outside of your own comfort the rest of the night. Yes?"

"Mhm, okay."

Hawthorne helped her step into the steaming water, kissing her hand as they let go, taking most of their magic with them. "Would you like me to leave?"

She shook her head, snatching their hand back and cradling it against her bare chest. "Stay."

Their free hand stroked her cheek. "Always."

That night, Hawthorne did not move from Rayne's side. The next morning, some time before noon they slipped out of bed, careful not to wake her and set to work.

Last night, they had decided that they would take Rayne away to the forest for a day, where she would be free from thinking about Bury or Persimmon. Nature would aid her healing, as it had aided theirs.

They spent the remainder of the morning preparing food for them both and rummaging through the garage for a suitable bag to carry everything they planned to bring to the mountains.

"House!" Hawthorne snapped, their head half buried in a pile of miscellaneous garbage Rayne's parents had insisted on keeping. "Is there a bag or something useful in all of this nonsense?"

"*Yes,*" The House answered, soft, subdued.

Hawthorne raised a brow. "Well, where is it?"

The House paused. *"**Must you go outside today? Our cherub could use a day of rest and recuperation. We can cradle her gently, both you and I, what do you say, wraith?**"*

Hawthorne opened their mouth to bite out a reply, but something tugged at the edge of their mind, something like memory. *No, it cannot be that. I have never forgotten anything.*

"House." They stepped away from the pile and ran their hand along the wall. "I know that despite your appetite for her, she means something to you. She needs some time away from this town, even if just a few hours of peace. Can you tell me where the bag is?"

The House sighed so deeply that the entirety of it quaked. *"**To your far right, under the large, red plastic container.**"*

Hawthorne patted the wall. "There we are. See how easy things can be between us?"

As they were leaving, The House shook again. *"**Hawthorne.**"*

They stopped in the doorway. *It has never called me by my name before.* "Yes?"

*"**She is not the only one that I care for,**"* It said. *"**I will keep the color of your eyes in the moss that grows along my sides. I have as much love for you, wraith, as I could have for anyone else.**"*

Love was still a word that Hawthorne was mulling over; they knew that they loved Rayne and told her as much, but did they love The House?

I feel a deep affection for it, yes. I would miss it were it to fall victim to flame or time. Perhaps that is a kind of love. I will ask Rayne about it later.

"A secret spot?" Rayne inquired, her breath against Hawthorne's neck as they carried her on their back. "I thought we were done with secrets between one another?"

Hawthorne chuckled; they did not have to see her to know that she was pouting at them, her nose scrunching in irritation. "We are done with secrets. I wanted to wait until the forest began to shake off the blanket of winter before I took you here."

Rayne huffed, resting her cheek against their spine.

She had seemed well enough when she arose this morning, but Hawthorne knew that there was more bubbling under the surface; their little wolf felt deeply, down to her bones. The death of her friend would not be something that she could shake off easily.

We will delay it at least another day, though.

Past their tree, there was another clearing, a field of wild violets that bloomed in spring. It was beautiful in its simplicity, and Hawthorne could not help but appreciate it. They knew Rayne would as well.

"We're here," Hawthorne announced, easing Rayne off their back. They observed her expression, the furrowing of her brow, the tension melting into a soft smile, and the moisture shining in her eyes.

Soft, misty sunlight shone down on them, a slight breeze making the pale purple flowers sway.

"It's beautiful."

Hawthorne kissed her cheek. "Come then, I did not bring us all this way to merely look at it." They held up the bag that they'd carried along with her. Inside, they'd tucked a few blankets to keep her skin from having to make direct contact with rough surfaces, tupperware filled with sandwiches, diced peaches, peeled oranges, chocolate, and a thermos of coffee.

Rayne watched them lay the blanket on the grass, close enough to the violets for them to be admired but not close enough to crush them. Her mouth pressed into a tight line when they took her hand and pulled her down onto the ground with them.

"You did this for me?"

The urge to joke, to tease, rose, but the look on her face was too vulnerable; she was baring herself to them, and that was a gift Hawthorne would never take for granted.

"Yes, of course," Hawthorne replied, squeezing her hand. "I intend to do much more for you for the entirety of your life."

Hawthorne spared a glance at the wedding ring Rayne had tattooed on their finger. Humans wore rings to symbolize their union and commitment to one another, but they wanted something that could never be removed, something that would follow them both wherever they went.

"I never thought that I would have this," Rayne admitted, blinking back her tears despite the gentle smile on her face. "I never expected that someone would care about me enough to stay. To keep staying. I never thought I'd have a friend or a spouse. Now you're here, and I don't know how I ever survived without you."

"We were separated for only a brief moment in the span of your life," Hawthorne answered. "A few years. I intend to make up for lost time. You will never be without me again."

"Promise," Rayne demanded.

Affection bloomed in their chest. *Such a demanding little thing.* "I promise. Nothing can keep me away. I love you, Rayne."

Rayne bit her lip, and before she placed the wall within her mind, they saw an image of Persimmon, followed by a sensation that reminded them of biting into something sour. *A feeling. I will have to ask her what it is called.*

"And I–I love you, Hawthorne."

I love you.

They knew that she loved them, could feel it in every moment that they spent together, but to hear it was another thing entirely.

A slow grin spread across their face. "Say it again."

She looked away, trying to hide the way her face mirrored theirs. "Don't you have super hearing?"

"I do." Hawthorne hooked an arm around her waist and slid her across the blanket to their side. "But I want to hear you repeat it."

"I love you," Rayne repeated, quieter, turning her face into their shoulder.

They caught her chin and tilted her face up. They traced her entire face with their eyes, the dark beauty mark just under the apple of her left cheek, the curve of her lips. *I will never tire of looking at you.* They did not attempt to hide the thought from her.

She lurched forward, breaking what little distance there was to kiss them, yanking them down to her by their hair. Hawthorne laughed into the kiss and fell back onto the blanket beneath, taking her with them. They had not considered bringing pillows to cushion her properly; instead, they positioned themself under her, acting as a shield against her and the ground.

Hawthorne's hand slipped under the oversized hoodie she'd stolen from them and traced along her spine, seeking the clasp of her bra, only to find her skin delightfully bare.

Trying to seduce me, little wolf?

You make it so easy, she thought back, neither of them willing to break the kiss as she attempted to pull the hoodie over her head. Hawthorne allowed her an entire second to do so before they were back on her, chasing her lips.

Their hand fell from her spine to her breast, thumbing the bud of her nipple. Rayne moaned into their mouth, and they devoured the sound. It was cruel, they reasoned, that they could not kiss her and admire her at the same time.

You and these perfect tits will be the end of me, Hawthorne thought to her. *Tell me that you're not wearing any underwear under all of those layers.*

I'm not wearing anything under these layers. Rayne emphasized the thought with a roll of her hips, grinding against the bulge of their cock in their jeans. Hawthorne groaned, punctuating the sound by teasing her nipple between their thumb and index finger.

Don't tease me today, Hawth, please.

If Hawthorne had one weakness, it was the sound of their wife begging for them. It didn't matter that she had started this; they would always give her what she asked for.

Remove your tights before I tear them off of you.

Rayne huffed against their mouth before pulling away. She carefully rolled them off and wiggled her way out of her tights and every layer that she piled on to protect her from the elements. Sunlight splashed against her back, filtering through the dark halo of her curls.

In the light, her hair was not black but a deep auburn; they had first caught sight of it on their wedding day and had been chasing after every chance to see it that they could get.

Every bit of her was breathtaking, the scars, the birthmarks, the dark curls between her legs; they were helpless to all of it.

Rayne didn't shy away from them as they marveled at her: when they'd first officially begun their relationship, she panicked every time that they looked at her for longer than a few seconds, convinced that they were about to point out some imperfection.

She'd been so shy and as cute as they had found all of her blushing, but that was not what they wanted from her. That was *not* who Rayne was, but who every vile human she spent her time around had forced her to be.

Their little wolf was not a raindrop but a hurricane, and though they could see it, she was still blind to herself, at least, for now. *I will do everything in my power to help her see herself as she truly is, without the cowl of shame others have wrapped her in.*

"Come here."

Rayne hesitated, looking around for something softer. "I don't know if I can here."

Hawthorne placed their hands on the ground at their sides, palms open. "Knees here. I'll hold you."

Her cheeks darkened, and sheepishly, she knelt into their palms while they supported her weight in their hands. Even in this form, their wife was nearly weightless. She felt around for the zipper of their pants, and then her hands were on them, warm and desperate.

They lowered her, the head of their cock seated at her entrance, before she reached between them and pushed their cock inside of her.

"That's right, take what you want," they said around a moan. Rayne pushed herself down, taking them deeper. Their head fell back against the blankets, swearing in their mother tongue. She drank every inch of them down, sucking them deeper into her orbit, in her. If it wasn't enough to have the warm haven of her cunt wrapped around them, the sounds that fell from her lips were nearly enough to bring them to the edge on their own.

Rayne pulled off of them only to slide all the way back down, riding their cock as if she was made for it. "Gods, look at you."

"You feel so good, Hawth," she groaned, and this time, when she slipped down onto them, the movement came with a circle of her hips. "I need more of you." Hawthorne bit down on their lip to keep from digging their claws into her knees, flipping her over, and pulling every little wanton noise from her.

Focusing with what little brainpower remained available to them, their shadows pushed out of their spine, snaked up their sides, and worked their way between Rayne's legs. The shadows solidified into a single tendril and immediately went to work on Rayne's swollen clit.

She melted, her back bowing, and the sounds that fell from her lips were driving them past the point of sanity. It took every ounce of restraint to keep from switching their positions, but this was how she wanted them, and that was precisely how they were going to give themself.

Rayne tightened around them, her entire body coiling like a snake as her orgasm crested. Her nails dug into the meat of their thighs, and Hawthorne followed her, her name the only prayer they'd ever uttered.

She collapsed on top of them, bringing their foreheads together. For a few minutes, they did nothing but breathe each other's air, sharing breath and pulses. Eventually, Hawthorne pulled out of her and set her down only a moment before she was in their lap.

"I feel guilty."

"Guilty?" Hawthorne asked against her hair. "For what?"

"For this. For being happy with you even though she's gone." Rayne worried her lower lip. "It's not fair."

Hawthorne swallowed their usual reminder of the truth of fairness, recognizing that Rayne needed something softer while the wound of her loss was still fresh. "Do you think that Persimmon would have preferred you to grieve her in misery for the rest of your days?"

Rayne hesitated. "No."

"She cared for you, did she not?"

Rayne swallowed. "Yes."

"Then," Hawthorne began, burying their nose in Rayne's hair. "Perhaps she would have been content to know that life goes on for you, that you have not lost joy."

She did not respond; instead, she ensured there was no space between their bodies. Hawthorne did not know if it was the correct thing to say, but it settled Rayne and the quiet storm of sadness that kept threatening to pull her under. *I will find the right thing to say if it brings her peace.*

The sun had begun its slow drip into the horizon by the time Rayne was ready to go home. She stretched while Hawthorne finished packing up the last of their items and tried not to notice how her hoodie rode up her stomach as she did so.

"I was half expecting to see that white rabbit again. I swear the thing's been following me," Rayne mused.

Hawthorne hummed, zipping up the backpack. "A white rabbit? That is rather uncommon. I can't say that I've seen one in these woods."

"It's a weird one, too. It's got these ugly red eyes, and it just stares at me."

Hawthorne froze. "You've been seeing a white rabbit... with red eyes?"

"Yeah," Rayne shrugged. "Why?"

No.

Hawthorne dropped the backpack, clearing the distance between them and startling a cry out of Rayne as they grabbed her face. "For how long?"

"A-A couple of weeks, I don't know," Rayne stammered. The air burst with the scent of her fear, and they knew they were scaring her, but she did not yet understand how scared she *should* be. "What's wrong?"

A couple of weeks.

Hawthorne thought back to what the last month of Rayne's life had looked like: the haze of bliss, the quiet nights, and the early mornings. She hadn't *done* anything. The killing shouldn't have been a problem; humans murdered one another all the time.

Unless it wasn't the killing.

Hawthorne's throat felt tight, itchy, as if there was a hand around it, and they could hear their own heartbeat, louder than they ever had before. It was a sensation that they had never experienced before, and they *hated* it.

They released Rayne's face and grabbed her hand, tugging her toward the shelter of the trees. "We have to go, Rayne. We need to get out of here, *now*."

Rayne slowed, digging her feet into the dirt as if she were strong enough to delay them. "Go where? Hawth, what's going on? Why are you acting like this?"

They didn't have time. If it had been weeks now, then there was not a second that they could waste getting Rayne out of this forest, out of this town. There might not be any refuge for them anywhere else, but Hawthorne had to try. *I won't lose her.*

"Rayne, listen to me," Hawthorne snapped. Rayne winced, and they wished they could take back the sharpness of their tone, but an apology would have to wait for another day. "We are leaving this town, this instant."

"Leaving? But what about House—"

"*House* will be fine. We don't have time for any of that; we need to leave."

"Where are we going, though?"

"Anywhere else!" they nearly shouted at her, and she shrank away from them. *Fuck.* Through the discomfort of the sensation rattling through them, they remembered how many people in life spoke to Rayne like that. Like she was a burden. Hawthorne refused to be one of them.

Hawthorne let go of her hand and cupped her cheek in their hand, smoothing their thumb along the small birthmark on her face. "I'm sorry. I don't want to talk to you like that ever. But I need you to listen to me, alright? We can't stay here anymore, and I don't have time to stop and explain it to you, but when we're safe—when you're safe—I will tell you everything. But right now, I *need* you to trust me. Okay?"

Rayne nodded up at them. "Okay."

"Alright. I am going to shed this body. I can move faster once I am free of it," Hawthorne tossed the backpack onto the ground. "You get on my back, and we'll go."

"*Oh, it is much too late for that now.*"

CHAPTER THIRTY-SIX
rayne

"*Oh, it is much too late for that now.*"

It was not the voice that set ice in Rayne's blood. It was the expression on Hawthorne's face that she'd never seen before.

They were *scared.*

The voice that spoke to them was not of any manëtu she'd heard; it was not soft like House's nor as deep as Hawthorne's; it was consuming, the voice of a god.

Before them, trees parted, and a white rabbit's head poked through the underbrush. Its head rotated, growing until it dwarfed Hawthorne. Pale fur split, and dozens of crimson roving eyes popped open. Legs stretched, and wings unfurled, littered with more eyes.

The creature sighed in relief and sat back on its haunches, its knees reaching well over Hawthorne's head. It leaned down, and in the center of its forehead, a final eye blinked open, settling on Rayne and Hawthorne.

It smiled, tilting its head at them. "Hello."

Rayne recognized that this monster was horrifying; she understood that, but she could not bring herself to focus on anything outside of the absolute terror on her husband's face. *I didn't know that they could feel fear. What could scare them?*

Hawthorne?

"Dresden," they breathed.

The creature, Dresden, grinned, the fur around its lips pulling back to reveal two sharp incisors larger than Rayne's head. "I will not have to introduce myself then. Good. A bit of ease is necessary in times of strife."

Hawthorne, Rayne tried again, grasping their arm. *Who is this?*

Hawthorne's attention remained fixed on Dresden even though their voice brushed against her mind. *Dresden. I didn't tell you more—I didn't have time. But your world has its hierarchies, as does ours. He sits at the top. Two more above him, but—*

Dresden's ear twitched, and his head inclined toward Rayne, leaning closer. Her reflection showed back in the pools of those red eyes, and her stomach clenched in fear.

He sniffed the air near her, and Rayne willed iron into her veins.

Hawthorne took Rayne's hand carefully and moved her behind them, stepping between her and Dresden.

"Now, now," Dresden barked a laugh. "We both know that if I were going to take the human, I would have. And *you* could do nothing about it."

The way Hawthorne's shoulders tensed in response told her that there was truth to what he said. *He is stronger than Hawthorne.* Rayne gripped Hawthorne's shirt to keep her hands from shaking.

"Hawthorne—that is the name you've chosen to be called now, yes? Yes, well. I have come to deliver a message for you and to enact your punishment on behalf of the Enforcer."

Punishment?

Enforcer?

Dresden cracked his neck and settled further back onto his hind legs. "You, Hawthorne, have violated ancient law and committed an Act of Wrath. Gone are the days when we smite mortals without predestined cause. *You* know better." He spoke as if he were reading from a script that he'd read dozens of times before. "The Enforcer has already passed her judgment, and so I've come for you."

For Hawthorne.

"No," Rayne spoke before her thoughts could catch up with her. "You won't touch them. I won't let you."

Dresden's laughter shook the forest, the very ground beneath trembling with his amusement. "Don't think that I have forgotten about you, little chimera, for it is *you* who did the deed. You should be grateful Hawthorne will take the punishment in your stead."

Rayne's mind scrambled to comprehend what he was saying. "Did what?"

Dresden shifted, lowering his head so that he could see the whole of her in his one eye. "The magic you used to tear those humans asunder, the man and his family. Did you think that there would be no consequence?"

The blood that Rayne had shed to avenge her dead friend. The blood that was still caught under her fingernails. *And now Hawthorne—*

"Wait, but—but I was the one who did it. Leave Hawthorne out of this!"

"Yes, but you used *their* magic. It is as if they did it themself," Dresden huffed, shifting to fix Hawthorne with his eye. "Is she truly so obtuse, or did you fail to equip her with the proper knowledge when you granted her your power?"

At Hawthorne's silence, Dresden shucked his teeth, tsking. "Another failure on your part, then it would seem. Nevertheless, I shall clean house. Come, Hawthorne. Make your parting words to the human, you've caught me in a temperate mood."

Parting. Hawthorne was going to—no.

Hawthorne turned to Rayne, their hands falling on her shoulders. *Rayne. I'm sorry. I didn't mean for any of this—*

I will not lose you. We stay together. Remember?

Please, Rayne, listen to me. He is not a fight you can win. Just turn around and walk back to the house. House will keep you safe. I don't want to make you, Rayne, but I will.

Rayne could hear them, could listen to the words, but none of it was sticking.

Hawthorne couldn't get hurt, and they couldn't get hurt because of a mistake *she'd* made.

"Ah, but before that," Dresden said, snapping his long, bony fingers. "I must return the human to her natural state. I will remove your influence from her, Hawthorne. Come here, human, this may make a mess."

At this, some switch seemed to flip within Hawthorne, and their human skin crumbled away. A growl, deep and warning, settled in their throat. "That could kill her. Leave it."

Dresden hummed, thoughtful and unbothered by Hawthorne's aggression. "It is a possibility, and I can see that you are quite... attached. I suppose that I could leave the human as she is." He smiled again, running a pale, white tongue along his teeth. "But I will require compensation, so tell me, what have you got to bargain with?"

This couldn't be happening, she *refused*. "You will *not* touch my husband," Rayne said, stepping out from Hawthorne's orbit to approach Dresden. She reached for her magic, the shadows, and folded them around herself, forging them into a knife.

"Rayne, wait!" Hawthorne hissed just in time for her to slam the blade of her darkness into Dresden's knee. At least, that had been her intent; instead, the blades hovered just over him, hesitating to strike.

"Oh, dear." Dresden cocked his head to the side. "Would you look at that?"

Rayne didn't realize what had happened until her head collided with the back of something hard and stars danced before her eyes. Shapes blurred with movement in front of her as the world gradually came back into focus. She was halfway across the clearing, her back soaked with water. Rayne clutched the grass, pulling herself to sit up.

Water? Her fingers brushed along the back of her neck and came back warm, stained red.

I'm bleeding.

Ahead of her, Hawthorne had shed their human skin completely, giving way to a nebulous cluster of dancing shadows in the shape of some canine. She could only make out their eyes and the glint of their teeth in the sunlight, bared at Dresden.

Dresden beamed at Hawthorne in delight, remaining rooted in place.

Rayne, snap out of it! You have to run. I can only buy you a few minutes, and you need to move! Hawthorne moved in front of her, growling at Dresden.

Rayne struggled to her knees, attempting to stand, but her vision swam, and the world tilted, knocking her back down. *I'm not—I can't leave you.*

I cannot defeat him, Rayne, and neither can you. Now, move! Hawthorne leapt forward, snapping at one of the eyes on the end of Dresden's wing. Dresden sighed and snatched Hawthorne by their throat, and they yelped.

"I tire of this. You've had your fun, Hawthorne. The time for play is over."

Her body moved of its own accord, and the shadows snatched her before she could think to move. Inside her, the magic thrummed, listening. *Make a weapon of me,* she whispered to it. *Whatever will cut this fucker down.*

It answered her, not with words but an image in her mind, so clear that she could feel the black ichor spilling down her wrist; a spear of obsidian cutting through the eye at the center of Dresden's forehead.

When she could see again, she was eye to eye with Dresden, surprise reflected in those red irises. Rayne's arms were above her head, her hands gripping something so tightly that she could feel her skin beginning to tear. The same spear she had seen in her mind, in the depths of her magic. *Holy shit.*

The sharp end of it hovered just above Dresden's eye, some invisible force keeping her from proceeding.

"You." Dresden marveled a moment before he snatched her with his other hand, his fingers squeezing the air out of her. His head turned at an unnatural angle, squinting as if to get a better look at her. "Odd. How did you manage something like that, human?"

Unable to find the words or the air, Rayne spat at his eye.

Dresden scoffed. "Disgusting things, you are," he murmured to himself. Across from her, Hawthorne bit and tore into Dresden's arm, clawing at any part of him that they could. Dresden's attention remained fixed on her. "No matter. Now, let's see. Where is it?"

He scrutinized her, every roving eye on his wing rolling toward her. "Ah, there it is." He loosened a finger from around her and plunged it into the flesh of her shoulder. Rayne screamed in agony, struggling against him as he continued to root around in her.

"Dresden, stop!"

"If the chimera dies, then that is her own failing." Dresden sighed. He pinched some nerve within her, and Rayne screamed until her voice left her. She did not see what was ripped from her, only felt its absence, like an amputation.

"Such dramatics." Dresden tossed her into the grass, and Rayne rolled onto her side, her limbs limp with exhaustion and slick with blood. "Be grateful it was I who did the deed, human. My better delights in terrorizing the flesh."

Rayne's eyes fluttered, her vision blurring into nothingness.

Rayne, open your eyes! You will not bleed out in the dirt like this. You're going to be okay. Just stay awake, do you understand me? Don't close your eyes—

Dresden's grip on Hawthorne tightened, constricting them, and then in a burst of shadow, they were gone. Rayne's eyes went wide, and she reached for the empty air, mouthing their name.

Wiping his hands on his knees, Dresden stood, his feet brushing close to Rayne's face as he did. Her world was blotted with black, her sight and consciousness slipping away from her.

"There, all done. It was fascinating to meet you, little witchling. We shall not do so again."

CHAPTER THIRTY-SEVEN
rayne

I t was not the drizzling rain, the water soaking her clothes, or the pain howling through every nerve that woke her. It was the *silence.*

Rayne groaned, rolling onto her back only to immediately regret the movement when pain answered. Her eyes blinked open, and she squinted against the overcast sky, painting everything a hazy gray. Dark clouds blotted the world above, lightning darting through her vision where the sun should have been. It was only moments before, when she had been with her husband.

Hawthorne.

Rayne jolted from the grass. *Hawthorne, are you okay?* she murmured down their connection, tugging at the thread.

Rayne's breath hitched. The usual comfort of her husband's end of the bond, the thread that remained taunt at all times, was slack, limp as a wilted flower.

Hawthorne! she thought again desperately. *Hawth, I need you to fucking answer me. Where are you?* The words echoed in her mind, frantic and raw. She listened, she waited for them to flutter against her mind as they always did. "Hawthorne," she whispered. "*Please.* I know you can hear me."

They have to hear me, Rayne insisted inwardly. *They have to know that I'm talking to them. They have to be here. Be here, please,* she begged in silence. At once, the memory of this afternoon came back to her, of white wings, the eyes of a rabbit, and blood. Her husband disappeared like a warm breath on a winter morning.

Rayne tried to get her feet, and her body immediately rejected the notion, smacking her back down. Her shoulder throbbed. The skin under her collarbone split, and through the ruined fabric of her hoodie, she could see the meat of her own flesh, red, open, and angry.

Every breath pulled at the wound; it would need stitches. It was the bonding mark that bled—the place where she and Hawthorne had become one, hemorrhaging into one another.

I need to find Hawthorne, Rayne told herself, panic rising with each breath. *I can't—I need to know they're okay.*

The world spun in protest, but she pushed past it, dragging herself to the nearest tree and using it to brace against.

Sound returned to her world: rain, thunder, the deep, melodic call of nearby bullfrogs. She could hear everything but the cold, limp end of what was once alive and shining between her and her husband.

It's daytime. Maybe that's why Hawthorne isn't answering me. They might be weakened after everything that happened. Maybe they're back at their tree.

It made sense, she reasoned. Her husband was made of shadow; it would make sense that if they were in some kind of weakened state, they would need to wait until night to come back out. To drag themselves out of the muck and mire.

I will meet them at their tree, Rayne decided, latching onto hope as she steadied herself.

Hawthorne crawled out from under their tree once a year with their human body, then had to return to that same soil; there had to be some secret regenerative aspect of their tree that they had not told her about.

Rayne moved much too slowly, her body refusing and struggling with the urgency with which she felt to find them. Her body ached, and her head throbbed, taking on a life of its own. Her legs were weak, trembling things, and every few feet, they bowed, nearly giving out on her.

Come on, body. For once in my life, don't fucking fail me.

Soon, but not nearly soon enough, she found herself at their tree, and she reached out toward it, toward them, to rest her palm against the damp, dark wood.

"Hawthorne?" she whispered. "Are you here?"

The forest remained silent, close, and yet an invisible wall had come between it and her.

She and Hawthorne.

Blood. Maybe they need an offering like before. That was what sustained them and kept them in their human skin. They might just be hungry or tired, like I am.

Rayne pressed her fingers into the open wound at her shoulder, letting the blood wet her fingers before she pressed both hands against the bark. "Hawthorne, I offer this blood to you and you alone," she murmured, closing her eyes and trying to envision that crimson thread, the nameless knot of magic and blood that kept them tied to one another.

I never had to think about it before. They were always just... there. But now she could not see it even in her mind's eye, even as she begged her husband to crawl up from the dirt and drink her down to the bone.

"Hawthorne," Rayne called again, her voice breaking. "Fucking answer me!"

Why aren't you answering me? Rayne screamed down their empty bond in her thoughts. *Where are you? Are you hurt?*

If they're hurt, then what if they can't hear me? Or what if they're... dead.

Rayne took a step back from their tree, her heart pounding over the sound of the same thought, playing on repeat in her mind.

What do I do?

Every bit of magic she possessed came from them; everything that she *knew* of magic came from them. If they were not here to guide her...

Rayne screamed with the thunder, splitting the air with her agony, as if the storm itself might shatter and show her the way back to what she'd lost.

"She's married, but I don't know how to reach her husband. I don't think there's anyone else to call for her. Thank you."

Who is that?

Rolling onto her side, her cheek was cushioned by something soft, pillow-like. *Am I back in the house? Where's Hawthorne?*

Fluorescent light hit her eyes first, shining down on her as they blinked open. Once they adjusted, her surroundings came into view. Baby blue walls, a pale green partition above, machines surrounding her, and an I.V. hooked up to her arm.

"What the fuck?" Her voice was all but gone, hoarse and ragged.

The partition moved, and Pastor Creary poked his head in. "Rayne. I didn't think you'd be up so soon. They said you'd be out for a while."

Rayne moved to sit up, immediately wincing.

"I wouldn't move too much if I were you. You were mighty banged up when we brought you in," he said, rubbing the back of his neck. "They stitched you up pretty good, but you're probably gonna be sore for a while."

"What happened? How long was I out?"

"Was hoping you could tell me. Looked like a mountain lion got you; you're lucky Mrs. Hamper saw you on her way into town. You'd passed out at the edge of the woods. She nearly missed you in the rain; you were all covered in dirt and grime. You've been out for a couple of days."

The forest. Dresden. Hawthorne.

Hawthorne.

She needed to get out of here.

Rayne moved and tried to swing her legs over the bed, but Pastor Creary moved to stop her, pressing a gentle hand to her good shoulder. "Whoa, now, don't go doing that. You're in no condition to—"

"Don't touch me!" Rayne hissed.

He stepped back, hands up in retreat. "Alright, alright. Just stay calm."

"I need to leave," she rasped. "I can't stay here. I have to go home."

"You damn-near died out there!"

I don't have time for this. Rayne ripped the sheets off her and grabbed for the I.V. line. Pastor Creary stopped her.

"Don't, you're gonna hurt yourself. Especially with your—well, your skin the way it is," he said. "I'll get the doctor. You can talk to him about wanting to leave."

"I'm leaving," Rayne repeated. *No matter what anyone says.*

The doctor and a few nurses tried to persuade her to stay, rambling on about how dangerous it was for her to be moving around in this state. Rayne heard none of it.

Finally, after signing what felt like dozens of papers, she was limping through the hospital lobby toward the exit.

"Rayne, wait!"

When Pastor Creary called for her, she didn't stop, didn't even so much as turn to acknowledge him. *I have to get home,* she thought. *Maybe Hawthorne is—*

"Let me give you a ride back into town, at least."

Rayne stopped, resting her good shoulder against the wall. "Why are you doing all this?" she asked, finally looking his way. "Thought you were all convinced I was consorting with the Devil?"

Pastor Creary shook his head. "Getting hurt is the most human thing in the world. Devil ain't got ahold of you yet, it seems."

Rayne glanced at him a moment before she continued hobbling out of the lobby. "Where's your car?"

Most of the ride was made in silence; he didn't attempt small talk, and Rayne was more grateful than she cared to admit. She kept her forehead pressed against the cool glass of the window pane, her eyes closed.

"There's been so much death in town lately," Pastor Creary said, breaking the car's peace. "It's unnatural. Now more than ever, it's important we all stick together. We've got the same roots at the end of the day, tilled from the same soil."

As they turned up the mountain, Rayne watched the trees pass them by, searching for any sign of Hawthorne.

"I won't ask you to come to church again," he continued, turning his eyes away from the road to look at her. Rayne shied closer to the door. "But don't isolate yourself. Whatever's out there is picking us off one by one. It doesn't care if we're loved or not. What happened with your store might have been an accident, but Persimmon—"

Nausea roiled in Rayne's stomach at the sound of her name. They passed the sign for Persimmon's garden that hung just over the entrance to the off-road where her home was. *Had been.*

The edges of the sign were blackened with smoke, somehow having survived the blaze.

The *only* thing that survived.

"—and then Lenny and his family. Tamera, the boys. God, it just breaks your heart."

Rayne pulled the latch of the door, yanking at it. "Stop the car."

"What? We've still got a mile at least, and you can't—" She yanked open the door, and he slammed on the brakes. "Jesus, Rayne! You can't just—"

"Thanks for the ride," she said, unlatching her seatbelt and sliding clumsily out of the car. Rayne nearly fell, her legs dangerously close to giving out on her. She steadied herself and began the long, painful walk to the house.

By the time Rayne reached her porch, she was panting and sweating from the exertion of the walk. She had no idea where her keys were and refused to look for them. "House," she breathed, wiping her mouth. "Open up. It's me."

She heard the shifting of the lock, and the door eased open for her, though the House remained silent.

"Hawthorne?" Rayne called, leaning heavily against the door as it closed. "Hawth, are you home?"

Please be here. Please.

The house was exactly as they'd left it before the two of them had gone off to the forest. The small pot of coffee Hawthorne had made for her was stale, with mold growing in it. Beside it on the counter was a small pile of orange peels, dried and browning around the edges. The last of their oranges sat in the fruit bowl, kissed with the green of rot.

They would never let an orange go to waste. The whole bowl would have been gone if—

Rayne dragged herself across the living room, not bothering with her shoes or the mud that she tracked onto the carpet.

At some point during her walk, her stitches had begun to bleed, sopping her tattered clothes with even more red. Beneath her, the floor began shifting and cracking under her feet as if to cradle her.

Rayne froze, her gaze hooked on the pile of blankets in front of the fireplace, where Hawthorne had held her the morning after Persimmon's death and let her cry and ruin their shirt.

Her knees finally gave way, and she used the edge of the couch to save herself from falling. She braced herself and then sank into it, lying back.

"You're bleeding, cherub." The House said finally, and the fire kicked to life.

At her House's voice, so soft and subdued, she broke. "They're gone, House," she whispered. "I think—I think they're dead."

The House sighed, and the couch pulled her deeper into its embrace. **"I know, sweetling, I know,"** it whispered. **"I'm sorry."**

With her voice having faded with every word she spoke, Rayne buried her face in the couch and sobbed silently.

I wish I had died with them.

CHAPTER THIRTY-EIGHT

rayne

*T*he night was black, the sort of darkness that vibrated with unseen life, and though she ran, it was not away from it, not in fear. Instead, she raced toward it, knowing that there were eyes somewhere in it watching her and looking back at her.

Look back at me, Hawthorne. Please.

The void smelled of rain, of moss, and beneath that, the sweet kiss of rot. Rayne walked barefoot through the grass, the dew kissing her skin. She was not entirely sure where she was going, but her feet seemed to understand the path. To know exactly where she needed to be. Around her, the forest screamed, animals shouting into the night as if they could call down the stubborn moon. But Grandmother Moon had long since turned her face away, forsaking them.

Brambles and thorns bit into her skin as she walked through the forest, though she felt no pain, even as the blood spiraled down her forearms and pooled between her fingers. Perhaps it was the blood that called them to her, alerted them to her presence because the wolves found her. Their eyes were as yellow as dandelions, peeking at her through the blackness, and their teeth glinted like unsheathed knives.

She wondered if she would feel herself churning in their stomach when they came for her.

*"**Sweetling,**"* The House crooned. Rayne shot up, feeling around, her eyes struggling to focus. *"Oh! Apologies, cherub. It was not my intent to startle you. Lay back, relax lest you agitate your wounds further."*

Rayne groaned, easing back into the couch cushions. She turned onto her side and curled her knees into her chest.

"Darling one, perhaps a bath now, hmm? Those cuts are deep and will fester if you do not tend to them."

"No," Rayne croaked.

"No?"

"I don't care. What does it matter if I rot here? I've lost them. Persimmon. Hawthorne." Her voice broke around the sound of her husband's name, and she buried herself deeper into the couch. "They're both gone."

"But you still draw breath, cherub. That must mean something."

Ignoring it, she rolled fully onto her side and let sleep claim her, drifting into a quiet, restless sleep.

In the morning, she didn't move; she didn't even bother to change position. She remained fixed in place. Her stomach growled, her throat ached with its dryness, but neither of the sensations was enough to tempt her to move. The House had lit its fireplace for her, coaxing her nearer to it, and yet Rayne did not move.

"Come, sweetness!" The House chirped at her with the morning robins. *"I can hear your stomach growling, and I can practically taste the desert of your throat. How about I boil some water for you and make you some tea? Fry you some eggs? Will you wake for me, little love?"*

"No, House," she whispered.

"And why not?"

"I don't want to. I don't want to do—" Her voice hitched, and she turned her foot back against the fabric. "Just, no."

"A shower then? You must clean your wounds. Infection will come for you before they do."

"They?" Rayne asked, turning her face back. "Who are they?"

The House shivered, and the couch sucked her in a little further. *"There are things, dear one, words that are impossible for me to say. But know that the town, the people will not wait for your grief to end."*

Of course. They're all still convinced that I'm the Devil.

Rayne rolled onto her back and stared at the ceiling. Her connection to Hawthorne was gone, the magic they'd gifted her had been ripped out. What did she have to protect herself, and more over, what was the point?

"I won't stop them."

The night came and went. Rayne had moved only once to drag herself into the kitchen, eyes heavily lidded from sleep and the dried salt on her skin, lips dry, to gulp down half a glass of water.

There was some part of her that longed to save itself that put the thought in her mind: *Go upstairs and fall asleep in bed. Stop punishing yourself.*

Upstairs in their shared bedroom, where Hawthorne's small collection of things lay, and the scent of them would still be heavy in the air.

No.

Rayne drank the rest of her water, staggered back into the living room, and lay back down on the ground where she belonged.

The sun became an enemy.

Rayne could not stomach its garish light seeping in through the windows of her home, washing her face as she lay on the couch, seeping into it like blood.

Every time she saw it, it meant another hour had passed without Hawthorne, and she was unable to do anything to bring them back.

The House whispered to her, but the words were lost, and for once, her precious House was not a secret friend but simply a house. The House she used to suffer in with her parents and had thrived in with her husband had changed again. She was left to suffer in a cage of wood and glass.

Alone.

The word reverberated in her mind, echoing in the empty shell of her. The life that they had built together was shattered, and now she was left lying in the remnants of it.

She felt *nothing.*

Sunlight moved through the sky until it disappeared over the horizon. Rayne didn't stir. The moon rose, its cool silver light slicing through the darkness, and still Rayne did not move. When the sun once again greeted her, this fact remained the same.

Rayne did not move until her body forced her to, and the day passed by her again. Sleep came as a thief in the night, though she hardly noticed.

The days came and went, slipping by as smoke between her fingers.

"Cherub, please," The House begged, shaking the couch enough to wake Rayne up. *"Just get up. Move. Do something. Do not allow yourself to give in to despair and rot."*

"Why do you care?" Rayne snapped. "Isn't this what you always wanted, to have me to yourself without having to worry about me going out into the world?"

The House sighed. *"Not at your expense, dove. You are not yourself."*

"It doesn't matter."

"It does to me. I need you. I have always needed you."

"Then have me, House."

The fire died, and the air chilled in response. *"You cannot mean that, cherub."*

"I gave you offerings before to keep you sustained. Just take them now, I don't care," Rayne replied, her eyes sliding closed.

Rayne slept uncomfortably, unsure of how long. But when she awoke, it was to the smell of peppermint, a sharp twinge of magic in the air. Her muscles ached, her body stiff. *I wonder if they've begun to entropy?*

She went to roll onto her side, but tension in her neck and ribs stilled her. *What?* Rayne lifted her head, struggling against the tightness. Across the living room, the window was cracked, and three long ivy branches had stretched across the living room and wrapped around her. House's ivy.

The branches tightened around her waist and had slipped up her back under her bandages and into the cut on her back. She shifted, and the leaves slid further under her skin. Rayne gritted her teeth more in discomfort than pain.

"House?"

"Yes, dear, cherub? Have you decided to rise? Shall I warm my oven for you?"

"Your ivy—?"

"Oh, yes! You said that I could have you. How strong and beautiful your blood is! My garden will bloom all over the mountain nourished by you!"

Oh. It's feeding on me. Eating me, Rayne thought, looking down at the ivy. There was a memory, a moment she remembered with Hawthorne, where they had warned her about how the House would eat her if she let it.

Tears burned the corners of her eyes. *Except they're not here anymore. So what does it matter?*

"I'm going back to sleep, House," Rayne murmured, nestling back into the safety of the couch.

The House sighed, disappointed. *"Alright. Sleep well, Rayne."*

CHAPTER THIRTY-NINE
rayne

The ivy had rooted itself in her, bringing lichen with it. She rarely woke, but she did; she lay there, dark eyes fixed to the ceiling of her house, tracing the patterns of Hawthorne's freckles into the wood.

Her body burned.

Does it matter? she thought, lifting her hand as much as the ivy would allow, stretching her muscles simply to test whether or not they'd begun to atrophy. *What difference does it make if I rot or if I burn?*

Beneath her, the House shifted, stretching like a cat awakening from its nap. She was moved as well, lifted only slightly before she was returned to her sunken tomb. She hardly felt the tug against her fused flesh, merging with the fabric.

The House sighed. ***"Still haven't found anything to move you then?"***

When she remained silent, it sighed again. ***"Keep your tongue if you must, I will speak enough for us both and fill this bitter air with something sweet."***

Rayne gave no inclination that she heard it, though it hardly seemed to mind. The House hummed what might have been a lullaby, the pipes and wood shifting and singing with the water heater in the basement.

"All things change and fade away," It said. ***"All will be by and by eventually. I will one day return to my roots and swell into the ground***

like spring rain. We will all be prey to something bigger. There is nothing so hungry as decay."

The words reverberated off the walls around her, thickening and slowing in the sun's dying light. *We will all be prey.*

"Not all," she whispered hoarsely. The memory of her husband hit her. She could see the soft, flickering glow of fireflies reflected back in their hazel eyes as they had lain across from her in the grass, their hand in hers. "Hawthorne. They weren't weak."

They weren't, and yet they had been laid low, crushed underfoot as a moth might have been.

And Persimmon. She had been strong, too.

Her friend had been terminated like a pest for a sin no greater than being seen in public as her friend, devoured by a coward.

But then there's me. Me, she thought. *Soft and weak as I am, I've killed. I tore Len to shreds.*

What rules then can there be if Hawthorne was cut down like wheat? If Len, who preyed upon Persimmon, can then be prey, what order can there truly be?

"No, they aren't," The House replied. *"And you, cherub? What are you?"*

"I'm—"

Aren't. Present tense. Like, Hawthorne is still here.

Since Rayne had returned, House had not once asked where Hawthorne was or what had happened to them.

"House," Rayne said with a grunt as she sat up as much as the ivy would allow. "How did you know that Hawthorne had died?"

"You told me."

"But—why didn't you seem surprised? Or ask me what happened to them?"

The House shifted, as if in discomfort, and the room warmed. *"I am merely a house, Rayne, and I've... seen it all."*

"What do you mean?"

The kitchen cabinet doors opened and closed. *"If the words were mine to give you, I would. But I am as ensnared as you."*

Rayne's brow furrowed, and she sat further up, the vines tugging uncomfortably at her flesh. "Ensnared in what?"

The cabinets snapped open and closed again. Upstairs, she could hear more doors doing the same. *"There is a Great Serpent at the end and beginning of time, devoured and being devoured,"* The House whispered. *"It is a cylinder that moves neither up nor down. A loop."*

"What are you saying?"

"There is no way forward and no way back. This moment, right where you are, is the only thing that matters. This choice. Do you understand?"

"Choice?" Rayne whispered, shaking her head. "What is there for me to choose? My only options are to stay here and rot or die with them."

"And if there was a third?"

A third? What could that possibly—

Rayne's breath caught, her heart stumbling over the thought. "Is Hawthorne alive, House?"

The House was silent, and even the snapping of the wood in the fireplace died down.

The room sweltered and sweat beaded at the nape of her neck.

"House." Rayne clutched the armrest of the couch. "Is. Hawthorne. Alive?"

"I am just a house, my cherub. I do not have answers for you. But if I did—"

It stopped and then was quieter. *"If I did, I would lead you straight to them."*

Lead you straight to them.

As if Hawthorne were somewhere. Somewhere she could reach them.

Rayne thought back to Dresden and how he'd spoken of Hawthorne's punishment. Never once had he mentioned death or called it a sentence.

It was punishment, something that they were meant to endure and live through. The truth of it had been right there in front of her the entire time.

The realization struck her all at once. Hawthorne had been alive this whole time, and here she had been, rotting away, giving up on them.

No. If Hawthorne were alive, then she would find them and bring them home. And even if she couldn't bring them back to her, then she would go to where they were and join them.

But how? I don't know what to do, and House can't or won't tell me.

She had no clue what to do from here, where to go, what her first step should even be in bringing her husband back, or making her way to where they were.

How do I find you? she thought to them, praying that even if they couldn't respond, they would at least be able to hear her and know that she had not forsaken them. That she was coming for them, however and whenever she could. *Hawthorne, if you can hear me, I promise you that I will figure this out. I will not leave you.*

But first, she needed to move. Hissing in discomfort, forced her body up straight, the vines pulled taut.

"What are you doing, my cherub?" The House crooned.

Rayne shifted, trying to move her arms beneath the ivy; the fabric and the roots moved with her, refusing her any give. Rayne finally allowed herself to look down and take in the full image of herself. An ocean of creeping ivy that dug into her skin like an ill-fitting garment.

"How long has it been? How long have I lain here and wasted time when I should have been searching for them?"

The House shuddered. *"It is nearly June, sweetness."*

June.

Hawthorne had been torn from her sometime in April—had she truly been rotting so long?

With her other arm, Rayne reached for the vines that had slithered into her veins through the I.V.'s entrance sight. She tugged, and the pain blindsided her; she released them with a cry.

"Cherub," The House chided. *"You made an offer, and I accepted. I cannot unearth myself. You shall have to do it."*

Rayne looked down at them and took a deep breath. *What's a little more pain? I can do this.* She gripped the vines once more. *I have to do this.*

Electricity shot through her veins, every nerve screaming along with her as the leaves and vines inched out of her, blood pooling down her arm.

When she finally pulled it free, it fell to the ground and recoiled back out of the open window, and her head fell back against the cushion in relief.

All this time. I was a whining, pathetic thing. No more.

Her fingers brushed along her neck; the ivy had tangled itself in bits of her hair. Rayne plucked the small pieces of lichen from her skin, pinching her eyes shut and flicking them toward the fire.

I was too weak to protect them.

White fur and bright red eyes flashed in her mind, the memory of Dresden and his unyielding smile. *I know the name of my enemy. I will keep the picture of him in the halls of my heart, and I will tear it to shreds with my bare hands.*

Rayne wrapped her fingers around the base of the vine at her neck, inhaled, and pulled. Her stomach ached, the pain settling so deeply within her that she almost vomited. Stubbornly, she bit her lip to keep from doing so, and when the vine was removed, she exhaled, panting as she wiped the sweat from her brow.

I was too stupid to realize that they're alive somewhere. I was wallowing when I should have been fighting.

She paused only a moment, allowing herself the briefest of breaths before she looked down at her legs and the dark moss that had grown along them as if she truly had been a rotten thing. Rayne reached down for a large chunk of the greenery on her thigh and picked until it peeled away, all bloody and raw. She screamed until she was sure her pain was enough to shatter glass, until her adrenaline had lifted her from the couch on trembling legs. But she was no calf taking its first steps; instead, a wolf relearning its environment and how it might find the nearest, weakest thing to wrap its jaws around.

Blood had seeped into everything: her clothes, the carpet, nothing was spared.

"Accept the blood that I've spilled as an offering, House," she said, reaching out to lean against the nearest wall. "Let it fortify us both. From this point forward, I will make a blade of myself."

The House exhaled, though she could feel it lapping at her blood in thirsty gulps. It shifted against her hand as if to hold it, and though it could not feel as she knew humans could, something like sadness radiated from it, like artificial heat.

"*Oh, my lovely funeral pyre,*" It whispered. "*I will never tire of watching you burn.*"

PART THREE
summer

CHAPTER FORTY
hawthorne

H awthorne was tired.

Time had slipped away from them and they could no longer be sure as to how long they had been here. It felt like weeks ago when they had awoken in a part of the Under that they'd never seen before. An orchard of black, barren trees, their barks made of shimmer obsidian.

It might have been beautiful if Hawthorne was not entangled in them. The branches of the trees knotted around their wrists and stabbed into their arms. Every movement that they made dug the stinging branches deeper.

The pain was more of an irritation, a buzzing discomfort, and somehow that made their situation worse. *I can bear pain but I cannot tolerate this itching, dull buzz.*

That was exactly why they were experiencing it. Punishment, Dresden had said. Everything about this was.

They were no more than a mayfly thrashing in a spider's web and yet that was the more merciful aspect of their torment.

"Hawthorne?"

"Fuck." They groaned, pinching their eyes closed. *Not again.*

Leaves crunched softly under footsteps and under the smell of ashes and dirt, almond with the floral kiss of roses hit their nose.

"Hawth, please," *her* voice hitched and she swallowed. They could even smell the salt of her tears, warmed by her skin. "It's you, isn't it? What happened?"

Gods, it sounds like her. The accent she's always fighting, the way she breathes.

Though they knew it was futile, they held their breath, hoping that she—*it* would leave. Instead, it swept closer, its hair brushed against their chest, her breath at their shoulder.

"Why won't you look at me?" It sniffled. "Hawthorne? It's me, Rayne."

You are not her.

They kept the thought to themself. The shapeshifter—ghost—whatever it was seemed to feed off of their responses. Sometimes when they remained silent, when they ignored it, it left sooner.

"Are you—" her voice broke, "—angry with me, like everyone else?"

It is not her. It is not her. It is not her.

Hawthorne turned their head away, squeezing their eyes shut tighter. The creature sobbed and rested its cheek against their chest. "I thought you loved me."

They bit down on their lip and focused on the feeling. *This is not real, it is not her. She knows I would never—*

No. I will not justify this. It is a mimic or some lower being. That is all. I will not allow it to taint my mind.

Instead, they focused on their last memory of her before destruction. She'd worn her hair down, like she always did when they were alone. Sunlight splashing against her skin, illuminating every beautiful scar. The dark birthmark dotted on her hip, her sternum...

"Would you even care if I died?"

"Get off of me!" they snarled, snapping their teeth at it. The thing before them was a perfect imitation of their wife, down to the beauty mark on the side of her face. An image of her plucked straight from their own mind, they were sure.

The creature pulled back, giggling. It hopped back down and blew them a kiss over its shoulder before skipping out of the orchard. There was no telling when it would return, using a different method to torture them with their wife's face.

Hawthorne exhaled, sagging against their bonds. *It does not matter how many times I see it. It still churns my stomach the way they mimic her likeness.*

When they'd first opened their eyes they had been dizzy, their memory hazy. They'd called for Rayne as she was the last thing that they could remember and then, all of it came crashing back to them.

Dresden. Rayne, bleeding out in the grass.

Hawthorne attempted everything that they could, tugged at every thread of magic available to them in an attempt to free themself. Then, they'd seen her. Bleeding and terrified, she had stumbled into the orchard. They fell for it the first time, desperate to get to her. The second time when she'd been angry, tearing through like a hurricane, they had believed it again. It was not until the dozenth time that Hawthorne realized it wasn't her.

It's never her.

But the knowledge never spared them the pain of seeing her again or quiet the longing that hurt more than any wound that could be dealt to them. At some point, early in their arrival, Dresden reappeared to deliver the full context of their sentence.

"Fifty years and a day as you are," he'd said, roving eyes looking everywhere else. "A rather light sentence, no?"

Fifty years and a day.

It *was* a light sentence in the span of Hawthorne's life—at least it should have—been but since their time with Rayne, they had learned to count the hours, minutes, seconds.

And Rayne. Fifty years was an entire lifetime to her. Their wife would be an old woman by the time that they were able to return above ground. *If she was even alive.*

Without the magic between them, Hawthorne would have no idea if she was dead or alive. They could feel nothing of her. The sharp static of her normally residing within their chest was silent, gone. They would scour the entire globe to ensure that she had not escaped to some faraway place, robbing them of even more time together.

The magic that solidified the bond between them had been strong, a blood pact interwoven with two vows of absolute devotion, but it wasn't impenetrable. No magic with a human being could ever be, but they had never expected to have it torn away from them.

Hawthorne had felt the severing, had felt the magic ripped out of them. *It fucking hurt.*

Hawthorne had never felt pain such as that before. The agony of that loss still reverberated throughout their bones.

Still, they could think only of Rayne. The shock alone of what she endured could have killed her.

No. She is not dead.

Their wife was stubborn, angry. She would be more indignant that something had almost killed her. She would stay alive out of spite, her rage would be the anchor that kept her locked in her world.

Still, she was only human. Her body could—

They yanked against the black webs that were tangled around their limbs, and as they did every time before, they shattered into tiny shards that stabbed into their flesh and tightened.

It was a wound to their pride to admit that Kings' magic overpowered their own, but more so that it was the only thing keeping them trapped, a prisoner within their own country. Pinned like a moth under a great glass. They could almost laugh about it if their wife was not at stake. They could remain here happily if they knew that she was alright, that she was not lost within the City of Shades.

Rayne as a shade.

Her soul, shifting through that dusty wasteland, with the misty veil of deathlessness over her hair...

When a human died, they were immediately taken to the City of Shades; a vast wasteland ripe with pear trees that reached up towards the sky, and the shades rotted at the base of them. At the edge of this city sat a river, the river that allowed humans to cross over to the next phase. All creatures, even Hawthorne, would eventually wade into the river to find what was next for them.

The shades that could not accept their deaths or refused to move on were forced to plant the seed of their souls into the dry, empty earth and wait. They would wait for the pear tree to grow, bear fruit and drop into their hands. Once they took a bite of it, life would begin for them again. They would reincarnate to learn all of their lessons again. The trees grew at their own rate, there was no way to tell how long a shade would lie there waiting in the dust.

But not Rayne. She would never accept the pear seed of her tree, nor would she wade into unknown waters without them. She would not fall in line. Rayne would not go gently into any of it.

Hawthorne smiled at the thought of her despite themself.

They could practically see her running her fingers along the fabric of her new reality, feeling for the loose thread so she could tear her way out. Rayne's temperament had always suited them well but they did not expect any of their kind to have the patience for her. She would find herself in trouble almost immediately.

I have to get to her before any of that can happen.

There was no bringing her back to life but they would find her and cross that great river with her. But she would have to wait for them. Getting to her was simple enough if she just stayed within the city and bit her tongue.

She won't.

CHAPTER FORTY-ONE
rayne

I feel more myself, Rayne thought as she watched the dirt and grime she'd scrubbed from her skin circle the drain. *Like I can think clearer.*

After redressing her wounds and popping a few ibuprofen, she got dressed and headed downstairs. The kitchen reeked of mold and rotten food. Braiding her hair back and out of her way, she set to cleaning it.

Hawthorne's nose is sensitive. I don't want them to come home and smell a festering house.

"I'll be back, House," Rayne said, peeling her rubber gloves off once she'd finally cleaned the kitchen.

"Where are you going, cherub?"

"Into town. Hawthorne needs oranges."

The floor rolled under her heel. **"Be careful."**

There was something in its tone that struck her but she said nothing, only ran her hand along its wall as she left.

Sitting behind the wheel of her car and driving back into town felt traitorous, Hawthorne was gone and Persimmon was—

Rayne kept her eyes glued to the road on the way down the mountain, forcing her attention anywhere but the blackened earth where her friend's house had once sat.

I promise that I'll mourn you properly, Persi. I just need to find Hawth first.

As she stopped at a light, the car beside her slowed just behind her before creeping up beside her. From the corner of her eye, she could see a man glaring at her, gesturing for her to roll down her window.

She rolled her eyes and kept her eyes ahead of her. *I'm not in the mood for your road rage, asshole.*

As she continued further downtown, she was met with similar glares, people seeming to recognize her car and stopping to stare.

When she'd finally made it to the parking lot, she double locked her car before heading inside. Right at the front door, beaming at her from the other side, sat a picture of Len Kappler, surrounded by flowers, balloons and small stuffed animals.

Like he was someone worth remembering.

Rayne stopped a few feet away from his memorial. *Look at you. Life time of treating people like shit, committed literal murder and you're still treated like the town fucking hero.*

"Figures," she grumbled.

She was preparing to "accidentally" knock it over with her shoulder when she realized that the entire store had their eyes on her. Every check out clerk, even the woman stocking milk in the dairy aisle had stopped, shaking her head as she watched Rayne.

Rayne scowled at them and turned away, ducking down the nearest aisle and out of sight.

What the fuck is their problem? Do I really look that bad?

She hadn't paused to consider what she must have looked like, bandaged, circles under her eyes, thinner than she'd ever been. She must have been a sight.

Whatever. It's not like they've never stared at me like this before. I should be used to it at this point.

Rayne snatched a basket from one of the aisle endcaps on her way to the produce. *I'll just buy them out of whatever oranges they've got. Hawthorne will probably want as many as they can get.*

Oranges and the occasional orange soda were the only real human food that Hawthorne was interested in. They hated the taste of any meat that she'd bought them. '*Inferior*', they'd called it, preferring to catch their own prey so that they could eat the meat raw.

Misty eyed, she couldn't keep herself from smiling at the thought of them. *I miss you so much.*

She wiped at her eyes with the sleeve of her shirt. *Crying in a grocery store. God, I'm a mess.*

Rayne shoveled as many oranges into her basket as she could carry. *Damn, I probably should have grabbed a cart.*

"You got some real balls showing up here."

Turning, Rayne came face to face with Terri Mckenny, her old kindergarten teacher. The only one in Bury. At her side, a little girl clung to her beige dress, face half hidden.

"Excuse me?" Rayne asked, looking from the child to her.

"After everything you've done, you think you can just stroll back into town?"

"And what exactly did I do?"

"You brought evil into town. Same evil that took Len Kappler."

Rayne looked around the store, at all of the eyes glued to her. *They're scared of me. All of them.*

She was no longer a woman but a plague.

Had I ever been anything different?

"Well damn," Rayne replied, cracking a smile. "You caught me."

Terri took a step back. "W-What?"

"I said that you caught me," Rayne repeated slowly. "I brought evil into this town, cursed this land and all you *fuckers* on it."

"Mama?" the little girl asked, her fist balling in her mother's skirt.

"Stay back, Ellie-May," Terri whispered, pushing her daughter further behind her. "It ain't safe."

"No, Ellie-May, your Mama's right. None of you are safe," Rayne mimicked, crouching so that she and the little girl were eye level. "See, it's people like your Mama and all the other people in town that are the reason bad things happen.

They'd rather point their fingers than look in a mirror. So when your Mama's burning in Hell, you remember that."

Ellie-May's eyes widened as they filled with tears and Terri gasped, yanking her daughter further away from Rayne. From her purse, she whipped out a small crucifix, a small goose feather and a raw turquoise bead tied together with a cord around it.

Goose feathers for the Creator's protection, turquoise for God's favor and a tether to the land. A strange mix of mountain superstition, indigenous belief, and religion.

Her tribe's stories and beliefs had bled into the land and the locals, but the sight of it stilled her. Her grandmother had a similar one that had hung over her front door.

"Get away from her, *witch*!"

Witch.

And yet I haven't got a drop of magic in my veins anymore.

Rayne smirked and grabbed her basket from the floor. "You're the one who came to me."

She made her way to the check out clerk, a teenage girl that she hardly recognized—someone's daughter whose name she'd yet to learn. Her name tag said Gabby.

Gabby stepped back against the wall behind her register as she could, looking at Rayne as if she were a wild animal.

"You gonna ring me up or what?" Rayne asked, amused.

"No," Todd Kappler, bleary eyed and haggard, stepped out from the storage room in front. "Just take it and go. Get the fuck out of here, Dorne."

If Rayne were kinder, more forgiving, she might have felt a stab of pity for Todd. She knew all too well the pain that came with losing a family member that you thought you'd have with you for the rest of your life.

But she was neither of those things, and Todd's brother had ripped away the only friend she'd ever had.

On her way out, Rayne toppled Len's picture over, nearly skipping to the parking lot, giddy off of the knowledge that apparently *she* was the thing that went bump in the night. *Hawthorne would be proud of me.* The idea cut down her amusement where it had stood. They would have been proud of her, if only she knew where they were so that she could tell them.

She imagined the ground beneath her blackening and cracking as she walked, falling away like burnt flesh.

This place could rot with her.

Oranges put away in the refrigerator, Rayne had made herself comfortable in front House's hearth, her legs crossed. "I don't understand why you can't just give me a straight answer."

The House sighed. *"It is not so simple. There is only so much I know and so much that I can do."*

"Do you know where they are?"

"No."

"But they're alive?"

The House hesitated and the fire dulled before returning to its former strength. *"As alive as you."*

Rayne ran her fingers through her hair in frustration. *The answer is yes but it doesn't want to answer me directly. I forgot how frustrating the way that spirits speak can be. Or maybe it can't tell me?*

"Okay so, if you don't know where they are, can you tell me how to get the information I need to find them?"

"If you are lost," The House whispered. *"Often times, the way forward is only found by looking back. Many paths are not new. We need only to think back on things that we have been told."*

"By Hawthorne?"

"Perhaps or perhaps further back."

Further back? Maybe when I was a child, something that my Mam'maw might have told me. Rayne closed her eyes and laid back on the carpet, taking a deep breath. She tried to imagine herself sitting in her grandmother's living room, the ruddy mustard colored carpet that smelled vaguely of roses and moth balls. Of her favorite recliner, the old emerald green velvet material of it, the soft ridges of it that fused to the shape of her grandmother's body.

The dolls of little indigenous girls in their beaded regalia that her grandmother went out of her way to buy because "*They never made dolls that looked like me when I was a girl*" and filled her house with them.

In her mind, Rayne could hear the gentle fall of September rain outside as it thudded softly against the roof and tapped against the oak leaves on the trees outside. Her mother had been all too delighted to drop her off at her grandmother's for the weekend and she had been careful to pretend that she didn't like it either, lest her mother decide to take the opportunity away from her. Rayne would have rather lived in that cramped little space across from her grandmother's sewing room, huddling between the iron boards than go back to that house with her parents.

"*Come here, little snap dragon,*" *her grandmother whispered as she handed Rayne a mug of hot chocolate, sweetened with mint syrup from the garden. "So you don't get cold."*

The mountain air was chilly, autumn's breath quickly turning into winter's bite even in the middle of September. Her grandmother had taken her place in her chair with no small amount of effort that Rayne had been too young to recognize as the early signs of disintegration. Instead, she had nestled into her grandmother's warmth, sitting down in front of her.

Her grandmother's dark eyes followed the rain outside, peering through the window through her thick glasses. "This is the sort of weather that those wisps wander through," she said in that hushed tone that Rayne knew to mean that there was a story coming. "You remember them?"

Rayne shook her head. "No," she lied.

Her grandmother smiled down at her and brushed some of her messy, frizzed curls out of her face. "Liar. You're lucky your tongue doesn't knot." She pretended to try to grab Rayne's tongue and she squealed with laughter.

Her grandmother patted her head and her gaze returned to the window. "I'll tell you again anyway. They're dangerous. They offer you anything that you want in the world."

"More dangerous than Old Scratch?" her younger self asked, pausing only to take a loud sip of her hot chocolate.

"Much more," her grandmother said, though the smile didn't leave her face. The smile that Rayne now knew to be only for her. "See, The Man in Black is scared of God. Won't do anything that will get him deep in trouble with the Man Upstairs. But the Neighbors, these wildings? They ain't got a God to be scared of."

Rayne wished that she could lean into the memory, live in it and stay there for the rest of her life. She focused harder on remembering how her grandmother had told her one went about finding the Neighbors.

"How do you meet them?" she'd asked.

"I will tell you, but only if you promise never to go and seek them out on your own."

She remembered promising but the rest of the memory faded, obscured by time. "Fuck!" Rayne sighed, blinking her eyes open. "I remembered a little bit of something that my Mam'maw said about the Neighbors. But not much."

"Maybe that is all you need," The House offered, neither confirming nor denying that she was on the right track.

"Okay, sure. Now I know about the Neighbors, what good does it do me if I don't know what to do with the knowledge?"

Distantly, the dull roar of voices and motors sounded, like they were coming up the driveway toward the house.

"They're coming for you, cherub," The House hissed. ***"Don't go out there. Stay with me, I will keep you safe, tuck you inside of me and hold you away from all of them."***

Of course they chose now to form an angry mob and chase me out of town. Like I don't have better things to do.

"I'm not afraid them, House. Let them come."

"No, you are not afraid of them," The House replied over the dull roar headed their way.

Rayne pressed a kiss to the wall of her House, where her husband always did the same in greeting of their home. It irritated the House, though she was sure that it loved the attention much more than it let on. If she closed her eyes, it was almost like she was kissing Hawthorne again.

But I won't have to wait for much longer. I will find them, she reminded herself as she opened the front door.

Outside, her lawn was filled to the brim with nearly half the town, some of them were praying, holding crucifixes while others simply looked enraged. Todd Kappler at the front of the line.

Next door, Mrs. Hamper stood on her porch, watching.

Old bitch.

"My birthday was in March," Rayne said, addressing the crowd. "I'm going to assume that's why you're all here because otherwise, you can get the fuck off my property."

"We're not going anywhere," said Todd, pointing a meaty finger at her. "You are, Dorne. Either by force or by choice. But today is your last day in this town."

"Is it now?" Rayne asked, tilting her head.

"Murderer!" a woman shouted.

"You killed my brother and his family. *Children*," Todd spat at her.

"Where's that demon husband of yours?"

"Keep my husband's name out of your damn mouth!" Rayne barked, stepping down onto the lawn.

"This ends now!"

They swarmed her, and Rayne laughed like a coyote.

CHAPTER FORTY-TWO
rayne

R ayne wanted to wash them all the way like the ants that they were, to devour them in shadow but when she reached for her magic, the well was dry.

She scrambled back desperate to get inside when she saw a twitch in the plum trees in her front lawn. Like nerves.

The branches grew long and sharp and whipped at the bodies around her, pushing them away from her. *House.*

Demon. Witch. Monster.

Every curse slung at her should have hurt, and maybe if she was still the timid creature that had wandered into town six months ago, they might have. Not now. Now if they wanted to hurt her, they'd have to kill her.

Rayne climbed the banister of her front porch and stood before them, ensuring that they could see her. "I've cursed this land, this town, and all of you. Every step you take on this soil only ensures your place in Hell with me!" Behind her the tree's branches snapped out in warning, hitting the few stragglers that were still too close. But as quickly as it had happened, it stopped.

"Have you all lost your minds?" a voice boomed. Pastor Creary moved through the crowd, pushing people out of his way until he was in front of the crowd. "This isn't any way to treat one of our own!"

"She ain't ours, she ain't even human!" Todd cried, wiping the blood from his cheek. "Or didn't you see her conjuring a moving tree out of nowhere?"

Pastor Creary stared at Todd as if he couldn't believe what he was hearing. "Todd, you're grieving. The mind can play cruel tricks—"

"No fucking trick!" he shouted. "I'm not the only one who saw it!"

Dozens of cries of agreement joined up with him and Pastor Creary eyed them all warily. "People. I understand that this is a terrifying time for all of us but we cannot start turning on each other. That's how sin begins, how true evil takes root. Now, I'm calling an emergency service down in the church and I expect to see all of you there."

"How can you defend her?" Terri asked, shaking her head. "After everything she's done?"

"I defend *all* of God's children. I don't get to decide who's worthy and who isn't. Or do you somehow know better than Our Lord?"

The accusation rippled through the crowd and quietly, they began to break off one by one, heading back into town.

Rayne waved. "See you in Hell."

"Stop it, Rayne!" Pastor Creary snapped, turning on her. "Don't antagonize them. They're scared and I can't blame them for that. But you sure don't do anything to help yourself out."

Rayne pursed her lips, staying silent until he gave up and left like the rest of them. Once she was alone, she raced inside and peppered the wall with kisses. "You brilliant, perfect, wonderful thing, you! I'll love you until my dying breath!"

"That will come sooner than either of us are prepared for if you keep up with your nonsense. Though I know there is more to come," The House sighed.

"I have to find Hawthorne, House. No matter what I have to do," she answered. "I know about the Neighbors now, but I don't know what to do with that, whether or not I should try to find them. And even if I do, then what do I do?"

The House did not immediately answer her and when it did, it was careful, quiet as if it were scared to be heard: ***"You gained magic by making a deal with our wraith, perhaps other things can be gained similarly."***

When Rayne reached back into her childhood, clammy palms snatching at the thread of what had been, her grandmother's warnings about the little people were minimal. Her grandmother did not like to speak of them and risk inviting their attention.

There were many things that her grandmother feared and had tried to instill that same carefulness in her as well.

"When you go looking into the dark, snapdragon," she'd murmured one after-noon, *fat summer rays splashing against her skin from the window. "There are a million eyes staring back at you and they don't forget."*

Danger be damned.

Sorry, Mam'maw, she thought, breaking her heart, she was sure as the twigs snapped beneath her heavy boots. But some promises need to be broken.

While she may not have remembered what her grandmother had told her about the Neighbors, she'd read enough fantasy novels to gather a general idea. If Gods could wear the skin of rabbits, who was to say that books couldn't act as instruction manuals?

From those books, there were consistent messages, things were consistently advised against:

Do not look at them.
Do not tell them your name.
Do not tell them where you live.
Never show fear.

Rayne glanced down at her phone. 10:37pm. She ran a hand through her tangled curls, swearing when her fingers snagged in the knots. *It's late. What time do faeries even come out?*

Everytime someone spoke of evil coming out, it was always at the stroke of midnight. But her grandmother spoke more of 1am. The Thirteenth Hour. Warning Rayne her against staying up to—it was when spirits came out to play. *It's all that I have. And it will have to be enough.*

Armed with nothing but a knife from the kitchen and a flashlight in her backpack, Rayne headed up the mouth of the holler.

No one came around these parts anymore whether it was for fear of spirits or mountain folk, Rayne wasn't sure. She hadn't been here since her grandmother's passing and the loss of her home. Rayne was grateful for the dark, it made it harder for her to see where her grandmother's house had once stood. Rayne kept her flashlight on the lowest setting, shining directly on her feet and no further. Shining a light through the trees was the quickest way to let everyone—human or other—know exactly where you were.

The dirt was wet and soft from rain and the air hung humid, thinning the higher she climbed. With the smell of it came tears for her husband and how long it had been since she'd seen them and how comforting it was to experience even a fraction of them.

"I miss you, Hawthorne," she whispered to the night air, her boots sloshing through the mud puddles she did not bother to avoid. "Things always kind of shitty before you and then, I guess I didn't realize just how much better my life was with you or how happy you made me."

There was a crossroads that led to the head of the holler, and if there were ever a place for a deal to be made, it would be there. She still had a long way to go and if she didn't look to either of her sides, she could pretend that Hawthorne was with her.

"I should have told you that I—I loved you sooner. You deserved to hear it, and often. But then again, look what happened. I said it and you disappeared.

I don't know if curses are real but I think my life might make a strong case for it," Rayne said, kicked at the dirt.

"It's not fair. Winter's gone, spring fell away which, I suppose I'm grateful for," Spring held no joy for her outside of the memory of their wedding. Her birthday fell less than a week after the Spring Solstice but she'd never enjoyed the day. Her parents had seen to that.

But now, she had her wedding to Hawthorne to think about. The pear blossoms, the gentle hum of honeybees and the way that Hawthorne's hazel eyes had held all of the beauty in the world. She would sever every vein, peel flesh from bone just to have that afternoon back. "I always hated it, the heat and how uncomfortable it made everything. But now I hate it because the whole world is alive and warm and blooming. And yet you're gone. Why should they get to live and be beautiful when you are nowhere to be seen?"

Rayne wished that the darkness would curl around her, brush tenderly against her delicate skin as it used to when they were here.

Take me with you, take me with you, take me with you, please. Just come back.

When Rayne finally approached the crossroads, she slowed to a stop. *I should check the time. I don't want to be too early or too late.* But when she pushed the power button on her phone, having turned it off to conserve her battery, it was dead. *Shit.*

Okay. Well, if I go back to charge my phone, I'll miss my window. But I also could be missing it now. Fuck it, I didn't come all this way to just turn tail.

Rayne stood at the center of the crossroad and turned her back to it as a way to ensure that she didn't meet the eye of whatever might answer her call.

"I—I have come to make a deal," she said, careful not to be too loud. The forest sang around her, alive with cicada song and crickets. Rayne listened closely for the sound of anything, anyone.

But the minutes dragged on and nothing answered her.

"I said I want to make a deal," she tried again. "Is anyone there?"

The moment that the question left her lips she regretted it; the air grew heavy with the presence of another. Behind her she could hear the sound of footsteps, slow and deliberate. The footsteps stopped just behind her and she held her breath to keep herself from trembling.

"I am here," said a soft, wet voice as if its throat was full of water. "Tell me of your deal."

"I-I have come to ask about my husband, Hawthorne. A shadow from this forest." Rayne exhaled.

"And what makes you think that I know where your husband is?" the thing asked.

"I do not need you to tell me where they are. I want to know how I can find them on my own."

The thing stepped closer and Rayne gripped the strap of her backpack tightly, forcing her eyes down. In the light at her feet, she could see the thing's shadow; thin legs and body bent at an unnatural angle. *Nope, nope, do not think about what it looks like. Hawthorne, think about Hawthorne!*

"A strange deal for a human to be making," the thing answered.

"Will you make it or not?"

"What have you got to offer in exchange for my knowledge?"

Shit! I didn't bring an offering. The Neighbors liked offerings; sweets, milk, honey. She hadn't thought to bring anything. But if this creature was anything like Hawthorne, it would sense her lack of preparation and see it as weakness. She could afford to be seen as weak. "I will trade whatever you want."

The creature was silent and then pressed impossibly close, she could feel its hair tickling against the back of her neck and she trembled.

You're not scared. You're not scared. You're not fucking scared!

"That is what you will offer me, whatever I'd like in exchange for knowledge?"

"Yes."

"You will get only three questions."

Three! Fuck. Okay, it's better than nothing. I will just have to be smart about this. "Fine. Have we got a deal?"

"Yes, our deal is struck. You may ask your questions."

She sighed and in the same breath her first question came tumbling out. "Is it possible for me to find Hawthorne?"

"Yes. Quite possible."

Rayne had to bite down on her lip to keep from crying in relief. *I can find them. I can do it.* "How can I find them?"

"You can find them by finding the one that took them," the creature said. "Follow the thread."

The one that took them. Dresden. But then what did the creature mean by thread? *Is it worth asking?*

"Your last question?" the creature purred, pressing closer and with it came the scent of rotting meat and damp, cold marshes.

"Give me a minute." Rayne chewed on her lower lip. *If I need to find Dresden to find Hawthorne then that should be what I focus on. Not them.*

"How do I find Dresden?"

"You do not find The Messenger—he finds you. You will need to be much more than you are if you aspire to capture the attention of a King."

Christ, that's cryptic. But at least I have my direction now. I need only decide my next step. She opened her mouth to thank the thing but thinking better of it, she said instead:

"Alright, okay. So, now what?"

Only the cicada song remained, the creature opting for silence.

"Aren't you going to take something from me or—?"

Rayne glanced down at the light on her feet and the creature's shadow was gone, leaving her alone again.

Magic came with a price, Hawthorne had always told her that but what they hadn't mentioned was that it apparently came with a hangover.

When she'd stumbled back home from the forest later than night, The House had been quiet and she'd been glad for it. She'd only had enough energy to toe off her boots, releasing her aching feet and collapse onto the couch before passing out.

Blinking awake, she rolled onto her back with a heavy groan. Sunlight was a dagger through her vision, obscuring what little she could see under the blanket of her exhaustion. Rayne covered her eyes with her arm, trying to shield herself from the light as she reached for a few more moments of peace.

Memories of the night before danced into her head reminding her that she had made a deal. *I made a deal and won... won what exactly? Hawthorne still isn't here.*

Rayne sighed and after a few minutes, she moved her arm from her eyes and sat up. Her vision righted itself but only slightly, the blurry vision within her right eye gradually adjusted and she could see just as she always did. But her left was dark, black, a closed thing. She blinked and rubbed at her eye. *Probably just dirt or something. Fuck, do I need a shower.*

But it would not set itself right, her vision would not change and the darkness did not subside. Tenderly, she brushed the pad of her fingers against the skin of her under eye lid and it felt empty.

She gasped and panic took the place of where her vision should have been and she shot to her feet, nearly stumbling over her shoes in her rush. *I need to get to a mirror.* The world was tilted, half gone and everything felt farther away than she remembered.

Rayne's shoulder knocked into the wall, frames falling and glass shattering behind her before she finally made it to the guest bathroom down the hall. She clutched the porcelain sink, staring down the drain as her chest heaved, giving herself a moment before she looked up and saw her reflection.

Her left eye was gone, an empty socket in its place.

Rayne screamed as if it would call her stolen eye back to her.

CHAPTER FORTY-THREE
hawthorne

E xhaustion was something that Hawthorne could handle, boredom too was something that they could tolerate but restless was a nightmare.

Day in and day out they thought of nothing but Rayne—*was she alive? Was she hiding? Is she looking for me?*

There was a selfish, greedy part of them that hoped she was looking for them. If the roles were reversed, there was nothing that Hawthorne wouldn't have done to find her. No place that they would not have searched, no deal that they would not have struck to get her back.

Deal.

The web of ancient magic entangling them in the branches of the tree would soon have them enclosed completely and still bound by the webs within. They couldn't get out but perhaps they didn't need to.

Favors were not something that Hawthorne liked to owe or use if they could help it, but it was the only true form of currency that their kind had. Hawthorne did not interfere much with the affairs of other spirits so they owed few favors, and had even less, but they would not hesitate to empty their entire hand for Rayne's sake.

They closed their eyes and whispered the name in their mother tongue—*Old Rusan*—savoring the sound of it on their lips. They spoke so rarely, they had forgotten how good the language felt on their lips. Words in the Underground carried and they would have to be mindful of what they said aloud. *"I require the favor that you owe."*

Ashen was one of the few creatures that—were they both human—Hawthorne might have considered to be a friend. She was a knocker that they'd known for centuries, the only tolerable one within the confines of the forest. A resident of the Underground and a creature birthed from the same black Earth as them. Distant cousin in a way.

It was not long before the whites of her eyes peered at them from the wall of rock near their head. Then gradually her head appeared, her skin like slate and her short hair blacker than a new moon. She blinked at them a moment before the rest of her face emerged. *"Nearly three centuries since we have spoken last and you come calling upon me as if I were some pet."*

"And yet you came."

Ashen shucked her teeth. *"But for what reason I cannot say. You know I cannot free you from this."*

"I did not ask you to," Hawthorne said, trying to keep their voice low. *"I have another thing which I would, however."*

"Name your favor then, cousin so I can be off. I dislike this part of the Under." Ashen sighed.

"I need you to go to the City of Shades for me," Hawthorne said. *"You must seek out a spirit for me and give her a message."*

"A shade?" She scoffed. "You send me to the in-between in search of a simple shade?"

"Yes. I know you dislike them but it is a message that must be delivered," Hawthorne pressed. They could not let on how much they needed this from Ashen lest the tables turn against them and they be the one that ended up owing her.

Ashen rolled her milky eyes. *"The name of your shade?"*

"Rayne Dorne. She has dark, curly hair and skin covered in scars. And she will most likely try to bite your head off if you get too close. Give her space."

Ashen blinked. *"And the message?"*

"*Tell her to wait at the edge of the river,*" Hawthorne whispered. "*To keep to herself and keep quiet. I will find her.*"

Ashen tilted her head curiously. "*My dear cousin, asking something of someone twice in one day. The end times are truly upon us.*"

"*Ashen.*"

"*Yes, yes. It will be done.*" She was already beginning to melt back into the earth. "*I will return here once I have done as you've asked. And then our score will be settled?*"

"*Yes, your debt will be paid,*" Hawthorne answered, nodding stiffly, and just as she had come, Ashen was gone and Hawthorne was alone.

Sleep had never been a friend to Hawthorne as it had never been something that they required. But their body was deteriorating and if they had to listen to one more false version of their wife, flitting in and out of their ear, their mind would be the next thing to go.

It was painful to see even the ghost of her, to catch a phantom whiff of the artificial rose scent and amaretto of her skin. The world was dizzyingly silent save for the phantoms that would come to haunt them. They would run their small hands up their arms, down their torso and whisper sweet nothings to them. Hawthorne tried to close their eyes, tried to drown out their voices.

They would have preferred to be flayed alive, over and over again than to hear the phantoms with her voice.

"*Do you miss me, Hawthorne?*" the specters asked in their ear. "*Do you feel guilty for how I've been blown apart? Will you kiss my rotting entrails in the dirt?*"

She isn't dead. A thought that had become a mantra, a prayer, a desperate plea. Their little wolf would still be alive and waiting for them when they returned. She would still be young and not an old woman with only a few years left in her world.

Though wouldn't that be the ultimate punishment? For them to be haunted by false images of Rayne, to dream of returning to her only for them to come back to a woman on her deathbed? That they would be separated unless they chose to cross that Great River with her. They would, without hesitation, but they did not know what lay on the other side of it.

What if there was nothing but emptiness? What if we are separated again?

"Hawthorne."

Their name jolted them from their misery and they blinked their eyes open. The phantoms were gone and in their place, the large, milky eyes of Ashen. *"How unlike you to wallow, cousin. I can smell your misery a mile away."*

"Did you find her?" they demanded much too loudly and then, quieter. *"Did you find Rayne?"*

Ashen sighed and stretched, the dirt around her shifting with the movement as she made a show of taking her time. " No, I did not. For there is no shade by that name."

Hawthorne's heart flew to their throat. "You are certain? You found none with her description and name? You searched the entirety of the City?"

"As per our agreement, yes, I did. Your Rayne Dorne, whoever she is, is alive. Or perhaps crossed the River earlier."

No, she wouldn't have gone anywhere without me. She's alive. Rayne is alive.

"Is that it then?" Ashen asked, lounging like a cat in the dirt. *"Is our deal complete?"*

"Yes. The debt has been paid." Hawthorne said distantly as their mind was sent reeling. Rayne was alive. Yet why could they find no relief in this knowledge?

"How long will you be kept so?"

"Fifty years and a day."

"Not long at all," Ashen said, turning back into her dirt. *"Good luck with your human, cousin. And perhaps consider a visit to your mother once you are free. You know how she is."*

Hawthorne did not hear her, all they could think of was their wife.

Rayne was alone with no idea whether Hawthorne was alive or dead. If she cared about them half as much as they expected her to—she was drowning.

Their little wolf was alive and that thought terrified them.

CHAPTER FORTY-FOUR
rayne

R ayne's stomach roiled with the image of what she'd been left with, of what she looked like. There had been no gore, no blood or mess smeared on her face. It was simply as if someone had reached down and plucked her eye straight from her skull without her knowledge, without her consent.

But then again who asks for consent before they rob you?

Rayne had kept her hand over her eye as she walked, not wanting to risk anything finding its way into the empty hole of her and she wanted to keep the bones of her dignity intact. She could practically hear the whispers in the town, could see even with her stilted vision the rotten frowns.

Did you see the Dorne girl? She wandered into the forest and came out without an eye—bet she sold it to Old Scratch. Bet he made her a deal before and now he's come down to collect his bounty. Look at her. Little fool is gonna need to be buried down by the river to wash clean those sins.

The House whimpered in the creaking of the archway, shifting as it awoke and stretched. *"My poor cherub. Why did you trade your eye away?"*

"I didn't trade my eye away!" Rayne bit back but the full weight of her conversation with the thing at the crossroads returned to her. *Anything you want.* "Son of a bitch!" she screamed.

The House hummed, cooing at her as if she were a baby bird. *"Half baked promises will always yield half baked rewards, my dove."*

"Where did I miscalculate? What was I supposed to say?" Rayne asked, sliding down the bathroom wall.

The House tsked softly. *"When making deals, sweetness, you must always know exactly what you're paying with. It seems you meant to offer an inch and instead gave a mile."*

"It's not fair!"

"Ah but it is. Anything stolen fairly may be kept so," The House continued. *"It is such a shame, I quite loved your eye. I will keep its color for you, in the dirt of my garden. The bark of my pear tree."*

Something in the way that it spoke felt weighted, as if it was holding a candle, able to illuminate the darkness behind her when she could only stumble in nothingness. It reminded her of the way that Hawthorne spoke – the language of spirits. She knew that the answer would not come in full, that it may not even be offered in a fraction, but desperation was an ugly thing and Rayne was hideous.

Rayne stumbled back down the hallway, mindful of the glass and felt around for her discarded shirt from the night before. She tore a strip of fabric from it and tied it around her head, covering her lost eye as best she could.

"Where are you going, cherub?"

"Back into the woods to find that—whatever it is. This deal was fucked and I'm not going to lose half of my sight and only receive some bogus answer in response."

The House sighed. *"Very well. You know I will be here upon your return."*

It was fury that spurred her movements, that fueled her as she stormed through the forest and repeated the same ritual that she had the first time. Rayne had asked her three questions and in exchange they had taken her fucking eye?

In what fucking world was that an equivalent exchange? The questions had not even truly given her a direction in which to go, a place to turn to begin the task of bringing her husband back to her. She had been duped and she sure as fuck was not going to let that slide.

Rayne did not know much of the good folk but she knew never to call or even think of them by what they were called. Her grandmother had always told her that, reminded her that they found it rude and the last thing that one wanted to do was offend one of Them.

Still. The fucker had taken her damned eye, and while she would have traded all of that and more to get Hawthorne back, she was no closer to her husband than she had been the day that they'd left.

But Rayne would not be had, she would not be torn apart for the sake of some creature's amusement.

This time Rayne left a few hours before sunset, giving herself enough time to easily get up the holler and wait at the crossroads with her new found disadvantage.

She sat in the dirt, watching the sun fade while her anger simmered.

Can I fight a faerie? she wondered, watching the moonlight splash against her outstretched legs. The moon painted her thick, black thigh highs silver, this time she had learned and fully charged her phone before she came and quickly turned it off before she left, ensuring that she would have ample battery life this time. Though her body was used to layers, the heat had sweat dampening her shirt.

When her phone began vibrating, alerting her that it was 12:55am, she stood, stretched, and turned to walk backwards toward the crossroad, the light at her feet from her flashlight the only thing to guide her.

Finally she stilled. It was not long before she felt the presence of another, the air weighted, a stone dropping into a lake.

But unlike before, the air did not fill with the scent of rotting meat but instead, peaches left in the summer sun too long, sweet and overwhelming. Rayne's eye watered at the intensity. She felt compelled to turn and face the creature for a different reason than she had the night before.

Her rage knotted in her fingers and she closed and flexed them, itching to punch at the thing that had tricked her. Though she couldn't see the thing, she felt it all the same.

"You could have at least told me that you were going to take my fucking eye, you conniving ass," she snapped at it.

Behind her, there was motion, a curtain drawing open and cool wind against her back. "I have never met the likes of you." Came a voice like fresh water over rock, a river running its course. It was nothing like what she had heard the night before. "Nor do I have any reason to take your eye, stranger."

Rayne nearly turned to face the thing. "We met last night and made a fucking deal!"

The thing laughed, a bird's chirp, a cricket chattering its legs. "Oh, I see. You met my sister then. If you were seeking me, you came out much too late and found yourself with her. That's terribly unfortunate for you."

Sister. Wrong hour. That would have made sense wouldn't it?

Or maybe... maybe she's trying to trick me?

The Neighbors were tricksters, shapeshifters, and it would not be entirely out of left field that one of them could easily pretend to be something that they were not. It was possible and she'd already been tricked before, but if the creature that she spoke to now was the one from last night, why not simply admit it?

Perhaps it's like one of those riddles. Like lady and the tiger, perhaps it doesn't matter what the answer is because either way my eye is gone and there are still deals to be made.

"But," the creature began, as if sensing the shift in her thoughts. "You are here now, girl-with-one-eye, which means you must have something you want. Something to trade."

Rayne swallowed and closed her eyes, envisioning what she wanted to say before she allowed the words to leave her mouth. *This time I will not lose.* "I have a husband, a shadow from this wood. Their name is Hawthorne. I need to get them back but I don't know how anything in this world works. I cannot navigate it like a child. I need knowledge."

"I imagine that you do," the thing purred like a cat. Rayne stared ahead even as she felt hair, long and silken brush against her bare arm. "But what has that got to do with me, girl?"

"I want to know how your world works so that I may move through it on my own. If you were to do that for me, what would you want in exchange?"

The creature hummed, a melodic albeit discomforting sound. Rayne could feel movement behind her, could hear the grass giving way to the weight of the other thing, but she kept her gaze fixed steadily ahead of her at the trees and the inky sky. "I will act as a mentor for you for three nights. We will meet here every night at this time and our session will end before my sister's hour can begin."

Yes! Rayne nearly leapt at the offer but then remembered herself, remembered her lost eye. "And in exchange?"

"In exchange, you will give me twelve years and a day off of your life."

"*What?*"

"To receive my help, you will offer me twelve years and a day off of your life's span. I will simply drink the energy from you. Painless, like a needle," the creature said slowly as if it was reveling in the explanation and the kick in her pulse. She had been foolish to consider that this thing, whatever it was, might have been different from the other at all. That it might have felt kindness or compassion for her and her plight. All spirits were the same. Hadn't Hawthorne told her that?

Every spirit was a greedy, ravenous thing and they would dig their fingers into the softest, weakness tissue that they could find.

"Do you know how long I'm going to live for?" Rayne asked, trying to think her way around any possible loopholes.

"I do not," the creature answered.

"So, I could potentially be giving you twelve years and a day off of my life when I'm only meant to live for another thirteen?"

"Potentially, yes."

"Why?"

"That is *not* part of the deal!" the thing hissed, sounding more like a snake now than a bird and Rayne swallowed. "But if you would like to know, perhaps we can add that to the cost?"

"No!" Rayne snapped and then, a moment later she sighed shakily. *I may be signing my own death certificate here but at least I can see Hawthorne again.*

"Alright. I will take the initial deal that you offered me. Your help in exchange for twelve years and a day of my life."

The thing chittered again and Rayne thought that it might have been laughing at her. She ground her teeth and waited, her hands balling into fists.

"The deal is struck then," it said finally. "Go home and rest, girl-with-one-eye. You will need it."

"That's it?" Rayne almost turned to face the creature but then quickly remembered herself. "We don't have to shake on it or something?"

It laughed again. "For my kind, our word is our bond. There is magic in a verbal accord."

"Oh." Rayne made sure to stick that somewhere in the mental files for later use. She was almost certain that it would come in handy for something else. Something told her that this was not going to be the only deal that she made with a spirit in the hunt for her husband.

Sleeping that night was nearly impossible and she found herself tossing and turning. What brief sleep that she did find was restless at best.

The House sang to her, a soft song of humming pipes and creaking floorboards that gradually had lulled her to sleep.

In the morning, the pain was worse than it had ever been. Her body ached in unfamiliar ways, joints that were sore, muscles that were tense where they never had been before.

She tried not to think too much of it and what it meant. Pain was nothing new to her and the loss of her eye had zapped more from her than she cared to admit.

She did not have time to worry about what she might have lost. All that Rayne could allow herself to think about was what she sought to gain.

Hawthorne.

The ending to their story together that she would get to write.

Over the next three nights like clockwork she went into the forest to seek out the spirit. She quietly named her Peach for her smell.

Peach was patient but not accommodating. She taught Rayne slowly, carefully but did not repeat her lessons. Rayne had only one chance to retain the information and tuck it away.

She listened and learned as much as she could of Hawthorne's world and the rules in which it operated. There was so much that her beast had not told her, and there was a pang of hurt that came with that knowledge. *Why did you keep a whole world from me?*

Rayne learned of the Kings—the most powerful spirits in this world. The First King, Dresden, she had already met. The Messenger.

The Second King, The Enforcer. Peach would not say the King's name but warned Rayne that for her sake, she hoped that their paths never crossed.

The Third King, the Sleeping King, Peach was even more tight lipped about. She simply shook her head and told Rayne that he was the worst of them all and that his presence meant the end of time for all living beings.

Peach told her of the favors in which spirits used for currency and she talked of the City of Shades. An underground city where all of the dead gathered to make their final choice.

A pear seed or wade through uncharted waters.

I would accept neither, Rayne thought. *I would not be reborn nor would I journey down that river without my husband's hand in mine.*

But most important of all that Peach told her was that if Rayne wanted to find Dresden and get his attention, she would need power. And power for a human could only be acquired by receiving it from spirits.

Her advice had ended there, and as Rayne made that journey home on the final night of her lessons, there was a rock of doubt within her gut. A feeling, like missing the last set of stairs on the way down. A misstep like the day before Len had killed Persimmon.

It doesn't matter, she thought, pressing through the woods. *There is only forward, there is only seeing Hawthorne again. Nothing else matters.*

Of the many stories and tales her grandmother had told, the way she spoke of cornfields always fascinated and terrified Rayne. Things about how the world was different behind the rows and that no one rightfully knew what lived there.

Only that it watched.

Her grandmother's stories had all proved to be right thus far and she'd saved Rayne whether she had meant to or not. *Maybe her prayers are still protecting me in a way.*

Though she was clearly giving her grandmother a run for her money. Especially now as she prepared to go back to the holler.

The chronic ache that she had become accustomed to dealing with when it came to her skin had only worsened since her deal with Peach. Since she had years of her life stolen from her, her body was exhausted and Rayne downed more ibuprofen than she ever had before, just to get through her days.

The cost was almost too steep.

Almost.

"I am leaving," Rayne announced, shoving a bottle of water into her backpack. "I will be gone for quite some time, I think. Hopefully back by morning."

"The forest?" The House whined in the shuddering of the refrigerator. *"Again? I am beginning to think that perhaps you do not love me at all, my cherub. That I am the thing you seek to avoid. Is it true?"*

Rayne sighed, moving through the living room and into the kitchen to brush her hands over the marble edge of the counter. "No, House," she began. "You are my home and I shall never desire to leave you. You know why I have to leave."

"Yes, I know."

Rayne pressed a kiss to the cool marble and House sighed in delight. *"I will be here and I will keep the lights on for you."*

"I love you, House," Rayne said with a gentle pat of its counter.

"I have always adored you, my little terror."

Rayne did not lock the door when she left now that she knew House could protect itself. Her House was safe.

She could not say the same for herself.

The walk was beginning to become second nature to her, she was certain that she had walked the path so many times now that there was a groove working into the land. A scar that she and her sorrow had mapped in the flesh of the world.

Time was not something that she could bring herself to comprehend, to grasp. What was the difference between seconds, minutes, and hours, if she spent them all alone?

Rayne could not know how long it had been since she had last touched her husband. All she knew was that winter had not come yet. *I will have you back before the first snow. We will watch it fall together.*

Twigs snapped under the heels of her aching feet as Rayne's thoughts drifted to her Mam'maw and her home at the mouth of the holler. She had been the single, solitary soul living between the town and the hungry mountains. She'd liked it that way too.

Perhaps it was the loneliness that led her to take the higher road, the left—Devil's side as her grandmother had always said. The old woman made herself a little crucifix of driftwood, twine, sea glass, and broken mirror pieces to stick at the top of the road.

"It'll trick the Devil, the dust demons, and any other haints," her Ma'amaw *had said while she sat in the kitchen polishing her good silver. "They can't help but stop and look at their reflections. Before they know it, they'll be trapped. Vanity is a terrible sin, snapdragon."*

Rayne smirked a bit to herself, unable to help it. Her grandmother had been drenched in her superstitions, they dripped off of her and she couldn't open her mouth without three or four old wives' tales stumbling out of her.

I miss it almost as much as I miss her.

The sun had reddened, bloodied, and set slowly in the sky with its scarlet eye on her, a reminder of her solitude. The light caught in the reflections of the mirrors, shining millions of little stars on the damp ground just up ahead.

What if I can't cross it?

The thought hit her so suddenly that she stopped dead in her tracks, staring up at her grandmother's charm stuck deep in the ground like a railroad spike. Rayne was not the same little girl who once walked this road freely, tossing baby carrots into the underbrush for rabbits. She had not been here since after her grandmother passed away and the house that they'd both cherished had been sold and quickly demolished.

The house that should have been Rayne's.

Everyone in town swore it was because the spirits didn't want the land tamed, refused to yield, and bit back. Before all of this Rayne had thought it was simply because they had realized that Bury was not the kind of town worth investing in but now she knew better.

This place was as haunted as she was.

Rayne stopped just at the crucifix and looked long and hard at it. She caught fragments of herself in the tiny pieces of mirror, the corner of an eye where crows had come to rest their feet, a deep set scowl, ruddy, dirty skin. She saw many things but nothing that made her want to look at herself longer than she had to.

She kept walking.

When she passed the plot of land where her grandmother's house used to stand, might still stand if it were not for the thing that birthed her being so full of poison, Rayne kept walking. She kept her head low and willed herself not to see it. Looking at it felt like staring directly into the eyes of everything that had ever been or gone wrong in her life.

She kept her eyes glued to the dirt as she trekked up the hill. The night had spilled over her and the forest, blacker than coffee and she was grateful for it.

Rayne did not know why she was walking this way, why she was following this calling, or even what it was. Her intuition was more like a stranger that spoke softly to her.

As she continued through the holler, came upon the cornfield, the one she had completely forgotten about.

Rayne had spent many autumn afternoons kicking fallen crabapples into the cornfield, hoping to rattle the entirety of it but too frightened to set foot in it.

Her grandmother's voice, as clear as day, sounded in her ear, as if her ghost was hollering at her from the grave. *"Don't you dare set foot in that corn at night, Rayne Cidney-Marie Dorne,"* she hissed and Rayne could practically see the wagging finger with it, her wispy, gray brows raised. *"You know damn well that you're never alone in the corn. What will you do when you see those eyes, hmm? Don't think you can come running, come hiding under my skirt!"*

The stories about the corn had been few and far between because of all things her mam'maw had come to fear, whatever walked behind the rows was the king of it. She remembered hushed words during the searing summer afternoons while her grandmother had burned sweetgrass. Stories about strange disappearances, people who walked into the rows and never came back.

"Why do you gotta go shaking your fists and kicking up dust into the eyes of bigger things?" the imagined ghost hissed. *"Why do you gotta go lookin' for trouble?"*

"It's what I'm good at," Rayne said to her grandmother's ghost. "That's all I can do."

"I raised you better," The ghost sighed, shaking its head, "You know better."

Rayne did know better but as she turned and set her path towards the corn field, she intended to find out.

CHAPTER FORTY-FIVE

rayne

T he world was different behind the rows.

The stalks of sweet corn grew long and tall, wild, and unbothered. This was nothing like the haunted corn maze that took place every October downtown where the path had been trodden, where the journey was as simple as following the path. Here there was nothing, she had to push her way through and step between the stalks, careful to keep herself from tripping over the fallen and decomposing ears.

If it weren't for the light of her flashlight at her feet, she surely would have broken an ankle.

Walking the rows was like running the labyrinth, but where was her minotaur? She kept no track of the time, had no way to do so, and yet she felt as though she had been stumbling around for years in the silence and the dark. Save for the sound of her boots crunching through the dirt and the snapping of the ears as she pushed them down. The world was oddly still, the air stagnant, heavy with the saccharine sting of rotting corn.

Something snapped in the distance and the stalks of corn shook with movement.

Oh, shit.

Her muscles tensed with the desire to run. But for better or for worse, she had decided that this thing would lead her to her husband. Fear had no place here for her any longer, if only her treacherous mind could get with the fucking program.

Rayne forced herself to walk slowly and evenly through the corn as the rustling continued, moving quicker and quicker her way.

Don't run, don't run, don't run.

Her heart slammed into her chest, blood rushing through her ears, surging through her veins and every instinct within her screaming.

The rustling caught up to her and then slowed until it was not behind her but beside her, whatever was on the other side of the rows was walking with her.

Breath sounded dangerously close to her blind side.

The Devil's side.

"Hello," she said lamely.

The Thing laughed like the kicking of an engine. "Hello, there," it said politely. "What's your name?"

"Don't have one," she replied with a shrug.

"A lie."

"Prove it," Rayne countered.

"Hmm. Why have you wandered so deep into my corn, nameless fool?"

"Does it matter?" she asked. "I'm here."

"No, I suppose it does not," The Thing said. "*You* are here and *I* will make a meal of you."

Rayne swallowed and did her best to appear calm, unphased by the threat though the bitter taste of fear rose in her throat. She could not falter here.

"I was hoping you'd say that," she said, clearing her throat. "You'd be doing me a service. Life has become bothersome, painful even, and I think that I've had my fill."

The Thing was silent for a moment before it spoke again. "You are strange. It is a shame that you have not given me your name. I might have liked to remember you."

"You could remember me still," she offered, her mind stretching, reaching in the ethers of thought to find a solution. "If you're up to a challenge. *A game.*"

The Creature stopped but Rayne did not, knowing somewhere within her that if she stopped moving in the presence of this predator that it would snatch her up. She could feel the thing listening, feeling her out, but she did not look back nor did she pretend to notice.

"Do you like games?" Rayne pressed though she knew the answer.

"Is there a creature alive that does not?" The Thing inquired and its steps resumed behind her until it was at her side again. "What sort of game?"

"A guessing game," Rayne said before her mind could catch up to her tongue. "The best kind."

"And what would I be guessing?" it asked and though it seemed as though it was trying to sound bored, she could hear the interest flickering in its voice.

"Not you, corn ghost," she said. "I shall guess something about you. What you are called, your name, perhaps?"

At this all attempts at hiding its interest melted away and she felt like a very fat mouse that had wandered into the den of a ravenous cat. "My name? What fun. The terms of this game?"

"You must answer my questions honestly and if I lose, you can eat me. All of me."

She felt The Thing frown. "That is hardly a reward as I was going to eat you anyhow. When I win, I should like to eat you and wear your skin and walk amongst the town as a thing reborn. Would you bargain your skin away?"

Yeah, you'd be getting more than you bargained for with this skin, I can assure you that much. But still, the thought unsettled her.

"Yes, I would, should you win," she said, though everything in her screamed in discomfort. "When I win, you will grant me your magic, in full, and it will be mine to wield."

The Thing chuckled and it was like cloth caught on a thorn. "Oh, I truly will need to get your name before I slip into your skin. Our deal is struck."

I will not lose this game. I will walk out of this unscathed and victorious. I can do this.

"I'd like for you to ask your questions now," The Thing said.

Rayne remained silent as she walked, her mind reaching for her grandmother and the listless void that was the stories of her childhood. Stories from the reservation that her grandmother tucked away and promised only to whisper in winter, lest the bugs come for her.

"Your eyes," Rayne asked. "What color are they?"

The Thing laughed. "As white as milk."

She cleared her throat to hide the shiver it sent down her spine. "And your skin?"

"It was once as black as the Earth on which you tread?" The Thing answered wistfully.

"And now?" she pressed.

"Whiter than the moon. The sight of me might blind you."

That tells me nothing! I need to find the right question.

"Given up, have you?" it taunted, laughing.

"Hardly! I am merely thinking."

"Think harder. I cannot spend all night waiting to eat you. Only so many hours in the night, you know."

She felt the creature recoil, heard the slight shuttering as it seemed to realize its own mistake. Rayne fought to hide her grin and pretended not to notice. *It can only move at night.* This narrowed down her choices quite a bit.

"Have you ever seen the sun?"

"Yes."

"Do you remember it?" Rayne inquired.

"Do you remember your birth?" The Thing hissed. "Do you remember the moment that you were thrust from your mother's womb into your world? No? Then do not ask me if I remember the sun. I do not."

It hasn't seen the sun since it was born. It can only move at night.

At this Rayne stopped and turned to face the general direction in where she believed The Thing to be. "I know you."

The Thing laughed and she heard it shifting in delighted anticipation, like a cat ready to pounce. "Do you? Say my name then."

"You are one of the Moon Eyed," she declared.

The Thing was silent for a few more moments before the shifting continued but much without its previous joy. "I am. But that is not my true name."

"I never said that I would guess your true name," she grinned. "We only agreed upon a name, something that you are called. You have said yourself that this is what you are."

The corn went silent, the rows breathed and moved and yet nothing made a sound. Rayne tensed, her muscles preparing for whatever was about to get thrown her way as uncertainty worked its way into her. *I was right, I know I was. I didn't mess this up. I didn't!*

"Very well then," The Thing said. "It seems you have won. And you were quite right, I *shall* remember you and I will gut you the next time I see you. Now." The rows to her left bowed, parting, and it began to move through, but remembering its remark about blinding her, she shielded her good eye.

"Clever," The Thing huffed.

The scent of burnt sugar and rotten corn filled the air, and she felt a fiery hand at her waist. Before she could move, a pair of lips against her mouth. They burned, searing against her skin and something slipped past her lips, bitter and burning her esophagus on the way down.

The Thing was gone, as if it had never been there, leaving only the scent of sugar and corn in its wake. Rayne turned and ran the entire way home, ignoring her screaming limbs.

The House was as curious as it was nosy and it immediately wondered why her lips were swollen, why she smelled of decay. She spoke nothing of what she'd done, she pretended not to know what it was talking about. But that night, she thrashed and kicked in her bed, her stomach aching as if she'd eaten an entire plate of sugar.

In her fitful sleep, she dreamt of her grandmother, seated at her window in her old rocking chair. The steady movement like the shucking of teeth. Her grandmother glanced her way with eyeless sockets to match her own misplaced eye. Her Mam'maw raked her skeletal fingers through her knee-length moon-light hair, tumbling over her frame just as spilled milk.

"Told you," Adele's ghost whispered, death rattle caught in her voice. "Now look at you, snapdragon. Your belly all full of magic and lies, both of 'em burning you up from the inside out like wildfire."

Rayne felt... wrong.

Her body ached but her head felt as though it were miles away.

The Creature in the Corn's magic felt nothing like Hawthorne's.

Hawthorne's power had been grounding, steady like the roots of a tree but this new magic made her nauseous, the vision in her good eye swimming and hindering her further. "I'm an idiot," she cried, burying her hands in her face. "I risked my life for nothing. And I still am no closer to finding Hawthorne than I was yesterday."

It was not until nightfall that the prize she'd won revealed itself.

The moment that the sky darkened, Rayne's vision sharpened and the world burst into more shades, shapes, and even sounds that she had ever imagined possible. A world that she had never imagined.

Outside, dozens of will-o-wisps drifted lazily on the air like jellyfish, the grass was filled with tiny hands holding and reaching for one another, even the sky danced with life. Everything was so beautifully, perfectly alive.

If the Moon Eyed could not see or function in the daylight, it would make sense that they would have a heightened sense of sight at night but this was beyond what she ever could have expected.

"House," Rayne whispered, reaching up to run her fingers along a wisp. "Is this what the world looks like for all of you, all of the time?"

"Yes, cherub. If you are seeing what I think you are."

When she turned back to face the House though the glass door on the porch she could see that a large mouth sat in the fireplace.

"I can see you!" she said, giddy.

"Am I beautiful?"

"Yes, House. The *most* beautiful."

Rayne tiptoed over the grass in her garden, careful now that she could see how tightly every blade clung to its companion.

"Rayne!"

She spun. "Hello?"

"Oh, you can hear me now!"

"Who—"

"The pear tree!"

Rayne slowly looked behind her where the pear tree sat in the back of her garden, the same one she and Hawthorne had stood before as their altar. *This can't be real.* After everything that Rayne had seen and heard, somehow the idea of a talking tree seemed too ridiculous to be true.

"You can talk?"

"And see and hear, yes."

Hadn't House told her that it could remember being a tree and even remember the soil it was tilled from? *Maybe a talking tree is just as ridiculous as a talking house.*

The pear tree spoke with not one voice but many, layering over one another in a chorus like an echo. *"You were wed under my blossoms, standing on my roots and now you act as if we are strangers? Come closer, Rayne. We are kin. And I have been hoping you would hear me."*

"Why?"

"I saw what happened—what one of us sees, we all see. Trees' interconnections are as old as the dirt. So, I have seen your loss and your journey. I want you and your shadow back here as you were. I like the look of you together."

"Can *you* help me?" Rayne's palm pressed against the tree's bark.

"Only offer insight, what you do with it has nothing to do with me," The tree replied but Rayne understood the gift for what it was. *"If you are to find a god, you would need something of equal strength for them to notice."*

Equal strength to a god. "Are you telling me that I need to become a god?"

The tree laughed, all of its voices following suit in a wave of laughter. "No, no. Humans cannot become what they are not. But if one were to lend it to you—"

Just as Rayne opened her mouth to ask what god would ever go out of their way to do that, the tree continued "*You already have the answer. Look to your blood, your roots.*"

My roots. My blood—Mam'maw. She must have told me about who I'm supposed to seek.

But who had her grandmother ever spoken of positively of other than the Creator?

There had been talk of ancestors but little else that Rayne could remember—everything else her Mam'maw had warned her against.

Later, she sat cross legged beneath the open window, near the hearth but not close enough for the heat to bother her. "House, do you ever remember anything I ever said about my grandmother?"

"Oh, plenty, cherub. You never stopped speaking of her even for a day. We would be here for weeks if I were to recount all you've said."

"But—did I ever mention a god or something that she told me about?" Rayne shook her head before resting it back against the wall. "Forget it. You couldn't tell me even if I did, right? Your rules or whatever that's keeping you from helping me."

"You were scared of thunderstorms. But—not after your time with her."

Thunderstorms?

Thunder.

Oh. But I could be wrong. It's been so long and I don't even know how I would go about getting his attention.

But it was a chance Rayne would have to take as helpful as The Creature in Corn's sight may have been but it was nowhere near powerful enough to do what needed to be done.

Hawthorne was waiting for her.

Shame nipped at Rayne's heels as she collected the small pieces of splintered bark into the pan she'd brought with her. *I should know how to do this, Mam'maw would have.*

As a child, her parents had discouraged her from following too closely in her grandmother's footsteps and that included speaking her and her mother's language. Her father had claimed it was to keep Rayne from becoming too vain but she couldn't understand how following the old ways could birth anything of the sort in her.

So, like everything else in her life, Rayne's language was fractured, ancestral practices that she should have carried with her were inkblots in her mind; there but obscuring everything.

The Thunder Being was a story that Rayne could not piece together fully but she remembered her grandmother whispering how he took pity on humans and fought to defend them.

Let's hope you're right, Mam'maw.

Rayne had no idea how to call him, but lightning struck bark had been something she'd seen more than once in her grandmother's home. *I think I even helped her collect some once.*

It will have to be enough.

If he was a "good" spirit then he would only come during the day so, armed with nothing but a pan, a grill lighter, and wood, she set off back into the forest. She cleansed herself as deeply as she could with water and smoke, her skin and hair reeking of burnt juniper. When she found a place comfortable enough in the forest, she sat.

"I have no idea what I'm doing," Rayne confessed. "Let's hope this works."

Lighting one of the pieces of wood on fire, she watched the smoke and leaned over it, pinching her eyes closed and whispering her prayer. Rayne prayed as hard and as genuinely as she could, giving her plight to the smoke so that it might reach the skies where he resided.

Rayne repeated the action over and over again, burning every piece of wood and praying. She did so until the sun's position in the sky shifting, slowly beginning the long process of its descent.

"Fuck!" Rayne exclaimed, tossing the lighter into the forest. "Why isn't this working? What am I doing wrong?"

She scrubbed her hands over her face before tossing the pan too. "Fuck this and fuck you gods! What use are you if you don't answer prayers?"

Overhead, thunder boomed in the clouds, and a bird, larger than Rayne had ever seen, fell out of the sky, cutting through the trees like lightning and standing before her. Closer to it now, Rayne realized that it was not a bird but a human figure with the arms of an eagle.

His black hair shone like a raven's wing, its skin nearly matched her own except bright, shining. But it was the eyes of the creature that alerted her to its true otherness. Eyes like smoke trapped under a glass; two grey voids.

"Are you—?"

"I am here."

The Thunder Being.

Pèthakhuwe.

His true name fell from her tongue, dripping with the language of her ancestors and he lit up with unrepressed pride. He smiled and it was sunlight cutting through an overcast sky. "Kàski hàch alënixsi? *Do you speak Lenape?*

Rayne swallowed the sudden lump in her throat at the sound of her grandmother's language, *her* language, on the tongue of a god. She hesitated, reaching for what little bit that she could.

"Òsòmi. Shék, mata wëlëluu." *Oh, yes. But it is not good,* she murmured, embarrassed by her stumbling tongue.

The Thunder Being winced. "English, then. I heard your prayer and I am here to answer it. To strike an accord."

"What do you want?"

"Easy, little crow. We must begin as friends do. Tell me your name."

Rayne pressed closer to the tree—she knew what power names held. The Thunder Being wanting it right off of the bat was a red flag.

"Ah, a show of trust is required. I will tell you something no one else will: it will always end this way. The path has been forged and the grove woven into the world cannot be undone."

What the fuck does that mean? Damn spirits and their spirit talk. "How do I know you're not lying to me?"

The Thunder Being frowned. "What reason have I to lie to a mortal? *You* prayed to *me.*"

"Yes and *you* answered which means *you* want something from *me.*"

"I feel pity for your plight. The loss of a spouse must be painful especially after everything you have lost."

Rayne crossed her arms over her chest. "And yet, you still want something from me."

The Thunder Being shrugged and stretched his wings. "Can both not be true?"

"I guess. So, let's hear it."

"Aht, your name first."

"Rayne Dorne."

"Well, Rayne Dorne, you need strength. I am here to offer you some of my own," he continued. "You shall be able to conduct my lightning. To shake the earth or tread quietly upon it. I will lend these gifts to you."

No. This was too good of an offer, there had to be some kind of catch. She knew how spirits operated now after having lost her eye and twelve years off her life, and she knew that there was no such thing as a *gift.* Even Hawthorne, who loved her more than any mortal had ever dared could not escape their nature. Anything that they gave her, they expected something in return be it her love, her pleasure, or her pain, they would always *collect.*

"What is it that you want from me in exchange? Name it in its entirety," Rayne demanded, stepping away from the tree.

"In exchange you will answer my call and heed me as you would the Creator."

Rayne chose to ignore his mention of the Creator for if He was real then she truly would never see her Mam'maw again. "You'd want me to worship you?"

Fat chance of that. Dark eyes narrowed into slits as she glared at the creature across from her. "Why me?"

"It is... good to hear the old language again, even if it is broken."

Well, that's not a damn answer but this deal is good. One that Rayne could not truly turn down and yet, she said "I have a counter offer for you."

The air crackled with his laughter, simmering with unnatural heat and the hairs on the back of Rayne's neck stood on edge. "You have my ear, little crow."

Rayne walked right up to him, leaving only a few feet between them. *I'm not scared of you, I can't be.* "I will leave offerings for you. I will build you an altar in the forest and refresh it every three months. I will sing what I remember of one of the old songs for you and in exchange, I keep what power you give me."

His wings beat against the air, blowing a harsh wind over her. She forced herself to stay exactly where she was, to keep her face straight.

"You dare to try and steal from a god?"

"It is not stolen if you give it to me."

"You will die if you try to hold onto this magic. Your feeble body is not made for power such as this."

Rayne shrugged. "If I die then no deal. But if I live then I keep it. I will still uphold my end of our bargain."

The Thunder Being scoffed. "You will refresh my altar once a month. On full moons, save for blood moons."

"I will."

He lifted into the sky, beating the air from his wings down on her. "Our accord is struck, Rayne Dorne. Prepare yourself. This will not be a pleasant experience for you."

"I've been running short on pleasant experiences lately. One more won't kill me."

"As you say then," The Thunder Being laughed, cracking his neck and stretching his massive wings over his head, blotting out the sun. The air hissed, crackling with electricity. "Once you have been hit, you may catch fire."

Rayne swallowed and dug her nails deep into her palm until little crescents were left in their wake. She whispered a single promise to herself, to Hawthorne, to every and any enemy she had ever had: "I will not burn."

The moment before impact she was hit with the scent of rotting lemons, something bitter with an underlay of rot; she had not known that lightning had a scent. It slammed her back against the tree and the trunk of it snapped sending her flying with it into the grass.

Her flesh boiled and glowing with an unnatural light that felt as though it was cooking her from the inside out. She screamed louder than any thunderstorm ever could.

CHAPTER FORTY-SIX
rayne

A gony came rushing back in waves, her eyes opened, the sun spitting in them, cicadas laughing at the grunt she made in response.

Though it was only the movement of her head, the slight inclination of her neck, white searing pain jolted through her. Like lightning.

Lightning.

She swore, hissed in pain and then laughed like the crow that The Thunder Being had crowned her. She had survived it, she had absorbed the lightning as if it had always belonged to her.

The Girl that Swallowed Lightning. The Girl Who Refused To Burn. The pain shot through her again, working to humble her.

The Girl Whose Bones Felt like Fucking Jelly.

The sun above her was pain, the ground beneath her more like a splinter against her back and her body alight with unadulterated agony. Still, she laughed over the cicadas and imagined dragging the sky down between her teeth.

See how I didn't burn? I told you, world. I'm rooted in you until you bring Hawthorne back to me or I rip the molar of them from your jaw.

The walk back was more of a crawl but gradually, it became a stumble, a hobble. She was recovering but the pain was just as great as it had been before. Rayne spoke to her husband, pretending that they were arm in arm, hand in hand in that holy palmers kiss. Loss had instilled a romance in her that she was not sure had existed before. *Sweaty, bloody, and alone and yet all you're quoting Shakespeare?*

"I will not be humbled," she sang to herself. "I will quote Shakespeare and bleed onto the grass if I like. I've earned it."

Rayne returned her attention to the ghost of her husband. "Did you see? I haven't died. Some fragile butterfly, huh?"

No response came as it hadn't for months and it did not feel right to put the words in their mouth, take the choice of wielding their silver tongue from them, so she continued.

"Would I seem different to you now?" she whispered. "Would you see me now, more scar tissue than girl and ask 'Where is the little wolf that I left behind? Who are you, crow thing? Where have you placed her, lightning bug? Did you—"

She choked on her tongue, pebbled and dry with emotion. Rayne moved from the tree she had been clinging to and limped carefully down the hill. She fell, palms out, held to catch herself from her face planting into the dirt.

You won't humble me, Universe. I've spilled too much blood today.

But where her skin once tore at the slightest bit of friction, her fall did not injure her. She brushed herself off and felt around her knees, her legs. No blood. *I didn't get hurt,* she marveled.

Rayne pulled down her ratty shirt to feel under the bandage where her stitches had been slowly healing. The wound site was gone and in its place, a pale scar. It stung a little when she traced her fingers near it, still tender.

Of course. I've got god magic in me now. What god could ever be so fragile?

Her laughter startled her with its suddenness, its intensity. *All it took was me being ripped apart for me to be rebuilt as something strong. Something capable.* Rayne doubled over, the forest swallowing her mirth.

"You've changed again, my cherub," The House whispered with her return. ***"Why is it that every time you leave me, you come back with less of yourself?"***

Rayne could not get into it now, she did not have the time or desire. Now that she had her new magic, her new powers, she was not going to wait another day to find her husband. It did not matter that she had no understanding of the new power that she possessed, she would figure it out and take it all in stride.

Somewhere between the waking and the walk, she had formulated a plan. A thread of one at least. Her mind had gone back to that afternoon where she had lost Hawthorne and what Dresden had said to her.

An Act of Wrath.

What she had done to Len and his family. Dresden had appeared the next day which meant that if she wanted him to come to her right away, she would have to do something worse.

And she would have to mean it.

Rayne didn't know what she would do just yet but what she did know was that either she would be returning with her husband or she would not be returning at all.

The House trembled. *"I can feel the horrors bubbling beneath your skin. Must you go out into the summer heat and chip more of yourself away?"*

Rayne remained silent as she entered the kitchen, heating some soup on the stove as she realized with painful gurgling of her gut that she had not eaten in what might have been days. Time was no longer a friend to her and everything blurred into one long, never ending day. A day without Hawthorne.

She fussed around the House, the entirety of it much too clean and perfect. As if no one had lived here in months.

Rayne did her best to ignore the House's gentle prodding and harsh coaxing as it tried to see what she was writing. She had grabbed a sheet of old letterhead from the guestroom and folded herself into the closet to write it. To keep from its prying eyes.

She didn't allow herself to wallow in any of the words that she scribbled down, she could not allow herself to feel the emotions of them fully. She didn't have the time to. But they existed and they were for her beloved House.

"Here," she said, when her task was finally complete. "If I haven't returned by the beginning of winter then you may open this letter. Not a day before."

The House pouted. *"Oh, let me read it now, cherub. Why are you so cruel with your affections?"*

Ignoring it, she pressed on, "Promise me, House," she repeated. "Promise that you will hold this between your rib cage until then."

"I swear by the moon in your hair and the stars in your eyes," it sighed. *"I will not open it before winter comes."*

Rayne smiled, pressed a kiss to the envelope and slipped it into the nearest air vent as gently as she could. The House shuddered in delight and then she felt it pout once more.

She caught a glimpse of herself in the hallway mirror and stopped in her tracks. The woman before her was not someone she had ever seen before. Rayne's curls, once dark, were streaked with white like falling stars. Her good eye was tired, deep bags under them and her cheeks hollow. In the corner of her good eye, crow's feet crinkled.

That's right. I'm older now. I felt it but I forgot that I would look it too.

"You're leaving me," The House whispered, pulling her attention away from the mirror.

"I am leaving, but not *you*. I will be back with our wraith."

"Have you found them then?" House purred, a curtain nuzzling against her as she passed by the door, securing her boots.

"Not yet. But I have a plan," Rayne explained. "Either way, I will not be returning without Hawthorne."

Rayne had to wait until night fell to do it. Such things, she reasoned, were done best under the cover of night.

When the sun fell below the treeline, Bury fell silent. A curfew most likely put in place to protect people from the evil that lurked in the dark.

She could have driven, it might have been smarter, and easier on this poorly stitched-together body. But she'd needed time to think. It would have been the human thing to do.

Rayne had shed that skin.

She walked in silence, with nothing but the dim light of the stars and the glow of the crescent moon used to be a comfort to her, the hum of the cicada song. And of it all, Hawthorne's ever-present hand in hers, guiding her through the darkest parts of the forest. She stretched her fingers.

Her hands were empty.

Balling them into fists, she headed into town.

It makes sense to start here. They will all come running and that way I do not have to chase them.

Rayne stood before the church, taking note of the three cars in the parking lot despite the dark. *One of those must belong to Pastor Creary. It's a shame that he will be first.*

With the shadows that she had kept beneath her skin before, reaching for them was a stab in the dark, a clumsy guess.

Lightning was sure.

Her finger tips sparked, her arm trembling with the force of it and unlike her husband's magic that she had to beg for, to root out, her lightning came when she called it. Rayne envisioned the church, struck, the roof collapsing and the base of the building on fire, and then it was.

The power whipped through her, cracking her spine with how forcefully it pulled her. It stung, a swarm of wasps all attacking her at once but it was all lost on the sound of her laughter.

She stumbled but quickly regained her footing, watching as fire consumed the building.

I did that. Me! The pathetic little butterfly!

"Rayne?"

She turned, her destruction silhouetted behind her. Pastor Creary gawked at her, but when he saw what lay behind her, he froze wide eyed, illuminated by the orange light of the fire. *Looks like he wasn't in there. Good for him.*

"What have you done?"

I don't have time for this. That won't be enough.

Rayne attempted to walk past him but he stood in her way, obscuring the path. She scowled. "Move."

"Your face looks so—you—it's been you this whole time."

Rayne pushed past him. "You can run if you'd like, I won't chase you. There's still time for you to get out of town."

He grabbed a fistful of her shirt. "I protected you from them and everyone was right. It's always been you!"

She looked down at his hand and then back at him slowly. "Don't touch me."

"Demon—!"

Light flashed, sparking from her palm and knocked her to the ground, spending Pastor Creary flying several feet away from her. Rayne scrunched her nose, covering her mouth with her sleeve to keep from smelling the burning flesh and melted fabric. "I did give you a chance to save yourself," she remarked to his corpse.

One down. The rest to go.

It was fitting that all of Bury should burn.

With Persimmon dead, there was nothing in this town worth salvaging. *I can't believe that I didn't see it before. But now, with only one eye, I see clearer than I ever have.*

It was a town worth burning and perhaps that was why it went up in flames so easily. Rayne moved slowly through the streets, back paths, cutting it all down. Each strike of lightning taking more from her than the one before it—a cost that she should have considered before but there was no helping it now.

She staggered from the street onto the curb, resting her forehead against the cool brick of the building closest to her, panting. Her heart hadn't slowed in its frantic thudding and it was becoming increasingly harder to breathe. "Fucking figures. The power of a god has clearly done nothing to shift my luck." *Where are you, Dresden, you fucker?*

You better get here before I keel over.

Surely the dozens of humans burnt alive or crushed in the rubble of her destruction had to be enough to catch his eye? *But what if it wasn't? What if I killed all of these people for nothing?*

"Mama!" Across the street, a little girl knelt in the rubble of what used to be the library, clinging to the arm of her mother, crushed beneath it. "Mama, wake up!"

Ellie May. Terri Mckninny's daughter.

Rayne's brow furrowed at the thought. *Glad her mother's dead, but her, she hasn't got anyone now, does she?* It was a cruelty Rayne had never intended to inflict.

She turned, resting her back against the building, leaning on it for support. "Ellie May Mckinny," Rayne called and the little girl jumped, squeezing her mother's hand. "Get out of here."

"But my—"

"Your Mama's in Heaven. Not your time yet. You know the way to the big welcome sign just outside of town?"

Ellie May nodded. "Good. Now, you start walking and don't stop until you see it."

She looked between Rayne and her mother. *Goddammit.* Rayne had never been good with kids and that certainly wasn't going to change now. "Get outta here before I send your ass to Heaven too!"

The girl screamed and took off running toward the edge of town.

Rayne looked around for any wisps that might have been near by, now that she could see them so easily, she'd learned that there was always one floating around somewhere.

"Wisp," she called, gesturing to one just over head. "Follow that girl. Don't let her get hurt. Keep her on the right path and don't leave her until someone finds her that'll keep her safe. Do that and I'll pay you something of equal value, nothing less and nothing more."

The wisp brushed against her hand before it darted off in the direction Elli May had gone.

Rayne sighed, closing her eyes a moment. *Alright, back to it. No rest for the wicked. Dresden still isn't here and it can't all have been for nothing.*

Pain was still very much something that Rayne could feel, she had come to find. In an attempt to be strategic, she had limped her way up the beginning of the mountain to get a better view of the town below and pick off any stragglers.

Every muscle was on fire, her joints screaming in agony, still she stood leaning against a tree to steady herself and watching the town she'd grown up in burn.

The ashes of it stung her eyes, streaking down her cheeks.

"Tears for what you've done?" asked a voice from behind her, like a needle into flesh. The hairs on the back of her neck rose, every cell in her body singing in memory of it.

Rayne turned to face him, all else forgotten in his presence. She'd worked so hard, broken her body into a dozen pieces, sold her life, traded her eye, all of it to get her right here.

"No," Rayne said with a smile of shattered glass. "All my tears have been spent."

CHAPTER FORTY-SEVEN

rayne

Dresden made a soft sound in his throat, sitting back on his hind legs, his wings tucked against his back. "You've changed. Something more about you now," he said, cocking his head to better fix her with the eye on his forehead. "Or less, perhaps."

"Where is my husband?" she hissed, voice cracked and raw from the black smoke rising like the souls of the dead behind her. "Where is Hawthorne?"

"I beg your pardon?"

"Hawthorne. Where have you hidden them?"

Dresden's wings unfurled, expanding to their full span, his eyes looking everywhere and nowhere. "You," He pointed to her and then the fire below, "did all of this to ask me *a question?* This is certainly the first time someone has gone to such lengths for my sake. There is a strange sort of flattery in it... although, there are no punishments that exist for the atrocities you've committed. We will have to create some."

"Tell me what you've done with them," she demanded, her hand clenching into a fist at her side. "I will not ask you again, King or not."

Dresden blinked at her again and his bleating laughter only fanned the flames of her anger. He folded in on himself, shrinking so that they were at eye level. "A little power and you think that you can demand things of me, witchling?"

Dresden gestured around them. "Look at what you've done! You were so weak that you could not even manage a spell to conjure me yourself! Instead like some *vampire*, you had to drain the life of an entire town in the hopes that I would even notice you." His laughter continued as he nearly doubled over.

"But you have come all this way so I will honor your journey and tell you the truth. With every eye of mine, I see all possibilities. And there is no world, no timeline where you see your husband again."

Each word that he spoke set a searing coal in her belly, burning her up. Rayne's breath caught in her throat, and the tears that had been claimed by the smoke began anew, though she could not allow herself to admit their genesis.

His words were the very root of her fear.

"You're lying." Rayne forced every ounce of conviction she could into her voice.

"Why would *I* waste my time lying to something such as *you*? The two of you shall remain parted. You will rot alone, become a portion for foxes. Then one day I will walk upon the earth of your grave and laugh to myself when I think of you both. I have seen it with all. Your fate is as sealed as those you condemned."

That she and Hawthorne would remain apart for the rest of eternity. That they were destined for loss, star-crossed to remain separated as the sun and moon.

Fate will make no fool of me.

With the amount of energy she'd exerted earlier, there was no way she could fight him. If she'd had a chance of doing so before, it was long gone now. It would have been smarter for her to attempt to outsmart him, to play the game of spirits.

Her body moved before the thought caught up with it, Rayne lunged for Dresden's head, digging her heels into his nose to steady herself.

"What are you—"

Rayne jammed her fingers into the eye seated at his forehead and with a feral cry pulled it as hard as she could, lightning sparking in her palm until the sinew snapped.

The scream that Dresden let out could have split the sky. He shook Rayne off of him, his hands flying to his face to nurse his wound. Ichor bubbled between his fingers. She tucked and rolled, dulling her landing.

His eye pulsed in her hand, no bigger than a grapefruit and it stared directly at her. Rayne stared in disbelief of what she'd just done. *I-I can't believe that worked. Guess you and your thousand eyes didn't see that coming, did you, fucker?*

"You wretch!" Dresden bellowed, shaking the ground as he writhed in the dirt. "I will spend the next century skinning you alive, piece by piece!"

Oh, shit!

Adrenaline surged through her and every ache or pain was quickly forgotten. Rayne bolted through the forest, cradling the bloody, pulpy rabbit eye to her chest. The thing kicked and pulsed within her palm as if it were desperate to return to its master.

Rayne dared a single look over her shoulder. Dresden was crawling through the dirt on his belly, his ears, twitching as he listened for her. His head snapped in her direction just as she looked over and he scrambled toward her. *Fast.*

She dove behind a tree just in time to dodge one of Dresden's massive wings sweeping through the forest as he miraculously moved in the wrong direction. "When I am done with you," he snarled, twigs snapped beneath his feet somewhere to her left. "The Fates themselves will pity you. I will show you new meanings to the word agony."

The eye was actively fighting against her now, vibrating against her chest. *Oh no you don't. You're staying with me. If you helped him see, you can do the same for me.*

Hand covering her mouth to hide her breathing, she tore her eye cover off and held the eye just above her own socket. *Please work.* Before she could talk herself out of it, Rayne pushed the eye against her socket.

The moment it touched her skin, it stung and for a moment the pain was too much for her to bear, her knees nearly giving on her as she struggled to stay hidden. The eye shrunk to accommodate and slithered inside of her socket with a wet squelch.

As quickly as it had come, the sensation was gone and her lost vision returned. Clearer than it had ever been before.

She didn't have time to focus on that though. She was going to use this same eye to get her husband back.

"Where is Hawthorne?" Rayne whispered to the night and her stolen eye, ignoring the screaming, bellowing creature that sought her blood. "Take me to them."

Instantly, a red thread emerged extending from her ring finger, where her wedding ring was branded into her skin. Redder than blood and warm, the thread glowed softly and knotted around her finger before slithering like a snake into the forest. "Hawthorne."

Rayne took off like a fool, the danger forgotten but not gone.

"You dare," Dresden snarled from somewhere behind her and she glanced over her shoulder to see the rage boiling in his scarlet eyes like the dying embers of a fire. "Put something of mine in that rotting body?"

Rayne reached for that power she had not yet explored and had no idea how to wield: silence. The Thunder Being had said that she could move through the world unheard. She could only think of the sweet pear tree that she had spoken to and the grass with all its little hands. Maybe they could hear her. "Hide me," Rayne begged, willing her prayer into the Earth. "Protect me from his sight. Let me move as silent as the grave. Cover me in a darkness that he cannot see through. Please."

Rayne felt the forest respond before she heard it, the tree branches creaking as if a great weight had settled on them and Dresden's shouts grew distant. "Chimera!" He cried miles away from her now.

"Thank you," she whispered to the soil and all of the beautiful worms that too must have done their part for her. Rayne ran, following her crimson-colored salvation deeper into the woods.

The thread led her to a clearing that she had never seen before, one that sat at the end of the river that ran through the mountains. The water from it collected in a small waterfall, tumbling down into another part of the river. Her thread continued through the waterfall to a cave directly behind it, with slippery rocks she would need to scale to get inside of it.

Rayne could still hear Dresden, an orchestra of rage and agony. *He will not find me before I find Hawthorne, of that I am sure.*

Once she and her wraith, her precious nightmare, were reunited, she did not care what happened to her. They could die, be torn apart at the exact same moment, none of it mattered to her as long as they were together.

Her journey over the rocks and behind the waterfall was not graceful but she moved with the determination of a woman possessed. Rayne had not been this close to her husband since that last afternoon in the field where she had been drowning in her love for them and luxuriating in their laughter.

Spring had barely come when they'd been ripped away from her and now summer was on its last legs.

The thread slithered deeper still into the cave, disappearing into darkness. The mouth of the cave was shaped like the mouth of a great beast, the jagged rocks there threatening to tear her apart. But if her husband rested in the belly of the monster, in the heart of hell, then so be it.

Rayne followed because she could do nothing else. Despite whatever fate may have been written for her, *this* was her path.

"I am going into the ground to meet you, Hawthorne," she swore into the darkness, praying that they could hear her. "Even if it is to a shared grave, you and I will be together again."

CHAPTER FORTY-EIGHT

rayne

D resden's bellowing screams shook the cave around her, growing closer.

The forest had only bought her time, not saved her. *I need to be faster.* The rabbit's eye even with its adjustments was ill suited for her skull and her peripheral vision was too vast. She swore, tripping over a rock and nearly slicing her hands open in an effort to catch herself.

Blood pooled somewhere that she could not see but felt against her hand all the same and then, the cut sewed itself up again as if she were a ragdoll. She felt the edges of her skin sliding back together as they knitted themselves up. Her stomach rolled with nausea at the sensation paired with the copper tang of blood and the acrid sting of her own fear. And magic. Magic.

"The thread!" she hissed, hands snatching at the air until they found purchase in the thickness of it and held fast.

Dresden's voice came again, undoubtedly nearer to the mouth of the cave. "I can smell your blood!"

No, Rayne thought, her breath catching as she tried to run, trying to find some way to move faster. *I will not be caught, I will not allow anymore obstacles between myself and my beast. I will not lose.*

Her body moved before her mind could will her to, something more feral taking over. With the thread in one hand, she used the other to feel her way along the wall of the cave, pressing deeper and deeper into the cave. The movement was slow, much too slow for her liking and she urged herself forward, faster but the darkness and her surroundings would not allow it.

Gradually, the sounds behind her faded away and the shape of the cave began to change. Only then did she rest, exhaustion pulling her under before she could even think to fight it.

Rayne didn't know how long she slept for, only that when she woke, her body was still sore but much less so. *Another benefit of god power, it seems.*

She'd fallen asleep with the thread squeezed in her palms and she nearly sobbed in relief to find it still there. Waiting for her to follow. *I'm coming.*

Space within the cave lessened the further she ventured in, movement became difficult. What had once been a cave was now a cavern, no larger than her body that she had to shimmy through. Every new movement alerted her as to how much smaller the space was becoming with every breath, how much less room she had with every passing second.

Her only companion was the sound of her panicked breathing in the silence and her trembling knees. The world squeezed her, tightening in on her again and she could feel the other side of the wall against her sternum, nearly trapping her like a moth under glass.

Rayne paused.

What if this path only continues to narrow? What if I keep going and I eventually am torn apart? Or squished? How will I save Hawthorne then?

Her breath came shorter and shorter as she thought about what lay ahead, desperately gulping up what little oxygen there was left in this place. "I can't go back," she dared to say aloud, her words tumbling out like rocks and swallowed by the jaws of the cave.

Clutching the thread as hard as she could, she kept going.

Dragging herself deeper into the Earth, the world began to change shape again, she could hear voices. Gossamer soft, they feathered against Rayne's ear. **"What do you think you'll find down here, girl?"**

You're alone in the dark, Rayne assured herself. *There is no one else here with you. Your mind is playing tricks on you.*

"Who are you, witch-child?"

"A rabbit eyed fool. She will sour the ground with her quest."

No one else is here, no one else could possibly be here, She assured herself. *Just keep moving, just keep going down. There is nowhere else to go but down.*

"Who are you to think that you can deny Fate?"

Hawthorne, Rayne thought to them, desperate to fill the space with anything other than the sound of her own breathing and call of strangers. *Do you remember the night before our wedding when we gave each other our wedding rings? When we tattooed one another, mixed our blood and made it so we'd never be apart again? We filled nearly half of a bowl with our blood and ink and I remember thinking that it was so much, too much. How foolish I was. We should have filled the bowl—how much blood would we have had to spill to be inseparable? For the only way for someone to have extracted Rayne from Hawthorne or Hawthorne from Rayne would be to split our very atoms? I want, should anyone or anything dare to separate you from I or I from you, that it would be felt through the entire world. The entire Universe. Please, let us be inevitable, let us be more brutal than any natural disaster. Let us be—*

A strand of Rayne's hair moved, as if some air had brushed past her. A breeze.

Rayne yanked on the thread as hard as she could, using it to pull herself the rest of the way through the cave, ignoring the screaming of her skin as it scraped against the walls.

The other end of the thread tugged back.

I found you.

Yanked out of the cave, Rayne found herself pulled down into a different type of darkness and she caught the briefest glance of light before she hit the water like a ton of bricks.

Thick water filled her nose as the air was knocked out of her lungs, tasting of moss and leaves. She released the thread and thrashed her legs, kicking toward the surface as hard as she could until she broke it, gasping and coughing up thick water.

She seemed to have landed in some underground swamp and she bobbed in the inky water like a buoy. Rayne paused only to seek the edge of the water and wade her way through it. The thread waited for her. She flopped out of it as ungracefully as possible and flipped onto her back, chest heaving and eyes pinched shut.

I made it... to wherever the fuck I am now.

Blinking the water out of her eyes, she stared up at wherever she had fallen through, finding a dark gray, dirt ceiling, rounded like a dome. There was a hole where she had crashed through and from the darkness of it, she could see dozens of listless, milky eyes staring back at her.

Rayne's hand flew over her mouth to catch her shriek and she rolled over onto her stomach, scrambling as far away from the eyes as she could. The grass beneath her was soaked and the air itself reeked with dampness. The thread was still waiting for her.

The swamps sat beneath a hill, black salt hay waving in an invisible breeze. At the top of it, a soft amber light glowed offering little comfort in darkness.

I have been fed a steady diet of nothing, Rayne thought. *I will take a fraction of anything over that.*

Swamp water squished in her boots and each step came as a clap of thunder, echoing in the silence. Rayne ignored it.

Her chest heaved with effort, each step up the sharp hill requiring more breath than the thin air around her was able to support.

When Rayne finally reached the hilltop, she doubled over, drinking down greedy gulps of air. "Fucking hell," she managed between breaths and when she finally found hers again, she allowed herself to look at what lay before her.

Clusters of jagged, prickling glass just as dark as the world around her shot up from the ground toward an invisible sky. Orbs of light flickered within them like candles and brightened a path that she could only just make out the edges of. Below her snow piled lazily, blanketing everything in white. Rayne knelt, scooping it into her palm. Confusion contorted her features as her hand remained sensationless. *Or maybe it's not my hand that's numb?*

She glanced over her shoulder down at the bog she'd landed in. The water had been real, still drenched her clothes and skin, and yet the snow was no more than a breeze on her flesh.

Strange. Armed with her breath and sopping boots, she began the trek into the strange glass. The glass was less of a collection of random spirals shooting up toward the sky and more like buildings, buildings that almost formed a city.

Though her feet lacked any sensation, another replaced what she should have been feeling, sound.

The sound of an entire world—laughter, hushed voices speaking in tones that she could not decipher. Air rushed past her like a train, and she dove out of the way, sliding on her stomach in the snow. Turning back to catch sight of whatever it had been, she blinked.

There was nothing. No one around her. No tracks in the snow outside of her own. Whatever was down here, even with The Thing in Corn's vision and Dresden's eye, she could not see them.

Or maybe they weren't meant to be seen.

The voices that had before been indifferent to her, honed in on her. Narrowing their invisible gazes like a ray of light through a magnifying lens.

"*Who are you?*" one of them asked.

"*How did you get here? You don't belong here.*"

Rayne hurried to her feet and dashed back down the path, deeper into the city of fractals.

"Hawthorne!" she called. "Hawthorne, where are you?"

Laughter billowed like smoke around her in response, and the invisible city leaned closer while a chorus of voices hissed, sang, and jeered a variety of questions

"*What makes you think you can come down here?*"

"*Did you think that you're better than any of us, that you can walk so untethered and free while the rest of us remain chained?*"

Rayne covered her ears because she couldn't answer. She was no one, she was nothing, she was desperate.

The familiar weight tugged into her chest, yanking her forward, and though she could not see the thread that bound her to Hawthorne, she felt it all the same. When she saw a clearing at the city's edge, she knew that they would be there.

Voices forgotten, Rayne ran as fast as her legs could carry her to the clearing of barren trees, and the massive body caught between them like a mayfly in a spider's web.

CHAPTER FORTY-NINE
hawthorne

H awthorne was tired.

Exhaustion was nothing that they had thought they could physically experience before their imprisonment. But now, after however many weeks, months—had it been months?

They were sure that this is what it must have felt like to be dead. But they were alive and being fed on by the trees.

If they had any sense of pride left, they might have been offended at such an idea that something dares to feed off of them. But Hawthorne could think of nothing that that wasn't *her*.

Rayne was alive and she was alone. They'd left her and that was a truth that set iron in their belly. This thought alone hurt more than the branches that had fused to their flesh, the branches that had pressed through their skin and tangled in their veins.

The Under had been noisier than usual but it was not entirely uncommon, nothing that would have alerted them to anything strange.

Footsteps, loud and clumsy, sounded through the orchard, trees shifting, swaying. A head poked through, searching for something. Hawthorne recognized the curl pattern, falling out of a loose braid.

Two in one day. Lucky me.

This phantom was different from the others, it hardly looked like Rayne. It was wearing a dirty, tattered sweatshirt and muddy, squelching boots. She never looked this unkempt, and the closer it got, the worse this recreation of her appeared. Her hair was too long and streaked with dozens of pearly white strands but worst of all was the phantom's face.

Its cheeks too hollow, there were lines on her face that didn't exist in reality but it was her eye that sparked their irritation. Her left eye was gone and replaced by a bulging, red eye. A rabbit's eye.

The phantom approached them slowly. "Hawthorne, is that you? You don't look like yourself."

They turned their face away, not wanting to look at this mutilation of Rayne another second. "Leave."

The phantom stopped and then, its hand flew to its mouth, the human eye growing misty while the rabbit one remained unblinking. "It is you."

The emotion in her voice— "You aren't her and we both know it. Just... stop."

"*It is* me, Hawth."

Hawth. None of them had used that nickname for them yet. *But that doesn't mean they won't. This isn't her.*

"If you step any closer," they warned, baring their teeth. "I will—"

The phantom knocked into them, wetting their stomach with tears as it wrapped its arms around their torso. "I was so scared that I'd never see you again."

Her scent was wrong. Yes, they could smell her usual scent but it was buried by a dozen others; stagnant water, ash, smoke, blood and *Bury*. None of the other ghosts had smelled of anything from the outside world, just her stolen scent.

Hawthorne shook their head. *I will not fall for this again. It is not her.*

"She never could have made it down here," they said, looking down at the ghost clinging to them.

"I did."

"She wouldn't know the way. Humans *can't* make it."

"I made my own way. I don't know if I'm human anymore."

It sounds so much like her. I cannot do this again if it is not her.

The phantom looked up at them, tears leaving trails through the dirt on her face. "What did they do to you?" She sniffled. "Why don't you recognize me?"

"I will not play your game."

The phantom wiped her face. "I don't care. I don't care that you don't believe it's me. I'm going to stay right here until you do."

Stubborn like her.

To prove its point, the phantom stood on the top of its toes, struggling to reach their lips, only just brushing them against theirs. Their body responded immediately, pulse racing and blood singing in their veins. "*Rayne.*"

Her fingers reached up to play at the end of their curls and she nuzzled against their chest. "Hi."

It took every ounce of restraint for them not to risk pulling against their bonds so that they could sweep her up. "What are you doing down here? Do you have any idea how dangerous it is?"

Rayne shook her head. "I had to find you. I thought you were dead and I had to see you. Where you go, I go, remember?"

Their chest felt as if it was splintering. "Yes, but you—how did you get here? How could you have found me?"

"I followed the red thread," she said, looking down at her ring finger. "It might have been there the whole time, I don't know. I couldn't see it before but now I can."

Hawthorne studied her rabbit eye closer, the thing simmered with power. Power beyond what Rayne should have been able to grasp. "Is that Dresden's eye?" She nodded. "How did you convince him to bargain it away?"

Rayne shrugged, sheepishly tucking a white curl behind her ear. "I didn't. I took it from him."

Took it. Affection for her flooded their senses and they leaned forward enough to brush their lips against her cheek. "You little brute."

"How do I get you out of this?" she asked, nodding toward the trees.

I should tell her to leave. She can't stay down here. Some part of her is mortal yet and that will bar her from residing here. I should but I can't.

Hawthorne should have told her to save herself and go back to the surface, promise to return for her when their time was up. She might still have a life somewhere.

But she was a criminal in every sense of the word now within their world. If she had truly stolen from a King, it was only a matter of time before they tracked her down. Hawthorne was already being punished, what was more?

I would rather suffer chasing freedom with her than spend another second apart.

"If we do this, they're going to come for us."

Rayne nodded. "Okay."

"It will be bad. Mercy is not something my kind is known for. We *will* suffer, both of us."

"As long as we're together."

If it were not for their bonds, Hawthorne might have fallen to their knees for her. They had never loved before her and there would never be an *after* Rayne. There was only this thing between them, hungry and holy.

"So," Rayne said, stepping away from them to assess the trees. "How do I get these things off of you?"

"I am not sure," they admitted. She stepped closer and reached for the branches that had worked into them, and they tried to shrink away from her. "Don't! They're parasitic. They will burn their way into you if you touch them."

"No," Rayne took a few more steps back and pointed her palm toward the left tree. The air hissed with magic. Her palm glowed red, her finger tips turning white. "I refuse to burn."

White flashed before their eyes, blinding them in a wave of heat and light. The tree squealed, releasing Hawthorne as it retreated back into the ground. Their arm hung limply at their side, fingers twitching as their nerves began the slow process of stitching themselves back together.

Rayne had been knocked into the dirt from the blow back of the blast. She exhaled, pulled herself to her feet and shook her hands. "Okay. One more."

This time Hawthorne was prepared enough to close their eyes, and when they were released, they fell to their knees, barely able to support themself.

"Hawth! You okay?" She rushed over to them, placing her hand at their spine to help hold them up.

"Fine. My body will repair itself as time goes on." They looked to Rayne, the lightning struck scars up along the backs of her hands. "You conjured that. You shouldn't be able to do that. A human cannot conjure."

"I know."

"Did you steal that too?"

Rayne shook her head. "It was a gift."

There is no such thing as a gift. "In exchange for what?"

She bit her lip, her fingers tapping against their back. "Can you stand?"

Hawthorne staggered to their feet, their muscles straining for a moment before they righted themself. Rayne remained pressed to their side, trying her best to support them despite the fact that in their current form, they nearly dwarfed her.

"Why do you look like that, are you hurt?"

Their appearance had hardly occurred to them during their captivity but now they could see why it might have alarmed her. Hawthorne was caught between forms, half in a human skin, half shadow, half animal. "No, I'm not hurt. I think when Dresden pulled me down, I was fighting, trying to shift out of his grasp and got stuck in the struggle. I should be able to shift once I'm stronger."

"Rayne," they reached down to trace a half clawed hand through the hair that had fallen into her face, "what did you pay for all of this? Why do you look so different? And *your* eye—where is your eye?"

"I lost it," she admitted, her lower trembling. "Bargained it away without meaning to. Everything else was on purpose. I traded a few years off of my life—"

"How many?"

"Twelve and a day."

Twelve years. Years that we should have had together. "Why would you do that?"

"How else was I going to find you?"

Me. She did all of this—her eye—her life—for me.

A new sensation trickled into their chest, cold and dense. They hated it. If the situation were different, if they were anywhere else, Hawthorne might have asked her what it meant.

Instead, their thumb traced along the seam of her lower lip. "We need to leave. To get above ground at least."

Rayne nodded. "I'm with you."

Although their strength was beginning to return, the pair of them were still moving much too slow for their liking. Rayne remained glued to their side, letting them lean against her for support though they tried desperately not to.

They caught her looking around at their surroundings, watching everything that they passed by. *Of course, she's curious.*

The Under was a strange concoction, a jumble of geography that was nearly impossible to navigate unless one was born here or belonged.

"I spent a decent portion of my childhood here," Hawthorne said before they cleared their throat. "Not where we are currently but deeper into the Under. There was a bog, and a forest nearby. I frequented the world above as much as I could. I did not like feeling caged."

There was much of their life that they should have shared with her; their mother, their sisters, and though they hated him, their father. *It is only occurring to me how unfair it was that I knew all of her and she knew so little of me.*

"I feel a deep affection for this place. I have not considered the Under my home for quite some time but it is a piece of me."

"Did you live somewhere else?"

"Yes. Far away with my... father for a time. He is from the coldest forest in the world, he resides there still. My mother lives here."

"Do you look like her?"

Hawthorne chuckled. "Hardly. I carry more of his traits than I do of hers."

Her hand coasted along their spine as far as she could reach at this position. "This is a beautiful place, strange as it is. I'm glad that I got to see it."

"I wish that I could show you more," Hawthorne said with a tight smile.

"I would have liked that."

"You will meet my mother, at least."

Rayne stopped. "What?"

Hawthorne stilled alongside her. "She is the only way out for us both. I do not have enough strength for the other path and you cannot travel that way. So, it must be hers."

Rayne's arms locked around herself. "Where is she?"

They nodded down the small hill to the thick bog expanding as far as the eye could see. "Down the way."

"Does she know about me, us?"

Hawthorne shook their head. "I have not been home in some time. A decade at least," they admitted. "And you will have to hold your breath as we approach. If she smells the air from your lungs before I introduce you, she will tear them out. She is fast despite her age."

They expected her eyes to go wide, for her to look up at them in fear as she often had when they told her of their kind. Instead, she set her mouth into a hard line and drew in a deep breath. "Alright. Tell me when."

Where has your fear gone?

When they were finally down the hill, Hawthorne paused and Rayne did the same. "Stay here. Hold your breath until I introduce you."

They took a few steps forward, angling themself in front of Rayne just in case. Hawthorne called for her in their mother tongue. "*Mother. I require an audience with you, please.*"

The surface of the water rippled and her arms emerged first, black as peat, and Hawthorne took a step back to accommodate for her size. Their mother hauled herself up to the edge of the bog, emerald amphibian eyes blinking up at them. She stretched her long, webbed legs out from under her and stood, crouching down to meet them. Her clammy skin was kissed with lichen, and moss had entangled itself in her soaked black curls. A dress of ferns clung loosely to her wrinkled body.

Hawthorne bowed their head, mindful to show her the proper respect she was due. She scoffed, reaching toward them with her webbed hands, smoothing their hair. "*Hello, child.*"

"Might we speak in English?" they asked so that Rayne could understand them.

"English? Why?"

Hawthorne gestured behind them to Rayne. "I am not alone. I have brought my wife. She is human. Please do not eat her." They looked over their shoulder and nodded to Rayne.

She exhaled and their mother's head snapped in her direction, sniffing the air. She squinted at Rayne, their wife's breath allowing her to be seen. "Human? Are you sure?"

"It is complicated."

"It must be, for you have been gone and now you return to me, married. To a human no less."

"I am sorry."

She waved a dismissive hand. "I am not displeased. I will meet her. Come, child."

Rayne stepped from behind them, walking to the edge of the water without hesitation. She glared up at their mother with her chin raised and her shoulders squared.

So much of her is changed. I will try to make space for the pieces of her that I have yet to meet.

"What is your name, daughter?" their mother asked, surprising Hawthorne. An acceptance of her already.

"I will not give it," Rayne replied. "Unless you offer yours."

Their mother smirked. "I will not give you mine either. How is it that you found your way down here?"

"I crawled."

She blinked, leaning closer. "For what purpose?"

Rayne did not answer her verbally, instead she reached for Hawthorne's hand, pulling it to her side.

Their mother's eyes followed the motion and she sat back, slipping partially into the water sloshing around her. "I see."

Their mother continued to fix Rayne with a hard look and their wife did not flinch, she did not look away.

"I am not displeased with this union," their mother said finally. Hawthorne was not presumptuous enough to believe that they could read their mother but she seemed to like Rayne already. "I do wish that you had told me. I would have liked to attend your nuptials. I bear no anger. I know how you are and I accept you. But that is how I know you have come to ask me for something."

"I have."

"Name it."

"We need to get topside. I do not have the strength to take us myself and she cannot go the other way. Some part of her is human still," they explained. "I would ask that you open the way for us and we will take The Ascent back."

Hawthorne's mother was one of the few liminal creatures that walked the earth. They were the gods of the in between. Their mother was *Goddess of Where Land Meets Water* and their father the *God of Where Dark Meets Light*. There were more, but Hawthorne knew little of them. All they knew was that some of them—like their mother—were just as old as The Three Kings if not older.

They were guardians of passage ways that connected realms and she was the only one who could get them out from The Under now.

"I know of your punishment, child," their mother sighed. "It pained me to hear of it. Were your sentence longer, I would have intervened."

"My crimes are not your burdens to bear."

Their mother tsked. "Motherhood is no *burden*. You are mine and no ruling will change what I will do for you. I fear no King."

"I know."

Their mother leaned down to kiss the top of their head. "I will do this for you, child. You owe me nothing. But hear me, I cannot hold the way open for you both for long. You must not dally. The Ascent is no easy journey. Walk sure and fast. If you falter, even I cannot save you." She slid fully back into the water as silently as she'd come.

Hawthorne glanced down at Rayne, her face damp. She was crying again.

"Hey. What's wrong?"

"She loves you," Rayne swallowed, wiping at her cheek. "She's doing this because she loves you."

Oh.

Of course this would hurt her.

Their wife had spent her entire life living outside of normal relationships, begging for scraps that were always begrudgingly given.

Hawthorne wished that they could tell her their mother would love her like a daughter; she wouldn't. Their kind did not do the sort of in-law relationships that humans did. While their mother may have accepted Rayne, she would never treat her with even a fraction of the affection that she gave Hawthorne.

It was the one thing they could never give her.

But what they could give her was themself. Hawthorne pulled her close and kissed her hair a dozen times. "I love *you*. Okay?" She nodded against them. "We need only make The Ascent and then we will be home. For however long we have it."

The bog water rippled and beneath them the ground shook; at water's edge a stone archway emerged, dripping in water and covered in moss.

Their mother's voice bellowed from the deep "Walk quickly, my dear. Do not stop. Do not look anywhere but ahead. Do not touch anything. Do not lose your footing. Do not speak no matter what you hear. When you have reached the end, there will be a light. Follow it."

"Thank you, Mother," they called after her.

"There are rules: the human must go first, our kind last. Good luck, child."

The human must go first.

CHAPTER FIFTY

rayne

*T*he human must go first.

Absolutely the fuck not! I spent months looking for Hawthorne, I'm not going to just dive headfirst into something without them.

Hawthorne must have already seen the defiance on her face, reaching for her hand. "Rayne—"

"No. No way."

"There is not another way for us to get out of here."

"But you said there was! What it is it? Tell me. I'm stronger than you think, we can—"

"*Rayne,*" they snapped, startling her as they gripped her face between their hands. "We can only go in one at a time. You are not alone. I will be in there with you. I know, *I know.* But we have to do this. We don't have time."

"It's not a trap?" Rayne whispered, hating how small and fragile she sounded to her own ear.

"It's not a trap. I am going to be exactly two steps behind you, you hear me?" She nodded and they kissed her forehead before releasing her. "Go."

Rayne looked back at them once before she stepped through the archway and into the dark.

The tunnel was a void. Even with Dresden's eye, she could see nothing.

If it were not for the motion of her feet on the ground, Rayne wouldn't have known anything was happening. Her footsteps made no sound, gobbled up by the nothingness. And as she listened for Hawthorne behind her...

Nothing.

The temptation to turn back tugged at her, prickling against her skin as winter chill. Was this really how things were supposed to be in this place? What if something had gone wrong and Hawthorne was not able to enter with her?

I can't turn around. They said that they were behind me. They have to be.

Rayne kept walking and the silence was deafening.

Everything around her was wrung out with lack. Lack of sound, lack of sensation, lack of scent, of sight. This place was a blackhole, eating away at the edges of her sanity—how long had she been walking?

Am I even moving anymore? Had I ever been?

She kept walking.

Gradually sound began to fill in around her until she was surrounded by a dull roar. To have nothing and then suddenly to have it all set her heart pounding, catching in her throat and ringing through her ears like drums.

A hiss of something shot by her ear and she started, faltering a moment at the suddenness of it but still she kept walking, refusing to allow her feet to stray from the path.

The sound of fire, of flickering flames and cracking heat followed her, just at her heels. Heat pricked at the back of her neck as she could feel the fire just at her back. *Am I going to burn to death in here?*

Screams, dozens of them, stabbed into her from all sides, assaulting her ears to the point of pain. They screamed her name, they called her a monster, a feral bitch and somewhere, a baby cried. Burning flesh filled her nose and she gagged, covering her nose and mouth. *It's just a memory,* she told herself, closing her eyes as tightly as she could to keep the smoke from getting into them. *It's not happening, nothing is burning. You're fine.*

The fire and the screams subsided after an eternity, and the silence closed in on her again.

Rayne kept walking.

"*They are not behind you.*" The voice of Hawthorne's mother slithered into her ear. "*You're walking all this way alone. They left you.*"

Rayne bit her lip and continued to gaze ahead into the emptiness. Hawthorne would never leave her of their own volition. She knew this.

"*But do you truly?*" her in-law continued. "*You have caused my beloved child nothing but trouble. They changed for you. They shrunk themselves down for you.*"

Her breath hitched in her throat as the words sunk into her gut.

There it was, the thought that had haunted her since the day that she had claimed Hawthorne, that they were lessening themselves for her sake.

Rayne dug her nails into the palms of her hands. *Hawthorne never does anything that they don't want to do. They love me.*

"*If they love you then why aren't they behind you?*"

Searing tears stung at her eyes, though she begged herself not to cry. Hawthorne was behind her, they had promised her that they would be and they had never once broken a promise to her. They would not start now.

Yet she could not shake the fear nipping at her heels. What if this had all been one big charade? A way for them to save her and sacrifice themselves?

She could not imagine Hawthorne breaking a promise to her but throwing themselves to the wind if it would save her? *That* they would do.

Every muscle in her body was poised to turn around and check to see if they were there, but Hawthorne's words kept her from doing so. The look that they'd had in their eyes, they looked *scared*. Whatever this hell path was, something about it had them worried.

She had no way of knowing where Hawthorne was, what was going through their mind.

"*Look what you've done now, snapdragon,*" her grandmother sighed into her ear, the soft scent of the roses from her garden and rotten crabapples blanketing her. "*I hardly recognize you anymore. Have you really forgotten everything that I taught you? All the love I tried to give you?*"

She's dead. She's been dead for years, you know this. Stop listening.

"How can I claim you now, broken girl? Monster child? Drunk on magic and lies. You've killed. You took so many lives, destroyed an entire town, and for what? A demon that will only drag you down to hell where I can never see you again? Did you think that I would be waiting for you in the flames, nhiluwès?"

"You're a murderer and you make me sick."

She knew that her grandmother was dead and that whatever was walking with her, speaking to her was not the kind old woman that had loved her. But there was a kernel of truth to the thing's words that she cut her teeth on no matter how she tried to swallow it.

Her grandmother would hate what she had become. *I don't think He'll listen but I hope the Creator has kept her blind. Never let her see what's left of me.*

The thing seemed to hear her silent plea and slipped back into the darkness, knife sheathed, and Rayne breathed a soft sigh of relief.

How far? She thought. *How much farther until we can be freed from this dreadful place? Until I can scream?*

"It's not fair, Ray. The way things worked out."

The sound of her voice nearly sent Rayne to her knees. She *almost* stopped. *Persimmon.*

From the corner of her eye, she caught sight of a coyote keeping pace with her; its fur illuminating its face. Green eyes stayed fixed on her.

"I loved my life, you know. I struggled and I worked so hard to make something that was mine, and after years, I finally had it. I was gonna adopt a kid, did you know that? I had so much love to give and I didn't want to waste it on a relationship. I wanted to raise a child and teach them to be gentle and kind and good. But then I met you. I met you and it ruined my life."

The tears that Rayne had successfully been fighting finally won out and her hand flew to her mouth to keep her from sobbing.

"I loved you. I thought I could fix you. I saw how lonely you were even if you didn't. I was trying to be good. I was so good. And I died for it. I died for you. You can't imagine how painful a fire is. I wasn't lucky, the smoke didn't get to me first. I loved my life and now it's over. I loved you and now I hate you with every bone in my body, Rayne Dorne. I hope that you burn."

True, all of it was true. Rayne had been the ruin of her friend. Her only friend. Persimmon had been so kind where Rayne had been cruel. It should have been her that died, perished in those flames.

But Persimmon, as angry as she must have been at Rayne, would never have wished something like that on her because Persimmon was *good*.

The thing at her side was not.

Without looking over her shoulder, Rayne reached her hand behind her into the darkness.

Hawthorne's hand found hers instantly as if they'd already been reaching for her.

Rayne didn't let go and they didn't pull away. She kept walking even though the voices told her that she was a fool for doing so and that all hope was lost. She kept walking. Their hand stayed locked within her own.

Gradually, as sand through a glass, light began to filter through the darkness until the outline of an exit made itself visible to her. Rayne wanted to race toward it, to tug Hawthorne from behind her and sprint into the light. But she kept her pace even, unsure as to whether or not this light meant anything at all or if it was just another cruel illusion of this hell.

But the closer that she got to it the more she began to realize that it was in fact real, that it was not just light but moonlight. Moonlight peeking through the mouth of a cave. They'd reached the end. They'd made it.

Rayne did not stop walking until they exited the cave, until they were illuminated fully in the light of the full moon, until they were blanketed by the humid summer air, until Hawthorne tugged on her hand.

Still, she was scared to turn around and look, terrified that this was the final part of their test. That she would fail Hawthorne and herself, that everything she did to get them back was for nothing.

"Rayne," they whispered, as if they too were frightened to speak. "Look at me."

She took a slow, steadying breath and turned. They opened their mouth to speak but whatever they were going to say was lost. The cicada song filled the silence as Rayne drank in her husband's appearance, truly for the first time.

They were not as she had ever seen them before, caught between their shadows and the human body that they had occupied. Their hair was mussed, still as dark as a winter's night, their eyes still sunlight filtered through leaves and their fingers still bore their wedding band. Stitched into their skin by her hand and hers had been by them.

She rushed into their arms, and in her suddenness, knocked them off of their feet and they tumbled into the grass with her. What could she say? How could she tell them what she had endured just for this? What would she have done simply to catch sight of them in the underworld?

Rayne was breathing for the first time in months.

Their fingers, half human, half shadow dug into her hair like homecoming. "I love you," Hawthorne said, an unfamiliar hitch in their voice at the confession that had spilled off of their tongue hundreds of times before. "I thought that I knew how much, but not before this. I never—"

"I found you." Was all that she could manage.

"I am sorry that you had to search."

There was more that she wanted to say, but not here, not yet. "I want to take you home," she said, pulling away enough to look up at her husband. "You're hurt and—will you let me?"

"Yes," they replied, planting a kiss against her forehead. "I will let you take me home, little wolf."

Little wolf.

Yes, that's who I am.

She was not the girl who had eaten lightning or the shadow that had brought flaming desolation upon the town. Those things belonged to her but they were not *who* she was. This was her. She was only real with them.

Rayne kissed them and it was clumsy, too hungry, too desperate and they nicked each other's lips with their teeth until they were raw. The kiss broke more when she needed to grab for air—she was not so much a spirit that breath no longer mattered to her. Hawthorne laughed like they used to in the dark, in the morning with their lips against the thicket of her hair.

She couldn't laugh yet. Not until she had locked the door to their house behind them, so instead, she grinned up at them and brushed their hair from their face. "Still good to walk?"

"Yes."

She rolled off of them and pulled them to their feet but they dwarfed her still and they both toppled over into the warm grass again. Her thoughts of saving her laughter were quickly forgotten as she dissolved into a pile of it with them.

Things felt easy again. She was alive.

When she finally got Hawthorne to their feet, they leaned heavily onto her and even so, she could feel them trying to hold back. Worried about crushing her as if she was still the fragile thing that they'd left behind. "Is this too much?"

Rayne shook her head. "I can carry you."

The procession through the woods was a slow one, both of them limping and Hawthorne leaning as much of their weight on her as she could bear. But she could bear it.

She could bear it all.

CHAPTER FIFTY-ONE
hawthorne

H awthorne stopped dead in their tracks. They could feel it, power thrumming against the humid summer night like a hummingbird's wings.

I didn't think that they would come for us this quickly.

This was not a battle that the two of them could win, but it did not matter to them. Not really. If it was to be the end of them, they would die by her side. Their blood would seep into the soil like a curse so that the earth might be plagued by their love.

Yes, they thought with a gentle squeeze of Rayne's hand. That was exactly how they wanted to meet their end. *I will rot with her until our bodies have become one nebulous coil of roots and spite and the taste of our names.*

They reached for her mind out of habit, remembering too late that there was no vein threaded between them any longer. And yet, they did not require it to read her, to see the tension in her like a coiling snake.

But Rayne was not the same woman that had clung to them when they had both been faced with the vastness of forces outside of their control. Now, she stood at their side, still within reach but her gaze was fixed on the sky, they could smell her magic crackling in the air around her, sizzling like burnt sugar.

She returned the simple gesture, a delicate sort of clinging before she slipped out of their grasp and they let her. Hawthorne had never held her back, never sought to keep her at their side if she did not choose it. They wanted her exactly as she was, unhindered and untethered to anything that she did not claim with her entire being.

"I told you that they would come," Hawthorne said.

"I know." She turned and flashed them a sheepish smile. "Doesn't mean I won't go down fighting."

The ends of her thick curls rose, responding to the static in the air, *her* static.

Standing a few feet away from them, under the silver light of the summer moon, they could see her better than they had in the inky blackness of the Underground. Everything about her had changed, not just her body but the way that she stood, the tension in her fists. "We aren't alone," she said. "It's very close, whatever it is."

The magic that lived within her now was not the magic that they had given her, it was all hers, all wild. The thought set an ache of longing and appreciation within them that they did not know how to alleviate.

She seemed so fearless. Gone was the cautious but feral thing that had captured their heart. She was still the love of their life but there was so much more to her now than there had been before. They couldn't look away from the woman that they'd known for her entire life and now had to meet again.

The air around them sang. "It seems that the two of you just can't behave. Tsk, tsk, Hawthorne."

At the mention of their name, Rayne ignited. Her hands still black and dusty from the Underground ignited with light. The sweet scent of her magic gave way to the acrid sting of her rage. Her power smelled of seared hair, so sharp that stung their eyes.

"Hawthorne stays with me," Rayne declared. It was not a request, no plea but a demand. "They are mine." Rayne was more lightning than girl and her power slunk around her shoulders, poised to strike.

She's the most beautiful thing I've ever seen.

Across from her in the clearing, a child appeared, sitting in the grass. "Is that so?" she asked, chin in her hand. "If memory serves, I had demanded at least fifty years for you, Hawthorne. And yet here you stand, not even a year later as if you desire nothing more than to be cut down again."

The child looked to be no older than five or six. Small, unassuming in appearance, but something in her piercing blue eyes of a viper. Black hair pulled back into a perfect bun, and a frilly, powder blue and white lace dress.

Like a doll.

"Who the fuck are—" Rayne's eyes went wide and she gasped, taking several steps back. Her magic faded as quickly as it had come. Her hand covered her mouth and she moved closer to Hawthorne.

"Rayne? What's happening?"

The little girl laughed, a keen, high pitched thing, the swan song of some wounded creature. She bared her teeth in something of a smile. "Oh, dear. You must be able to see through my glamour with that stolen eye. You can see me as I really am."

She stretched and strolled over to them. "I will answer your crude question. I am The Enforcer. But Primrose will do for now."

The memory of Dresden resurged: *Be grateful that you have not met my better.*

I had expected Dresden. Not her.

Hawthorne shifted between, angling themself in front of Rayne. "What do you want, Primrose?"

Her lip quirked. "Prim, if you please. I just want to talk to you and your little chimera," she said, dusting the dirt off of her dress. "She's caused quite a bit of trouble in your absence, you know."

They tensed and she rolled her eyes "Oh, relax. You and I both know that if I wanted to harm her, she'd be dead before she set foot in the grass and you'd be back in your cage. I am here to talk, nothing more."

"We are listening."

"I am… surprised at the levels that your human has gone to break you out of your prison. I am not easily surprised. So, for that rarity, I'd like to offer a gift.

But first, I must request that you return Dresden's eye. He's quite sore without it." She opened her tiny palm. "You may give it to me and I shall see that he gets it."

"No." Rayne kept her hand over Dresden's eye, shielding herself from Prim's true form. "I don't think I will."

"I am trying to be civil. So, I am asking for it *nicely*."

"I won it. I will not give it back."

"You stole it," Prim corrected.

"Fairly. He was trying to kill me, I challenged him and I won."

"He was doing his job," Prim countered. "Under *my* orders."

"Then he should consider this an occupational hazard," Rayne shot back.

"I will have the eye." Prim's tiny fingers twitched.

"Then take it."

Hawthorne tensed, squeezing Rayne's hand. *What are you doing? Why are you inviting destruction?*

Primrose remained exactly where she was, making no move to smite either Rayne or them.

"Or," Rayne continued. "Can't you? Since I acquired it fairly, it is mine, isn't it? That's why you're asking."

Prim's smile was tight, her hands locking behind her back. She bounced on her heels. "Look at you, a mortal understanding our world."

Rayne cast a quick glance at Hawthorne and gave their hand a squeeze in return. "I've had a change of heart. I will give back the eye."

Prim grinned, clapping in delight. "There's a girl! Now—"

"As a favor to you," Rayne finished.

Oh, you mad, perfect, beautiful thing.

Primrose's grin fell and her eyes darkened, shifting from their electric blue to nearly black. But then her smile returned and her eyes returned to their original color. "As a favor, then. I will be in your debt, Rayne Dorne."

Had anyone ever been owed something from a King? She might be the first.

"Now. I'll need that eye."

Rayne blinked and took a step back. "You mean just... take it out?"

"How else will I get it? I can even do you the honor of removing it myself. You need only consent—"

"No," Hawthorne pressed themself between Rayne and the elder god. "Absolutely not."

Prim rolled her tidal waves eyes though her dagger of a grin remained. "Oh, don't be dull. It won't hurt." She cracked her fingers and her teeth caught in the moonlight. "I am quite the professional, you'll come to find."

Primrose was in the business of punishment, that was *all* she did. She would butcher Rayne.

Rayne grasped their hand, her knuckles turning white with the strength of her grasp. Hawthorne was intimately aware of how their wife wore her fear, the trembling of her hands, the tapping of her fingers, and the worrying of her bottom lip until it bled.

No matter how much venom she spat, Rayne was scared of Prim. Every movement she made reaffirmed what they knew she was thinking:

Don't let her touch me.

Hawthorne ran their thumb over her hand and gave it a reassuring squeeze in return.

Hawthorne was aware they did not yet understand the extent of what Rayne had suffered for the magic within her, but what they did know was that she was done sacrificing for them.

The rabbit eye that sat in her skull was for *them*, everything she had done, become, and lost was for *them*.

They paused, silent as their mind raced for a solution and the same sickening one kept playing on repeat.

I will have to take it out myself.

Hawthorne had hurt their wife once before, accidentally when she had been a child, unaware of how delicate her disease had left her skin. It was a violence that they swore they would never commit against her again. The idea of not only hurting her, but ripping something as vital as an eye from her set a wave of disgust off in them. They had never vomited before, but the idea of doing this to her made them think that they could.

But what was the alternative? Hand her over to this mad god that was waiting to hack into her like a vulture into carrion?

Of all the things that they would endure for her sake, another's greedy hands digging into her was not one of them.

"A moment, if you would, my King?" Hawthorne requested, hoping that it would tickle the prideful part of her.

Prim raised a brow but made a satisfied noise in her throat, most likely pleased by the honorific. "Only a moment." She turned on her heel and slipped away from them.

"Rayne," Hawthorne began their joined hands to their lips and kissing hers. "Would you forgive me if I took it from you?"

"The eye?" she asked and they nodded, watching her as she worried her lip. After a breath, she met their gaze. "There is nothing to forgive."

Hawthorne's heart ached with everything that they longed to tell her but time and the fates were not on their side tonight. Instead, they pressed another kiss into the back of her hand and mouthed '*I love you.*'

They turned away from Rayne and Primrose was there, waiting with her hands folded patiently in front of her. "Well?"

"I will extract it and give you the eye myself."

Primrose frowned. "And deny my fun?"

"I will get you the eye. Do you agree to it?"

She groaned and crouched into the dirt. "Fine. But be careful. One scratch on it and you will both pay dearly."

She turned her back to them but Hawthorne's attention was already back on their wife, smoothing some of her hair out of her face, she nuzzled her nose into their hand.

"This is going to hurt regardless of how it's done," they admitted, tracing their finger along the inflamed skin around her stolen eye.

"Real magic always does," she offered with a sheepish grin. She would be the death of them.

They kissed her forehead. "I will be gentle."

"Don't. Just do what you need to do. I'll be fine." Courageous only because she didn't know anything better. *I'll love you into the earth and back.*

"Hand on my shoulder," Hawthorne said and their wife obeyed immediately. They would never get over that flutter of satisfaction when she dropped all of her bravado and fire and just listened to them. Their fingers slid into her hair to keep her in place. "Two taps if?"

"If I can't do it," she finished.

They smoothed their thumb over her cheek. "I've got you. Cover your other eye." She nodded and they both took a deep breath.

Their magic was weak, a fluttering, flickering thing where there had once been a wildfire of power. They concentrated on their breath, breathed until their breath was an extension of their darkness that blanketed them both.

Hawthorne could feel the eye's power vibrating, thrumming defiantly against what it seemed to sense coming. To remove such a delicate organ and keep it intact enough to be returned and reattached to its owner took a certain kind of magic. It could not simply be torn out, it had to be compelled, caressed and then at that moment of surrender, plucked out.

How their brute of a wife had managed to wretch it from Dres without destroying it completely was a mystery to them.

Hawthorne yearned for the power to heal, to soothe and create rather than destroy. Always when it came to Rayne they felt that longing for something that they never once desired. This process would have been simpler, easier for her that they could heal as they took.

With a dozen silent apologies, they slid the dagger of their fingers into the socket of her eye. Rayne bit down on her lip, her nails digging into the flesh of their shoulder. Even underneath the iron cast of their concentration, their admiration for their wife threatened to sink them completely.

The eye pulsed against their finger, and Hawthorne started, accidentally pulling back. Rayne shrieked and Hawthorne swore. "It's okay, I've got you," they assured her, readjusting their grip on her hair. The eye practically hissed at them from within her skull, like it was fighting their attempt at extraction.

Behind them, Prim giggled.

They would just have to try harder than they had originally anticipated and hurt their wife more than they were comfortable doing. She was trembling and the hand grip at their shoulder was loosening with each passing second. *I need to hurry this up.*

Hardening themselves, they dug deeper in, and ignored the scent of her blood, the sound of it squelching between their fingers even over her screams. Hawthorne tried to compel the cursed little thing into their fingers, hoping to just magnetize it to them but it pulled away. Actually pushed away from them like a cornered animal. They snarled in frustration. Between her screaming, Primrose's infernal laughter and whatever was wrong with this eye, their focus was fraying at the edges.

The eye kept moving and lurching away from their grasp, refusing to allow them to get a proper grip on it and repelling what magic they were apparently wasting on it. *Fuck.* Her arm went limp, sliding from their shoulder but they couldn't allow it to distract them or this would only end worse for her. "Almost. Stay with me, Rayne."

The cursed thing within her skull pulled back, the trauma of losing its first master too fresh and it fought back against their grip. And it fought back hard, kicking around their fingers like a thing possessed. The damned eye would have bitten them had it had any teeth. It made sense that it had bonded to Rayne so quickly.

Fuck, fuck, fuck! "I know, baby. I can't stop now, I'm almost there. Just stay with me, okay?" they asked, struggling to keep their voice as even and calm as possible.

"Ok-a-ay," she said as her legs gave way and she would have collapsed into the grass if not for their iron grip on her. They moved with her, easing her onto the ground.

"Don't you pass out on me. I need you to stay awake." She made the faintest of noises in response. "Just stay awake for me, please?"

They dug their fingers into her hair, tightening their grip on her. Without giving either of them a moment to adjust, they turned their fingers within the socket, tearing everything that they could and pulled. Rayne howled like a wounded wolf and thrashed against their hold on her.

The irises of Dresden's hideous eye were scarlet and burning and it tried to jump from between their fingers. Despite its small size, it felt like an anchor in their hand, trying to pull them down into the dirt. Hawthorne held it fast and still it fought against their grasp. From between their fingers it peeked out and set its fiery, angry gaze on them. They hadn't liked it looking at them from within Rayne, but they hated it even more outside of her.

Rayne screamed again, kicking and thrashing against the grass, drawing their attention back to her.

"Prim!" they called, holding out the pulsing, ugly thing out to her. She appeared at their side, plucking it from their grasp delicately, as one might hold a child.

"Hmm. Well enough," she said, turning it between her fingers, but Hawthorne's attention was elsewhere, completely fixated on their trembling wife.

Hawthorne eased her into their arms, pulling her close as they rubbed soothing circles into her hair and trying to ignore the blood that had matted into it. She was trembling so badly that her teeth were chattering. Magic or not, she was still not fully a spirit. Still closer to delicate than they could bear. "Good job, baby. You did so well, you know that?" they crooned into her ear, wiping some of the blood off of her cheeks with their other hand before it could dry there.

She hiccupped against their side, breaking their heart all over again.

They glanced at Prim and she rolled her eyes but turned away.

Hawthorne reached for that last bit of magic that they had available to them and allowed it to wash over their wife, covering her like molasses. They had never used this power on her in full since she'd lost Persimmon. They wanted nothing of her that she did not willingly give them, but her pain? Hawthorne would take that from her in an instant.

It worked into her hair, dripped down her neck and down into her shoulders. "I've got you," they whispered into her ear, their darkness pulling her into them, compelling her to listen. Her sobs died down, gradually stopping completely as her shoulders dropped and she melted into their side. She sighed, exhaling a tight breath. "That's my girl. Your eye is fine, it doesn't hurt. Nothing hurts, you feel comfortable—right?"

"Yeah." She leaned her head against their chest.

They kept their magic around her, dripping over her in gentle, coaxing waves. They just needed her calm and comfortable long enough to figure out where to go from here, what to do next. Their magic wouldn't work for long, they could grant her barely an hour of peace before they were completely spent.

There was no way that they hadn't caused her some kind of internal damage. She needed to be tended to.

Can I even take her to a hospital? Will human medicine work on her now that she's half in my world and half in her own?

Her sighs, softer than the surrounding cicada song were still drenched in the dregs of their magic and they struggled to keep their attention pinned on the archaic god before them. They would find a way to spare her no matter what the cost. *I will cut as many deals, will dice myself into as many pieces as I can and shove my hands into the hands of anyone who will hear me out.*

Hawthorne was no stranger to this world.

Rayne may have had to fumble around in the dark to seek out answers but they did not.

"Prim." When they turned their head, the little girl was at their side, crouching over Rayne with a grin that set an array of nerves off with them. They pulled their wife closer and warred with the urge to bear their teeth at the elder creature. Hawthorne loathed authority but authority that took joy in its own power? They would rather be a shade.

Hawthorne had never been preyed upon. Their place within the food chain had always been solid, as unyielding as oak and yet they felt now like a leaf caught in the wind.

"Yes, Hawthorne?" she asked, warm honey oozing onto a dagger's edge. "Something you required of me? Oh, don't look at me like that. I've been nothing but helpful to you both, have I not?"

Ignoring the barbed question, they pressed forward. "Let me ask your favor in her stead."

At this, it was her turn to frown at them.

Prim shucked her teeth around an excuse. "It is not yours to ask," she said with a shrug. "The girl is owed not you."

"She is incapable of asking."

"Ah, but it was never specified in which state she was able to request the favor." Primrose sang.

"I am her husband. I am as much her as she is me. Our rules—"

Primrose snarled, her face dangerously close to their own. The scent of the ocean hit them but there was something beneath it, rotten as low tide. "Do not speak to me of rules, shadow!" She spat with venom that surely could have curled flesh from bone. "I was there when they were written. I have seen the beginning of our kind and I know the end. *Do not condescend to me.*"

Primrose sat back on her heels and began picking at her nails, her attention diverted. "Prove the union."

Hawthorne nodded down to Rayne's arms, hanging limply at her side. "Her left ring finger. It bears my magic, interwoven with my blood. You will find the same mark on my own finger with her. We wove the spell together and our House was the witness. You may ask it, if you so choose."

Prim sighed, picked at her nails for a moment longer and then looked down at the dark band tattooed into their wife's finger with magic. The blood bond between them may have been severed but their marriage contract was not.

Her hand ghosted Rayne's and before their eyes the blood magic kicked to life, their finger throbbed as the red thread of magic shimmered, burning like falling stars as it wrapped around their finger and tied around hers.

Primrose's expression remained unchanged as she allowed the magic to slip away into the night, and though it was still there, it could no longer be seen. "She must consent to your asking." Prim answered tightly after a few moments. "Do you consent to Hawthorne speaking in your place?"

"Mhm. Yeah," Rayne answered dreamily.

Prim sighed. "Ask your favor and make it quick."

"Give her a new eye, a human one that works just as well as the other to last her the rest of her life. Do not cause her anymore pain in the process and relieve her from the pain and damage of the extraction."

"Is that all?" Prim's cheek rested in the palm of her hand. "How dull."

"Will you honor it or not?" Hawthorne grit out.

"Our score will be settled after this?" she asked, rocking back and forth on her heels.

"Yes, the debt will be repaid and we will be even," Hawthorne said.

"Then it is done," Prim looked down at Rayne. "Turn her face towards me and then look away."

Gently, they hooked their finger under Rayne's chin and turned her face to Prim.

As soon as they looked away the scent of salt spray and damp sand filled the air. Some of the spirits had whispered that The Enforcer had crawled out from the sea, half storm and murky water. That she was the first creature to ever swim the oceans.

"There. All done," Prim said a few seconds later, wiping her hands on her dress. They knew that her power was immense but the quickness and ease in which she had worked her magic still surprised them.

Hawthorne caught Rayne's chin and her glazed eyes met theirs. Human eyes. Her left, the newer of the pair, was a few shades too light to match the sunkissed soil of her other eye. It was like the terracotta pots that the flowers inside of the sunroom in the House sat on. They'd forgotten to mention the color of her eyes, to make them match and of course Prim had taken that and run with it. *Annoying wretch.*

Rayne smiled up at them, still under the influence of their magic. They were hesitant to pull it off of her, even with Prim's favor. They kissed her forehead.

"Hmm, color's a bit off but it will work all the same," Prim shrugged, placing her hands on her knees as she rose and turned to walk away. Then she stopped abruptly and snapped her fingers. "Oh, yes! My gift, I'd almost forgotten."

She was in Hawthorne's face again, only a breath away with that wild grin of hers once more. "Will you accept it in her stead as well, oh noble husband?"

"Yes." Hawthorne did not like the joy glinting in her wicked blue eyes at their agreement but Rayne was in no state to accept anything.

"I'm told you sent a knocker into the City of Shades to seek her out, to find her soul and deliver a message." Primrose wagged her finger at them. "That simply won't do."

Shit.

Hawthorne hadn't considered that the Kings would have bothered keeping an eye on them once they'd been tossed into the Underground. Apparently they'd been mistaken. They clutched Rayne closer to their side, earning another contented sigh from her.

"We can't have you two tearing down the walls of the Veil to get back to one another when she inevitably must choose between the River or the Pears." Primrose continued, not waiting for their response.

Hawthorne felt something foreign and cold work its way up their spine and coil around their neck. *Magic.* Ironclad. Salt water slowly dripped into the back of their throat.

They coughed, grasping at their throat. Rayne must have felt the same sensation as she began coughing, spitting up water.

"Shh. Your King is speaking, darkling." She giggled. "This gift is for both of you after all."

Prim's eyes brightened and a lightning storm began behind those two blue daggers, clouds gathering within her as if she were a tempest herself. When she spoke again, her voice was the very sky, crashing down upon them.

"Since you refuse to be separated then you never shall be. She will live as you do and you shall die as she does. Your lives are inextricably tied from now until the end of time." With every word she spoke, Hawthorne felt themselves being stitched into some invisible patchwork, bound to some larger picture yet unseen.

"You shall be as The Great Serpent. There is no way forward and no way back. You shall walk this path until every star has collapsed. It is over for you the moment that it starts and *it will always end this way.*"

All of the magic left her at once, her stormy eyes melted back into their cutting blue and whatever tether that had been snapped all at once. Hawthorne spat up seawater.

Rayne gasped, spitting the salt water into the grass, gagging.

"The gift has been given. It can never be taken back!" Primrose laughed, spinning in the grass, arms above her head, reaching for the moon.

As she spun, she began to melt away, lessening and lessening until she began to disappear into the moonlight. "You will see me again but *I* won't be me and *you* will still be you." Her mouth, the only remaining piece of her, unmoving, grinning like a blade through skin. "*Again, again and again and again.*"

Her humming and her grin remained long after the rest of her had melted into the night and the taste of saltwater left their tongue.

CHAPTER FIFTY-TWO
hawthorne

Hawthorne held Rayne for a long time, waiting, listening. When they were sure that the night was filled with only crickets, only then did they brush her hair from her face and carefully remove their magic from her.

Rayne blinked up at them as if roused from a nap instead of nearly bleeding out in the dirt. "You're here," she whispered.

"Where else would I be?" they asked, brushing their nose against hers. She smiled and it shattered their composure. "You're so fucking beautiful."

She laughed and pushed against them, sitting up. "Are you flirting with me?"

They leaned down to kiss the top of her head. "Am I forbidden from flirting with my wife now?"

"Never," she shot back, brushing some of their dark curls from their face. "Are you okay?"

"I will be once we are home," Hawthorne admitted, placing their hand over hers. "And you, little wolf?"

"I will be once we get home."

Hawthorne brushed their thumb along her cheek. "Your eye, it doesn't look the way that it did before. It's different. Lighter."

"Oh." She bit her lip and met their gaze. "Is it ugly?"

"Never."

"Home, my beast?" Rayne offered.

Hawthorne stole a kiss. "Home."

They both struggled to their feet, clinging to one another, arms encircling the other's waist to stay up right.

"We look like shit," Rayne laughed, nuzzling their side. "Like absolute trash."

"Speak for yourself," Hawthorne chuckled. "I think blood and dirt suit us well."

"House is going to kill us both. You, especially."

Hawthorne laughed. "I am ready for my lashes."

The walk home was silent and Hawthorne tried not to ruin it with all of the things that they longed to say to her. How they wished that they could just sit with her and give her every thought that she had occupied in their time apart. But they wanted to go home first, they wanted that almost as badly as they wanted to fold into their wife and forget the world.

She bore their weight silently and every time that she stumbled, she would bite her lip stubbornly, right herself and keep moving. Rayne did not ask them for anything.

They were not sure if it was anger or determination that kept her moving but they were glad for it because almost as soon as they had set into the forest toward their House, they were there.

Hawthorne had spent weeks dreaming of this exact moment; of walking up the off white stairs and standing in front of that white door, impeded by frosted glass, but now that they were, something heavy anchored in their chest. Rooting them in place even as Rayne slipped out from under their arm to open the door.

They did not realize how long they must have been standing there, staring up at the House until Rayne placed her palm against their chest. "Hawth? Are you okay?"

Hawthorne nodded, smiled a little down at her. "Just needed a moment."

Rayne nodded, moving to the side to make room for them.

"What's that?" The House's voice came from the stairs, creaking like old bones. *"Is that our wraith, come to grace us with their presence?"*

"Yes, House. It's m—"

The floor beneath their feet snapped and groaned, bucking like a wild horse. *"I will have none of you! You think that you can waltz back into our lives so long after the music has stopped playing?"*

"House," Rayne snarled, but they stopped her.

"Say what you need to say," they said, focusing their attention on the rowdy, temperamental thing that they lived in.

"You will not come here tracking mud and smelling of the rot and earth and demand that I say my piece!" it snapped *"You left us without leaving a light on. You left us for all this time and now you think that you can just come back."*

Rayne's mouth was drawn into a hard line and her hands balled into fists. Was she angry? They couldn't be sure, and that plucked a thread of nervousness within them. Coming home was supposed to be the easy part. The fight was over, they could just ease back into their life with one another.

They just needed to get over the bumps, handle the small hiccups as they arose. This was just one and they would make it past.

"I am here now, House," they said, the only olive tree branch that they could think of extending. "I did not want to leave either of you and you know this. I won't be gone again. I cannot change that I left, but I am here now."

Hawthorne brushed their fingers along the frame of the door, the way that they used to after one of their long trips into the forest. Like ruffling the soft feathers of a bird, the House shuttered and shivered under their touch and it felt like forgiveness.

"You do not need to forgive me. But will you at least let me inside for the night? We can talk about everything in the morning, can't we, oh *darling, treasured* House?" they crooned and the House cooed like a turtle dove.

"I suppose. But light my fire, give me sweet rosemary and mint sprigs to feed off of. No, don't look at me that way. I care not that it is summer."

Hawthorne stole a glance at their wife and she seemed calmer, the fists having dissolved into fingers pressing into her sides.

They offered her their hand. "Shall we see what we can scrounge up from the garden?"

Something dark flashed across her expression and they worried that they had misstepped. "It's a little overgrown."

"Why should I care about that?" they said in an attempt at humor, but then her lips curled upward and they were sure that they were on the right path.

The way home.

CHAPTER FIFTY-THREE
hawthorne

The two of them laid beside each other on the couch, exhausted. The House creaked with life, warming the skeleton of what had once been her tomb. Hawthorne had brought life back with them from the Underground.

Absently, Hawthorne stroked Rayne's legs as they met her gaze.

They had believed that they would never see this House again. That they would never enjoy the gentle life that they had carved out with Rayne. Hawthorne had known that they would find Rayne again, no matter what the circumstances or cost, but to return here, to this?

That they had feared was gone forever.

And yet here they were with her, after nearly six months apart. Alone without the fear of being watched, or needing to stay on their guard. There was still the matter of the gift that Prim had given them both. *We can talk about that in the morning.*

I don't want to think about anything other than Rayne.

They took the opportunity to really look at her, to drink her after all this time. So much of her had changed. But still they could recognize her. The full pout of her lips, her thick lashes, the birth marks at her left cheekbone. Tiny things about her appearance that acted as a comfort to them, a harbor that they could always set port in.

Hawthorne wished that they could erase whatever it was that had caused her face to change so drastically, be it time or magic, but they would give anything to see her looking as she had before.

They thought back to that morning on the day in which they had been torn away from her. She had just lost Persimmon but she had curled close to them and smiled sleepily up at them. She had looked so peaceful despite her pain and they just wanted to see that soft, stubborn joy on her again.

Rayne was staring back at them, similarly she seemed to be drinking them in as well. They wondered if they looked as they had before or if, like their wife, they had changed in appearance. Their gazes met and they still had to take an extra moment to catch their breath when they looked at her. Her mismatched gaze. Warm, sunkissed earth and terracotta. Just another reminder of how different she was.

They both moved at once, them reaching for her waist and her bringing them in for a kiss. She straddled them and their hands slid from her waist to the swell of her ass. Her fingers found purchase in their hair and she kissed them as if she was trying to wretch their breath straight from their lungs.

Gods, I missed her.

Rayne's breath pelted their skin when she pulled away. Her forehead had come to rest at the crook of their neck.

She felt lighter than they remembered. A frown accompanied the thought of her having missed meals and not taking care of herself due to her concern for them.

The long-sleeved shirt she wore was one that she had donned frequently when they were together, she had gone from swimming in the dark fabric to drowning in it.

"Are you alright?" they murmured against her hair, their hand coasting down between her shoulder blades. They found the muscles there, tenser than they remembered, and carefully they worked their fingers against them.

Rayne nodded immediately, her arms locked around their neck. Familiar fingers weaved into their hair. "Yes," her voice was porcelain against the floor, a shattered thing. "I'm fine."

There was a part of them that wanted to call her on the lie, press against her lying tongue until she confessed her truth. But there was another part of them that realized that they did not know *if* she was lying.

The Rayne Dorne of six months ago was an easy read, every tell on display before them. But this Rayne, terror, monster, was a language that they didn't speak. She had been birthed from their absence.

So, Hawthorne swallowed their inquiry and in its place, another spawned. "Can I see you?" they asked, drawing gentle patterns in her back.

While she did not pull away from them, she did not press closer. She remained still. Numb.

"Okay, if you want," she whispered back, her lips against their ear.

"Of course I do," Hawthorne pulled back enough so that they could look down at her, meet her mismatched gaze and on reflex, their hands caught her cheeks. "But do you?"

Her eyes cut away from them but again, she did not remove herself from their grasp or make any indication that she desired to be free of them. "Yes."

Something is wrong. The memory of the ghosts in the shape of her hit them like a ton of bricks. *What if this had all been an elaborate ruse?* The creatures had been good at donning the cloak of her and taunting them. Using their words to weave them the cruelest of fantasies.

What if that's all this is? What if I'm still there, trapped between those damned trees?

It wasn't impossible, it simply would have had to have been the illusion of the century. While they would not put it past any of the Kings to do such a thing, it seemed a complete waste to do so to them. They were a minor god, a lesser thing. But then again...

Rayne had crossed every border, shattered every glass ceiling.

This is real. She is real. It's her.

Hawthorne released her face and instead moved to ease her shirt off of her. As expected, she wore nothing more than a velvet bralette beneath it. They sighed, relieved at the fragment of familiarity, thumb coming to stroke the soft fabric with reverence.

Rayne remained as still as ever. Like a corpse. Their throat constricted and for a moment, they thought that they might vomit. It was a disgustingly human act but they felt less than immortal.

"Rayne?" they tried again, brushing their thumbs along her cheek. Her eyes closed at the contact and she inhaled. *Am I hurting you? Are you uncomfortable with me now?*

They wanted to ask her, they wanted to know what was so different now, whether or not they were misstepping or if this was the way back to one another.

But this peace was delicate. They could feel that. Hawthorne was balancing on an invisible scale. They just wanted to know if they were about to dive head first in the wrong direction or guide them both back to shore.

Hawthorne waited for her to open her eyes and look at them, to see them as they were, as she always had. They waited for her to nuzzle her cheek against their palm as if she couldn't bear the space between them. Like she used to do.

But her eyes didn't open. As if she couldn't bear to look at them.

Is it my fault? they wanted to ask. *Have I done this to you?* Instead, they said "Rayne, can you look at me?"

She remained still, unmoved, and just before they could open their mouth to beg, she looked at them and they melted. At least, for the few seconds that she held it before her dark eyes drifted away, past them.

Should I drop it? Should I try again?

Hawthorne did not want to ogle their wife as if she were something to be studied, but they could not control the way that they looked at her, and took everything in. The map of her body that they had once known more intimately than anything else was gone. Unrecognizable amongst the new landscape of her.

So many new scars that they practically devoured her older ones. The angriest of which started at her sternum and splintered out and up, ending at the base of her collarbone. Like lightning.

"What happened?" they whispered, hand hovering over her dark skin, over the place where her scar began.

"The House," she said, leaning forward so that their hand could come into contact with her warm skin. "I let it eat me."

Hawthorne wanted to be angry at the House, but like them, it could only do what was in its nature. They rested their head against her chest. "I'm sorry."

"It's okay," she said, tangling her hands in their hair again. "It isn't your fault,"

Stop acting like this is fine, like it's okay that you're in shambles and had to glue yourself back together! It was only when they got halfway through the thought that they realized that she could not hear them. They were screaming down a hallway, alone in an abandoned building where their bond used to live.

"I don't know what to do," they confessed, their throat as dry as the rolling summer heat outside. The soft scent of dried sweat clung to her skin and they closed their eyes, breathing in as much of it as they could.

"You don't have to." She ground her nails into their shoulders, digging her claws into them. "I thought I was never going to see you again. You were just gone," she whispered and latched onto them so tightly that had they been human, she might have actually hurt them. They would welcome any pain that she saw fit to grant them.

Hawthorne swallowed something hard in their throat and pulled her closer, kissing her temple. "I know. I'm sorry."

"I'm sorry." She shook her head and her vice-like grip began to bite into them. They let it. "It was all because of me."

There was a thread that could be followed, events that could be pulled apart and dissected for what they were. But they could not, would not allow the blame to rest on her shoulders.

"Don't." Hawthorne didn't give her a chance to say something that would only cleave them both in two. Instead, they kissed her.

Rayne started and then paused before tentatively returning their kiss. Like she had forgotten what it was like to be kissed at all.

I would have crawled home to you.

The chaotic, demanding little hands that they were used to were nowhere to be found. Instead, Rayne threaded her finger through their hair slowly as if she were weaving a tapestry.

They wished that they could weave their way back into her just as easily. They longed to reestablish the bond that had been snapped between them. But they were exhausted and their magic was clumsy. The bonding spells required patience, a delicate hand, and a focused mind.

Hawthorne possessed none of these things as their wife filled their awareness. Her hair, thick and untamed as ever, brushed against their arm as they held her. Her heart was pounding so loudly against the outside of their ribcage, her pulse fluttering like the wings of a butterfly against their skin. She was so deliciously and perfectly alive.

Still human. Safe.

Hawthorne squeezed her closer. They broke the kiss to canvas the column of her throat and revel in the feeling of that living pulse beating under their mouth. Rayne kept them close, her grip on their hair digging deeper all of a sudden.

"You're here?" Rayne whispered once the kiss had been broken enough to allow her to breathe. Her words came like a sigh of relief.

"I'm here," they assured her.

The sound of her beating heart, playing a song for them both drew their attention and their hand came to rest on her ribs.

"You're alive."

She nodded, placing her hand over theirs and then, guiding it under the velvet of her bralette. "I'm alive."

Hawthorne hesitated, fingers freezing in place. They wanted to see Rayne, to bury themself in the garden of her body but how could they do so when they couldn't read her?

What if she is doing this out of some misplaced sense of obligation?

"I want to," she announced, shattering the doubt that they felt as easily as she shattered everything else around her. Rayne unwound a hand from their hair to peel off her bralette and discard it behind her.

The rest of the room, the entire world, dissolved in a moment. There was nothing that existed outside of her orbit. Hawthorne lost themself to her gravitational pull and gave into the sweet salt scent of her skin as they buried their head between her breasts. The drumline of her beating heart pulled them further and further into her but it wasn't close enough. They wanted to slide their clawed thumb into her skin and split it, smoothing it apart like orange skin until they found the fruit of her heart.

I just need to see it. I just need to know that it's there and beating. She isn't a figment or fraction.

Hawthorne's tongue lavished the dark bud of her nipple with their attention. Rayne's grip on their hair remained and so they followed her as she arched back onto the couch.

Her moans were soft, quiet, and almost timid, but they were a song that she sang just for them and they had committed to memory.

There was a story they remembered Rayne had been fond of as a child: Little Red Riding Hood. They couldn't help but wonder if the little girl had felt relief when she saw light in the windows of her grandmother's house. If that light in the darkness had been a reminder of home, of safety, only for her to have been met with a hungry wolf.

Do you feel that way, Rayne? Safe here with me, lights on, surrounded by the comfort of home only to be devoured?

I will be that light in the dark, they whispered down their silent bond. *I will be that house in the middle of the woods, a candle always lit for you, and I will be the wolf that eats you with care.*

Their hungry mouth sought the taste of her and as they licked their way down to her stomach, the softness that they were accustomed to having there had disappeared. It would return. *She will come back, we both will.*

Her fingers dug into their hair again but they could tell from the motion, she was trying to keep them from roving down lower.

"No," she murmured. "Closer. Come here."

Hawthorne obeyed and aligned themself between her legs, their chests pressed against one another and their bodies slotted together. Both of them exhaled at the meeting of skin, pressure melting off of the other.

Rayne yanked them down again and they followed, floating close enough to her lips that they were sharing breath but far enough that she still spoke, could still stop this if she wanted to.

"I missed you," she confessed, all but taking their breath away. "Nothing felt real without you."

Hawthorne swept the curtain of her hair out of her face, taking a moment to appreciate the ocean of white that lived within it now, like a meteor shower on a winter's night. "I missed you too. You were the only thought that I could manage."

They kissed again and their fingers remained tangled in her hair while one of her hands slipped between them to tear at her pants. When they made a move to help her, she bit their bottom lip in warning.

Stubborn. Past them would have teased her, prodded at the little rebellion to see what else they could draw out of her. But now they needed her, they needed those teeth.

Hawthorne's tongue slid into her mouth and for a second her hand between them stilled only to return to tearing off her clothes with renewed vigor until she was completely naked between them.

She ground her cunt against them and the unexpected friction stole their breath from them with dizzying ease. "I want you."

Hawthorne was still caught between their shadow self and their human form, bits of darkness twisting and mingling with their human flesh. Their fingers were half human, half clawed, tipped in black. In the illumination of artificial lights, truly seeing each other for the first time in months, it suddenly felt like too much. A thing too grand to even conceptualize.

"Like this? Are you sure?"

"Hawthorne, I need us to be close again."

They knew what she meant this time, knew exactly what she wanted because they wanted the same. Needed the same as her.

Rayne wrapped her legs around them to lock them both in place and they held as much of their weight on their forearms as they could to keep from crushing her. She hardly allowed them enough space to reach between them to slide into her. Something swelled in their chest, sharp and biting at the back of their throat as they watched her face, forcing themself to keep their eyes open so that they did not miss a single moment or a single expression that crossed her gorgeous face.

Her warmth dragged them in and the tight walls of her cunt clenched around them as they pulled out and sunk back in. Her hands were all over them as if she didn't know what to do with them anymore. She dug her nails into their chest, keeping just a breath of space between them but the other hand rested at the base of their neck, trying to drag them closer.

"Do you need me to slow down?"

"No," she hissed and her body decided for her, arms locking around their neck and forcing them as close as they could possibly be to her. "I'm sorry. I don't know what I'm doing anymore."

They pulled out and slid into her once more, stretching her around their thick cock with a groan of restraint. They wanted to hide in her, to rut into her until they forgot about the last six months and they could simply imagine that they had been here, folded in the sanctuary of their shared bed.

"Don't," they murmured low in her ear. Their thumb found her clit and she gasped, sharp and perfect. "I want all of you, I don't care what that means. How it looks."

She whimpered and they chased the sound, rolling their hips against hers in long, deep strokes as they circled her clit with the pad of their thumb. She circled with them and it was like that last day that they'd spent together. When they had danced, and clumsy as she was, she found their rhythm and followed.

She always followed even if it meant waltzing right off of the edge of a cliff.

A small jolt of pain caught their attention and the scent of blood—their blood—that followed. Rayne was staring up at them, hips still following their perfect dance of friction, and her eyes caught in the light, reflecting back at them. Her hands latched onto their wrists, bracketing her to the couch and she had dug so deeply into their skin that she had broken it. Beads of blood pricked at their skin but they could not take their eyes off of her.

"Stay."

Hawthorne broke, and with them came the gossamer thread of control that they'd been clinging to as they fucked her. They caged her against them and stole her lips, taking every bit of herself that she had offered. Their hips pistoned into hers and she met every thrust with the song of their name. She bit at their lips, taking more of their blood like she was coming to collect on a debt.

Hawthorne, without stopping, repositioned them to hook one of her legs over their shoulder and their cock slid impossibly deeper within her.

They were drowning. The taste of salt accompanied her lips. Her tears were not something that they could ever forget the taste of. They understood her tears and yet were as confused as ever about why she shed them.

What does it mean when you cry like that? Are you telling me something?

"Oh, fuck, Hawthorne," she hissed around the sound of a sob, throwing her head back. "Hawthorne, please—"

It was the animal in them that brought them to the dark veins of her throat and the rapid pulse that they found there. Their teeth grazed against it and they heard it quicken, a rabbit desperately trying to escape a fox.

It was the monster in them that bit her as they increased the intensity of their thumb at her clit. When she came, scattering like flower petals, it was with their name on her tongue and her blood in their mouth.

The air filled with the sharp sting of black pepper and mint. A familiar, sweet agony snapped through their veins like wildfire. Like *magic*.

Hawthorne came apart with a strangled cry, unfurling like yarn as the thread of what was once them and theirs was knitted back into her, back into an us. A tear stitched closed. They collapsed onto her, mindful of their weight even in the throes of their pleasure.

Rayne cried out with them, hand flying to her neck but not the fresh wound at her neck but to her bond mark, red and angry.

Why do I smell magic? Rayne's voice came as a bull in the china shop of their thoughts.

They blinked and eased back slowly as if the thing that they hoped between them might shatter at any sudden movement.

Rayne? they thought down the bond, and it was everything. The hallway was now an open door. The abandoned house was now a room flooded with light. Can you hear me?

Their wife's eyes flooded with tears. *I hear you.*

Hawthorne held her so fast and so hard that they both fell off of the couch awkwardly onto the floor. Their massive legs were still half on it and Rayne entangled herself in them like vines, her sobs coming like the summer rain.

They wanted to cry with her for nothing else other than the fact that they did not want her to have to do anything without them anymore. Instead, they held her, kissed every bit of skin, every strand of hair, and made a dozen vows to her until her tears lessened and her sobs subsided. Until she resembled the little wolf that they left behind, curling herself as close as their bodies would allow.

It was her stomach that broke the silence, gurgling loudly.

Rayne snorted, giggling, and pearls of her raspy laughter bubbling out of her like she couldn't contain it.

The world begins and ends in that sound, they thought and she smiled meekly at them, brushing some of her dark hair behind her ear.

"Do you have any food in the house?" they asked.

"I think I might have some pasta or something. Let me—"

"No, baby. Let me find you something quick and then in the morning, I will cook you the biggest breakfast that there ever was. Okay?"

Rayne's smile widened until her teeth showed but it was not a bearing of them but a smile that was too big to be contained. "Okay."

I love you. I love you. I love you. They held onto the thoughts greedily. Right now, their adoration of her was just for them, but in the morning, they would give it all back to her.

Withdrawing from her was a herculean task, but they endured it because it meant that they could carry her to bed and lay her down and spend the night buried in her scent. That had been their fantasy, the daydream that they had wandered into during their torture.

Walking into the kitchen, they were alarmed by the cleanliness of it.

She could have simply been giving in to her anxiety. Cleaning until her head hurt from the chemicals. I'll ask her about it in the morning.

Hawthorne swung open some of the cabinets where Rayne usually kept her snacks; chocolate, granola bars, instant noodles, dried kiwis, anything. But they found nothing. All of the cabinets were barren.

Frowning, they moved to the refrigerator and the moment that the door opened, they were hit with a wave of oranges.

From top to bottom, the refrigerator was filled. Even a six-pack of orange soda on the top shelf, but save for that, only oranges.

The sickeningly sweet scent of rot wafted up, knocking them in the face. All of the oranges were in varying states of decay but every single one of them had gone bad.

Rotten.

All of this food was for them.

And yet her cabinets were bare, she had left nothing for herself. *All of this, for me. Everything she's done to herself has been for me.*

Hawthorne stared, swallowing a sudden lump in their throat. They gripped the handle of the door hard but still their hands shook. The world blurred, smearing and bleeding into itself.

What is wrong with my eyes?

Moisture, foreign and unwelcome cut down their cheeks, pooling at their chin. Hawthorne wanted to touch it, to wipe it away, but their damned hands would not stop their treacherous trembling.

"Hawthorne?" Rayne called out to them softly, over the symphony of emotions they did not recognize. "What is it?"

They flexed their fingers and forced one hand from the handle and into the refrigerator to grab her an orange that only just started to go bad.

Hawthorne closed the door to the refrigerator and swallowed the taste of salt and rotten citrus. They could not bring themself to look at her yet or for her to see them like this. Hawthorne wiped their tears away and began the work of peeling the orange for her.

Never before had the scent of it made them sick, never had the mere sight of them brought a wave of weariness.

"In the morning, Rayne," their voice cracking under the impossible weight of everything, "we will talk about it in the morning."

EPILOGUE

Her grandmother loved her.

The girl knew this, but she did not know why her grandmother refused to let her stay out after dark. She watched as her grandmother flicked off the remaining lights and lit the candles along the walls to beat back the darkness.

It was a practice from before the girl was born, but one her grandmother had kept up for all of her nine years. She remained silent as she nestled on the couch, pulling the blankets up to her chin as she waited for her grandmother to join her on the sofa. The scent of apricots and warm sugar hit her nose, and she wanted to fold into the smell.

When her grandmother shuffled into the room, she came bearing two mugs of sweet cherry tea and a plate of raspberry shortbread cookies. With hands much sturdier than her age should have allowed for, she placed the contents down on the glass coffee table and sat beside her.

The little girl opened the blanket, and her grandmother grinned, then settled under it with her. "Hey, Gram. Can I ask you something?"

"Go on, Christina," Her grandmother said, reaching for her tea.

"How come we never go outside?" Christina asked. "Even when the weather's nice?"

Her Gram laughed, patting her leg. "We got outside plenty, and you know it."

"Yeah, but not at night."

Her grandmother paused for a moment, took a slow sip of her tea, and closed her eyes. "No, not at night."

"How come?"

Christina shared everything with her grandmother; there was not a thought in her head that her grandmother hadn't heard at least a dozen times. But her Gram, there were moments when Christina was sure secrets were bubbling beneath her wrinkled skin.

"Bad things happen at night around here. We're too close to Bury for anyone to be safe after dark. I know that, your mother knows that, and I want *you* to know it too."

"Bury is where you grew up, right?"

"Yes."

"Is it—bad there?"

Her grandmother placed her tea down on the coaster on the table. "Didn't use to be. Used to be the most beautiful little town. But now—well, I've told you, ain't nothing out that way."

Christina pouted. "But, I wanna see it."

Her grandmother chuckled. "There's not much to see anymore."

"But there is something," She pressed. "Just tell me what I *would* see *if* we went."

"What if we watched some TV instead, hmm?"

"Please, Grandma May?" Christina pleaded, looking up at the old woman with the most pathetic look she could muster. Her grandmother didn't like her full name; she said it reminded her of bad times. It made Christina sad. Ellie May was the prettiest name in the world as far as she was concerned.

"Alright, alright. But then," Grandma May placed her tea back onto its coaster on the table. "No more. I don't like to dwell on that place too long. It might—well, might attract the attention of things that should be left alone."

"Like what?"

"The Dorne Witch, for starters."

"A witch?"

Grandma May hushed her. "Do you want to hear what you'd see if you were there or not?" Christina nodded, making a show of zipping her mouth closed and throwing away the key. "If you went out to Bury now, you wouldn't see a town. Most of it was destroyed in the fire, and no one ever bothered to rebuild it. Now, nature's reclaimed it, and maybe that's for the better."

Why! Christina wanted to demand, but she knew her Gram would scold her.

"You'd see mountains. It's God's country out there for sure. It was the most beautiful place in the world once upon a time."

"What happened to it, Gram?"

"Well, most of it burned down. See, the fire worked its way up the mines and into the mountain. Now, they say the ground is still burning, like Hell. But that kinda thing doesn't just happen. I think someone started it."

"Was it The Dorne Witch?" She asked, all attempts at hiding her curiosity gone.

"I'd bet." Grandma May's smile didn't look so happy, and Christina frowned.

"But why would she do that?"

Her Gram sighed. "I don't know. Some people are just born wrong, I think."

"Who is she?"

Her grandmother sat back on the couch, though her spine remained perfectly straight. "She used to live there in town with all of us. But she was evil. She hurt people. Like my Mama."

Grandma May always got misty-eyed when she spoke about her Mama, and her hands started to shake something fierce. Christina held her hand to steady her, resting her cheek against her grandmother's shoulder. "I'm sorry your Mama died, Gram."

Grandma May kissed her hair. "You don't have anything to be sorry about. That witch is the one who'll be sorry. God always punishes the wicked."

Christina swallowed. Her Gram always spoke of God and His love, but she rarely spoke of wickedness. *But what does evil really mean?* Christina thought. *Just bad?* "How do you know she hurt your Mama?"

"I saw it with my own eyes," Grandma May replied, her attention had moved from Christina to the window. She stared at it as if, even through the blinds, she could see something Christina couldn't. "Once you've seen lightning up close, smelled skin burning off the bone, you never forget it."

Terror chilled Christina's skin, and she clutched at her grandmother's hand. She'd never thought about either of those things, and she didn't like the images that they conjured up in her mind. "Gram?"

"I still see her sometimes, in my dreams, along with that town. She's out there, I know she is," her grandmother whispered, but she wasn't looking at Christina; she didn't seem to be speaking to her either. "Even after all this time, all these years. Why didn't she kill me? I thought it might have been mercy, but—"

"Gram!" Christina squeezed her grandmother's hand, and she turned to Christina, her eyes wide and shining, her thin cheeks slick with tears. She blinked at Christina, awaking from some personal nightmare.

"Oh, I'm sorry, dear. I got a little carried away, didn't I?" Grandma May wiped at her cheeks, laughing a little to herself.

Christina hugged her grandmother's side. "It's okay, Gram. I'm sorry. We can watch TV now."

That night, after her grandmother had gone to sleep, Christina slipped out of bed. *Why did Gram look like that when she talked about the witch?* She thought as she tiptoed from her bed to the window on the other side of the room. *What had she been looking at?*

Pushing back the blinds, Christina stared into the darkness of the surrounding forest, moonlight blotting through the trees from the full moon. Shadow and light shifted together in the breeze, and Christina squinted to get a better look.

She gasped, her hand flying to her mouth as she stumbled back away from the window and dove into her bed. Christina pinched her eyes closed and yanked her blankets over her head to shield herself from what she'd seen.

Just at the edge of the tree line, a woman with starlight caught in her hair, streaking it white, stood perfectly still. Behind her, the shadows curled, wrapping around her, and the woman turned, stepping into them with open arms.

ACKNOWLEDGEMENTS

While I did not name Rayne's illness explicitly, it is a rare skin condition that I also have, known as **Epidermolysis Bullosa.** If you are interested in learning more or donating, you can do so by visiting https://www.debra.org/

When I first began writing this story, I didn't think anyone would read it. It started as a strange little novella that I was going to write quietly, throw into the void, and see what happened. I'm glad none of that happened. While this story ended up taking on a life of its own, it never would have had the room to do so if not for my three brilliant critique partners — Nico, Morgan, and Harper.

Nico, this book would not exist without you, hands down. Your support, willingness to listen, and refusal to let me give up pushed me through so much of the process. Thank you for cheering for me even when I can't cheer for myself. (Also for being Hawthorne's number one fan) You've been here every step of the way, and I don't have enough words in which to thank you. Thank you for always (*lovingly*) bullying me into betting on myself.

Morgan, there are so many things about this book that would not have been possible without you. You have been such an integral part of every piece that has gone into this work. Thank you for every ounce of your support and your steadfastness in all that you do. Your enthusiasm is contagious and has helped me far more than you know. I have no idea what I would do without you.

Harper, hi twin. You were the very first person to read this story, and your consistent enthusiasm for everything I shared with you has fueled so much of my writing, especially when I was struggling. You have given me some of the best advice I could have asked for, and I don't know how I would have made it without your openness and constant willingness to help. Thank you for always encouraging me to chase the excitement, the weird, and the whimsical.

Mikaila, I could honestly write an entire page just for you and all you've helped with. So I will just say: thank you for everything.

Dylan, I told you this was happening, so you can't be mad about it. Thank you for always listening to my mad rambling, reminding me to be normal, and supporting all the weird stuff I'm doing. I'm glad I met you.

Steph, thank you so much for all of your enthusiasm. You've always been so pumped for anything I shared with you. I am so happy that I met you.

A special thank you to Val, B, and Alex for being so excited about this story from day one. Huge thank you to all my beta and ARC readers—you are all wonderful.

ABOUT THE AUTHOR

Roslyn Reed is an adult horror, romance, and speculative fiction author. Her work centers on character-driven stories, feminine rage, body horror, and the terror of falling in love. There is nothing she loves more than writing about terrible women and the monsters who adore them.

www.ingramcontent.com/pod-product-compliance
Lightning Source LLC
Chambersburg PA
CBHW022028120726
47901CB00003BA/875